CAL

When duty calls

By
Leighton Harding

Other Books by Leighton Harding

CALVERT SERIES
State Secrets
Secret Assignment
Calvert's War of 1812

Havoc
Beyond Honour
Tirpitz Nemesis
Hunt the Bear

The Red Silk Dressing Gown   A Guy Ransome Murder
Death on TV   A Guy Ransome Murder

APPENDIX

ILLUSTRATIONS

Plymouth Harbour

West Coast France

Brest Harbour

Cherbourg Harbour

St. Valery-sur-Somme

HMS Snipe

For those interested in knowing the various sails and rigging mentioned in this book, along with uniforms, Duty rosters, naval times and list of most common nautical terms, please log onto www.leighton harding.com

CHAPTER 1

1791

As the 74 gun ship-of-the-line HMS *Challenger* manoeuvred her way out of the Hamoaze and into Plymouth Sound, William Calvert watched all that went on around him. He was standing on the quarter-deck as a supernumerary Master's Mate. He had only been signed on a couple of weeks earlier, yet it all felt very familiar.

Now nearly 17, Will had gone to sea on his father's merchant ship at the age of 12. They went wherever there was cargo to be traded; the Far East, North America, the Baltic, the wine ports of France and Portugal, and the distant reaches of the Mediterranean. When his father had died, he had decided to offer his skills to the Royal Navy. With a letter of recommendation from a friend of his father's Will had set off to the Hamoaze where the Navy's ships were moored.

Discovering that the naval captain to whom he had the letter of recommendation had sailed only days before, Will had enquired where he needed to go to volunteer for the Navy. The seaman leaning on a bollard at the top of the steps grinned at him.

"Run like the clappers, mate! Only an idiot volunteers!"

Although extremely nervous, he managed to put on a brave face. After all these Tars were no different to the men who had manned his father's ships. Will explained patiently to the bored man that he wanted to be a Sailing Master. The seaman looked him up and down, before spitting out a chew of tobacco.

"Listen Laddie, you's not to run until you can swim!"

This rather perplexed Will.

"So, where should I go to become a Sailing Master?"

By now other seaman had climbed up the steps from their ship's barge to see what was going on.

"What makes you think you could be a sailing master?" Asked a newly joined Tar.

"Because I have been navigating since I was thirteen. I have been round the world!"

"Doesn't mean the Navy would want you. We's want experience, that's what we's want!"

"But surely if I have the experience, someone would employ me. I can fix a position by the stars or the sun, and I know all about sail handling and the weather."

"So does this lot, not the stars bit, but the sail handling, don't we boys?"

There was a rowdy chorus of approval. However Will was experienced enough dealing with rough sailors to be able to stand his ground. He grinned at the men surrounding him.

"Yes, but with you in charge, wouldn't this lot jump ship when you got on a lee shore?" Will said; pointing at his tormentor.

There was general laughter, as the sailors appreciated the spirit of the lad who could stand his ground. Suddenly the lounging seaman shot to attention. Indeed the other sailors who had congregated around Will to overhear what was going on did the same. Will turned to see who had caused the change in attitude to find an officer standing behind him. Will had no idea what rank he held, as he wasn't cognisant to the various uniforms and their ranks. It was obvious that the erect, smartly dressed officer required respect.

The middle aged Gentleman in the blue uniform had a beak of a nose and two startlingly blue intelligent eyes that had the hint of a smile. He was a big man in all senses of the word, imposing even. His skin was weathered, but his confident relaxed manner gave him an air of authority. The Officer had obviously overheard the banter.

"So you know all about navigation do you young man?" Asked the Officer; with a smile.

"Yes Sir! My father was a Merchant Master and he taught me."

"So how does one determine one's Longitude?"

He was jesting, but when William took him seriously and explained that you did so by taking a Noon sight coupled with the use of the Chronometer and the angle; you determined the Longitude. The Officer became interested. What Will didn't realise was that this gentleman was a senior Post Captain.

Will suddenly remembered the letter and produced it. The Captain read the letter and then regarded the young man before him with greater interest. A young man of average height, he had muscular shoulders with a mop of dark hair tied in a queue with a lock of hair that kept falling over his right eye. The young man had a ready smile and the soft pale blue intelligent eyes had a hint of mischief about them. The Captain had noted the way this young fellow had responded to the sailors' taunts.

As it turned out, the Captain could do with a Master's Mate. His ships' Master was getting old and the second Master was due for promotion, so there was a presumed vacancy about to appear, and the Captain was not a man to let chances go by. A back-up would be to every-bodies advantage. Obviously it was William's lucky day.

The Captain took him with him in his gig and they were rowed out past the massive sides of ships-of-the-line anchored in the Hamoaze to the Third Rate Line of Battle ship, HMS *Challenger*. Will sat between the Captain and a Midshipman, whilst a sailor stood to the tiller and gave the commands to the oarsmen. A furtive glance at the Midshipman confirmed Will's opinion that the fellow was younger than him.

There was a challenge from *Challenger*.

Answered by the Midshipman at Will's side shouting. *"Challenger."*

A quietly spoken word from the seaman at the tiller and

the bowman hauled in his oar and stood up with a boathook. The wooden sides of the ship seemed to tower over them as they drew alongside. Will watched in awe as the oars were tossed into the air at a word of command from the tiller and they drew silkily alongside the big hull. Once the painters had been secured, the Captain rapidly ascended the boarding steps mounted on the side of the ship with the aid of a pair of ropes that hung down on either side; to disappear through an imposing entry port. Will waited expecting to be told to follow, but the gig was 'walked' forward a foot or so and only then was he ordered to climb the narrow steps up the entire side of the ship, passing the entry port.

Arriving at the gallery that ran from the forecastle to the quarter-deck on either side of the ship, Will was faced by a giant of a man at the top who barked.

"Who the ******* are you?"

The man was dressed in a red coat with a stand-up collar. The coat had white lapels and cross belts. Will was so surprised he was lost for words. Suddenly a panting young man appeared who informed the giant in a breathless but superior way that the lad was here on the orders of the Captain. The giant's tune changed radically. He sprung to attention and motioned Will forward.

"Hello, I'm Pike…Midshipman Pike, what's your name?" Asked the young man.

"Calvert, William Calvert, Sir."

The Midshipman smiled. "You don't say Sir to me; you call me Pike, or may be when we are better acquainted by my Christian name." But he failed to elucidate the name.

"Follow me!" Pike said and clattered down a ladderway to the deck below. Pike appeared to be younger than Will with unruly mouse coloured hair that escaped from below his hat. He was a good foot shorter than Will, and not as sturdy a build, but he had a pleasant and open manner.

Will gazed about him. Ranged on either side were cannons mounted on wheeled carriages with heavy rope lanyards attached to the ship's side. It was all familiar to him, though there were many more guns and they seemed much bigger than those on his father's ship. As they made their way aft Will passed the ship's great double faced steering wheel. Pike stopped outside a cabin that gave straight out onto the deck just aft of the wheel under the companionway up to another half deck. Pike respectfully tapped on the door. A frail stooping elderly man appeared. His lank grey hair was tied untidily back from a yellow sunken skinned face. There were red blotches on the cheeks, but under great bushy eyebrows, the dark eyes were sharp.

"What is it now Pike?" Asked the man.

"Master, the Captain wants you to find out just how much this fellow knows about navigation. When you have finished, he requires you to report to him."

Will gathered that this must be the Sailing Master.

The man lent forward and peered at Will. "Alright come in here!" He commanded; shuffling backwards with a permanently bent back into the cabin. Will followed him and discovered it wasn't a cabin at all. It was a dark cubicle with ranged against the ship's side a table with cubby holes beneath and shelves above. On the table was a chart of Plymouth Sound spread out and held in place by four squashed lead balls. The light came from a small rectangular scuttle in the side above the chart table.

"Right what is that?" Asked the man pointing at the chart; followed by a hacking cough.

Will was surprised to be asked such a simple question. "A chart of the Sound, Sir."

The man grunted. "And that?" The Master pointed at a triangular wooden object with an arm attached to the top and mirrors mounted on the sides, which hung from a peg in the ship's side...

"That's an Octant! I'm surprised you aren't using a Sextant!" Blurted out Will.

The man gave Will a sharp look and then pointed at a wooden box at the back of the table. "And that?"

"Looks like a compass box; Sir!"

"So how do you know where you are on the chart?"

"Well Sir, this close to land, by taking bearings on known charted shore positions. Things like church spires, or headlands. Three are needed for an accurate fix."

"And how would you do that?"

"By using a Pelorus either on a compass or on a card, but the later would have to be aligned with the ships head."

"And at sea, out of sight of the land?"

"If the weather is clear enough by Noon sights, or in between by plotting the course sailed from the Traverse Board."

"Right! What is Longitude?"

"They are lines drawn between the two poles that bisect the equator at right angles. Each line of Longitude is 15 degrees either side of the prime Meridian, or an hour's difference."

The man grunted. "So if I gave you a reading could you plot the position on a chart?"

Will hesitated for a moment: was it a trick question? "What readings would they be Sir?"

The Master pulled out a battered old logbook and flicked through its pages." Know what this is?"

"The ships log?"

"Correct! Now let me look out the correct chart."

Again he started to cough badly. Finally he seemed to be able to fight back and gain control. He counted across the charts under the table, and then down, to pull out a chart which when unrolled Will recognised as the Western Approaches to the English Channel. From the log book the Master wrote down a series of jottings.

"There!"

"Excuse me Sir, but what was the last known position before this reading was taken?"

"What do you want that for?"

"Because unless I'm mistaken this will give us the Longitude but not the Latitude."

For the first time the Master smiled. "So we were here.

At 10 o'clock by Dead Reckoning." The Master said; making a mark on the chart.

Will lent over the chart table and asked. "At what height was the observer?"

"15 feet!" Came back the reply.

"What was the mean speed of the ship for the two hours in question?"

The Master consulted his log. "7 Knots, course east north east."

Will wrote down the hour, minute and seconds from the note, then asked for the Chronometer error and added this when told. He then drew a line below that and entered the observed altitude and asked for the index error. The Master laughed for the first time and gave it to him, followed without being asked by the correction. From this Will obtained the True altitude and subtracted it from 90 which he was then able to transpose onto the chart.

"So what about tides, young man?" Asked the Master; but it was in a friendly tone.

"We are three days ahead of Neaps, Sir. That means we shall have less of a variation in the heights of the tide. And the tides obey the phases of the Moon."

"And where did you learn all this wisdom?"

"My father was a ship owner and master. He took me to sea with him when I was twelve and taught me."

"So where did he trade?"

"The Far East, India, China and the North Americas and all over Europe and the Med."

"And you have visited them all?"

"Yes Sir!"

"And what about sails?"

Will immediately gave a list of the sails normally carried by a similar ship to the one they were aboard from bow to stern. He then added the fore and aft sails, followed by the various studding sails. The Master patted Will on the shoulder and told him to wait there.

Will positioned himself by the door so he could observe

what was going on the deck outside. He was fascinated to see a young man dressed like Pike appear up the hatchway before the wheel, stand waiting and turn the sand glass, just as it ran out. At the same time a seaman stepped up and gave six strikes to the ship's bell on the forecastle. Both then disappeared. An officer appeared up the companionway, the same ladderway as the midshipman had used, placed his hat on his head and proceeded to stroll off down the deck checking various things as he went. Seamen were standing about tidying up the sheets and becks and other lines, whilst chatting amongst themselves.

CHAPTER 2

Pike came back to ask how things had gone. Will replied that he did not know, but the Master had told him to wait where he was. Pike took the opportunity to show off his knowledge of his ship. He explained that *Challenger* was what was termed a Third Rate ship-of-the-line with 26 twenty-four pounder cannons on her gun-deck and 26 eighteen pounders on the upper deck. He also pointed out various features, which were familiar to Will, who remained quietly listening.

It wasn't until the bell and glass routine had been repeated, but this time seven bells sounded, that the Master came back. After a hacking cough into a handkerchief, the Master explained that Will was to follow Pike, and that Pike was to take Will to the First-Lieutenant to be signed on as a Masters Mate. Will politely thanked the Master.

Pike quickly led Will down the ladderway that the officer had emerged from into the shadowy world below. The Gun Ports were open, so Will was able to see he was being led aft. Large cannons sat on their carriages with their muzzles lashed close up to the side of the ship, just above their respective gun-ports and between them as far as the eye could see, tables hung from the deck head with seaman lounging about them. They passed a huge capstan and then came to a partition right across the ship. Pike knocked on a panelled door and after a minute or so it was opened by an officer.

"Sir, could you ask the First Lieutenant to attend; Captain's request!"

The officer gave a weary shrug and disappeared. A minute later an older man appeared buttoning his waistcoat. "Yes Pike?"

"Captain's compliments; he requests that you sign this fellow as a Master's Mate. Name of Calvert. Sir!"

The First Lieutenant was a tall angular fellow with a scar across one cheek, which pulled down one eye, giving him an appearance of leering the whole time. Will felt that this officer had an air of quiet confidence about him; his straw coloured hair was pulled back and tied in a neat black bag at the nap of his neck. Despite his slightly piratical look, he had a warm smile.

"Calvert is it?" He asked. "Follow me!" He led the way into the Wardroom, where officers were lounging about reading or in groups talking and drinking. Ignoring and ignored by everybody, the First Lieutenant went to a desk at the side and pulled out a book. He flicked over the pages and then dipped a quill pen in the ink well and asked. "Christian name?"

"William, Sir.

The First Lieutenant wrote William Calvert, Masters Mate."

"Age?"

"Sixteen, nearly seventeen. Sir!"

"Date of birth?"

Will gave it, and the First Lieutenant wrote in the book.

"That's it; you are signed on, now you have to swear to obey all orders given to you by an officer."

William placed his hand on the Bible and was sworn in.

"Come!" Commanded the First Lieutenant. Will followed him and found himself back at the door with the hovering

Pike.

"See that Mr Calvert gets a uniform today and show him the ropes." And with that he was gone.

"Oh Lord! That means an interview with Mr Trotter!"

"Who is Mr Trotter?" Asked Will; as he followed Pike down another ladderway.

"The Purser – guardian of the ship's purse. Getting money from him is worse than squeezing a stone!"

Pike took a lantern off a hook, and they descended further. They found the Purser in the ship's inky black hold, taking an audit of supplies. He looked up with a bad tempered scowl. "What do you want now, Pike!"

"First Lieutenant's compliments – this is Mr Calvert, our new Master's Mate. He needs a uniform."

"Well - send him to a tailor."

"For that, Sir, he requires money."

"Then bring him back later!"

"The First Lieutenant desires that he is taken ashore now, Sir."

"Oh he does, does he?" But he turned and picking up his candle lantern led the way back up to his cabin. By the light of day, Will was able to see that the Purser was a short spare man with thinning gingery hair. On an upturned nose a pair of metal rimmed glasses appeared to have slipped from a non-existent bridge, revealing two poppy eyes of a strange mixture of brown and gold. He seemed to have to peer at everything.

"This is the Orlop deck; where the surgeon works during a battle. It's painted red so it won't show the blood!" Advised Pike in a whisper.

Pike held up a hand in warning and the two of them waited outside the Purser's door.

The Purser re-appeared with a note. "Give this to the usual outfitters."

"Thank you, Sir!" Said Will; and Pike led him back to the upper deck.

Once ashore; the two made their way to the tailors, where Will was able to purchase a second-hand Midshipman's jacket. The collar had to be changed and white piping added to the front edge, pocket and behind the cuff buttons. The coat would be available within two hours. Will under Pike's instruction also ordered breeches and stockings, together with the order for a new jacket. Next it was to a cobbler to obtain suitable foot-ware. With the necessary bribe offered, Will would be able to collect a couple of suitable pairs the next day.

"I better collect my sea-chest." Said Will.

"You have a sea-chest?" Queried; a very surprised Pike.

"Well yes, it was my father's."

"And where is this chest of yours?"

"At my Aunt's house, overlooking the port, near the Barbican."

To save money the couple decided to walk as the weather was set fair. It was during their walk that Will got to know more of Mister Pike. He had been a Midshipman for eighteen or so months. His Uncle had secured him the position as he knew their Captain. Pike's family was the poor relation, so the introduction had been a great relief to the family. Pike admitted that he found the mathematics needed for navigation troublesome. Will offered to help in any way, which endeared him to Pike.

Will's Aunt insisted that they partook of some sustenance whilst the maid was sent to fetch the carter. Refreshed from lunch, the trip back to the Dockyard with Will's sea-chest was a jolly affair. They sat on the back of the cart and chatted away, waving and exchanging ribald remarks with any pretty girls they passed.

They returned to the tailor and Will changed into his uniform. Unfortunately the boots that Will was wearing really didn't go with the uniform, which caused Pike much amusement. Back on board, Will was introduced to the other members of the Gunroom. The gunroom being set a deck below the wardroom used by the Midshipmen and the

'Young men'; who hoped to become Midshipmen. The Captain of the Gunroom was the Gunner, a thick-set man with a weathered and grizzled face. He greeted Will with no great enthusiasm. Next was the Carpenter a kindly stooped man who had a warm smile. What really surprised Will was the number of young men lounging about dressed like Pike. It turned out that there were up to 20 Midshipmen normally assigned to the Gunroom of a third rate. Will was introduced to each one present and greeted with varying degrees of friendliness or indifference. Finally Pike introduced the two other Master's Mates aboard. Will was surprised to find that they were both around his own age. It emerged later that the Second Master was being sent to another ship as Master. Now Will was bound for the West Indies as *Challenger* was part of a squadron due to sail to that area.

CHAPTER 3

Although in that year, 1791, Britain was at peace, the country had been building up its Navy both as a result of the American War of Independence and the ever growing ambitions of the French. Now with France in the turmoil of a revolution, the British Government was undecided as to what might happen next. HMS *Challenger* left Plymouth for the West Indies; along with other ships-of-the-line and their attendant frigates. For Will it was an adventure as well as a learning curve. It took him a few weeks to settle down and become familiar with the routine. There had been a couple of weeks in harbour, during which Will had explored every corner of the ship. It soon became obvious that the two other Mates were nowhere near as proficient in any area as Will. Now in the middle of the Atlantic he found himself virtually doing the job of Second Master. The Master was not a well man, and more and more responsibility seemed to devolve onto Will. Because there were now three Master's Mates, the Master decided that Will should spend most of his time assisting him, and that he should not adhere to the normal watch keeping pattern.

The Master had explained in detail the methods he employed in stowing everything below decks to achieve the perfect trim; which was so important to the ship's handling. This was nothing new to Will, who had learnt the lessons of loading on his father's ship. He did not mention this, however. Will was always alongside the Master when he was consulted as to the sails carried for different winds and courses, and he noted the answers carefully. He soon got to know the Lieutenants from the First Lieutenant down. There were seven of them, and not all were that brilliant at navigation. At midday, weather permitting, Will would join the Captain and Master on the Quarter-deck with his father's sextant taking the Noon sight alongside the First Lieutenant and any other officers and Midshipmen who could get their hands on a sextant. In practice he soon stood in for the Master when he was too ill to appear.

Will's foul weather gear drew many comments, some appreciative, some ribald. He wore his father's coat which was made of fine canvas, treated with beeswax and oil to make it more waterproof. The multi-layered collars reminiscent of a coachman's protected the shoulders, whilst the double breasted front withstood the waves. The high collar that reached almost to the eyes could be buttoned up the front. The cuffs could be tightened with leather straps. The skirt of the coat reached to below the knees and more leather straps beneath prevented it from flying up in the wind. On his head he wore the widest brimmed southwester anybody could remember.

Challenger and the squadron headed south towards the Canaries before picking up the warm North East Trades which was to carry them across the Atlantic to the West Indies. By the time they had reached the Canaries, the Captain and most of the officers had begun to appreciate just how good Will was at navigation. On the other hand the crew had come realise that his seamanship was extraordinary.

When on duty he would constantly monitor the sails. Holding up a piece of wood in front of him, he would use it to judge the distance to the ship in line ahead. If any adjustment was needed he would walk forward and have a quiet word with the leading hand in charge of that particular sheet, brace, bowline or tack that needed to be adjusted. He knew each sailor by name. He would compliment them when they did the adjustment themselves. Often he would crack a joke as he turned away, leaving the seaman in good spirits. He seemed to have an uncanny knack of knowing what the wind was likely to do, so sails would be taken in before there was a risk to the topmen.

When they arrived in the West Indies there was no going ashore. The Captain was fearful for the crew as there were fevers that were rife at the time. The squadron was always on the move. The Second Master went to join another ship, so Will was promoted Temporary Acting Second Master. There were constantly problems to be solved as well as dangerous reefs to avoid. Will concentrated on building a dossier of his own charts to those he had inherited from his father. He sought permission to visit other ships when they were moored anywhere close by, to borrow charts so he could copy them. He enlisted the aid of *Challenger's* Young Gentlemen in the copying process. These were boys who went to sea at an early age to learn the duties of an officer. They hoped to be made Midshipmen, and start the slow crawl up the ranks. It was the Master's job to instruct these young fellows, so Will found himself doing most of the teaching. He showed them the method his father had taught him, which was to place a blank piece of paper fixed to the front of the chart and then by flicking the paper up and down fast you could position the mark to exactly correspond with the one on the chart below. It took time, but it worked well.

Almost exactly a year after HMS *Challenger* had arrived in

the West Indies, the fleet was anchored in Falmouth Harbour, a bay at the southern tip of the island of Antigua. The mercury was falling fast, and all the officers feared that they were in for a bad storm. Will was deputising for the Master who was confined to his cabin in a very poor way.

"So what do you think, young Calvert?" Asked the Captain; as he came onto the quarterdeck, where Will was watching the cloud formations, book and lead in hand. He was getting used to being asked his opinion. At first he had been nervous about saying too much. Then one day he was called to the Captain's cabin.

"Ah! Calvert, a word in your shell like! You tend be rather reticent. It does you no favours. I have come to realise that you are outstanding at your vocation. If you want to get on in this man's navy, you will have to be more assertive. Certainty inspires confidence. Even if you are not that confident, don't let others realise. You can always change your mind, but dithering will cause people to doubt your ability."

"Thank you Sir. I shall make sure I follow your instruction!"

"Good! You have the ability; you just need the confidence in yourself. Don't be modest; come out with it!"

"Aye Sir!"

So now Will immediately responded.

"I think we can expect a hurricane, Sir. I doubt it will pass over us, more likely to be quite a few miles to the north, but I should imagine we will get some very strong winds on the side of it."

The Captain nodded, and Will added.

"Where or when it will strike is in the hands of the Almighty!"

"So what would you advise, if you were Master?" Asked the Captain, and he did not seem to be testing Will, rather actually consulting him.

"When I was last here... not this harbour, but further south, we made for a bay like this and then tied ourselves to every rock and palm tree we could find. We had all our anchors laid as far out as possible."

"And?" The Captain waited.

"It faded out, so we never experienced a full blown hurricane, just a very bad storm. This time though the winds are building and the clouds are ominous. I would suggest we put out as many warps to solid objects on the shore all round, and put our anchors out as far as possible to give us as firm a hold as possible." He looked to see if he was going too far, but the Captain was nodding his head.

"I would further suggest Sir that we take down the yards and the top masts."

"Thank you, Calvert, very interesting. Tried to speak to the Master, but he wasn't really well enough to speak. Terrible cough he has got. I did not realise you had been through this before!"

When the order was given, there was a certain amount of scoffing by the Lieutenants present. One of the officers pointed out that nobody else was taking such drastic measures. The Captain who happened to arrive on the scene at that moment silenced them.

"Mr Calvert is the Master, we shall do as he suggests!"

Will noticed the slip of the tongue, and felt very proud of the Captain's trust.

Anchors were set as far out as possible in every direction. Warps were rowed out and secured round rocks and stout trees ashore, ignoring the protests of some other ship's captains. The Boatswain' Mates were everywhere, exhorting the crew to ever greater efforts in securing everything. Below the Purser was supervising the securing of the stores. The boats were hauled up and extra lines tightly lashed over them. Yards came down; topmasts were lowered and lashed twice over to their masts

Gradually during the day the clouds turned blacker and more menacing and the winds began to increase in force.

Even in their comparatively sheltered bay, the waves began to build, becoming short and steep with spume blowing off their tops. Day turned to night! The rigging started to sound like piano wires, a raucous cacophony of ill matched notes and loud howls, like baying wolves. *Challenger* seemed determined to break free from the bonds that held her. She thrashed this way and that, throwing anybody on the move across the decks. Then came the rain; the horizontal, lancing blades that meant anybody on deck had to hide their faces, whilst their hands and bodies were tortured. One had to cling onto any secure object to stay erect. All around them the other ships were suffering; yards left up were torn from their masts to crash down causing damage below. Ship's boats still in the water were smashed against the sides of their ships. Anchors dragged free letting ships swing into their near neighbours. Still the wind; still the screaming, shrieking wind! There seemed to be no let up to the misery! Then quite suddenly the wind dropped, the clouds parted and the sun broke through highlighting the damage wrought by the storm. Will had been correct; the eye of the hurricane had passed to the north.

The hurricane might have passed to the north of the island, but the damage to the houses on the islands and many of the ships that had not taken sufficient precautions was extensive. One frigate managed to break loose and crash into the flag-ship. *Challenger* was bounced about severely, but no major damage was done.

The squadron a few days later sailed up the west coast of the islands and they were able to see for themselves the amount of damage that a tropical storm could wreak. It had passed over Haiti and then veered north to bypass Jamaica, hitting the southern coast of Cuba. Even from the sea the devastation to the palms could be seen. Flotsam told its own story. The squadron finally anchored off Freetown.

It was whilst they were at anchor in the bay off Freetown that Will was ordered to attend the flag-ship. No reason was given, but wearing his best uniform he was duly rowed over to the flag-ship. On arrival he gave his name and was taken by a midshipman to wait outside the Captain's quarters. After sometime he was called and found himself facing a panel made up of a senior Post Captain and three of the Masters from the other ships-of-the-line. Will knew them all, because he had borrowed charts from them. He had chatted to each of them getting to know them as well as time would permit. When any two Masters were gathered together they would swap opinions and ideas on any subject to do with the safe handling of ships.

"Mister Calvert?" The Post Captain asked; although Will knew he was known to the Captain.

"Sir!"

"We are a specially convened Board to adjudge whether or not you should be certified as a Master."

Will's surprise was apparent.

"I believe that you are known to the Masters, here present?"

"Sir!" Replied Will; smiling nervously at each in turn.

"You are presently?" The Captain continued.

"Master's Mate; Sir"

"That is not what is written here!" The Captain checked a paper in front of him on the table. "It says 'Acting Second Master' is that correct?"

"Aye, Sir!"

"So how long have you been acting as Second Master?"

"About three months, Sir."

"And how often do you act as Master?"

"Well Sir, Mr Luke is indisposed at the moment, so I have been acting for him for all that time. At present we are short of a second Master."

"In other words, you are acting as the Master of one of His Majesty's ships-of-the-line?"

"If you put it like that, yes Sir!"

The Captain sat back, smiled at Will for the first time and turned to the Masters beside him. "Any questions gentlemen?"

The Flagship's Master cleared his throat. "I think Captain; with all due respect, we can save our time here. Mr Calvert has been navigating some of the trickiest waters in the area for the past three months. His Captain I know has put him up for Master, which knowing that Gentleman means that he has the highest regard for this young man's ability. I realise that he is rather young to be a Master, but I don't think that should be put in the way of such outstanding ability."

The Master of another one of the 74s added. "I understand that it was your suggestion as to the disposition of the anchors, kedges and warps of *Challenger* during the recent hurricane."

"That is correct Sir!"

"And that you suggested the lowering of the yards and topmasts, which action being the first ship to do so, was copied by many of the other ships in the fleet?"

"Yes Sir!"

"We are all agreed then Gentlemen? Good! Congratulations Mr Calvert. You are now a certified Master!" Said the Post Captain.

"Thank you Sir!"

"The Certificate will be sent over when it has been made out. When we return to Britain your Captain will make it his business to ensure you get your Warrant."

"Thank you Sir. Thank you all Gentlemen."

The Masters all stood up and came round to shake Will's hand. The Captain rang a bell, and as he came to shake Will's hand a steward came in bearing a tray with a decanter and glasses. Will found himself drinking the finest Claret with the Board members.

Will was now the Master, a member of the Wardroom and paid the rate, His predecessor, Mr Luke had been shipped back to England, too sick to continue. A Masters Mate had been poached from another ship to act as Second

Master under Will.

Wardroom life was very different to that of the gunroom. The Lieutenants were generally much older and the conversation more adult. James Crick, the First Lieutenant was the senior officer and made sure that arguments were few and far between. His piratical appearance belied a kind and thoughtful character. It was he who made sure that Will was made to feel at ease. There were a couple of the younger Lieutenants who seemed to consider themselves too superior to talk to him in the wardroom, but the rest tended to ignore them. It was really only at meal times that he was in the wardroom as he had so many duties to perform. At anchor, he tended to keep out of the wardroom and use his cubicle as a refuge.

Then at last the orders to return to Britain arrived. HMS *Challenger* was amongst the fleet on their way back, when some hundred miles south of Bermuda a vicious storm blew up. Will advised that warps should be streamed from the bows and that the spanker sail be set, double reefed. The Officer of the watch was disagreeing with him, when the Captain appeared and ordered that the Sailing Master's orders were to be obeyed. Will had the topsails, normally set in such conditions taken down, together with the upper yards. HMS *Challenger* lay head to wind; the warps with old sails attached acting as sheet anchors and together with the spanker set on the mizzen mast, she rode the waves head on. Even with these precautions the ship staggered from one wave top to the next, burying her bowsprit and bows deep into the oncoming waves, and then; just when there seemed no hope of ending a headlong dive to the bottom of the ocean, she would shake herself free, tossing gallons of water over her decks. Up on deck everybody was lashed to masts or binnacle. Down below the safest place to be was in a hammock. Pots and pans clattered this way and that, but nobody dared to try and silence them. The hull protested loudly, groaning at the punishment that was being inflicted upon it.

In the bad visibility they lost touch with most of the other members of the fleet. Those that they could see between squalls were suffering far worse than *Challenger*. Most were under topsails, so the wind and waves were driving the ships before them, which meant there was no control. Those that could be seen were rolling badly and many had already lost sails and rigging.

The Captain spent the six hours at the peak of the storm beside Will, close to the wheel. One had to shout to be heard, but at one point the Captain grabbed Will's arm and pointed to Larboard. There rolling badly, her foretopmast gone was a frigate. Even as they watched she rolled nearly on her beam ends, before righting herself, to repeat the performance the other way. It looked as if she might well flounder. Then the rain came down again and she was lost from sight.

When the storm had abated a bit and the rain had gone, it was an empty horizon that greeted them at first light. For the first time it was possible to send a look-out up the mast. He reported that there was only one ship in sight. Gradually the yards were hoisted back up and sail set. After three hours it was possible to clearly identify the ship as the flag-ship. *Challenger* took up station on the flag-ship, but it was clear to see that the flag-ship had suffered. It wasn't until two days later that all the ships of the fleet were accounted for. Over half had major damage to their rigging. One of the frigates had lost a topmast and had no topsails to set. Only one other ship appeared to have weathered the storm as well as *Challenger*.

"Who taught you to ride a storm in that manner?" Asked the Captain; later.

"My father always did that, in all the oceans." Will answered; quietly.

"Humph! Merchant Captain of course....years of experience!"

CHAPTER 4

When HMS *Challenger* finally docked in Plymouth it was for a complete refit. As a result Will expected to be cast off on half pay, if he was lucky. However Britain was now at war with France. Every ship was needed. The Master, Mr Luck, now much restored to health, would return to stay with the ship; which was normal practice. Gradually the Lieutenants disappeared to other ships. Will was granted a week's leave, so went to visit his mother at Fowey. This involved taking a ferry across the Tamar and then hiring a mount to ride to Fowey. Will was not a good rider. He found the journey made him very saddle-sore. He didn't dare to ride at anything faster than a trot.

Luckily the weather was fair, with scudding clouds, with otherwise a blue sky and plenty of sunshine. Everything seemed to Will to be exaggerated green and verdant. The birds were singing; rabbits hopped about un-phased by the lone rider or his mount. Labourers smiled and waved their hats as the naval officer rode by. The younger girls in the few villages stood suggestively or blew him kisses.

It had taken a whole day, with frequent stops to reach Bodinnick, the hamlet on the opposite side of the river to Fowey. He had to persuade the gnarled old ferryman to carry him across, because he arrived so late in the day. Will recognised the old boy from when he was a youth. His face was like dark tanned hide, and his knuckles twisted with age. He wore a thread-bare coarse serge jacket that might once have been dark blue, but was now so faded as to be difficult to really tell its original colour. On his greasy hair there perched what might have once been a leather cap, but it was now so old it had no recognisable shape. His sail cloth breeches were untied and his feet bare.

They were only halfway across when the ferryman stopped rowing and leaned on his oars.

"I's know you, doesn't I?" He said frowning, his steely

eyes fixed on Will. "You's young Calvert, Cap'an William's son, isn't you?"

"That's me!" Replied Will with a grin.

The ferryman started to pull on the oars again. "Your Uncle Judd, he drowned you know. He was so drunk he fell off the quay... stupid sod! Blind drunk as usual: why anyone bought him a drink, I'll never know....always cadging, that one. Used to turn and walk away if I saw him coming. He would pester the life out of you!"

Will did not think there was any suitable comment to make, so remained silent. Uncle Judd had been the reason he had left Fowey, as the drunken man had threatened to get even on him because his father had not allowed a drunk on any of his ships.

After a bit the ferryman spoke again. "So, you in the Merchant now?"

"No Royal Navy."

The ferryman looked puzzled. "What are you then, you's wearing a sort of uniform, I supposes."

"Ship's Master." Responded Will.

"That mean you is the Captain?" The ferryman looked totally disbelieving.

"No, just responsible for sailing and navigation, that's all."

"So what's the Captain do?"

"He's in command of everything, especially fighting the ship."

When he finally got to Fowey, he said goodbye to the ferryman, thanking him for working so late. He slung his bag over his shoulder and made his way up the steep hill to the family home. When Mrs Calvert came to the door of the house, she nearly fainted. There before her stood her son, but now he was a man. His face was brown from the sun, the cheeky good humour still there, but with a much more mature facade. He seemed to have broadened out and his uniform was no longer loose around him. He had an air of confidence which had not been there before. She threw her arms around his neck and kissed him, before dragging him into the house.

He found that not only was his mother in good health, but that she was being courted by a local farmer. She had a cheerful air about her, which was very different from the sad widow he had left. His mother was ecstatic at seeing him, and admired his uniform, asking him if this was a Masters Mates uniform. When he told her he was a warranted Master in his own right, she could hardly believe her ears. Immediately she set to, to cook up a game pie, with all the vegetables available. A tankard of ale was gleaned from the local Inn down the road. She insisted that he sat in what had been his father's chair and regale her with tales of his exploits. The next morning he became the centre of attention amongst the ladies of Fowey, especially the younger ones. They would walk past in pairs giggling and batting their eyes in his direction. He found that the few girls that he had known were now grown up; some were married and had changed beyond recognition. A few recognised him, or had been told about him, so stopped to say hello. He was flattered, but knew well he had no time for such flirtations, even though some seemed to be very pretty. Boys that he had played with as a youth, when not at sea, greeted him as a stranger, but still insisted that he drank with them in the various Inns. Most were fishermen; a few worked the quays, whilst others worked on the land. His mother insisted that he walked all the way to her suitor's farm, so Will could meet him. Will was not used to walking on land and found the distance tiring. The Farmer seemed to be a good sort, shy, but warm hearted, even if he did have a decided stammer. He was shorter than Will had expected, but made up for it with massively strong arms and torso. What surprised Will was that this his mother's suitor, seemed to be more prosperous than most of the folk about. He wore a well cut tweed riding jacket over clean riding breeches, held round the calf by highly polished brown leather gaiters. He was going bald above a strangely cherubic face with weather induced rosy cheeks. His eyes were hooded by bushy eyebrows that had yet to go as grey as his hair. He spoke little, but ordered wine for Will to drink. Will's mother did most of the talking, whilst the farmer sat and smiled approvingly sucking on his clay pipe. He was a widower who now obviously doted on Mrs Calvert. When the time came to return to Fowey, Mr Chegwidden, for that was his name, insisted that he drive Will and his mother home. A farm worker was called for and a quarter-of-an-hour later a smart dog cart was brought to the front of the farm house. It was drawn by a meaty cob with a trussed tail, tied with ribbon, and a shining harness. The cob's coat was so well brushed, that even Will noticed and remarked upon it to the delight of the owner. It was quite obvious that the fellow adored Mrs Calvert, so Will's mind was put at rest.

Will was so worried about getting back, that he only spent four days with his mother, before setting out on the return trip.

On arriving back on board *Challenger* he discovered that there was a signal for him. He was to join the Frigate *Artful* whose new Captain, James Crick, had been the First Lieutenant on *Challenger*. He was to be the Master. Now, according to the Navy's unique way of putting things, he ranked equal but below the Lieutenants, however he would be paid more. He would have two Master's Mates of his own as well as his own servant. He was in reality the second most responsible person onboard. Unlike a ship-of-the-line, a frigate didn't rate a Second Master. There was an added bonus; in another packet was his Warrant from the Navy Board.

Artful was one of the frigates assigned to the Channel fleet. She lay to a buoy higher up the Tamar River, one of a number of frigates being prepared for sea. Together with sixteen other frigates she was to be part of Admiral Howe's command.

One of *Challenger's* cutters was assigned the job of rowing Will up river to where the frigate *Artful* was moored. It was one of those days, so common to the South-West where the earlier rain had given way to a bright sunlit afternoon. Around them the gulls wheeled hopefully, as the oarsmen in perfect time drove the cutter against the weakening ebb tide. The frigate when she appeared from behind a fellow frigate looked to be in good order. Her figurehead appeared freshly painted and the gilt-work gleamed in the sun.

The lookouts aboard *Artful* must have been on their toes, because there was an officer peering down at them as they drew alongside. On arriving with his sea chest he was greeted at the top of the ship's side by a young Lieutenant not much older than himself who enquired rather briskly as who he might be!

"William Calvert, Master!" Replied Will; fixing the Lieutenant with a direct look.

"Oh! Right….err; welcome aboard. I'm Craddock. What ship are you off?"

"HMS *Challenger*" Replied Will; amused at the reaction this had upon the Lieutenant who must realise that Will would be well known to their Captain. A Midshipman was summoned to show Will to his cabin. As Will followed the young Midshipman he established that he was called John Preston and had just been made up from 'young gentleman' to Midshipman, and that he was immensely proud of the fact. All around them the sides were freshly painted and the decks holy-stoned within an inch of their lives. Obviously the First Lieutenant had an eye for the detail.

Will had a cabin to himself, but unlike *Challenger's* canvas screens, these cabins had wooden permanent walls and doors. There were no guns on this deck, so the partitions remained during any action. Will's cabin was right at the stern opposite the First Lieutenant's cabin. It was dark down here because unlike a wardroom on a ship-of-the-line with stern windows, the cabin spaces were off the gunroom on the gun-deck. The only light came from the grating overhead to the upper deck. What light reached into the cabin did so through the open area at the top of the cabin walls. Will's cabin had a fold-down desk built against the partition; whilst in the centre hung a cot suspended from the beam above. The walls were whitewashed to reflect what light was available. To see properly, you had to light a candle lantern that hung from a hook on the beam overhead. In front of the desk was a folding chair with a canvas seat. Preston seemed impressed by the space, and Will gathered that this was the first time the Midshipman had been inside an officer's cabin.

There was the noise of a chest being dragged along the deck and a young boy appeared in the doorway with Will's sea-chest. The boy gave a sort of half bow and then stood up very straight at attention.

"This is your servant….." Preston said; forgetting or not knowing the boys name.

"And you are?" Asked Will with a smile to encourage the lad.

"Thomas Tucker, Sir"

"Well Thomas Tucker, perhaps you would be so kind as to push my chest into that corner."

Tucker flushed bright red, but did as he had been asked. Having finished the boy stood undecided by the chest.

"That's fine, thank you Tucker; that will be all." Will said.

The boy gave a bob and fled, much to Will's amusement. He realised that Preston was still there and turned to him.

"Would you like to be shown round the ship, Mr Calvert?" Asked Preston.

"Very kind of you, but I think I can manage. Perhaps you would be so good as to inform the Captain and First Lieutenant that I am come aboard."

"Aye, Aye Sir!" Preston turned and ran off.

Emerging from his cabin Will found nobody about in the gunroom. He could hear the noise from the mess deck forward, separated as it was by just a thin partition. Unlike *Challenger* the partitions would remain when the ship went into action as the mess deck was only just above the waterline and not pierced for gun ports. His cabin appeared to be larger than most of the others, but he soon discovered that the quarter gallery was next to his cabin. This meant that the officer's heads was right next door, with all its attendant noises.

Will decided to go up on to the quarter-deck, so that he would be more available to the Captain if called. Looking along the upper deck as he climbed the ladderway, Will counted 28 eighteen pound guns ranged up neatly either side. He knew from viewing the ship from the longboat that had brought him, that the forecastle and quarterdeck also had guns, but they would be carronades, short lighter guns firing heavier shot. Astern he could see a marine sentry outside the door to the Captain's quarters. Will strolled forwards along the upperdeck nodding to members of the crew who seeing his plain blue Warrant officer's coat stood to attention as he passed. He took a turn round the foremast and then back towards the stern. As he approached the capstan, the door to the Captain's quarters opened and a Lieutenant emerged and spoke to the marine sentry as he donned his hat.

"Mr Calvert!" Shouted the marine.

"Aye!" Shouted back Will, but he didn't change his pace.

The Lieutenant came to meet him and put out a hand to shake Will's.

"Hunter, First Lieutenant, pleased to have you aboard. The Captain desires your presence." The First Lieutenant was a stout party who filled his uniform with a ruddy countenance, but had a warm smile.

Will shook his hand saying. "William Calvert, Sailing Master."

To Will's surprise Hunter fell in step beside him until they reached the Marine.

"Mr Calvert, the Master." Hunter told the Marine.

"Mr Calvert the Master and the First Lieutenant!" Announced the Marine; in a sonorous shout, coming to attention and bringing his musket to the present.

Hunter opened the door and stood aside to let Will through first.

They were in the Captain's dining cabin, where the table was set for five. The highly polished table gleamed reflecting the silver cutlery and the sparkling decanters with their squat bases. The chairs were fairly delicate and reflected the new fashion. The light came through the open door to the Captain's day cabin, where they found the Captain at his desk. The floor was covered in canvas painted in black and white squares, whilst on the window seat all across the stern, comfortable cushions gave a civilised air to the cabin. Two high winged button backed armchairs were positioned at either quarter. The desk was brass bound at the corners.

"Will, welcome aboard!" A smiling Captain Crick stood up from his seat to greet them. "I see you have met Number One already. Had a good leave?"

"Yes thank you Sir. And may I congratulate you Sir!" Said Will; shaking the Captain's hand.

"I think we are both to be congratulated, don't you. Sit down gentlemen." The Captain indicated the window seat that ran the whole width below the stern windows.

"I have explained to Number One all about you, so he is up to speed. I am afraid we are still short on crew... as always, but we have been promised some from the Holding Hulks. Lieutenant Simmons is with the Press at this moment, though I doubt we shall net many seamen. When we have enough crew we are to join Admiral Howe's Channel Fleet. If you haven't got charts for the French coast, especially the Atlantic coast, I suggest, Will, you try and get hold of them as soon as possible, by hook or by crook."

"I have a pretty wide selection, thank you Sir." Replied Will; glowing with the reflected enthusiasm radiating from the Captain.

"I understand the Purser is still ashore, but we have been promised the ordinance barge tomorrow and the victuals in the late afternoon."

"Excuse me Sir, but when did *Artful* last have a refit?" Asked Will.

The Captain laughed. "Hear that Number One? No messing about straight down to the nitty gritty. She has just had a minor refit; cordage and paintwork. I understand she was allowed into dry dock to have her bottom scrubbed and the copper checked. The carpenter assures me the timbers are sound. Any questions Number One?"

"Not at the moment Sir." Replied the First Lieutenant.

"I am inviting the senior members of the wardroom to dine with me tonight. I know it is unusual to have dinner in the evening, but I thought it a good idea to get to know each other when there was no work to follow. So I shall be seeing both of you this evening."

Will and Hunter rose together and made their way out onto the upper deck. Instinctively Will made for the cubicle set to the starboard side behind the ladderway to the quarter deck. This was where the Master always kept his charts and instruments. Hunter followed him.

"I doubt if the previous Master left any charts behind." Commented Hunter,

"Nor do I, I just wanted to see what it is like. Could do with a good clean out by the looks of things. I shall have to find the Master's Mates if I have any."

"Oh you have two, both young lads of sixteen. I checked their mathematics just in case, but to be honest with you, navigation is not my strong point, I am afraid."

Will grinned. "Thank God, you would put me out of a job!"

Both laughed together and Will felt relieved that at least the two most senior officers of the ship were friendly. To Will's surprise the First Lieutenant pulled the door shut behind them.

"Just to warn you; Lieutenant Simmons, who is the officer out with the Press, is... how can I put it.... frankly a snob! He thinks he's the best thing the navy has ever had! He thinks he knows it all, which he most certainly doesn't.

Don't let him brow beat you. You may be, frankly, young for your position, but the Captain really rates you, so remember that."

"Thank you… thank you very much. Fore-warned is fore-armed!"

The First Lieutenant left and Will emerged to button-hole a petty officer to ask him to pass the word for the two Master's mates to attend him. In doing so he asked the petty officer's name, to store away for future use. A few minutes later two scruffily dressed young men appeared at the door to the cabin.

"You must be my Master's Mates?"

"Sir!" They said in unison.

"So who are you?"

The taller of the two who had a mop of blonde hair replied first. "Samuel Jackson, Sir"

"Ezekiel Granger, Sir." The second boy was short and chubby with red hair.

"Right… the first thing is - this is the Chart Room as far as I am concerned. This is how we refer to this space in future. At the moment it is a disgrace. You will clean it thoroughly from top to bottom and then you will clean yourselves. I will not tolerate members of my team dressed in a slovenly manner. It indicates a slovenly mind, and therefore a person who is liable to be slip shod and make errors. There cannot be errors in our trade. Too many lives depend upon us. Is that clear? If you haven't got any better apparel, you must see the Purser."

"Yes Sir!" Came the reply in unison.

Will left them to it and sought out the Boatswain.

CHAPTER 5

Will found the Boatswain on the mess deck' enjoying a chew of tobacco. He was a swarthy faced individual of about 40 years with his dark hair tied neatly back in a queue. When he stood up to greet Will as he introduced himself, he appeared to be above average height with powerful arms. His ready smile was to Will encouraging.

"I heard about you from the Captain." The Boatswain said after giving his name as Hughes.

Will invited him to join him with the Captains of each mast to review the state of the rigging.

"Not that I doubt that it is fully up to the mark with you in charge Mr Hughes, but you will allow that the ultimate responsibility lies with myself. It should also give me a chance to assess the Captains of the tops."

There was subtle pause as Hughes weighed up the request, but he relaxed. "Both watches?" He enquired.

"Aye! If they are both aboard."

Hughes turned and with a powerful voice shouted. "Captain's of the Tops, both watches, to your masts."

Will could hear the murmur from forward and then the sound of feet clattering up the ladderway forward.

"They didn't expect that!" Remarked Hughes with a laugh as he followed Will up the after companionway to the quarter deck.

"I suggest we work aft, don't you Boatswain?"

"Aye Sir, as you wish. Stand to! We will be with you next." Hughes told the two captains standing at the base of the main mast.

Will and Hughes made their way up the starboard gallery, past the cutters on their cradles, forward to the foremast. Here two fit young, but veteran seamen stood rigidly to attention. One was dressed in a checked shirt with a waistcoat over. He had the long trousers favoured by seamen, but his instead of being loose around the leg; had been sewn fairly tightly. His shoes were highly polished. The other wore petty-coat breeches with a horizontally striped 'frock' or jumper. Both had their hair tied tightly back in queues.

"Captains of the fore-tops Spicer and Phillips. Mr Calvert the Master." Hughes said as way of introduction.

"Good day Gentlemen. Since I am responsible up top, I should be grateful if you could show me around up there and we shall inspect the cordage as a matter of routine. I know you will have done so yourselves as well as Mr Hughes, but I am required by their Lordships to do so myself."

Both men knuckled their brows and ran for the opposing shrouds and started to climb the ratlines. Will dropped his coat to the deck and followed up the starboard side. He was grateful that he was wearing shoes rather than boots as he quickly made his way up the ratlines. Instead of using the easy way up to the foretop through the 'lubber's hole', he climbed up by way of the futtock shrouds. He knew by using this route he would show the captains-of-the-tops that he was not afraid of the height. To use the futtock shrouds you were suspended hanging on by your hands with your feet inboard of your body. Once on the Top, he was greeted with approving looks from the two Captains. The one called Phillips open mouth revealed a set of blackened gums and no teeth. Will then proceeded to inspect every part of the rigging forcing open the cordage with a marlin spike to check the quality of the ropes. As he did so he chatted amiably with both the captains establishing a rapport. He then made his way up to the fore-gallant mast. The Boatswain stayed at the foot of the mast where he was able to listen and join in with the banter. The two Captains stayed on the top staring up at the unusual sight of a Master actually climbing the top mast.

Having inspected the foremast he climbed down and

then ascended the Main Mast, using the same method to arrive at the Top. He continued his checking, even moving out on the yards to check them. When he was out on the Main-topsail yard there was a shout from below through a voice trumpet. "What's that man doing on that yard? Get down this instant!"

Will peered down to see a Lieutenant he hadn't met, eyes shaded by one hand glaring up at him. Will was quite amused, so just gave a friendly wave.

"Get that man down this instant, or I shall want to know the reason!" The Lieutenant screamed.

Will waved again. "Lieutenant Simmons?" Asked Will; of the nearest Captain-of-the-Top. The man smirked. "Aye Sir! You got him in one!"

Will looked down again and saw Hunter emerge onto the quarter deck and have words with the Lieutenant, who turned and stalked away.

Will repeated the process at the mizzen mast, before finally strolling with the Boatswain to the stern end of the quarter deck.

"I commend you on the rigging Mr Hughes. I suggest though that we have the yards down whilst we may and give them an extra coating of varnish. I rather feel that once we are at sea, it will be some time before we can do the job again. I am not criticising in anyway, you understand, it's just that we are at war and I know we shall be joining Admiral Howe's Squadron out in the Atlantic where the weather is not kind to the spars."

"I agree Sir. We'll be started immediately."

Will nodded his thanks with a smile. "I also commend you for the smart turn out of your captains, does you great credit Mr Hughes."

Hughes beamed with satisfaction, and Will knew that he had managed to get the Boatswain on his side.

Later when Will was in his cabin he could hear Lieutenant Craddock who had greeted him as he arrived aboard talking to someone he called Simmons, asking how he had got on with the Press.

"Bloody stupid idea to do it during the day, I say." Came the reply.

"I thought it rather clever, nobody would be expecting it." Craddock replied.

There was a snort of contempt and a door slammed. Will was in his cabin dressing for dinner. He had hung up those items of clothing which he felt needed to be hung rather than kept in his sea chest. He had changed his shirt and put on a new collar, around which he tied his black stock. He had no way of telling how it looked, he could only feel, there was no looking glass in the cabin. He heard a door open so made his way out into the Gunroom.

"Hello again. Sorry about the way I greeted you when you came aboard. I'm James, James Craddock. We were expecting a new Master, but I suppose I expected a wizen old cove."

Will put out his hand and shook the Lieutenant's saying. "Understandable; I am rather young to be a Master, but then we are at war!"

"Quite! Are you dining with the Captain tonight?"

"That I am and I understand that you are too."

"Shall we make our way up then? Simmons will be there already trying to impress the Captain!"

Will gathered there was no love lost between the two junior Lieutenants.

"I have no glass, is my cravat tied alright?"Asked Will.

Craddock peered at Will closely. "It's fine!"

"Thanks!"

"The First Lieutenant - excellent fellow, you will get along with him, I know." Continued Craddock; as they moved out of the gunroom.

"Yes I've met him, seems a very reliable and dependable fellow."

In a low voice Craddock added. "The Captain seems really on the ball, but you must know that having been with him on *Challenger.*"

"A very fine seaman!" Responded Will; anxious not to say too much.

Will and Craddock made their way up the ladderway to the upperdeck, where Will paused to check on the Chart Room. Earlier after his inspection he had sought out the carpenter to have shelves made and a better arrangement below the table for his charts. He was glad to see that at least the tools were there which indicated work might commence the next morning. He had also asked for a couple of trestle tables to be made up. As Master, Will was responsible for the education of the young men and midshipmen in navigation and other skills. The tables would be set up outside his chart room for an hour each day after the crews' and gunroom dinner, so he could teach.

After having been announced by the Marine on duty; the pair made their way through the dining cabin to the captain's day cabin. Here they found Simmons all by himself gazing out of the windows. He turned to see who had entered and immediately it was apparent he was disappointed. He was tall and slim with blonde hair that flopped over his eyes. His nose was definitely patrician, but the chin receded, which gave him a rather pinched look.

"Simmons, have you met Mr Calvert our Master."

"No - Mr Calvert." He managed by saying the word in a lazy drawl to make the 'Mister' sound contemptuous, as he turned back to look out of the window as if bored with idea of having to make conversation with his inferiors.

"Hello you lot!" Came Hunter's voice, from behind them. Hunter joined Will and Craddock. He nudged both before addressing Simmons.

"I understand you made a complete hash of things this afternoon, Simmons."

Simmons whirled round, fury written all over his face. He was just about to say something when his expression changed completely.

"Good evening Sir!" He said looking past the three of them. An ingratiating smile on his lips, which Will noticed did not reach his eyes.

"Good evening!" The Captain said crossing to meet them, followed by his servant who picked up a tray with cut glass wine goblets already filled with red wine.

There was a noise behind them and two more officers appeared, both dressed in a similar fashion to Will.

"Right, I don't think you will have met Surgeon Cunningham and our Purser Mr Greet. Our new Master, Mr Calvert."

The Surgeon, stepped forward to shake Will's hand. He was a tall thin man of middle age with an air of studiousness about him. His iron grey hair was cut short, which obviously meant he was used to wearing a wig when ashore. He had piercing green-blue eyes, with laughter creases at the corners. The Purser was so unlike a sailor as to be unreal. He had a round totally bald head and he peered at one through pebble glasses. His neck did not seem to exist, as his chest and stomach seemed to be attached to the head in the shape of an egg, from which protruded a pair of very short thin legs.

"I suggest we sample this wine before sitting down to dinner. I gather the rest of you have met Will here? He is late off *Challenger*." Said Captain Crick.

There was a murmur of assent and hellos as each received his glass from the servant

"Very disappointing afternoon, Simmons?" Said the Captain; once everybody had a glass in his hand.

"Yes Sir. Only managed to pick up one seaman. Everybody seemed to have protections; I am sure they were forged. The Press Lieutenant wasn't happy missing his dinner."

The Captain didn't comment; he turned to Hunter.

"Word is that we shall be sailing in company with *Justina*. Interesting to see how we perform against her. She boasts of being fast."

"At least we will start on equal terms, both having clean bottoms!" Commented Hunter.

Will standing next to Simmons could almost feel the resentment emanating from the man. He had wondered why none of the other officers could stand the man. He was to understand during the course of the meal.

After their pre-meal drink they sat down to dinner. The Captain placed Hunter on his left and Will on his right, leaving a fretting Simmons to find a place for himself. Craddock didn't seem to mind where he sat. As it turned out Simmons sat next to Hunter so Will was able to see his expression easily.

Every-time Simmons spoke he seemed to distain the present company. He couldn't wait to mention his meeting Mr Pitt at his Aunt's.

"No doubt you told him how to win the war!" The Captain jested; and immediately turned the conversation away from that subject.

Simmons didn't seem to be able to refrain from name dropping, which was obviously a reason why the others were bored by him. Every time he mentioned his aunt it was to accentuate the 'Lady' part.

Will kept very quiet, letting the conversation flow around him, unless asked a direct question. As was the normal convention at such gatherings, virtually no mention was made of ship-board affairs. Since Will knew nothing much of what was going on ashore, other than in Cornwall, he had precious little to contribute.

Then came the moment when Simmons asked "What's your accent?"

Will was caught completely off guard. The Captain spoke before Will had a chance to reply. "The same as Sir Francis Drake's, and most of our finest mariners. My mother's family came from the same part of the country. In fact it might have been Will's Grand-father who was so kind to mine. My grandfather was caught poaching. A deadly sin!

The Squire, Sir James Calvert, in questioning my grandfather found that the family was starving, so let him off and told him to ask for food, not to steal it - remarkable man!"

The put-down had its effect on Simmons, who realised his attempt to patronise Will had failed. Hunter winked at Will, showing his support. The battle lines were obviously drawn.

CHAPTER 6

The next morning on his way up to the quarter-deck, Will met another senior member of the crew, the Gunner, who on seeing Will said. "I know you; you're Will Calvert off the *Challenger*, aren't you?"

Will admitted he was, but he failed to recognise the man.

"Guns off *Challenger* is a mate of mine, told me to look out for you, you would go far, and here you are!" And he laughed at his own joke. His name turned out to be Basil Fortune. He was a short bulky character with a bald head and virtually no eyebrows. He seemed to be of a jovial nature.

On mounting to the quarter-deck; Will found Lieutenant Simmons shouting and swearing. Nobody seemed to be paying much attention to him as the ordinance barge was manoeuvred alongside. Will decided to remove himself and met Hunter on his way down the ladderway. "Stupid Bugger, Guns is in charge of this!" Hunter muttered under his breath.

Will went to the chartroom to discover one of the carpenter's mates putting up the shelves he had requested. It would be sometime before he could bring his equipment and charts up, so he set off for the forecastle to inspect the anchors that were catted. He also checked the mooring ropes to the buoy whilst he was there. The Hamoaze is a notoriously difficult port to leave if the wind is from the South or South East. Will knew it from the past, but he hadn't been responsible for leaving this harbour in an adverse wind. He took the opportunity to examine both sides of the Tamar carefully with a telescope. Where they were moored at the northern end of the buoyed area would mean that they had to pass all the ships-of-the-line. It was important not to make a hash of things. Nominally the Captain would be in charge, but it was also up to Will to advise him as Sailing Master.

After the crew's dinner, taken at the normal time of one o'clock in the forenoon, it was the victualling barge that lay alongside. The Purser was everywhere fussing about everything. Craddock was on duty, so the actual hoisting aboard was carried out in a calm and efficient manner. Will was responsible for the trim of the ship, so also ultimately responsible for where the barrels should be stowed. The Purser though seemed to have taken it upon himself to decide. Rather than cause any hostility Will watched and made a mental note of the stowage. The Purser was efficient, but didn't seem to pay any regard to the weight of the barrels as they were lowered into the hold.

It took most of the afternoon for the loading to be completed. Will then asked Hunter if he could borrow a ship's boat and crew. Hunter didn't ask for a reason, he just ordered one of the midshipmen to oblige. It was a cutter that was manned with a coxswain in command, nominally under the direction of a young midshipman, by the name of Cranfield.

Once Will was seated in the stern, he asked to be taken to the Cornish side of the river. This seemed to greatly perplex the young midshipman, but the coxswain just steered the cutter as near the shore line as was prudent. Once they were level with *Artful*, Will asked them to stop rowing. He studied the way *Artful* sat in the water. After a bit he said to the Midshipman. "How do you think she looks?"

"*Artful* Sir? Very fine, very fine indeed Sir!"

"Now look again, notice anything?"

After a moment's consideration the reply came. "No Sir!"

"I am sure if we asked the coxswain, he would know. Wouldn't you Mr Frobisher?"

The Midshipman seemed amazed that Will knew the man's name. The Coxswain grinned at the midshipman. "She be down at the foot Sir."

"Exactly!" Agreed Will. "If you look closely at the water line you will see that she is bow down. Now that, if left as it is would affect the way she handles and sails. Right let's get back aboard and do something about it Mr Cranfield."

Back aboard Will sought out the Purser. "Thank you so much for seeing to the victualling Mr Greet, unfortunately we shall have to make a few adjustments to alter the trim."

He had expected resentment, but he got abject apologises.

"Off course, of course, I was so concentrating on getting everything aboard I forgot to consult you. The last Master just left it to me."

"Well I'm sure you made a very fine job of it, but this time we are bow heavy. You wouldn't realise it unless you viewed the ship from some way off." So together they recalled the loading crew and with much muttering from the crew, plus Craddock's help had some of the barrels moved, until Will thought they might have achieved a balanced trim.

This time Cranfield, the Midshipman, was waiting eagerly to return to the cutter.

"Excuse me asking Sir, but how did you know my name and the coxswain's name?"

"I make it a rule to try and remember as many names as possible. You were pointed out to me. Mr Frobisher I met on the mess-deck, when I made myself known to the crew. It helps if the men feel you have enough respect for them to bother to remember their names."

"Thank you, Sir, I'll try and remember that!" The young Middy said as he started to descend to the cutter. Frobisher met Will with.

"She feel better from here already, Sir!"

Indeed the *Artful* now sat poised upon the water. Will studied the trim from the bow and the stern to make sure she was trimmed level as well, and was satisfied.

That evening Will met the last member of the wardroom, the marine subaltern, Spencer Wiggins. Wiggins was not much older than Will, tall and well built with a merry fresh faced countenance under a mop of sandy hair tied hard back in a queue. This meant that his ears appeared to be at right angles to his head like a loving cup's. He was ribbed unmercifully by the Surgeon about his amorous adventures ashore, but took it all in good part. Will couldn't help but compare his reactions to those of Simmons. The later sat with a leg nonchalantly thrown over the arm of his chair appearing to be studying a newspaper. Hunter sat at the head of the table writing up his journal, which reminded Will that he must write up the ship's log, even though the ship was moored. Since the chartroom was still being revamped, Will took a fresh candle and retired to his cabin to write up the official log as well as his own Journal.

CHAPTER 7

Will was summoned to the Captain's cabin, where he found not only the commissioned officers, but all the warrant officers and senior petty officers. The Captain welcomed them all aboard and then introduced the First Lieutenant, Hunter, then Craddock, Simmons and Will himself. He didn't stop there; he also named each of the warrant officers and petty officers present. The only officer not present was the Subaltern of Marines Spencer Wiggins, who Will knew was on duty outside.

The Captain then addressed them with regard to how he saw discipline being maintained aboard. He indicated the Purser, Mr Greet, and stated that the Purser had on his instruction purchased enough coloured shirts for each of the landmen.

"Each Landman is to wear the shirt at all times on duty. You Petty Officers are to allocate a trained seaman to work alongside each newcomer to show him his job. I don't want to be confronted by a Landman being 'started' just because he doesn't know what the order requires of him. Because we are at war, it is imperative that we train everybody as quickly as possible. I know that we don't have our full compliment as yet, but we shall begin training immediately. We shall exercise the guns – without firing them - twice a day, anchored or at sea. I want the top-men to take their new men with them and show them how to furl and unfurl the sails. The afterguard is to be shown what sheets, tacks and braces do and how to work together. Once a day we shall man the capstan – of course not actually taking in the anchor – but so each man knows where and what to do. Make sure that they are taught to fit the 'swifters' correctly.

I shall address the crew later when we are nearer the full compliment and ready for sea. In the meantime, mess captains are to read their messes their rights and inform them as to how they can complain, if they think they are being treated unfairly. The First Lieutenant has given you your divisions; please make sure the messes know which division they are in. There is a good reason for this – if a man thinks he has a method of redressing a grievance he is a happier man. It also means we sort out the habitual complainers from the justified ones. Don't think this is going to be a lax ship; it certainly won't be, but a crew who work and fight together are going to get the best out of the ship. That is all for the moment, thank you gentlemen."

Everybody filed out, little groups forming to discuss what the Captain had said.

Three days later the Captain addressed the ship's company after the morning service, it being Sunday.

"Gentlemen, I'm your Captain – Captain Crick." He then went on to introduce each officer and warrant officer by name. Then he continued.

"I know some of you are here against your will. I can't apologise for that because our country is at war. Don't blame the officers or your petty officers; it has nothing to do with them. Blame the French; they declared war on our country again. I understand that they intend to try and invade our country. It is up to us, His Majesty's Navy to make sure that doesn't happen. It is therefore vital that His Majesty's ships are manned. You who are new to the ways of the navy will find it difficult to adapt. New skills have to be learned. Luckily your fellow seamen are some of the best in our Navy."

There was a ragged cheer from the old hands.

"I have as you know instructed that all new hands wear coloured shirts. This is not an insult, so don't take it as such. It is so the quartermasters and boatswains mates can see immediately that you are a Landman, and therefore probably at a loss as to what you should be doing. I like a happy ship, so this means that the warrant officers won't mistakenly take you for a shirker. But this won't last! If you fail to obey an order, you will be punished, once we have established that you should know what the order demanded. That is why you have each been given a mentor. A mentor is somebody who works alongside you and shows you what is what. Very soon we shall be ordered to sea. It is highly likely that we shall meet a French warship bent on hurting us. That is why we have been practising our respective jobs. We must be faster and more accurate in the use of our guns, we must also be better at handling the sails to outwit the Frenchy. Remember they want our land, our women and children. We are not going to let them!"

A cheer went up from the crew, and Will gazing at the sea of faces realised that all had joined in.

"Just one other matter. I know from experience that life at sea is hard. It is especially hard if you don't eat well. Unfortunately it is not up to me to appoint the cook. I am sure their Lordships found us a good one. Your officers shall be eating the same food as you will be in your messes, so it better be good!" The Captain ended with a smile and a wave.

Another cheer went up, this time even more heartfelt.

The orders had arrived. *Artful* in company with *Justina* was to join Admiral Howe's fleet off Brest. It couldn't have come at a worse time as far as the wind and weather were concerned. The wind was from the south and the barometer was falling.

The Captain sent for Will, who arrived clutching a chart of Plymouth Sound and the Hamoaze.

"Ah Will, I need to pick your brains. First time in command and I have to take her out in an opposing wind with all and sundry waiting to see us make a pig's ear of it. Any ideas?"

Will walked over to the table and spread his charts. Then he produced a circular piece of card with six points of the compass marked off either side of an arrow.

"Trust you to come up with something new!" Commented the Captain."

Will laid the card over the chart near to the Hamoaze.

"The wind's from the south-south-west: so it is the first part that will be most difficult. Directly we are here at the southern end of the Hamoaze and turning to Larboard we shall have the wind just aft of our beam. When we come abreast of Mount Wise we have to turn to starboard, we will have the same problem as we will have had in the Hamoaze. I suggest that we need to sail that part close hauled on our fore and aft sails. Ten cables past Devil's Point, here in the Narrows, we will have a choice. The tide will be right for either continuing straight on or using the Drake Channel. I strongly advise using Drake's Channel, there are rocks on the 'Bridge' here, between St Nicholas Island and Ravenness Point. So it is the first part that is most taxing. If I might propose a method that might give us most control?"

"Go ahead!" Said the Captain: gazing down at the chart.

"If we pass a line through the mooring eye and back on

the same side bow and another from the stern to the mooring buoy and back, we could then, using just our foresails, inch up against the beginning of the tide as it turns to ebb. We hold the ship on the new bow line, so we can free the mooring warp. Once we are ready we cast off our temporary bow line and take up the stern one. Then we put the helm over so as to turn the bows to starboard to catch the tide. The tide since it will have only just turned won't be too strong. We let the tide turn us using the stern-line to hold us. We only hoist fore and aft sails for the first part. We detach the stern-line once we are facing downstream. With just the two jibs, main and mizzen staysails plus the spanker set we will have just enough to give us sufficient steerage with the tide pushing us from astern."

The Captain straightened up and regarded Will for a long moment. "You had this all worked out long ago didn't you?"

"Yes Sir."

"Very good, Master, so be it!"

Will turned to go, but the Captain called after him. "Thank you; not the way I would have attempted it, but I think you are right!"

Will knew that as far as the rest of the officers were concerned they would remain ignorant of his input. He didn't expect praise, it was his job.

The final preparations for leaving were made. *Justina* as the senior ship would leave first. They watched from the quarter-deck as she unfurled her sails from their yards. The tide had yet to turn when *Justina* let go her mooring ropes which meant she had the remains of the tide pushing her up river as well as the wind. She managed to sail past *Artful* before trying to turn. Here she got into difficulties, she was carried sideways up the river before she managed to come head to tide and the wind. She was carried stern first still further up the river. Because technically *Justina* had cast off, it was now time for *Artful* to do the same. The Captain waited until *Justina* finally managed to make it downstream past *Artful*, then he gave the order to haul in on the two headsails, but to keep them full. The wind gave her way and she nudged up to the buoy where the buoy-jumper undid the mooring warp. The ship now came up taught on the temporary bow line, which was let go and hauled in. She was now held by the stern-line. The sheets were eased. Since the tide was now slack and just starting to turn, she swung across the stream still firmly held to the buoy by the stern line. Once the turning tide had pushed her head round, the sheets were hauled across to the opposite side and tightened and the stern line let slip. As close to the wind as she could sail on fore and aft sails alone, she ghosted past the Port Admiral's flagship to turn neatly to larboard where the square sails were released and she picked up speed to steer calmly through the narrows. Then the topsails and top gallant sheets were eased and she sailed on her fore and afters, before again sheeting in the topsails and top gallants out into the Sound.

Since this was the first time that the Captain had taken his own frigate to sea, there was considerable pleasure to be seen on the faces of the crew; they had shown a more experienced Captain the way to do it!

Later Craddock confided in Will that Simmons had scathingly commented when they had started out on fore and aft sails alone: 'For God's sake we're a frigate not a bloody sloop!" Now he had to eat his words after witnessing the hash the other frigate had made of the departure.

CHAPTER 8

It was the start of a long period of being at sea. They finally joined up with the other frigates on patrol after a week of searching. *Artful* had played follow my leader to *Justina* the whole time, so they weren't to blame when they finally caught up with the senior frigate. It was too rough for a meeting of the Captains, so they were signalled to detach and go with the Outer Squadron. This group of frigates were forming a line within signalling distance of each other and patrolling up and down waiting for any French ships to try to escape from Brest.

The Inner squadron would sail close to the French coast to try to gain as much information as possible. The Inner Squadron of five or six frigates and a couple of smaller sloops were to reconnoitre individually. The Channel Fleet, made up of the ships-of-the-line stayed off Spithead, as free as possible of any dangers of storms, but ready to sail as a fleet if information was delivered back to them that the French Fleet had broken out. The news would be rushed back from the frigates by the smaller faster sloops.

Whatever the weather, the frigates ploughed backwards and forwards. Will settled into the routine, always busy and occupied. He soon learned the strengths and weaknesses of the watch keeping officers. Hunter was experienced and professional. Craddock, although fairly green, learnt fast and was popular amongst the crew. Simmons was lazy and abusive. The crew resented him almost to a man. You could observe the way the crew responded to the differing methods of command. Hunter was confident and hardly ever raised his voice, giving his commands through the various time honoured channels. Craddock could be a bit diffident, but wasn't above asking advice from the senior members of the crew. Simmons on the other hand shouted and screamed at everybody.

Blockade duty in the north Biscay area is the worst possible posting. The sea is unpredictable and you can have gales and rough seas for days. Navigation is a nightmare, as very often there is total cloud coverage. The discomfort is another matter. Everything seems to be permanently damp. There is no escape. Even your hammock or cot feels damp when you finally manage to climb into it exhausted. Trying to estimate or plot a position is a constant battle to hold the chart and the instruments from sliding away. Eating means that stews are the order of the day, as they can be spooned from a bowl held close to the mouth. On really bad days it is impossible and dangerous to keep the cook's range alight, so it is even worse. Drinking requires that the mug is never full; it must have enough room for the liquid to slop about in it as the ship heaves itself over another wave. Perhaps the only redeeming feature was that when possible the supply ships brought fresh meat and vegetables, as it was only a couple of days sail from Plymouth and Falmouth. The crew would also have a ready supply of beer to keep them satisfied.

On deck, unless one is lucky with the weather, the sea is being constantly scooped up and thrown back across the deck at you. It is one hand for yourself and another for the boat. The canvas waterproofs were anything but waterproof. You were soaked to the skin within seconds and had to stand the rest of the watch shaking with cold, and there was no prospect of a warm fire to dry yourself off. All you could do was to rub yourself down to get the circulation going again, and look forward to your tot of rum, or if an officer, a brandy to warm your inner self.

Conversely you would suddenly get a bright warm day, with the sun shining, but no time to put out clothes to dry, as rain laden clouds would build in the west advancing, in your direction. Thomas Tucker, Will's servant spent hours wiping Will's instruments to try and keep them dry. Will had experimental foul weather clothing, based on his late father's, which he paid the sailmakers' mates to cut out and sew together to see if the quartermasters' lives could be improved in a small way. Sail cloth was in most cases far too stiff and uncomfortable to suit. He tried lighter material impregnated with various ingredients including a mixture of candle wax and cooking oil. All his designs featured high collars with buttoned fronts that came up to just below the eyes. The skirts fell right down to nearly touch the deck. They did meet with some approval, but sailors are very resistant to change.

The frigates had difficulty in the bad weather keeping station. The Senior Captain of the squadron kept pouring scorn on Will's and therefore *Artful's* repeated lowering of upper yards and top masts. That was until after yet another signal berating them, the lead frigate's top masts were torn off in a particularly fierce gust. The signals ceased.

Tedium is the worst enemy to a crew on patrol. Will was probably the least affected, as he was constantly on the go. There being no Second Master, he was on call day or night. He spent a great deal of time trying to bring the relatively inexperienced Master's Mates up to speed, so as to relieve the pressure on himself. He took to having a hammock rigged in the chartroom, so he was instantly ready for any eventuality.

They had been enjoying a few days of moderate seas, and clear skies. The wind was now beginning to build and Will could see from the clouds to the West that the weather was going to get a lot worse. He turned to the Officer-of-the-Watch, who happened to be Lieutenant Simmons. Knowing how prickly the Lieutenant tended to be, Will said.

"Wind is going to get stronger, I advise that we furl the Top Gallants and reef the Topsails."

"I have the Watch!" Replied Simmons; stalking away from Will to the bulwarks.

Will took another glance to the West and then into the chartroom to plot their noon position on the chart and bring the Journal up to date.

As he was finishing the journal entry he felt that *Artful* was not behaving quite as he would have expected. She seemed to be heeling over rather more than would be usual and the noises weren't right.

Will grabbed his oilskin from the back of the chartroom door and put it on as he went back out to the quarterdeck.

One look confirmed his worst suspicions. The Frigate was carrying too much sail.

He was just in time to hear the Boatswain ask if he

should take in the topgallants, Simmons told him to mind his place. The Boatswain was an old tar and immensely experienced. Will who was just coming onto the quarterdeck realised immediately that the action had not been taken. Without stopping to consult Simmons, he shouted at the Boatswain.

"Take those Top-Gallants in - NOW!"

Simmons screamed at Will. "Mind your place, you fucking peasant!"

"And reef the Top-sails!" Will added.

As the topmen raced to the ratlines, Simmons swung round at Will.

"How dare you! I am the officer-of-the-watch. I am your senior!" He screamed.

"Then look to your ship!" Countered Will; turning to see what was happening aloft.

Simmons grabbed Will by the front of his oil skin.

"You'll pay for this you little turd!" He shouted; then he released his right hand and closing his fist swung his arm back in preparation to punch Will in the face. Will was a stronger build than the Lieutenant and grabbed Simmons' wrist that was holding on to him and brought up his other arm to turn the punch aside.

The Boatswain moved forward to protect Will from a screaming demented Simmons.

Because of the worsening weather both the First Lieutenant and the Captain had decided to come on deck. They both caught the end of the incident and the resulting tussle.

Simmons was fixated on the supposed insult, rather than on the reason and failed to see the approach of the two senior officers.

"Lieutenant Simmons, leave the quarterdeck this instant and wait for me in my cabin." Commanded the Captain; in a low threatening growl.

"I have the Watch!" Called Hunter; from beside the quartermasters at the wheel.

The Boatswain had arrived on the quarterdeck panting.

"Thank God you came on deck Mister Calvert!" He gasped.

"What exactly is going on?" Asked the Captain; looking straight at the duty Masters Mate as spume from a wave crest soaked him.

"Err... well I am afraid that Lieutenant Simmons took exception to the Master giving the order for the topgallants to be taken in. Lieutenant Simmons lost his rag, Sir!"

"Mister Calvert?" The Captain turned to Will.

"Exactly as the Mate says, Sir. The Topgallants should have been furled earlier and I was afeared that we could lose our topmasts. I had advised Lieutenant Simmons to take in sail earlier, but he had obviously ignored me!"

The Captain looked sharply at the First Lieutenant, who spoke up.

"I didn't get the first part, but I gather that is what happened." He turned to the nearest Quartermaster.

"Were you here on duty when Mister Calvert advised the Officer-of-the-watch to reduce sail?"

"Aye Sir! Mister Calvert said to take in the Topgallants and reef the Topsails, Sir. Lieutenant Simmons shouted he had the watch, Sir!"

"And you?" The Captain asked Cranfield the Middy on watch.

"Aye Sir! Mister Calvert advised Lieutenant Simmons to take in the Top-Gallants and reef the Topsails. We were all surprised when he didn't do it. I asked if I should relay the order to the Boatswain and was told to shut my trap! Then the Mate here repeated the advice and was told to get out of his sight – that is Lieutenant Simmons sight, Sir."

"Mister Calvert?" Enquired the Captain.

"It didn't cross my mind that he wouldn't do so in this wind; Sir! I took it that he meant he had the watch and would do just that."

"You happy to take over this watch Number One; whilst I deal with this?"

"Aye Sir!"

Will was a bit shaken by the altercation. He might be a year or so younger than Simmons, but he was the Sailing Master, so it was his responsibility to advise the other officers. He had never dreamt that Simmons would take the advice as an insult.

Just as the Captain was leaving the quarterdeck an extra strong gust struck the frigate. All glanced up at the masts to see that the Top Gallants were safely furled and all topsails reefed.

The Captain gave a wry smile to the assembled group around the wheel as the frigate righted herself.

"Somebody seems to be looking after us!"

Later that evening Simmons was nowhere to be seen in the wardroom. Will didn't ask, he just raised an eyebrow in question and Wiggins the Marine Subaltern jerked a thumb towards Simmons' shut cabin door. Now with a gale blowing there was only cold food to sustain him and a shot of brandy, before he made his way back up on deck.

"Can you take the watch, whilst I just pop down and change into dry and warmer clothes?" Asked Hunter; as Will joined him on the quarterdeck. Normally the Commissioned Officers took turns with the watch, Will being available at all times in theory to advise them.

"Certainly!" Replied Will; as more spume came thrusting up covering all beside the helm. He took it as a compliment in his ability that the Number One should swiftly show his seal of approval.

Ten minutes later Hunter returned, this time properly dressed against the elements.

"Rotten night!" Shouted Hunter.

"Going to get worse before Midnight, then it should slowly get better."

Hunter glanced at him. He had never quite worked out

Will's uncanny ability to accurately predict the weather. He didn't know that Will back referenced different situations from his personal journal, so as to be able to predict the weather better.

Two weeks later they met up with the leader of their group, who signalled that *Artful* was to return to Plymouth to re-victual. Simmons hadn't reappeared so Will found himself alternating watches with Craddock. The wind was not kind to them when they arrived in Plymouth Sound, so they hoisted a signal to be re-victualled and tacked back and forth across the Sound. Cawsand on the western side of Plymouth Sound, the one refuge that could be used was too exposed. They would have to carry on to Torbay to get any respite from the stormy weather, but the Captain hoped that they could place their order and a hoy might just be able to get round with the supplies when the sea calmed down. After an hour a small sloop appeared from behind St Nicholas Island sometimes referred to as Drakes Island. When the small vessel finally luffed up alongside *Artful*, it was possible to shout across using speaking trumpets. With some difficulty the vessel managed to come close enough on the leeward side for a line to be thrown and then a canvas bag with the written requirements successfully exchanged. The Captain informed the sloop's Captain that *Artful* would proceed to Torbay and that the urgently required victuals should be delivered there as soon as was possible.

Artful then sailed on to round Start Point and at last found fairly calm waters close in near other ships of the fleet sheltering at anchor in Torbay. The main part of the Channel Squadron was here, so the Captain's gig was prepared and the Captain was rowed over to the flagship.

On his return the Captain brought with him the Master-at-Arms from the flagship together with two burly marines. Simmons was brought up and taken away to the flagship to await a Court Martial.

That night the wardroom entertained the Captain, though

on rather meagre rations, and there was a great deal of laughter in a new relaxed atmosphere. Will could but ponder on the effect of removing one person from a closed group and its effect.

Two days later the hoy arrived and *Artful* was resupplied. The Admiral's Flag Lieutenant arrived and went below to have a word with the Captain. Soon after he had left, the crew were called to quarters for leaving harbour. *Artful* left with fresh supplies, but no replacement for Simmons. As a result Will was called to the Captain's cabin once the ship was settled on her course back towards Ushant and the Brest Patrol.

"Ah Will, come in!" Said the Captain: after Will had been announced by the marine on duty at the Captain's door.

Will crossed towards the Captain's desk, but the Captain had stood up and came to meet Will.

"Will, this is off the record so to speak, but since Simmons is still on the books officially, we aren't allowed a replacement. I told the Admiral that I was quite happy to promote you to Acting Lieutenant until such time as the Court Martial is completed. It is highly unusual, but then these are unusual times. He asked me about your abilities and I was happy to inform him that I considered you to be an outstanding officer. I pointed out to him that I had served with you in *Challenger,* and that you had already been acting as the third Lieutenant in reality, and that I considered you to be of great benefit to the ship. I realise that you are undertaking two jobs at the same time, but I saw no deterioration in your navigation or other duties. However this arrangement could be greatly to your benefit in the long run when you are put up for a Commission."

Will was stunned. It had never occurred to him, that he might make the leap to Commissioned Officer, and therefore the long chain up the command ladder. He mumbled a self-conscious thank-you, and was grateful to regain the quarter-deck.

CHAPTER 9

When they met up once more with the squadron leader, they were informed that they were to change places with another frigate that needed to be re-supplied and that they would now be charged with patrolling inshore. This time they were on their own and not sailing as part of a squadron. Their remit was intelligence and reconnaissance. Their area was from Brest in the North to the River Loire in the south. Three frigates were already on their way south to check out the area that included Rochefort, another French base, and the River Gironde. The orders were to stop and search all vessels that might be supplying the French Fleet or war effort. They were to seek out and attack any French men-of-war.

Will set a course to take them close to the 'Bec de la Chevre' on the French chart, or the Cap de la Chevre, on the English version. They would then swing into the Bay of Douarnenez; do a sweep around it and then out and round the Point de Raz, inshore of the Island called Ile de Seine. Where, if they didn't time it right, they could meet strong adverse tides. The Captain pouring over the chart beside Will in the chart room commented that he doubted very much that anything of any significance would be found in the Bay. The river at the south eastern corner, could hide a frigate, but according to the chart there was precious little to recommend it.

He was proved right, they luffed up outside the entrance and sent in a ship's 25ft cutter, but there was no sign of anything bigger than a fishing smack. As night was approaching they anchored close to the shore.

That evening in the wardroom there was a discussion about the use of cutters to investigate the bays and river mouths. Hunter was worried that a cutter could get caught in cross fire from forces on shore; it was very vulnerable. The Subaltern, who was normally quiet during such discussions and always seemed very languid, spoke up.

"Why don't we disguise the boat and crew?"

Hunter turned to him. "How do you mean?"

"Well if we painted the cutter bright colours and all our fellows were dressed like natives, how are the Frenchies to know who we are?"

"I never thought a marine would discard his uniform!" Laughed the Surgeon.

"Normally no – but these are unusual times. Remember it wasn't so long ago this part of the country was up in arms on the side of the king." The Subaltern grinned at the assembly under the swinging lantern.

"We really need people who can speak French, but in a local accent." Commented the Purser: who had been listening intently.

"Could we find enough weird clothes for the cutter's crew?" Asked Hunter.

"Most of the crew look pretty weird to me anyway! It's my marines who need to be disguised; as well as the cutter – far too Admiralty regulation." The Subaltern interjected.

"Do you think you could take in a cutter with your marines doing the rowing? That would mean that they could have sufficient firepower to counter a threat." Will added to the discussion.

There was general agreement and after their evening meal had been finished, Hunter went up to put the idea to the Captain.

"Marines rowing a longboat! I have got to see this!" Was the Captain's first comment.

"Spencer was all for it. I gather that he is pretty certain that they can get by. Perhaps not quite what an Admiral would expect, but he points out that locals probably wouldn't be keen on perfection. The Purser has agreed to provide the costumes from his store."

"Well, Will was pointing out the number of small bays and river mouths for which he had no large scale charts or any pilot information. He was very concerned about us going in too close, and getting stuck. The only way we can check them out is with the longboat, so I think the idea has merit. You have my permission to personalise the boat to be used. Will has charts of the larger places where it is more likely that a ship of any significance could hide. We need to identify the places we can ignore to save time. I suggest we call for the Master and see what he thinks."

So Will was summoned to bring his charts to the Captain's cabin, where they were spread out. They identified seven likely places in the first stretch to the Passage de la Teignouse, where a ship the size of a sloop or frigate could possibly lie up. In the Biscay area an onshore breeze normally blows in the afternoon and then slowly veers to a North Westerly later in the afternoon. Using the winds they decided that it was best if they made passage in the late afternoon and stand off during the night, then dropping the cutter off at first light, search further south and then return for the boat midday.

Hunter suddenly had an idea. "What if we could snaffle a local fishing boat, large enough for the crew to sleep aboard and then they could explore the inlets, leaving us free to inspect the larger places. It could save a lot of time."

"And where would you expect to find such a ship?" Asked the Captain.

"Loctudy looks the first." Replied Will; pointing to the chart. At that moment a midshipman was announced and gave Lieutenant Craddock's compliments, but the Raz de Seine was coming up fast on the larboard bow. Will hoped his calculations were correct, and that the tides would indeed be in their favour.

They rounded the Point du Van, and there ahead of them lay the Ile de Seine with a narrow channel of only about a mile and a half of water between the island and the mainland with dangerous rocky outcrops. It was a passage that Will would not have attempted in other than the finest weather and with the tides just right. They were blessed with a moderate breeze and a calm sea. Will had judged the tides correctly, but it still necessitated constantly taking bearings. Once through they turned to run south-east along the coast. The slight haze was now lifting and they began to get a clearer view of the rocky coast. They followed the coast about a mile off, near enough to be able to see clearly if there were any hide-holes. Rounding the point de Penmarch they turned East to follow the coast. They dropped anchor off the village of Loctudy and sent in the cutter to investigate the river mouth.

When the cutter returned, Midshipman Bright' in command reported that there a few small coasting vessels further up, but that they didn't look as if they were in any state to go to sea. There seemed to be no craft of a reasonable size suitable for their purposes. Soon they were off the entrance to the river Odet. There was a Fort on the Western side marked on the chart, so they made sure that they kept a minimum of 1½miles off. Since it was still light, but there seemed little activity the Captain decided that they pretend to sail past. As night fell they retraced their course to lie off the entrance. Undercover of the darkness, the longboat, not yet repainted, was lowered and a handpicked group of marines and able-seamen, dressed in weird garments all of a dark colour dropped down to man the oars. The Subaltern and the Corporal of marines followed. Muskets and ammunition together with a swivel gun were lowered to them and the party set out to row up the river. Extra lookouts were posted and the ship settled down to wait.

Hunter came to see Will and suggested that it wasn't fair on Will to have to do turn and turnabout watches as well as his duties as Master. He proposed that he took every alternative one of Will's watches.

"I know the Captain is keen that you are recorded as having had a lot of experience as Officer of the Watch, but I don't want you to get too washed out!"

CHAPTER 10

At what would have been two bells of the morning watch, four o'clock in the morning, but they weren't sounding them so close to the enemy shore, the longboat arrived back, rowed by half the number of oarsmen as had left. An hour later they were joined by a small fishing smack of some 40ft in length. The smell of rotting fish was pretty awful, but it appeared to be a sound vessel. The Midshipman, John Fairley, who had been nominally in-charge, was cock-a-hoop. The Coxswain was rather more restrained in his description, but it was obvious that it would suit better than the longboat. Apparently they had come across the smack anchored about seven cables up-river. The longboat had towed the smack to the river mouth where there was sufficient room for the smack's sails to be set. The smack had to tack its way out to *Artful* whereas the longboat had taken the direct route.

Will's Master's Mates and the Young Men were hauled out of their hammocks and put to copying what large scale charts they had of the coast and its ports. Before first light *Artful* hauled up her anchor and slipped out of the estuary mouth and back to sea towing the smack.

It was decided that the senior midshipman Gregory Yates should be in command of the smack with Spencer Wiggins in charge of the reconnaissance party. When the sun was up, the smack dropped her tow line and made for the coast. On board was one of the Masters Mates, Ezekiel Granger, who was instructed to chart and draw as much of the uncharted areas as possible. It was agreed that they should rendezvous off the northern coast of the Ile de Groix in two days time, weather permitting. The Captain instructed them to take enough provisions for two weeks as insurance. The smack was provided with two swivel guns as well as extra muskets. Two of *Artful's* crew who happened to be Royalist

Frenchmen, were included in-case they were challenged. *Artful* would patrol the mouth of the estuary that led up to Port Louis, at the mouth of the river marked as the Le Scorff and then down to the mouth of the River La Vilaine and back. The smack would investigate all the smaller places in between.

The places where the smack would look were too dangerous for a ship like *Artful* to navigate without a really large scale and reliable chart or local knowledge.

Having watched the smack sail away towards the coast, Will had to inform the Captain that the weather was set to change for the worse. With the Iles de Mouton and the islands of Genan to the South-West, it was no place to be. They therefore made their way South and then out further to the West, well away from any hazards. A day later they were under a minimum of sails riding out a storm. The clouds seemed to reach down to the sea, and the rain came in waves of penetrating ferocity. For Will it was a period of calm. There was nothing within miles for them to run into, and the ship was riding the waves well. He actually managed to force himself to go down to his cabin and sleep in his cot. He was now confident in the remaining officers, and knew that they would not take risks.

Three days later the storm blew itself out. At noon they were able to plot their position both from a noon day sight and the outline of Belle Isle. *Artful* would arrive off the entrance to the Vilaine just as it was getting dark, so they stood out to sea. Will planned to be at the mouth of the Vilaine at four bells of the Forenoon Watch (1000). He was counting on it being a clear starry night so he would be able to navigate by the stars, taking regular fixes. If it clouded over they would have to estimate their position and stay well out to sea until dawn. Luckily it remained cloudless with a moderate sea so at each bell the Officer-of-the-Watch and two midshipmen took fixes. Will had decided to take the middle watch which since it started at midnight would mean he would be on duty when they should alter course south of

Belle Ile and have the tricky passage to pass the island of Hoedic and the rocks of Les Cardinaux. It is a very dangerous coast, there are masses of hidden rocks far out off the Passage de Teignouse that marks the southernmost tip of the Quiberon peninsular and the islands beyond. Go too far towards the main coast of France and you have more rocks to contend with.

At two bells the shoreline was obvious and as they closed, Will had everybody trying to find the spire of the Church of Billiers and to the east the Abbey de Prières. This according to his father's notes was the conspicuous marks on which to approach.

Should be approached on a course NE half E.

Note: At entrance to river is shoal or bar. Entrance to La Grande Accroche – River Vilaine –should not be attempted at other than flood tide. Rocks to S ½ cable from point. River subject to silting. Max depth approx 1 fathom at flood. Narrow winding river widens about a mile inland, with gorge like conditions. Should only be attempted by smaller vessels; preferably with sweeps.

"He says there is a large shoal astride the entrance called La Grande Accroche which has only half a fathom depth in places. There are also rocks off the southern side of the entrance. We won't be able to enter the river itself, because it silts badly, so one would need a pilot. Looking at his chart I think we could get quite near the northern side where the Abbaye is situated and be able to see up the river." Will told the Captain.

"Very good!" The Captain said; still searching for the Church spire.

"There Sir, right on the bow. It's just showing through the mist." Cried one of the Midshipmen; excitedly.

"Got it! Thank you Mr Sweet. I think you are right." The Captain regarded the compass. He then made a few alterations to the course until they were on the correct heading.

They coasted in towards the shore with their courses furled. The wind was from west, which meant that they could reasonably predict that they would be able to make their way out without having to tack. As they neared the Point de Penlan they could see clearly up the river until it bent away about four miles inland. There were a number of small trading vessels anchored waiting for the tide, but no French naval vessels as far as they could make out. Nobody appeared ready to come out and challenge them. This part of the Coast of France was not as heavily fortified as the North. Satisfied, they wore round and headed south about a mile out, apprehensive about the rocks mentioned in Will's father's notes. They ignored Le Croisic as the entrance would have been too difficult for any frigate.

By late afternoon they had made their way out into the Atlantic again, making sure they were well away from the rock infested coast. Next morning found them turning east to close the shore. To enter the mouth of the River Loire it is necessary to keep to the northern side as there are sand banks in the middle of the channel. Suddenly Will felt a searing pain and was thrown backwards against the starboard side hammocks and collapsed to the deck. The next thing he remembered was hearing the Surgeon saying.

"Get a couple more buckets of water." Will found he was blind - all he could see was red. He gasped as a bucket of cold water was thrown on his face. "And another!" He heard the Surgeon say and again the stinging pain.

"Now keep still Mr Calvert!" Said the Surgeon and blinking Will could at last make out vaguely a face peering down at him with a lantern swinging behind. Somehow he must be below decks, but he couldn't remember how he had got there.

"The leather!" Came the Surgeon's voice and a round thick piece of evil tasting leather was forced into his mouth. Strong hands held his arms and legs, whilst a very strong grip was taken of his head. Next something terrible was thrust up one nostril, the pain so bad that he passed out.

The next thing he knew was waking up with the deck-head a couple of feet above him.

"You awake Sir?" The voice of his servant Tucker, coming from somewhere to his right. Will tried to turn, but his head began to swim and he shut his eyes.

"Where am I Tucker?" He crocked, the taste of blood still filling his mouth.

"In your cot, Sir. You had your nose bashed in. First Lieutenant says it was a splinter off the spanker boom."

"How come?"

"There was a shore battery, what didn't take kindly to us. Hit the spanker boom and a great piece of it wacked you across the face. You are bandaged now, but apparently the Surgeon had to gouge out airways both sides."

"It bloody well hurts like hell!" Cried Will.

"Bound to Sir. I'll get you some brandy shall I?"

"Thank you, Tucker, but I doubt it will kill the pain!"

He heard Tucker moving off and then Hunter's voice.

"Well you would be the first to be injured in action, wouldn't you Will?" It was said with a chuckle.

Will tried to grin, but winced with the pain.

"Painful?" Asked Hunter; sounding sympatric.

"Very!" Grunted Will; finding it hard to breathe.

Surgeon will be here soon. Just patching up a couple of crew who took minor wounds.

"What happened?" Asked Will.

"A battery opened up from the shore. One of their first shots hit the spanker boom and a very large piece, like a big splinter, came whirling off and struck you full in the face. You were thrown across the quarterdeck – nearly knocked the Captain over! You passed out and were carried down to the Orlop. We returned fire, which the Frenchies didn't like, so they stopped firing. We had a look around and sailed out, this time we fired first, which kept them very quiet. Now we are safely back at sea. The Captain didn't fancy trying to make passage between Belle Ile and the island of Hoedic, so we are going the long way round."

"Many hurt?" Asked Will.

"Five in all; but only from small splinters. The French cannon must have been shooting a little too high, because besides the spanker boom, they caught the main course yard."

At that moment the Surgeon arrived, Hunter moved aside to let the Surgeon get to the side of the cot, where he peered down at Will.

"A lot of pain?"

"Rather a lot!"

"Well your nose was pretty badly smashed up. Pushed right back into your face, I had to force passages either side by pushing up the cartilage from inside. Rather painful procedure, I'm afraid, but necessary if you were going to be able to breathe through your nose again. You passed out with the pain, which was to be expected. Nature being kind! I couldn't give you anything until you regained consciousness. Now I am going to give you some Laudanum, which will probably send you to sleep, but will help with the pain. I don't want to give you too much, because I am of the opinion that it can become addictive."

The Surgeon proceeded to put a hand under Will's head and gently lift him up before offering him a tumbler. Will sipped slowly until it was gone. The Surgeon then lowered him gently back onto his cot mattress.

The next day in the afternoon watch, the smack was seen tacking her way towards them. After rendezvousing, the smack was taken in tow and *Artful* made her way back South giving the Point de Conguel a wide berth. Without Will, the Captain had no desire to attempt the Passage de Teignouse to reach Quiberon Bay. Instead he followed Will's charted route from a couple of days earlier. Not wanting to put the smack at risk, *Artful* kept well to the South so if there were any defences at the mouth of the entrance to the Morbihan, they would not realise that the smack had anything to do with the hostile frigate. Rested, the smack crew returned to their craft and set off to explore the inner waterways of the Morbihan. Later in the day from close off shore *Artful's* lookouts on the tops could see well into the area. There were no tall masts which might have given away the presence of a warship. The Morbihan is a large inland sea, divided from the sea by low lying land, so it was absolutely essential to check carefully. A whole fleet could be holed up in the south eastern section. *Artful* cruised up and down waiting for the smack to reappear, but by dusk, there was no sign of her. *Artful* therefore made short runs within the Bay of Quiberon that night. Late in the morning the smack reappeared through the narrow entrance channel. The Midshipman in charge, Gregory Yates, shamefacedly admitted that they had run aground on a falling tide and had been stuck. However there was no sign of any naval forces present.

CHAPTER 11

Since Will was indisposed, the Captain decided to leave the Bay by heading towards the ancient port of Le Croisic on the Brittany coast, before turning out to sea. This meant that it would take a day longer before they were heading north once more, but he felt prudence was called for. On the second day well out to sea, those on the quarter deck were surprised to see a bandaged Will climbing up the ladderway from the upper deck.

"You fit enough?" Asked Craddock; who had the watch.

"Can't stand being cooped up any longer." Replied Will.

"Well I suppose it is one way of getting out of your watches. How are you feeling?"

"Sore, very sore and it is quite difficult to breathe through the nose. But Sawbones says that it's the swelling and will go down soon."

"Better not show your face to the enemy, they would

turn and run a mile!" Joked Craddock; smartly coming to attention at the sight of the Captain coming up the ladderway to the quarterdeck.

"Hello Will, good to see you back on your feet! Pretty sore I imagine?"

"Yes Sir, very painful, though the Laudanum helps. Where are we Sir?"

"About halfway between Ile de Groix and Point Penmarch. We should be seeing the Iles de Glènan on the starboard side in about an hour"

"What time do you expect us to be passing Point Penmarch?"

"Should be there by six this evening. We shall be standing out to sea so we are well clear of land during the night."

Will took himself off to the chartroom, where he found one of his Mates pouring over the chart. Will regarded the chart and then the log.

"Who's been filling the log?" He asked.

"First Lieutenant, Sir"

Will flicked back through the last few entries.

"Keep a check on the wind direction and the weather to the West!" He said as he left the chartroom. He didn't really feel up to anything more.

The next morning Will felt better, he could breathe more easily. He even felt like some breakfast, which drew some witty comments from his fellow mess-mates.

Back in the chartroom his feelings of the night before were confirmed. He went back up to the quarterdeck and tried to sniff the air, but soon realised that was impossible. He stood for some time watching the clouds and the sea. He then went to see the Captain.

"We are going to have a southerly wind this morning and it will gradually move round to the southeast about noon. It would be the ideal time for the French to try and leave Brest."

"Really? Rather further south than normal for this time of year?" Commented the Captain.

"All the same I am pretty certain that is what will happen."

"Right we'd better get up there pretty quickly! Thank you Will; you're obviously feeling better! I am afraid though Will that your eye sockets are blue black, must have terrible bruising. How's the breathing?"

"Better, thank you Sir. I am sorry if my appearance troubles you."

"Will, it doesn't trouble me at all, I just hope you are fit enough to resume work. Might frighten the French though - if we come up with them!"

Will found it painful to smile, so he made a small bow and retreated.

With the wind from the south-west and quite strong with a rolling swell capped with foam, the Captain had all sails set. Running with all her kites up; as Will referred to them, meant that *Artful* was making good speed. Royals were set as well as spritsails and studding sails. Though the tide was against them as it was one hour after High Water, it made very little difference to her progress.

The Captain had cleared the decks for action, the gun ports were still shut, but the men stood ready by their guns. Hunter and Craddock were still on the quarterdeck. Craddock would be in charge of the forecastle carronades, Hunter the main armament, whilst Spencer Wiggins would be in charge of the quarterdeck carronades. Will was in his place close to the quartermasters at the wheel and within earshot of the Captain. The Boatswain was standing close to the quarterdeck rail ready to make any adjustments to the sails. It was a routine that was observed first thing every morning. The only unusual part of it was that they didn't normally approach a possible engagement under full sail, but the Captain was eager to get to the mouth of the Brest Harbour as quickly as possible.

They had made good progress after rounding the Point de Raz early in the morning. Now they were fast approaching the Point de Pen-Huir, the southernmost point of the Camaret Peninsular, from where they should be able to see if any ships had left Brest Harbour. Will was now piloting *Artful*. As they reached the headland abeam, they altered course to take the inshore passage between the mainland and the rocks. They had to sail within half a mile of the French coast before turning 20° to larboard as they came abreast of the Roche du Lion, a rocky outcrop with a hole through the centre. They were now in the Toulinguet Passage between the rock and the Point de Toulinguet. As they came round the point, still under full sail, the foretop lookout shouted out that two ships were preparing to leave the Brest inlet. On the quarterdeck all with telescopes to hand raised them to see the masts of two ships showing above the low lying peninsular of the Goulet de Brest which forms the southern side of the narrow passage entrance to Brest Harbour.

"Kites in, Mr Hughes, the Captain called to the Boatswain. Mr Cranfield, be so good as to hoist my personal ensign!" The Midshipman ran to the flag locker. Will stopped himself from frowning; it hurt too much, as he didn't understand what the Captain was talking about.

"Boats out! Larboard side only"

It was normal when preparing to do battle for the ships boats to be put in the water and left to fend for themselves, until they could be retrieved. The last thing anybody wanted was the extra danger of fragments of boat flying about. Dropping the boats on the larboard side meant that it would be harder for the French ships to see what was happening.

"Mr Calvert we shall keep the courses set for the moment – let's try and confuse the issue. Number One, don't open the ports until I give the word. Lieutenant Craddock, you can go forward now, but don't fire until we are really close. Load shot, then grape alternatively down the line. Number

One I want low, high, low. I intend to turn across the leading frigates bows at the last minute when we are close up. Will, I will give you the word when I want the Courses furled, but leave them be for the moment."

Will considered how the Captain was so calm. He realised that he had seen it all before during the two previous wars, but even so this was the first time he had been in command in action with enemy ships, as far as Will knew. The keeping up of the Courses was a master stroke. No French Captain would suspect an oncoming vessel to be aggressive, as all ships furled their courses before engaging the enemy.

"Sail on the horizon to west!" Called the maintop lookout.

"Hoist signal flag No. 1 from the larboard yard, if you please Mr Cranfield." The No.1 pennant was Lord Howe's Code for 'Enemy in sight'.

"Number One, don't bother to run out the guns, have them close up to the ports ready to fire. No need to run them right out for the first shots. If you can't hear me, open the ports when we turn."

Hunter waited to see if there were any more orders. He had already passed the order for the type of shot required. It was obviously the Captain's intention to confuse the French, cross their bows at the last minute so being able to attack one of the weakest parts of a ship, the bows. By firing low first he would be aiming to blow a hole below or close to the water line. The high shot was to rake the upper deck. They had practised this routine every day, without normally firing the guns.

A lucky shot fired at the bows or stern could pass down the whole length of the deck up-ending guns, causing untold injury and confusion. There was not much point in a close action in using bar shot to damage the rigging. The Carronades on the forecastle would be using grape to inflict as much injury and confusion as possible. The Gunner had explained how he liked to work his guns. He drilled into each gun captain the necessity of aiming at a chosen target;

that was whilst you could still see a target. When they had found a convenient rock outcrop they would practise their aim and be able to judge their precision.

Will moved closer to the Captain so he alone would hear him.

"Batteries on either side of the entrance, Sir!"

"Good point! - Number One, warn your Larboard guns that their first target will be the battery on north shore."

"Grape and shot Sir?" Asked Hunter.

"Absolutely! Try and put them off their aim!"

This was Will's first real taste of ship-to-ship action. In the Malacca Straits, his father's ship had repelled pirates, but it had been uneven odds. He was surprised how slowly everything seemed to be unfolding. He realised that as they would be slowing down from their speed of 10 knots, even with the fresh breeze, it was going to take them another quarter of an hour to twenty minutes to close.

"Mr Bright, keep a sharp lookout on the fort to starboard. Mr Sweet, keep a sharp lookout on the fort to larboard on the North shore." Said the Captain to the Midshipmen.

Aye, aye Sirs chirped from the two as they gathered up telescopes and rushed to the hammocks surrounding the quarter deck which were put there as a protection against musket fire.

"Spencer, please keep your marines in those red coats out of sight; yourself included. And none of your marines in the tops please. Tell Mr Fortune I want muskets taken up by the top-men now. Have them lashed to the mast. When the courses are furled tell him to order the top-men to stay in the tops and be ready with the muskets, but not to be showing any weapons until we turn. Mr Hughes, you heard that, top-men to take up muskets. They can go up directly they have been issued the weapons and be prepared to furl the courses on my command." The Captain spoke calmly. Will wondered how the Captain felt. He, himself, had butterflies in his stomach. To take his mind off the immediate, he took bearings on three distinct points of reference and went down to where his chartroom had been to plot the position and note the time on the chart for writing up later in the ships log. There was nothing left. Where his chart table had been, an 18 pounder sat ready for action. Everything, including the Captain's cabin's walls and furniture had been stowed below. He took his chart to where the Captain's chair had normally been in front of the stern windows. He laid the chart on the deck and marked the position on the chart, before returning to the quarter-deck.

CHAPTER 12

On the quarter deck nothing seemed to have changed. Hunter was still beside the Captain, glass to his eye surveying the scene. Now clearly to be seen from the quarter-deck were the masts and top sails of the two French frigates coming through the narrow passage that led from the port of Brest. From his chart Will knew that there were tricky rocks on the southern side, which reduced the room for manoeuvre. Where it looked likely *Artful* would meet the first of the frigates, which were in line ahead, there was slightly less than one nautical mile from north to south in which to manoeuvre. To the south there was a shallow area of sand and rocks, whilst to the north there were rocky outcrops off the Point de Berthenum. He would have to keep reminding himself of those points even in the midst of the battle that was sure to follow.

The French frigates were both under topsails and staysails only, with a couple of their jibs set. Their gun ports were shut like those of *Artful*.

"Of course with the wind in this direction, they can't see our ensign anyway. May be the batteries can." Said the Captain; more to himself than anybody else.

Artful wasn't wearing a pennant. Earlier in their expedition south, the pennant had got caught up in the rigging and nearly brought down one of the top-men. The flag which in Will's opinion was ridiculously long had got torn to shreds and a new one was not yet finished. As a result, fortuitously, the only identification of nationality was the ensign, and *Artful* was flying the Captain's own flag, which was some sort of coat of arms on a white background.

The silence was almost palpable. All that could be heard were the creaks of the rigging and the general sounds of a ship at sea. There was no shouting. There were no Boatswains mate's pipes. The Captain had from the first pointed out that in battle the noise was so great that nothing could be heard above it. He had therefore insisted on a series of hand signals. Midshipman Yates was already on the upper deck checking the big guns with Midshipman Bright to assist. Midshipman Preston was with Cranfield on the forecastle. Midshipman Fairley stood respectfully behind the Captain and Will on the quarter-deck, ready to do whatever was ordered, but normally would deal with the flag signals.

The Captains of each part would look to their relevant officer to see what signal he was making. Otherwise the age old custom of runners was employed, but that took time. Because they were short of watch keeping officers, the Captain had decided that Wiggins, the marine subaltern should command the quarterdeck carronades, Craddock the forecastle carronades, and Hunter would command the main gun-deck. Will as Master had to be on the quarter deck to look after the sailing of the ship, so he also should double as the watch keeping officer who would have normally been Hunter. If the Captain was killed or wounded Hunter was to be sent for. The Gunner would be down in the powder store in his crimson soft slippers.

Will glanced up at the main mast top and could see the top-men making their way out across the main course's yards. Still *Artful* and the French frigates closed. If *Artful* kept to the same course now she would pass to windward of the leading French frigate, which was just at the mouth of Le Goulet, with a rocky area to the south of her. The wind was backing so it would be normal for the French frigate to alter course to head west instead of south-west to gain from the wind. The French Captain would think nothing of the strange frigate making to pass her to windward. *Artful* was now heading directly towards the Point du Petit Minou which was on the northern side of the entrance.

"Probably still thinks we are one of theirs." Commented Hunter his eye still glued to his glass.

"Why?" Asked Will.

"*Artful's* design is based on a captured French frigate; same lines." Hunter explained without taking his eyes from his glass. After a short pause he added.

"Second French frigate is making a signal!"

"Mr Cranfield, make up any set of flags you like that don't mean anything!" Ordered the Captain.

"Furl the Courses!" Followed immediately.

Crouching just behind them the Captain's clerk had taken up his position to note down everything that happened, especially the orders.

Down the Starboard gallery, which ran from the quarter-deck to the forecastle, crouched the marines behind the stacked hammocks ready with their muskets under the command of the marine sergeant. Wiggins had briefed the sergeant to have every other marine fire then drop down to reload being replaced by the alternative marine. It meant that their fire would be constant instead of in waves.

On board the leading French frigate, the *L'homme d'honneur*, the new captain was taking her out for the first time. He had achieved command because his father was a prominent member of the Jacobin Party in Paris. He had never commanded anything larger than a small sloop. His crew was cobbled together from all over the country. Most of the experienced French naval officers had left the country or been beheaded. The First Lieutenant was more experienced, he had been a junior lieutenant on a ship-of-the-line, but he was terrified of putting a foot wrong because of his Captain's connections. When asked if the frigate approaching them was friendly, he had pointed out that it was hardly likely that an enemy frigate would be rushing into the harbour under full sail and without her gun ports being open for action. He thought she was probably being chased by a pack of British frigates, which were known to be blockading the harbour.

Below decks the crew were trying to find their allotted messes. The cannons weren't even loaded and there were no gun-power canisters or shot set out ready for action.

It was *L'homme d'honneur's* first outing after a refit.

It was a very junior French officer who asked if he should hoist a challenge, but when told to do that, didn't know which flags to hoist, because he had forgotten to bring his code book up with him.

In another five minutes *Artful* would be passing the French frigate if they stayed on their present course. Everybody aboard *Artful* was keyed up for the forthcoming action.

"Open the skylight!" The Captain ordered unexpectedly.

"Edward, time to go to your station and may God have mercy upon us this day." Said the Captain; speaking to Hunter. Hunter touched his hat and dropped down to the Upper deck to command the guns. *Artful* was less than a cable away from the leading French frigate. If she kept on this course she would pass the Frenchman larboard side to larboard side. She was approximately a mile off the Petit Minou.

"Stand-by to Starboard your helm, Quartermaster! - Mr Hedges, stand-by." The Experienced Boatswain grinned at the Captain and nodded his head. He had been through all this many times. He strolled to his position on the forecastle.

The seconds seemed to tick by in an age of suspense.

"Starboard the helm!" This perversely, meant that the wheel was turned to larboard so that *Artful* swung to larboard. It was a hang-over from the days when all ships had tillers. She would now pass across the bows of the oncoming French frigate. The two ships were now within minutes of passing each other.

The noise of the Gun ports on the deck below smacking open resounded against the hull. Will turned to see the Captain's ensign float to the deck and be replaced by the British Ensign.

The first of the 18 pounders barked, closely followed by the first of the forecastle carronades. The noise was incredible! Will could see clearly the bows of the French frigate as *Artful's* cannons and carronades fired. The bows of the French frigate seemed to disintegrate before his eyes. He could see that the hull of the Frenchman was open to the water; then smoke obscured everything before being blown away. There was a pinging sound, but he failed to notice its significance. The first six to eight starboard side guns on the upper deck had wrought havoc with the French frigate; she was already starting to dip. Beneath him he felt the ship shudder and wondered why. The smoke from *Artful's* guns was being whipped away towards the bows by the wind. Again *Artful* seemed to shake strangely. The North Battery must be finding its target.

Suddenly Will realised that the Captain wasn't beside him any longer. Glancing round he saw that the Captain was lying on the deck against the scuppers with a burly marine private draped across him. There was no sign of life. Will turned back and realised he was the only naval officer on the quarter deck. He should send for Hunter.

They were still heading towards the North shore!

If they continued on this course they would be sailing away from their targets.

"Larboard the helm!" He shouted right against the

quartermaster's ear. Then bending to the open skylight he shouted to anybody below. "Tell the First Lieutenant we are going round; watch the fort on the north shore! Oh, and that he is needed on the quarterdeck!" He heard no acknowledgement. As he stood up he felt as if his right arm had been punched, but took no notice as he was concentrating on the French frigate which was now passing down their starboard side. Beside him the stern carronades under Wiggin's direction were firing across the Frenchman's quarterdeck.

"Send for the First Lieutenant!" He ordered and a young gentleman ran forward. Suddenly the foremast of the French frigate shattered, which puzzled Will for a moment. Looking up he appreciated the reason, there was a round hole in the spanker above him; the North Shore Battery must have hit their own frigate.

"Mid-ships! Shouted Will into the ear of the nearest Quartermaster. *Artful* responded and the masts of the leading French frigate were now passing down their starboard side, seen only above the smoke.

Will suddenly realised that if they continued they would be broadside to broadside with the second French Frigate and have the North Fort wreaking havoc to their larboard side. He decided to turn *Artful* so she would pass between the stern of the leading French frigate and the bows of the second. The two weakest points of any fighting ship.

He tried to gauge the position of the leading French frigate from her mizzen mast, just visible above the smoke.

"Larboard your helm!" He ordered; now completely oblivious to the fact that the First Lieutenant had not yet gained the quarterdeck. He was concentrating on trying to put *Artful* in the best possible position to fight.

Now they were turning to pass astern of the first French frigate, the cannons below were once again firing. Each time they blasted a hole in the side of the French frigate Wiggin's carronades fired into the hole. The smoke began to roll over the quarter-deck and Will's eyes began to smart. Now he couldn't see the enemy. He couldn't even wipe his eyes because of the bandaging across his nose. He glanced up and realised he could still see the tops of the enemy's masts, so gauge their relative positions.

The roar of *Artful's* cannons and carronades came like somebody striking a bell. One –pause-two-pause-three-pause, and so on as each gun captain waited for a target. *Artful* was going to scrape past the stern of the leading French frigate. There was no point in boarding as he knew the ship would sink. The starboard 18 pounders on the deck below seemed to have stopped firing. The larboard side bow carronades were opening up on the second French frigate. Then the larboard cannons started to fire one after the other, almost in a ripple of fire. As *Artful* rounded the stern of the leading French frigate the starboard cannons below Will opened up and he could hear smashing glass; it must be the ornate windows of the French frigate. The Frenchman was so close it felt as if you could have leant out and touched her. All around the stern behind him the marines were popping up, firing and dropping back to re-load, whilst another reared up to fire. He realised that the strange sound he was now hearing were screams coming from the leading French Frigate.

Will swivelled round to see what was happening on the larboard side. In a brief clearing of the smoke he caught a glimpse of the second French frigate's bows: they weren't there! There was nothing to see. It was as if the front of the ship including her bowsprit had been sliced off at the foremast. The danger now lay with the shore batteries. Oddly the northern one seemed to have stopped firing. The second French frigate must be in the way. Why hadn't the south battery fired?

"Larboard your helm!" He shouted again and made a rotating signal with his hand for the benefit of the quartermasters. As the wind punched aside the smoke, Will could see that he had called for the turn at exactly the right time. They would pass down the larboard side of the first French frigate, or what remained of her, with the yards nearly brushing each other.

"Midships!" Cried Will; realising that if they kept turning they were going to ram the French frigate. There was still no sign of Hunter. The quartermaster beside Will crumbled to the deck. Will without thinking stepped over him and took his place to help and instruct the remaining three seamen manning the wheel. The stricken quartermaster was dragged away from Will's feet.

"No point in trying to take her, she is doomed!" The Captain's voice beside Will made him jump. Will turned to see a white faced Captain leaning heavily on the arm of Midshipman Sweet.

"What happened?" Asked Will.

"I think the marine must have been hit and he fell against me. I must have knocked myself out hitting the deck. You did well Will, very well! But why didn't you call for Hunter?"

"Immediately I realised you were down I passed the order for him to come to the quarterdeck, Sir. In fact I sent one of the crew below as well when he didn't appear."

Captain Crick surveyed the scene, and then turned to Will.

"You passed between the two frigates?"

"Yes Sir!"

"My God Will, that was absolutely the right thing to do. I hope I should have thought to do the same in the heat of the battle."

He regard Will for moment, then exclaimed.

"You're hit!"

Will looked down at his right arm and saw that indeed blood was dripping down his sleeve from a wound in his upper arm to the deck.

"Better go and see the Surgeon!" Said the Captain.

Hunter arrived on the quarter deck.

"You all right up here?" He asked looking at the same

time at the battery to the south which was now firing uselessly at them, their cannon balls bouncing across the water like five stones to drop a hundred yards astern.

Aboard the *L'homme d'honneur* the shock pulverised any immediate reaction. The approaching frigate suddenly seemed to decide to pass across their bows! What the Hell was he thinking of? Then the gun ports opening alerting them to danger. The frigate seemed to lurch as if brakes had been applied suddenly. Before they had time to think the bows of their ship were beyond repair. Men were thrown to the deck. Below decks there was chaos. Guns were up ended and sent hurtling like demented weapons spinning down the deck flattening anybody in their way. Grape shot, unimpaired by any bulkhead screamed down the gun-deck killing and wounding indiscriminately. The Captain lost it and cowered against the hammocks by the side of the quarter-deck. The First Lieutenant was one of the first to be hit by the carronades from the bows of the British Frigate. There was nobody to command the ship.

On the second French frigate, things happen slightly more slowly. The Captain was more experienced than his Senior Officer in the leading frigate; but he didn't have relations in high places! He was more cautious than the other Captain, he had sent his crew to quarters, but he was hampered by the narrowness of the channel. He ordered an alteration to starboard, but had to counter it almost immediately when he realised that it would put his ship across the line of fire from the northern fort. He couldn't turn the other way, because he would run against the rocks. He couldn't stop; he just had to continue, aware of the danger from the swiftly turning British frigate that could bring its guns to bare long before they could retaliate.

What surprised him was the accuracy of the British frigate's guns. Just two fired at the Northern fort and these seemed to find their target, because for a while the fort stopped firing. Then the British waited, not a gun was fired wildly. It felt as if he was in a shooting alley. Each British cannon seemed to pick their target carefully and soon the whole bow section of his ship was decimated. What was so annoying was that not one of his cannons was in a position to fire. The ship was sinking and sinking fast. The screams and groans from below told their own story. He watched in dismay, but a certain amount of admiration as the British frigate circled back past his leader's ship, without firing a gun. The Captain called for a telescope and focused it on the stern of the British frigate. He read *Artful*.

"Qu'est que le mot anglais 'Artful' en Français?"

"C'est un petit malin!" Responded one of the Lieutenants."

"Oui, un roublard!" (Yes, an artful dodger). Nodded the Captain.

In the relative silence after the battle, *Artful* slid past the leading French frigate, the crew starring at close quarters at the awful damage they had wrought.

The Captain turned away from looking at his defeated adversary and addressed his First Lieutenant. "What's the damage?"

"Four killed, eight wounded, not including the Master here, or yourself, Sir."

"I'm alright, just must have got knocked out. What about the ship?"

"She received a direct hit on one of the carronades and one between the first and second larboard 18 pounders. Two of the crew of Craddock's carronade were killed and three wounded. One Marine is dead and a powder monkey also, killed next to the cannon. The damage is repairable the Carpenter says."

CHAPTER 13

After having his wound seen to by the Surgeon, who's parting words were. "Why you have to be in the thick it of each time, God only knows. I hope, for your sake, that this will be the last for a long time!" Will returned to the quarterdeck just in time to see a line of four British frigates approaching on the starboard bow.

There were a series of thumps and bangs as the gun ports were shut. *Artful* was changing back to cruising mode.

As the British Squadron leader's frigate passed a cable length away on the starboard side, a mighty cheer went up from her crew who were lining the side.

"Glorious action this day! I think it reads." Said a bemused Cranfield; trying to read the flag hoist. *Artful's* crew stood waving back, lined up on the gallery.

"It was rather successful!" Commented the smiling Captain; revelling in the reflected glory.

As each frigate sailed past in line, the cheers were repeated. The squadron leader put about and fell in line behind *Artful.*

"I rather think he would like to take the lead!" Remarked the Captain; giving the orders for the sails to be loosened, so that their progress was slowed. As the Squadron leader drew alongside, the Senior Captain could be seen taking up a speaking trumpet.

"What damage?" He shouted.

Artful's Captain replied, again using a speaking trumpet.

"Four dead, three wounded, one carronade damaged, one bower anchor and cable lost. Will now have to return to pick up our boats."

"Incredible! We witnessed it from a far, remarkable piece of work! Heartiest Congratulations."

There was a pause, and then back came the Senior

Captain.

"Make course for Plymouth to have repairs and replacements. Sending across dispatches for Lord Howe; as soon as ready. Fall in line astern after retrieving your boats." With that he waved and stepped down from his perch in the mizzen shrouds.

In the lee of the isle of Ushant, The squadron leader's cutter brought over the dispatches for Lord Howe, as well as the usual ones for the dockyard in Plymouth and requests to the Board of Admiralty in London. That night *Artful* left the squadron and sailed through the night back to find Lord Howe's fleet, which could be either at Spithead, or sheltering nearer in Torbay. It was unfortunate that the fleet was anchored at the Spithead, so it took another day before they were able to drop anchor near the fleet.

Even as they approached the signal flags on the Flagship were instructing *Artful's* Captain to report.

As *Artful* dropped her anchor, the reply was flying from the main-yard. Captain Crick went below to his quarters to change as the gig was lowered and brought alongside the starboard entry port. The Captain's coxswain made sure that everything was up to his usual high standards. Hunter and the side part stood by the entry to see the Captain over the side. The usual pipes were sounded and the Captain dropped expertly into the gig.

When *Artful's* gig pulled alongside the flagship, the Captain hoisted himself up the high sides to be met by the Admiral's Flag Lieutenant.

The Flag-Lieutenant's expression said it all. "You've seen some action?"

"Yes!" Was *Artful's* Captain's succinct reply.

He was led down to the Admiral's quarters, where the Admiral stood by the windows with his Flag Captain.

"Ah Crick, what news?"

"Sank two French frigates trying to escape from Brest."

"Two frigates, but there doesn't appear to be much

damage to your ship!"

"Well we had four killed and some wounded, including the Master, and we lost a Carronade and a bower anchor. Otherwise we came out of it rather well, thanks mainly to our Master Mr Calvert, who took over command right at the beginning when I was knocked out."

"Knocked out! How come?"

"A marine was hit just in front of me and he fell back on me. I must have hit my head really hard, because I was knocked out. Came round to find our Master had literally run rings around the French-men."

"Obviously a good man to have around! Where was the First Lieutenant?"

"As you know, we are short of officers due to Simmons, so Lieutenant Hunter was commanding the guns. Mr Calvert called for him to take over, but the message got lost in the melee, even though it was repeated. Mr Calvert was there and took charge."

"So how did you achieve this feat?"

"The wind was likely to go round to the southeast, so it made sense to go in close to Brest to see if the fleet was preparing to try and make a run for it. We saw that two ships were about to leave, so decided to make sure that they did not go very far." And he went on to explain the beginning of the action. He explained that Mr Calvert had recounted what had happened after he had been struck down. He continued. "Lieutenant Hunter's gun crew's were brilliant. A masterful piece of disciplined gunnery; they used every shot to inflict the utmost damage." The Captain added.

The Flag Captain asked. "How were you so sure the wind would be right for an exit by the French?"

"Mr Calvert predicted it, Sir!"

"I must meet this Mr Calvert of yours." Said Admiral Howe, before calling for refreshment and gestured to Captain Crick to take a seat, whilst he read the report.

Will retired to his cubicle; he had all the paperwork to complete as well as bringing the ship's log up-to-date. He found it difficult to write as his right arm above the elbow was heavily bandaged and his fingers felt stiff. He persevered though it was tough going. Once he had cleared the official paperwork he wrote up his own journal, before joining his fellow officers in the gunroom.

The next day they sailed out their remaining anchor and turned for Plymouth. For once the winds were kind to them and they were able to sail straight into the Sound, round Drake's Island and coast through the Narrows to reach the Hamoaze. One of the cutters had been lowered in the Sound and towed behind them as they entered the harbour. Now it was crewed to take the buoy jumper out to the buoy. It was a tricky operation slowing the frigate under sail and then manoeuvre into position at just the right speed. The Captain indicated what he wanted and it was up to Will to give the necessary commands at precisely the right time. Everybody aboard knew that the rest of the ships in the Hamoaze would be watching them, ready to hoist critical hoists if they found fault. It very nearly went wrong, when the oarsman of the cutter had trouble getting into a position where the buoy jumper could reeve the necessary light cable which was attached to the main warp. *Artful* was almost in irons when finally the cable was retrieved and the main warp could be pulled back through the eye of the buoy and made fast.

As the light was fading it would have been just possible to see that the Port Admiral was requesting *Artful's* Captain to attend him. However where their buoy was positioned they couldn't see the flag-ship. Luckily another frigate was moored within hailing distance so although the flagship was obscured to *Artful* by the frigate; they were able to relay the signal.

Will having completed his paperwork with regard to the voyage, now had to attend to the other duties which fell upon his shoulders. He spent a couple of hours in the bilges with the Purser, evaluating the amount of room left for more stores and where they should be stowed. He joined the other officers later for the evening meal, where Hunter was trying to fathom out how many shots they had fired and what shot they had used. Craddock suggested it was best to overestimate, so they would have enough for any adventure in the future.

It took a week for the Dockyard to mend the damage to the larboard Cathead and replace the anchor and cable. During that time, they were re-victualled and re-armed.

CHAPTER 14

It was back to the routine of six months with the squadron sailing backwards and forwards in all weathers off the Brest Estuary, and then another six months searching inshore down the coast. They saw little action, and the only respite was every two months a trip back to Plymouth to re-supply. The inshore work was the most interesting, because they were more likely to be in action. They stopped any craft that might be taking supplies for the navy or armies of France. Under the menace of the frigate's cannons, few refused to stop and be searched. Those that did suffered the fate of being target practice for *Artful's* gunners. It was noticeable that the French were trying to sail individual Prames, Chaloupes, Peniches, and Caiques around the coast. Obviously they hoped that they would be mistaken for local vessels, but most were straight off the slip. What these shallow draft boats could be intended for was a matter of conjecture. They were almost always empty. Most clung to the coast trying to make life difficult for a frigate to approach. Those that were captured were blown up, as it wasn't worth taking them. The crews were then transferred to another captured vessel and sent back to port. Any weapons were ditched over the side. As autumn drew to a close, there were virtually no attempts at trying to take such vessels round the Brittany coast. On reflection it was obvious that they did not want to risk the passage through

thc Chenal du Four, the North West tip of France, in winter.
[Prames: two or three masted flat bottomed craft: Up to 20 guns. Chaloupes: Two masted gunboat. Peniche: 60ft gunboat with 2 Howitzers, flat bottomed. Caique; Rowed flat bottomed troop carrier.]

Winter was upon them: the sea and wind were having an effect upon the rigging and hull. *Artful* was noticeably slower and Will was worried about the state of the fixed rigging as well as the running rigging, which kept having to be replaced or repaired. The Boatswain was constantly drawing Will's attention to defects. They had been patrolling the area for two years without a refit.

They were nearing the end of their time, when one of the vessels they intercepted and searched told them that a French frigate was holed up and hiding behind a headland just to the north of their position.

Artful had duly flogged her way up into Quiberon Bay, but had discovered nothing. On beginning to beat their way out; the lookouts reported two ships rounding the southern tip of the bay. Obviously, the information had been a lure to bring them north into this bay so that the two French frigates could trap *Artful*. Suffering from two years of being constantly at sea, *Artful* was now slow and tired. The pumps were permanently manned and her rigging had been spliced, and re-spliced. *Artful*, close inshore would have to tack into the wind to face her two opponents. With patched sails and doubtful rigging there seemed no doubt as to the outcome of the confrontation. The two French ships were spilling the wind to retain their advantageous positions, ready to pounce.

From inside his cubicle, Will could clearly hear the noise of the frigate preparing for battle. It always seemed that one's senses were heightened before an engagement. The sharp cracks as the gun ports were raised, the sound of the wheels of the gun carriages as they were hauled out, together with the cussing and swearing of the gun crews immediately above him. He could hear the feet of the seamen overhead preparing the splinter nets to cover the upper deck. William turned from his notes, to study the chart in front of him once again.

Could he be correct? Was he sure enough to advise the Captain? He remembered what the Captain of *Challenger* had told him; be assertive. But was his idea too risky? Self doubt is a terrible thing. Will shook his head almost to try and clear it. Once again he peered closely at the chart in front of him. He had used other charts copied from the same enemy collection. They had all been correct to the last detail. Beside him the flimsy partitions which formed part of the walls to his small chartroom were suddenly removed. He considered for a moment rechecking and then rolled up the chart. Dodging out from the remains of his cubicle, close to the Captain's Cabin on the upper deck, he ran up the ladderway to the quarter-deck of the frigate. He stood waiting for the Captain to notice him. As he did so, he looked to where everybody else was gazing. Looming on the near horizon, were the two French frigates, and they still had the wind in their favour.

For that area of the French coast the day was unusually brilliant, with only a slight swell, but a modest wind. Will knew that normally the Captain would not think twice about engaging a superior force. This time the odds were stacked impossibly high against them. The two privateer frigates, because that was what they appeared to be, not only had the wind gauge, they would have superior fire power and room to manoeuvre. *Artful* was bottled up with no chance of getting to a favourable position.

The tension on the quarter-deck was palpable. The Captain and his Lieutenants all had spy glasses to their eyes studying the opposition. Will gave a polite cough to try and attract the Captain's attention. Everybody on the quarter-deck ignored him. Running out of time Will had to speak out.

"Excuse me, Sir, but I think I might have a remedy to our predicament!"

The Captain lowered his glass; everybody within ear shot swivelled round to look at Will.

"I doubt that very much Mr Calvert, but what is it?"

"Sir, I have checked and rechecked. In about twenty minutes there should be enough depth for us to get between the Island and the mainland. I have interpolated the captured charts, especially the Local Merchant's. We should have a window of ten minutes to get through with a depth below the keel of two feet; after having allowed for the extra we draw due to our leakage."

The Captain turned to regard the narrow channel between what was an island only at high tide and the mainland.

"What tide is it again?"

"Just before Springs, Sir."

"Are you certain of this?" Queried the Captain; doubt showing in his expression.

"As positive as one can be about these things, Sir."

"Twenty minutes you say?"

"Twenty minutes! We must be at the entrance to the channel then, otherwise we shall be trapped by the tide turning. It runs out very fast after it has turned."

The Captain put up his glass again and focussed it on first one and then the other of the French frigates.

"The buggers are just toying with us!"

"We are heavily out gunned, Sir!" Commented the First Lieutenant; in an unusually candid aside.

"You can say that again! Well, better to live to fight another day, than court disaster. The old girl is feeling her age. One ball hitting the waterline and she will sink like a stone. No doubt some land lubber will say we should engage the enemy, but I think that their Lords of the Admiralty will appreciate our predicament. They are precious short of frigates, as it is! All right Mr Calvert we shall try it your way. How long before we need to go-about to make the channel on time?"

"Eighteen minutes by my reckoning, Sir."

"Stand-by to go about in eight minutes! We should be expected to tack at about then anyway. Make it look as if we are going to head for the island side of the bay, before turning at the last minute for the channel."

"Sir? Might I suggest that we move the Larboard guns to Starboard as we enter? It will give us another foot to play with!" Added Will; now emboldened.

"See to it Mr Fortune!" Ordered the Captain; to the Gunnery Officer.

"Now let us take a closer look at this chart of yours Mr Calvert."

It was impossible to read the chart in the necessary detail with the wind blowing across the quarter-deck. Will naturally stood aside and let the Captain descend to the Upper deck where Will's small chart cubicle had been situated. Now only the chart table fixed to the side of the hull remained.

Will unrolled and spread the chart out on the table. The chart was of Will's own making. Painstakingly worked up from both British and captured French Charts. Will had long ago encouraged the boarding parties to always bring back any charts they could find. Under the Articles of War, he wasn't allowed to keep them, but there was nothing said about copying them. The copies he added to his growing collection. Six months previously they had managed to capture a French Merchantman which had provided a number of charts of this particular part of the French coast. The narrow channel they were now studying had featured on one of the charts. On the British charts there was no passage shown. The French chart was meticulously notated, and rubbed out plots could still be seen, which Will had assumed meant that they had used it frequently. What had been the greatest difficulty was converting what the French took as datum and transposing it to what the British Navy used as datum.

"There is a rock halfway through, which luckily has to be passed on the leeward side. There is not much room, but the Merchantman's keel depth was greater than ours." Will pointed to the rock's position on the chart.

"Well you haven't let us down yet. Let's hope you haven't this time. Although I must admit the odds on us being able to fight our way out past the two Frenchies are about zero!"

Will started to take bearings off the chart that would be needed to ensure that they were in the correct positions at the right time. The Captain left him to his work, knowing Will's attention to detail in everything he did when it came to navigation.

Will carried his own John Adams compass out to the quarter-deck. It had been his late father's and was equipped with a pelorus. [Pelorus: A circular ring fitted over the compass with two sights for taking bearings.]

All the Midshipmen knew what to do when Will arrived on the quarter-deck with his brass bound wooden box that housed the compass. Each time Will said "Check!" one Midshipman would read off the bearing which a Master's Mate noted down. Conversely, as in this case, the Middy would provide the next required bearing so Will could set the pelorus and wait for the ship to arrive at the point where an alteration was required.

Directly Will was settled he started to check their position. He waited until *Artful* had gone about, and then checked for the moment that they would have to alter course. The first thing he had to get right was the course *Artful* had to sail to reach the entrance to the channel. When the moment came he gave the compass bearing. The First Lieutenant then gave the orders for the helmsmen until they had settled on the correct course. Immediately they entered the channel he called out changes to be made which were passed onto the helmsmen. The guns were now being hauled across the Upper Deck so as to give the frigate more of a list to Starboard. With the wind on their Larboard Quarter they had the benefit of one of the best points of sailing. From

Will's notes the next bearing was called out by another Midshipman. Directly Will saw through his Pelorus that they had reached that bearing; he signalled the alteration of course. The channel was twisty and they seemed to rush up it, despite the fact that *Artful* could only manage just over three-quarters of her designed top speed due to all the growth on her bottom, although she had copper plates all over it. The Captain had posted a look-out on the end of their bowsprit, whilst chains-men were calling out the soundings all the time. Some of the Midshipmen looked at each other apprehensively as the called fathom depths grew shallower and shallower. Will was well aware of the atmosphere around him. He tried to ignore the butterflies in his stomach and appear confident.

Just as Will called for "Hard to Larboard!" the lookout on the bowsprit shouted a warning of a rock directly ahead. The next moment before the officers had gathered the situation, Will called "Hard a Starboard!" They all felt the grating sound as the ship's hull brushed along the side of the rock.

"Clean our bottom a bit!" Remarked the Captain; to ease the tension.

"Midships!" Called Will. *Artful* came slowly around as if she was tired of all these sudden alterations. The soundings were still very close to zero, when they all felt the old girl shudder as she slid across the bottom. She stuttered to a halt for a heart stopping moment and then the wind in the tightly sheeted sails pushed her further over and she shook herself free.

Just as she reached deeper water, the stern lookout called out that a French frigate was in sight. The bulk of the island had obscured the two French frigates as *Artful* had manoeuvred her way through the channel. Now clear for all to see was one of the French frigates heading for the channel.

"What do you think, Mr Calvert?" Asked the Captain.

"If I am right, they will be able to make the first part of the channel, if they have the right charts, but as you felt, the tide has turned and if she does try it, I am very pleased to report that she will be there for a very long time!"

"Take her up into the wind Number One; if the Frenchman tries anything, let him think that we shall be waiting for them with our broadside ready!"

"Aye Sir, but we shall need to replace the Larboard Guns, Sir!"

"Just so!"

The Gunner who had just reached the quarter deck turned and could be heard passing the order to his Mate; from there the order could be heard repeated. Next thing, the larboard gun-ports could be heard being raised as the cannons snouts began to appear.

Artful came up into the wind, her sails flapping as she lost the wind. You didn't need a telescope to be able to see that the French frigate realised the danger at the last minute. Not only did she face a hazardous channel, but at the end of it *Artful* sat waiting with a full broadside. The Frenchman came up into the wind and turned away.

Luckily *Artful* just had enough way for her to be turned, her foresails were backed bringing the bows round so the sails filled again and they gathered speed away from the channel. The island, when it was an island and not a spit of land, was large enough to mean that the French frigates would have to beat their way out of the bay, before being able to round the southern tip of the island and the associated rocks. By that time *Artful* would be a speck on the horizon. The French frigates would now not be able to catch *Artful* for many hours. Even if the French tried to follow, there was a good chance that the British fleet blockading the harbour of Brest would be within signalling distance. British Frigates would be dispatched to face the enemy.

"Well done Mr Calvert! Spared the old girl and many lives. Now I think we need a course to steer to rejoin the fleet."

Will knuckled his brow and followed the Captain off the quarter-deck to review his chart. Once he had plotted the course Will emerged from below to find that the Second Officer had the watch. Will gave him the course to steer and since it was also his responsibility, he scrutinised the sails set. Satisfied, Will called his Mate on duty and led the way down to where his cubicle was being re-erected, to write up the ship's log and his own journal, from the times set down by the Mate. Will was meticulous about keeping both up to date. He noted everything, even down to the sea birds he had seen in his journal. He especially noted the clouds, their form, speed and direction. He would draw little sketches of their shape. From this he had built up an encyclopaedic knowledge of the weather and what to expect in the hours ahead. It was the same with the tides. Every detail that he could glean was noted and reviewed.

Will was just finishing when the Captain popped his head in and said. "How long before we shall be in the general area of the patrols?"

"Two hours, thirty five minutes to the edge of their scheduled area, Sir."

"Very good!" He turned as if to leave but stopped, then said.

"I shall be putting you up for confirmed rank the first chance I get. It is not the first time you have got us out of a thorny problem. I am hoping that this time the Admiral relents and lets *Artful* have the necessary repairs. She deserves them as well as needing them! I fancy that we could all do with a bit of leave. Thank you again, Lieutenant; a brilliant piece of navigation!"

The year was 1795. William Calvert was just about to have his twentieth birthday.

CHAPTER 15

After the timely extraction of *Artful* from the trap, she was ordered to return to Plymouth for a complete refit. This would mean that the ship's company would be dispersed to different ships. There were endless discussions in the gunroom about where each of them might be sent. As Will was the Master of *Artful*, it would be normal for him to stay aboard, even when the ship was in dock, along with the standing officers, the Boatswain, Purser, Carpenter and Sailmaker.

They sat anchored in a fitful sea off Cawsand for three days before they could finally make the passage into the Drake Channel, through the Narrows and into the Hamoaze, where they were ordered to moor to a buoy. The Captain set off for the Port Admiral's Flagship and was gone until late into the evening. The Gunroom decided to ask him to join them for a final dinner the next day, before any of them were ordered to other ships.

The next day a surreal atmosphere seemed to settle over *Artful*. The crew moved about quietly, as if apprehensive as to their future. The crew had welded into a taut united fighting unit. Now at the whim of the Senior Officers somewhere else, they would be split up and have to make new friends and allies. Only the Warrant officers would remain. Even the Boatswain's Mates didn't seem to have the will to rebuke anybody, even if a rope wasn't tidied away to their usual high standards. The crew moved in groups, stopping to chat with other groups, only to move on. Even when the rum was drawn, there wasn't the usual banter and high spirits.

When it came to the Gunroom Dinner, the same strange feeling seemed to haunt them. The Captain had graciously accepted their kind invitation, but came with no news. Many toasts were made to the ship and the individuals. *Artful* had been an exceptionally happy ship. There had been hardly any flogging, or need of severe discipline. It had seemed that immediately Lieutenant Simmons had been removed from the scene, the ship had heaved a massed sigh of relief and settled down to a steady routine.

The Captain did have news of Simmons, he had been Courts-Martialed and had been severely reprimanded and lost his seniority, which meant he remained a Lieutenant, but was relegated to the back of the queue for promotion.

The following day, just as Will and his fellow officers had finished their meal, a young gentleman knocked on the gunroom door with a message that Mr Calvert was to report to the Captain. Will picked up his hat and proceeded up the one flight of steps to the captain's cabin. The marine on guard announced him as he approached the doorway.

"Ah Will!" Said Captain Crick; looking up with a broad smile. "I have something here for you." Crick lifted a ledger and sorted through some papers below to retrieve a signal form. He handed this to Will, still folded.

Will thanked the Captain.

"Well read it, Will!!" Commented the Captain.

Will unfolded the signal.

It was from the Admiralty. It stated in just a few words that it was hereby confirmed by their Lords of the Admiralty that Lieutenant William Calvert had been promoted to the rank of Lieutenant with seniority from the date of Lord Howe's original signal. This meant that Will had been a Lieutenant for the last eighteen months.

"Been sitting here with the Port Admiral for months awaiting our return." Said Crick.

"My gig is at your disposal. Get yourself ashore and into the proper rig.. We will celebrate this evening in fine style!"

Will thanked his Captain and re-folding the signal; he pocketed it and made his way down to his cabin. From his sea chest he took out a purse of sovereigns and then made his way up to the quarterdeck. Craddock had the watch.

"The Captain's coxswain has been waiting for you! Going ashore?"

Will nodded and made his way to the side where he descended to the gig.

It felt extraordinary to be climbing the very steps where he had first joined the Navy all those years ago. The Naval Tailors was just as he remembered it.

"Good Afternoon Sir. What can we do for you?" The same tailor asked as Will adjusted his eyes to the gloom.

"I need two Lieutenant's Uniforms, shirts, hose and cravats." Stated Will.

The Tailor put his head on one side. "Been promoted have we?"

"Eighteen months ago, but been unable to get ashore long enough to get a uniform made up."

"Well then we must certainly cause you no extra delay."

"I don't suppose you have second hand uniform I could purchase immediately, so as to give you more time?"Asked Will.

"Well now! Let me think, you are ordering two new uniforms and the clothes to go with them, so perhaps this once, I might break our golden rule."

Will's expression asked the question. The Tailor chuckled. "We don't encourage the selling of second hand. We normally keep such things for the needy. I do happen to have a uniform which might fit you. The officer in question made Post a few months ago. Now I seem to remember that we made the uniform you are wearing for you. Must have seen a considerable amount of sea-time, me-thinks! Right let me measure you for your new coats"

Will was measured in every direction. A junior arrived with the second hand uniform, which fitted Will fairly well. Will retrieved his purse and papers from his Master's coat and was fitted with his new officer's sword. He paid for the second hand uniform and a deposit on the new clothes.

Then he went down the street to the Cobbler, where he ordered two pairs of hessian boots and two pairs of new shoes.

There was no sign of *Artful's* gig at the steps, so he had to pay a boatman to take him back out to the ship.

CHAPTER 16

Back aboard *Artful*, Will was greeted by a very surprised quartermaster. The quartermaster just stood there with his mouth open, not knowing what to say. Will was much amused by the man's reaction. But he didn't bother to explain. In the gun-room there was even greater surprise.

"Good God Will. What are you dressed like that for?" Asked Craddock.

"Because apparently I have been a Lieutenant, a commissioned Lieutenant for the last year, but nobody thought to tell me - or the Captain."

"Well, my heartiest congratulations! I suppose that means that you'll be leaving *Artful*." Commented Hunter.

"Thank you! I suppose you're right, I hadn't thought of that! I had thought that I would be staying aboard, as usual, being the Master. But now you mention it I suppose I'll have to go to a new ship."

"Join the club, old boy!" Said Spencer; folding his paper.

"How come your uniform looks as if you've been wearing it for three years?" Asked the Purser.

"I managed to get a second-hand uniform. I'm having two others made for me now. One will be ready tomorrow. I hope I won't be called to the flagship before it arrives."

"Nothing ever moves that quickly, dear boy!" Commented the Surgeon.

"Doubt if we will be re-assigned until *Artful* is in the dockyard – who would move her?" Asked Craddock.

"They could always tow here over!" Responded Hunter; picking up his hat to go on duty.

Three days later, the signal came for *Artful* to be moved to the dockyard quay. The Captain took control, commenting that he didn't have a Master to assist him anymore; with a big grin for Will's benefit.

Once they were tied up and everything had been tidied away, the job of taking down the yards and upper spars fell to Will to organise. He might be a Lieutenant now, but he was still thought of as the authority on such procedures, along with the Boatswain. It was routine that the crew knew only too well. They had done it hundreds of times, as Will hated the idea of being caught 'over sparred' in a gale. He always advised the Captain earlier, rather than later. First the yards were quickly lowered to the gallery level, and stored against the bulwarks. Then the tackle that held the stays taut had to be let go. First the top gallant masts were lowered to deck level and stowed; then the gallant masts, or top masts were lowered, leaving only the fixed masts. It meant that an immense amount of cordage had to be neatly coiled up, secured with hemp ties, marked and stowed carefully, where each could be identified easily.

Halfway through, Will realised that all the cordage would probably be removed, once the ship was in dock, but he still insisted it was correctly and neatly stowed. To each tightly bound stay a white cotton rag was attached with the identity clearly written on it.

Next came the difficult job of retrieving the outer part of the bowsprit, which had to be manoeuvred slowly inboard without it crashing into the dirty river water streaming past. For this, the fore topmast preventer stay was re-attached to the mast just above the futtocks and used to take the weight, whilst the martingale stays were used to inch the sprit back aboard.

There had been no instruction regarding the guns, so they were left where they were.

Only one yard was left up, and this was the main course

yard, which would now be used to hoist the remaining stores out of the hold. Before the Purser got his hands on it, Will had the ships boats hoisted ashore.

Halfway through proceedings which would last two days, a signal came for the Captain to repair to the Port Admirals flagship. Because *Artful* no longer had her boats, the flag captain sent over a boat to collect the Captain. It was obvious to the whole ship's company that this was the beginning of the end.

The Captain was a way for two hours before he returned. He summoned the commissioned officers to his cabin, where he announced that he had been given command of a third rate ship-of-the-line, which was a step up the career ladder. Wine was brought and they all drank his health. He had been a popular captain. They were going to miss him.

The next day the Captain was piped ashore with a rousing cheer from the crew. Hunter was now nominally in command. Just after the Captain had left a signal came for both Hunter and Will to attend the flagship. This time no such honour of a boat was provided, they had to summon a skiff and pay for it to take them across. Hunter was the first to be seen and emerged to say that he was to be second lieutenant on a first rate ship-of-the-line. He was obviously disappointed, he had hoped for a frigate command. Next Will was seen by the Flag Captain.

Will was handed his next commission which was to HMS *Victory* a first-rate ship-of-the-line which was refitting at Portsmouth. After the usual formalities Will found himself back on the deck wondering how to get to Portsmouth. He had never been further East than Devon by land. He fell to talking to another Lieutenant who was waiting to be taken ashore, and asked his advice. He suggested a signal sloop might be about to leave taking signals from Plymouth to the Channel Fleet which would probably be anchored at the Spithead. If this was the case it would be faster and more comfortable than the Stage.

Once ashore it took only minutes to find out that there was indeed a Brig-sloop about to clear for the Spithead.

Will grabbed the first available skiff and paid to be rowed out to the Brig-sloop lying at anchor. He was met by an elderly Lieutenant, who obviously had a chip on his shoulder, but wasn't averse to taking Will for a payment, which was of course highly irregular. Will had to bite the bullet, and reflected that it was probably cheaper than by stage coach. It was a mad rush back to *Artful*, where he kept the skiff waiting whilst he had his chests hoisted down along with his servant, Thomas Tucker, as he said his goodbyes.

The Brig-sloop was surprisingly fast. The Lieutenant in command might appear past his prime, but he was a seaman through and through. It was late evening when the Brig passed the Mew stone in a slack tide. The wind was from the South West, and the Brig seemed to pick up her skirts and fly. Will retired to the hammock he had been given in what passed for the captain's cabin. The Lieutenant spent the whole night on deck, and when Will put his head up the next morning it was to find that the Needles were clearly in sight on the starboard bow.

The Lieutenant was a man of few words. He nodded to Will as he came on deck. "Two hours before High Water!" Was all he said. Will knew this meant that they would have the tide in their favour as they sailed up the Solent. The Lieutenant then stooped to the binnacle which was fitted with a pelorus. He was taking bearings on Hurst Castle and the Needles themselves. It was important to make sure that they were to the East of the Shingles, a sand bank on the larboard side as you enter the channel up to the Solent. Once between Hurst Castle and what was known as Cliff End on the Isle of Wight, the Lieutenant relaxed.

An hour later and they rounded Egypt Point, and there set out in front of them was the Fleet at anchor at Spithead. It was an impressive sight. The entire Channel Fleet was anchored in an orderly manner. The Brig-sloop anchored as near the Flagship as possible and Will, together with Tucker and the signals, was rowed across. The officer of the watch was rather surprised to greet an extra Lieutenant at the gangway, but once apprised of the situation arranged for one of the Flagship's longboats to take Will ashore.

Towering above every other group of masts in Portsmouth Harbour, were the masts of one particular ship, whose hull was impossible to see until they were virtually up to the dockyard lock gates.

This then was the mighty *H.M.S. Victory* that Will was joining. *HMS Victory* was a First Rate Ship-of-the-Line. She had been Flagship to many a notable Admiral. Will was put ashore with a member of the crew to help Tucker manage his sea-chests. He made his way towards the towering hull, realising that the ship looked ready for sea. All her standing rigging looked shiny new, and her paint-work and gilding shone in the faint sunlight. A gangway ran from her entry port to the quayside. Tucker and the crew-man deposited Will's sea-chests at the bottom of the gangway. The crew-man knuckled his forehead and ran back to join his ship, leaving Tucker to guard the chests.

Will eyed the gangway and the ornate entry port in the high bulging side of the great ship, which sloped inwards towards the top. A massive anchor was suspended from the Cathead. Through the three rows of open gun-ports, cannons lashed tight up to the sides could be glimpsed. Will swallowed hard, took hold of his scabbard to stop his sword swinging about and tripping him up. Then he sauntered up the gangway, not wanting to appear like a novice. He was grateful that he was wearing the second-hand uniform. The tarnished gold braid spoke of sea-time. Will raised his hat as he automatically ducked his head as he entered the ornate entry port and was greeted by the smallest Midshipman he had ever met. Marine sentries at either side came to attention, their muskets held vertically close to the side.

"Good morning, Sir!" Chirped the Midshipman. "Your

business Sir?"

"Lieutenant Calvert, joining His Majesty's Ship Victory." Replied Will formally.

The Midshipman's air of self importance vanished. He was obviously new to his profession.

"You take me to see the First Lieutenant." Whispered Will; leaning forward so it would appear that the marines beside the entry port might not be able to hear.

The young Midshipman flushed bright scarlet. "I'll take you to the First Lieutenant." He said in a louder voice, and turned on his heel.

Will winked at the Quartermaster standing to one side, who returned a broad smile. The news would soon be all round the messes, that the new Lieutenant had helped the raw Midshipman. It could do no harm.

Will caught up with the Midshipman, who turned to thank him, before informing Will that his name was Owens.

They were halfway aft towards the wardroom on the middle gun deck, when Owens stopped to ask a Boatswain's Mate if he knew the whereabouts of the First Lieutenant. It transpired that the Officer in question had last been seen on the quarterdeck, so Owens turned back past the aft capstan and led Will up a companionway stairs to the quarterdeck. Standing talking to another officer was the First Lieutenant who noticed Will arrive on deck. Owens interrupted the conversation by announcing Lieutenant Calvert. The First Lieutenant frowned at the interruption.

"One moment!" He said to the officer he had been speaking to and turned to Will.

"Lieutenant Calvert from *Artful?* Welcome aboard. I shall only be a moment." And he turned to continue his instruction to the other Lieutenant. Once he had finished, the First Lieutenant took Will's hand and shook it.

"You made very good time!" He said.

"I came by sea." Explained Will.

The First Lieutenant stared at Will in surprise and then roared with laughter. "My God, what a brilliant idea! How did you manage it?"

"I hitched a lift on a Brig-Sloop which was delivering signals. I was lucky – the timing was right."

"Frankly I did not think you would make it. We are ordered to sail in three days time to join the Med. Fleet. *Victory* will be the flagship. My name is Fraser, by the way. Captain Knight is the captain. Come; let me introduce you to the wardroom."

As they made their way down to the middle gun deck again, Will asked. "Whose flag are we flying?"

Fraser stopped and said quietly. "Admiral Hood's at this moment, though I am not sure for how long! But don't ask - all rumours at the present time."

Will was introduced to the rest of the wardroom, and made sure that he made a note of the names of his fellow officers. He discovered that he wasn't the most junior commissioned officer. There were two who had only just been made up from Midshipman.

Will was to learn very quickly that *Artful's* adventures were known to the officers of *Victory*, although his part in the famous action was obviously not known. He felt it prudent to let it remain that way. The First Lieutenant informed him that he would be responsible for the forward section of the guns on the middle gun deck. After checking that his chests had been stowed in his cabin off the wardroom, Will decided to check out his area of responsibility. He wandered forward on the middle gun deck.

"At ease Gentlemen!" He said as he came to the mess tables and the seamen seated between the guns. "I'm Lieutenant Calvert, late of the frigate *Artful*. I will be in charge of this area whilst the guns are manned, so I thought I better make myself familiar with the surroundings."

The tension that he had felt eased and one of the tars stood up. "I'm the Gun Captain here Sir. Tompkins the name."

"Very good Mr Tompkins – have you served on this ship for long?"

"Joined a month or so gone, Sir."

"Ah! So you haven't exercised the guns yet? What ship were you on before?"

"HMS *Stately*– 64 Guns, Sir. Captain Douglas."

"So you've served in the Far East?"

"Aye Sir!"

"Then we have something in common, Tompkins, but for the moment – how many Landmen do you have in your gun crews?"

"Twenty-two, Sir.

"Then, if I might, I suggest you appoint a mentor for each one, and check that they have been shown exactly what is expected of them, before we first go to action stations."

"Aye Sir."

"How many are we short?"

Tompkins looked a bit baffled by the question. "Not rightly sure, Sir!"

"Then I suggest you work it out and let me know later in the day – I shall be back during the first dog watch."

Tompkins knuckled his forehead, as Will turned away.

Later in the Wardroom, Will was able to ascertain that *Victory* would be calling at Plymouth, to take on more crew, before setting sail for the Mediterranean. He might get his second new uniform after-all.

The Wardroom of *Victory* had a very dispirit assembly. Besides the eight Lieutenants, there were the Surgeon, Purser, Master, Second Master, together with a Captain and a Subaltern of Marines. Will kept his own council; he watched and listened to his fellow inmates of the wardroom. He was gauging each of the characters. Fraser, the First Lieutenant, a fellow of average height and build, had a weather beaten face and eyelids that drooped, giving him a permanently tired look. He was apparently due for advancement to Post Captain, but in the meantime remained as the number one in

Victory. He was extremely experienced and well respected by the others in the wardroom.

The next most senior Lieutenant was named Locke. He was an elderly gentleman, who enjoyed a tipple, but was also worldly wise. He was as thin as a wraith with a balding head whose few remaining hairs he tried to keep brushed across his tope. He said little, but when he spoke, it was to the point. Next in seniority was a short stocky north countryman named Spenser, with an 's' rather than a 'c'. A point he always made clear when giving his name. All three of the most senior Lieutenants had served in the War against the Americans.

The Fourth Lieutenant reminded Will of Lieutenant Simmons. Lieutenant Fellowes was opinionated and bad mannered. He was tall and thin with a large patrician nose, over an almost girlish pair of lips and virtually no chin. He obviously considered himself to be superior to those around him. He sported the highest wings to his collars, Will had ever seen, offset by an exaggeratedly complicatedly tied cravat. This meant that he could never bring what little chin he had down to look at anything, which gave him a permanent air of looking down his nose at everything. Apparently his family had large estates in middle England, and he was related to a Marquis. His side kick was a timid fellow called Dundas, who seemed to accept Fellowes bullying tactics, and agreed with everything Fellowes said. Dundas was short with flaming red hair over a pinched face. It didn't help that when stressed he had a pronounced stammer.

The two junior Lieutenants to Will were of a very different nature. The Hon Richard Gaunt, Will's immediate Junior, was a languid fellow, who seemed to view life with an air of amused detachment. He had an open friendly expression with mousey coloured hair, which tended to come free from its queue to flop over a high forehead set over a pair of sparkling light blue amused eyes. He was about the same age as Will, and despite their very different backgrounds, they got on very well. The most junior Lieutenant was Simon Cartwright. Although an older man, he unfortunately was very shy, and suffered the butt of Fellowes barbs. He was also very short, of which it was very evident he was acutely conscious.

Then there was the Master, Mr Blair, an elderly weather-beaten Scotsman with the bandiest legs Will had ever seen. He had a Second Master who was a very tall thin Irishman, Mr O'Connell. The pair seemed to stick together and were rarely in the wardroom except at meal times.

There should have been a Surgeon, but apparently he would be joining at Plymouth.

The final make up of the wardroom were the two Marine Officers, a Captain and a Subaltern; Messrs Richards and Keen. This pair; in their bright scarlet coats were a comedy double act. Nothing seemed to phase them or worry them. Then finally there was the Purser – Mr Briant – a bald bespectacled fellow with a large stomach, who bustled everywhere, muttering to himself.

CHAPTER 17

Victory's wardroom was very different from the dark cramped gunroom of the frigate. Windows right across the stern bathed it in light which reached into the individual cabins. Will had to share his cabin space with a long 24 pounder cannon, which restricted the space available to him considerably. Will spent very little time in the wardroom during the two days that Victory remained in harbour. He had no specific responsibility. He spent the time getting to know the ship, and the men who held responsible positions amongst the crew. The Boatswain, a giant of a man, turned out to come from Cornwall, so there was an immediate rapport between them. The man's name was Helyer, but the crew universally called him Mr Hell, which he seemed to enjoy. There was little need for him to say anything twice, as his deep voice carried the length of the ship, without seemingly being raised. He was an imposing figure. When he discovered that Will had served on *Artful*, he was keen to find out all the detail. The Gunner was a fellow by the name of Rivers, who it turned out, had his very young son aboard. Will actively sought Rivers out to consult him about the guns which would come under his control. Rivers was a fund of knowledge and finding that Will was eager to learn, readily helped in every way.

Victory had to be warped out of the dockyard, with heavy horses attached to the lines. Once she was free of the dock, she hoisted sail and in a light westerly slowly made her way out through the narrow entrance to Portsmouth Harbour. Once at sea, gun drill was called. It did not go well! Tompkins was distraught. He had only six seasoned seaman for the fourteen guns under his command on the middle gun deck. Although they were only required to exercise one side at a time, it meant that only six out of seven guns had a mentor and since a gun crew was normally twelve men, divided into two – for either side. There were too few to go round. Even counting the untrained landmen, they were thirteen men short. It was a shambles. Tompkins was hoarse from shouting instructions. They did not fire the guns, but it was obvious that there were problems that would be noticed on the quarterdeck. Will made notes; there was no point in him putting his oar in! When the gun crews had been stood down, Will was summoned to the quarterdeck to report to the First Lieutenant.

"Bloody shambles – Calvert" The First Lieutenant said, in clear hearing of the Captain, to whom Will had yet to be introduced.

"Complete shambles – I totally agree!" Replied Will in a clear voice.

"So how come?"

"I think you will find that a disproportionate number of landmen have been assigned to the forward middle-deck guns. There are only six – six – experienced seamen. There are 65 landmen, who have never touched cannon before, let alone fired one. Tompkins the Gun Captain has tried mentoring the landmen, but there are not enough experienced men to go round. I just wondered how the other decks faired."

Fraser looked quickly at the un-named Captain, then back to Will. "So how many men are there in all?

"Seventy-one! I know we are not up to strength, but I would have thought that there were more experienced men than just six available, if they were shared out equally.

"Edward, who was responsible for assigning the gun crews?" Asked Fraser of Lieutenant Locke who was standing near-by.

"Lieutenant Dundas!" Came the instant reply.

"Have Lieutenant Dundas and Mr Rivers attend me!" Ordered Fraser. One of the twenty-four Midshipmen aboard *Victory* fled in haste.

"Follow me!" Fraser said to Will and proceeded to climb the steps up to the Poop deck. They waited patiently for a good five minutes before the head of a panting Dundas appeared above the top step of the Poop deck, closely followed by a calm Mr Rivers.

"You wanted me, number one?" Asked Dundas; eyes darting this way and that.

"You were responsible for dividing the crews for the guns?"

"Yes err." Replied Dundas; a very worried look appearing on his face.

"So how come so many landmen were sent to the forward middle-deck?"

"Well, err; we are very short of experienced men." He said diffidently.

"So what proportion of experienced hands did you allocate to the forward lower gun deck?"

Dundas looked really frightened. "I would have to check my records."

"Well give us a rough idea." Fraser spoke mildly, but there was a hint of menace about him.

"Well, err.... Lieutenant Fellowes insisted that he had a full complement of experienced men, Sir!"

"Ah! And you do everything Fellowes tells you to, even if you know it is wrong?"

"Well Sir, he is my senior!"

"No Lieutenant, you do the right thing, and if you aren't sure what is the right thing, then you ask me, or Lieutenant Locke. Dismissed!"

Dundas rushed off.

"Mr Rivers, perhaps you could divide out the experienced men, this time."

Mr Rivers knuckled his brow and nodded to Will, as if suggesting he followed him below.

"Lieutenant, you may go back to your station." Fraser said to Will.

Will thanked Fraser and left. As he climbed down to the quarter-deck he heard the call go out for Lieutenant Fellowes to attend the First Lieutenant on the poop deck.

Will passed Fellowes on the upper deck heading in the opposite direction. He looked very smug. "Had a little difficulty then?" He asked as he walked past. Will ignored him. Rivers made a face that said it all.

Will did not know what was said on the poop, but the immediate result was a change round of personnel, overseen by Mr Rivers and confirmed by Lieutenant Locke.

In the first dog watch, hands were called to exercise the opposite side guns. This time each of the seven guns had three experienced seaman and six landmen to each gun. Tompkins was everywhere; goading and making sure each gun performed as well as could be expected. Mr Rivers stood near Will, quietly watching. This time the performance was fair. The guns were rolled out together and ready to fire at the same time as those below them. Again Will stood and made notes. He neither praised the men nor scolded them.

He preferred to have a quiet word with Tompkins when the gunners were stood down.

Later that afternoon Fraser called Will over and thanked him for being straight and to the point.

"I hope I did not let you down, Sir!" Said Will.

"Not at-all. There was nothing you could do about the problem. It was the first time you had supervised the guns. How were you to know that the idiot had bowed to his colleague's machinations? Watch out for Fellowes, he took it badly - the reprimand, and I have a suspicion he might blame you!"

'Thank you Sir!"

At supper, Lieutenant Fellowes had the watch with Lieutenant Lock, so was not present when Will eat. It wasn't until breakfast next morning that Fellowes had a chance to have a go at Will.

"Had to go running to the First Lieutenant, didn't we!" Was the comment, but before Will even had a chance to reply, Locke was at Fellowes.

"I suggest that you rethink that remark Fellowes. Lieutenant Calvert is far and away more experienced in the matter of gunnery and ship handling than you. You should consider yourself lucky you are not on report to the Captain, because your behaviour in bullying poor old Dundas into giving you a majority of the most experienced gun-crews; could jeopardise the ship if we run across a French Fleet on our way to Plymouth. Your guns might have operated well, but overall our performance would have lost us the ship. Remember we are all in this together, not for our personal glory!"

There was a general muttering of agreement around the wardroom table, and Fellowes found himself the odd one out. He got up and left the wardroom.

Will wondered how Locke had known of his experience. He had not told anyone, and there was no way his papers could have got to the ship before he did.

It was early evening when *Victory* coasted into Plymouth Sound. Will stood to one side of the quarterdeck, managing to keep out of the way, as the Master brought the huge vessel to anchor off Cawsand Beach. The next day they made their way up the Hamoaze to a buoy.

Victory would only stay a matter of days in Plymouth, to take on more crew from the hulks and those who had been taken from ships under repair. Will was surprised to see a boat full of *Artful's* crew brought alongside. He hastened to the gallery where the sailors appeared from below. There were smiles all round when they recognised Will. They even managed a small cheer, before they were bundled away to be assigned to their various messes.

Later Will found that half-a-dozen had been placed in the forward middle-deck mess and therefore would be handling his guns. Will now had a hundred men to service the guns on the forward middle-deck, and half of them knew what they were doing.

Now there would be an improvement; *Artful's* gunnery had been superb.

Later that afternoon, Will was summoned to see the Captain. When Will reported at the cabin door and was announced, he found Captain Knight sitting at his desk with the First Lieutenant standing at his shoulder.

"Ah! Lieutenant Calvert, sorry not to have seen you before, but as it turns out, it is probably in your favour. Just had your service record delivered, together with a letter from Captain Crick: seems to think very highly of you!"

Fraser smiled at Will over the Captain's shoulder. Will stayed silent and impassive.

"Hope you will live up to your reputation, aboard my ship!"

"Very sound man, Captain Crick – good judge of character!" Added Fraser.

Will took it that the interview was over and bowed his

head in acknowledgement, before taking a step back to turn to leave.

As Will stepped out of the Captain's day cabin, he was joined by Fraser.

"A word Will." Said Fraser; guiding Will to the larboard rail; out of earshot of others.

"I read Crick's letter. I did not realise that you were that experienced, or for that matter had been in charge when *Artful* sank the two French frigates."

"Hardly in-charge, it just transpired that way. The Captain was temporarily out of action, and as we were short on officers, I was there on the quarterdeck as Master as well as the Officer-of-the-watch. It all happened very quickly! I just did what seemed necessary at the time."

"And what about that extraordinary business of navigating the impassable channel?"

Added Fraser.

"I was acting as Master – I had the right charts – it seemed expedient."

Fraser clapped Will on the back. "Glad to have you aboard!" Then he strode off forward.

CHAPTER 18

It would take rather more time than expected for *Victory* to complete victualling and taking on gunpowder, during which period, Will took advantage of the time to visit his mother, now married and living on the farm above Looe. Rather than travelling overland, Will hired a small fishing boat, about the same size as the one in which he had originally set sail for Plymouth all those years ago. He took with him a young Midshipman by the name of Herries, who came from the same part of the world. Thomas Tucker acted as crew. This meant that he did not have to hire extra crew. Passing through Looe, Will was hardly recognised. He realised he had grown from a boy to a man. The young women of the fishing village were very interested in this young naval officer, despite the fact that he had a pugilist's nose. He was pleased to find that his mother was in reasonable health and seemed to be happy enough. She was now married to her wealthy farmer. He was welcoming but just as quiet, a man of few words. She was horrified at the sight of his broken nose, but immensely proud of Will in his Lieutenant's uniform, and showed him off to all her friends that evening, as Will was off the next day.

Back aboard *Victory*, Will took his turn at covering other officer's watches, so they too could spend time ashore. He was pacing the quarterdeck on a windy grey clouded day when Mr Blair came up to him.

"I understand from the First Lieutenant that you were a Master."

Will nodded.

"And that it was you who extracted *Artful* from that trap?"

Again Will smiled and nodded agreement.

"Have you been Master on anything larger than a frigate?"Blair seemed genuinely interested.

"I was Master aboard *Challenger* in the West Indies." Replied Will.

"Ah! Good! It is really very comforting to know that there is at least one Lieutenant who is a proper seaman aboard!" Mr Blair commented; slapping Will on the back, before striding off.

Then finally came the day when they let slip the mooring line, and slid down the Narrows, past Devil's Point, turned into Drake Channel, and finally into the Sound and out to the Western Approaches. It seemed very strange not to be on the quarterdeck managing the whole business. Will had his duties, but they were nothing like as responsible.

Whilst visiting his mother, Will had learnt that his Aunt had died. The family home in Plymouth now belonged to him. He had taken advantage of the time spent in Plymouth to visit the house, before putting it up for sale. Together with Tucker he had filled a chest with books from the library and got then taken round by boat to *Victory*. He now had probably the largest library aboard. It was to prove a great bonus, to be able to while away the off-duty hours reading great literature.

It took over a week to make Gibraltar, as the Bay of Biscay, was not very friendly. The weather was squally and overcast with fluky winds. It took a bit of getting used to, the change in motion. *Artful* had been very lively. *Victory* was much more ponderous in her movements. Each day on the voyage out, the gun crews had been exercised. Sometimes they actually fired the guns, but without using shot. Will's crew, with the addition of the experienced seamen, managed to out-perform Fellowes crew below. They fired their guns and had them sponged out, reloaded and run-out a good thirty seconds before their arch rivals. Mr Rivers even came down to watch them the last time they practiced firing before sighting Corsica. Tompkins was overjoyed, when given a grudging compliment by the Gunner himself. Will was insistent that the crews changed places, so that each man could do any of the necessary jobs, in case men were killed in action.

At other times Will took his turn on watch. He was surprised to learn that Fellowes and Dundas always had a senior Lieutenant on duty with them as well as a Master's Mate. Will discovered that when it was his watch; he always seemed to be the senior officer on the quarterdeck. It was the Master who let slip that the other two were not trusted to sail the ship unsupervised. Will, however, because he had been a Master was considered fully capable of handling the great ship by himself. This wasn't strictly true, because he always had either the Master or the Second Master available to advise him and their mates. Will enjoyed the power of the great ship; he often gazed up at the massive array of canvas above his head. The Honourable Richard Gaunt (no relation to Will's Aunt), was his number two. He spent the whole time quizzing Will about what should be done and why. Will enjoyed his company as well as his enthusiasm. The Master seemed to prefer to be around when Will had the watch, but hastily informed Gaunt that it wasn't because he did not trust Will, rather that he enjoyed the company of another real Navigator.

Unlike the other officers, Will liked to find out about the crew around him. He often talked to the quartermasters at the wheel, discussing the feel of the ship and her performance. They were experienced seamen and had all been on *Victory* for a long time, even during her refit.

Will had the watch when the lookout first sighted the great mass of the Rock. They were approaching Tarifa Island on the larboard side, with Africa clearly visible on the Starboard.

Will had been here before, but it was new to Gaunt, who gazed in awe at the narrow channel that divided the two continents and the great Rock rising up out of the sea ahead of them. Will walked over to Gaunt and explained that they had the advantage of the tide, as it was near high water, so the tidal stream was in their favour. The best place was where they were, in the centre of the channel. The supporting frigates were now much closer to *Victory* than at any time during their voyage out. Will had increased the number of lookouts, just in case the French had managed to breakout from Toulon. Now both the Captain and the First Lieutenant emerged to see what was going on.

"Fine day for it at last Calvert." Remarked Captain Knight as he surveyed the horizon with a glass.

"Aye Sir, I was explaining to Lieutenant Gaunt that we had arrived at the right time as the tide was in our favour."

Knight took the scope from his eye and looked over the side. "Right!" He commented and then turned to greet Rear Admiral Mann, who was coming out of his quarters. The Admiral had hardly appeared on deck during their voyage south. Will, as officer-of-the-watch held his position, whilst others withdrew to the gunwales. He heard the Admiral ask after the officer by the wheel, but didn't hear any more as both the Captain and Admiral climbed to the poop-deck. .

Will had expected Fraser to take over, but Fraser just smiled at Will and joined the Master on the opposite side. Will was left to give the commands. He waited a few minutes and then calmly ordered the Boatswain to have the Royals taken in. Pipes sounded and the topmen leapt to their respective shrouds to climb to the very top yard.

He then gave the order "Starboard ten" which meant that the ship would turn ten degrees to larboard. "Man the Braces!" The braces controlled the angle of the yards to the masts. There was no need for him to order the sheets adjusted, because the Boatswain and the Boatswain's mates were already making sure the necessary tightening and loosening was under way.

Out of the corner of his eye Will saw the Captain come down from the poop-deck, glance his way, before returning to his scrutiny of the shore. Fraser finished conversing with the Master and ambled over to join the Captain, though he did not speak to him. The Master came over to join Will.

"Fraser's letting the Captain see that you know what you're doing!" The Master whispered out of the corner of his mouth, before returning an evil smelling pipe to the mouth in question.

It remained that way for the next hour. More officers came onto the quarterdeck, but the Captain remained on deck, though he later took up a position on the poop deck above. Fraser seemed to content himself with leaning on the larboard bulwarks, watching the Spanish mainland pass-by.

Finally when it was time to turn north into the bay of Algeciras, Fraser walked over to Will and said quietly. "I have her!"

Will stepped aside to become an observer. Lieutenant Locke would be in charge of the anchor party, assisted by Cartwright. Spenser and Fellowes walked forward to their positions by the Main and Foremasts respectively. Dundas was nominally in charge of the Mizzen mast. Nearer the time, Will would descend to the upper gun deck to supervise the checking of the anchor cable as it was run out, making sure it did not rush out too fast and foul the anchor.

There were a number of merchant ships anchored off the rock and its harbour. Inshore Will spied at least two sets of masts belonging to third-rates. *Victory* would be by far the largest ship in the anchorage. The orders went out for the Courses to be furled. Fraser was obviously going to use the Topsails as he approached the anchorage, which made sense as they were less likely to be affected by any local vapours coming off the Rock. As *Victory* swung to Starboard to head in towards the anchorage, Will dropped down the companionway to the upper deck. Here the experienced crew stood by watched over by the Captain of the forecastle. Will had no intention of saying anything so long as the whole operation went smoothly.

As usual the forecastle crew was made up of the older and therefore more experienced seamen. They knew exactly what was expected of them. The anchor cable was flaked out along the deck, with stoppers to check its passage as necessary. The anchor itself had been un-catted and now hung by its cable ready to be released. Now the crew stood ready to let go the anchor, by chopping through its restraint. At last the order was passed down, the boarding axe sliced through the lanyard holding the anchor and it splashed into the sea, followed by a snaking cable. Everyone had to watch out to make sure they were not caught by the eyes of the cable as each flake was released. Finally the order came to snuff it. Expertly another line was whipped around the cable and secured. It brought the cable up short. *Victory* was now pulling her anchor across the bottom, until the sheer weight of the cable and anchor ploughing into the seabed held her.

Victory took the opportunity of loading fresh victuals and water, before setting out for Corsica.

CHAPTER 19

It was May when *Victory* arrived at San Fiorenzo Bay on the northwest coast of Corsica to join the Mediterranean Fleet blockading Toulon. Not all the fleet was there because most of the frigates were patrolling off the coast of France. It was still quite an impressive sight as there were a number of ships-of-the-line already anchored in the charming bay.

Victory didn't stay long in the Bay. She sailed to join the blockading fleet off Toulon, under Vice Admiral Hotham aboard *Britannia*. *Victory* would normally have expected to be the flagship, but for some reason Admiral Hotham preferred otherwise. There the fleet sailed backwards and forwards, mostly in sight of land, waiting for the French fleet to come out.

No longer being the Master, Will had to stand-by and watch the provisioning at sea routine. The Merchantman would sail up close astern of the *Victory* , whose crew would drop a line attached to a small barrel into the sea and let it drift aft to hopeful end up at the bows of the merchantman. Here a poor fellow stood on the Martingale Guy holding onto the Whisker or as the seaman referred to it the 'Dolphin Striker' with one hand, whilst with the other trying to catch hold of the streamed line with a boat-hook. It always took a number of tries, before the line was caught and passed up to the bows of the merchantman, where a towing cable was attached. Then the seaman on *Victory's* deck marched aft hauling in the cable. Already rigged around the stern would be a strop which was temporarily secured to the stern rail of the poop. A bowline knot would then be made in the towing cable around the strop. Once ready the strop would be dropped into the water and the merchantman signalled to secure the cable. At that point the merchantman eased her sails and became towed by the great ship.

Cutters were then dropped either side of *Victory* and

allowed to fall back to the towed merchant. Once loaded the cutters would then be hauled forward to *Victory*; their cargo hoisted out, so that the cutters could be drifted astern for more. It was a tricky operation overseen by the Master - Mr Blair.

In April the wardroom learnt that six French seventy-fours with four frigates had managed to escape from Brest and make it all the way to Toulon to join the French Fleet there. By the officers calculations this meant that the French now had about 19-20 ships of the line based in Toulon. So the fleets in general numbers were nearly balanced except for the fact that there were two Neapolitan 74s with the British fleet.

Then in the middle of May rumours filtered through that Intelligence had found out that there had been a mutiny amongst the French fleet. It explained why half of the fleet were anchored in Toulon Roads.

The question on everybody's mind was how this would affect things. In June they were to find out. Early on June the 8th, cannon fire could be heard. The order was given to prepare to sea. *Victory* was one of the first to haul up her anchor. The 64 gun *Agamemnon* under command of Captain Nelson had managed to out sail the French to warn the British fleet anchored in Fiorenzo Bay. The French must have realised that they were out gunned. The British had six three deckers! The French turned and fled. The winds were fluky, and it wasn't until four days later that the British fleet learnt from their Corvettes that the French having sheltered in Frejus Bay were now South of the Islands of the Hyères.

Next morning contact was made and the British led by *Victory*, closely followed by *Culloden* and *Cumberland*, chased after them. Once again the Mediterranean weather started to play its tricks. The French hit a calm and soon the three leading British ships were up with the tail-enders. Will was at his station with the middle-deck guns. *Victory* was leading the attack, and Will could see through the open ports that she was drawing to a parallel course with the last of the French ships. Then the wind shifted around to the North and the rest of the French ships altered course onto a new tack.

The order was relayed down to the Middle Gun deck "Open fire!"

Will raised his arm and the first of the gun captains pulled his gunlock lanyard. As each Cannon fired, there was a bark of the gun as it kicked back like a startled animal to be caught by its breeching rope. Immediately at every gun, with the poise of a ballet dancer the number two in the gun crew leapt forward and pushed his sponge down the barrel to extinguish any residue left in the barrel. As he was doing this the gun captain pricked the touchhole to make sure it was clear. No2, the second loader, inserted the charge down the barrel followed instantly by a wad to hold it. Both were then rammed home to be followed by the ball and another wad, As this was happening the gun captain had pricked the charge through the touchhole and inserted a goose quill filled with powder, The rest of the gun crew were already hauling on the gun tackle to bring the cannon up through the gun port ready for firing. If any alteration of angle or elevation was needed this was done as the gun was run out.

One thing that Will had made sure Tompkins insisted on; was the position of each member of the gun crew. There had to be a routine movement. Each man had to make sure he took up a set position for each phase of the operation, so nobody would be falling over anybody else. The powder monkey had to place the charge box in exactly the same position every time; and the same was true of the balls and wads. Similarly the powder monkeys and ball bearers had to mount the ladderway on a set side and go down on the other. It was a routine drummed into each crew every day.

Immediately the first broadsides were exchanged; instinctively many members of Will's gun crew ducked, as the ship vibrated from the impact of the enemy balls striking the rigging and hull. As usual the French seemed to be aiming at the rigging, because down below Will could feel the shivers reacting throughout the hull, but there was little in the way of damage being done to his own deck.

Will only heard afterwards, that the French had taken advantage of the wind backing and coming from the North instead of from the South-West, to turn onto a new tack where they would be able to fire at the oncoming British ships.

Now they were assailed by more than one French ship. Will was concentrating on the French opponent, which he had seen was a 74 gun ship-of-the-line. Now he couldn't see a thing. The wind made sure that the smoke from the 32 pounders on the deck below mingled with their own to obliterate everything. Around 2pm, there was a shout from above; the Frenchman had lowered his colours. Two French frigates rushed in to try and take the French 74 in tow. *Victory* laid down such a barrage of fire, that the two frigates were forced to abandon the attempt.

It was the first time Will had commanded guns in an action below decks. The noise was incredible, leaving one deaf. The smoke from the guns filtered back into the gundeck, making one cough and the eyes smart. The gun crews worked tirelessly, swearing and shouting encouragement to each other. Sweat poured from their bare backs; the heat was like being inside a furnace. Will stood to the rear of his section. The idea was that one would be able to see exactly what was going on, but after the first broadside, it was obvious he could see very little and control even less. Nobody noticed him, as they were concentrating on their guns. Marines staggered past carrying the shot, whilst the 'powder monkeys' emerged with their boxed charges from behind the thick 'dreadnought' cloth screens erected around the ladderway to prevent sparks dropping down to the magazine below. If he moved forward he would only get in the way. He had supervised the training, now it was up to the gun crews themselves.

Then other French ships turned their attention on trying to intercede. Suddenly more smoke than would have been usual, could be seen coming from the fore of the French 74. Then there was a terrific explosion. Everybody concluded that the magazine must have gone up.

By this time *Victory* had slowed due to the damage to her rigging. *Victory's* boats were recovered and manned to try and save some of the French survivors of the explosion. The fighting had stopped, almost as if the explosion had so surprised both sides that they stopped their conflict.

Then there was muttering from the gun-crews. They stood about, faces and bodies blackened by the smoke with lines where the sweat had run in rivulets down their bodies. They had hoped to take the Frenchman and gain some prize money. They had just heard that their prize had blown-up. Will was surprised that *Victory* wasn't going after the other French ships. It was what he had expected. Word came for the gun-crews to stand-down, and Will made his way up to the quarter-deck to discover that Admiral Hotham had signalled from *Britannia,* that the whole fleet would now retire.

Nobody could understand why the British ships had not pressed their advantage.

One of the officers in the crowd on the quarterdeck was heard to say.

"The whole French line might have been cut off from land, taken or destroyed; and even afterwards, they might have been followed into Frejus Bay, and wholly destroyed. [The Royal Navy. Vol 4, Clowes]

Victory retired to Fiorenzo Bay, where the riggers and ship-wrights worked tirelessly to repair the damage and make her fit for another round.

Once the major damage had been repaired, it was back to sea. *Victory*, recently out from England was in a better state than many of the other ships. There was an acute shortage of supplies. Many of the crews were sick, and the lack of decent victuals, caused much grumbling below decks.

Will found blockade duty very boring and tiring. He had been used to blockade duty onboard *Artful*, but then he had always been in the thick of it. Now he was just one of a number of watch-keeping officers. It was a continuous repetitive need to keep station, with frequent tacking or wearing. At night it was an even greater strain. There was a break in the middle of October, when Vice Admiral Linzee hoisted his pennant in place of Rear Admiral Mann aboard *Victory*, otherwise the blockade duty continued.

At last there came a minor distraction, which was the arrival of the frigate *HMS Lively* with Admiral Jervis, come to take command of the fleet. Due to the light winds, the frigate had great difficulty in setting her anchors.

Finally Admiral Jervis came aboard, to take over command of the whole fleet. Previously *Britannia* had been the flagship of Vice Admiral Hotham, and his successor Vice Admiral Parker. Now *Victory* was the flagship, and Jervis had brought with him two new captains. There was a Fleet Captain, a Captain Calder, whilst Captain Grey took over as captain of *Victory* herself.

Victory settled down to blockading Toulon once more. The monotonous regime affected the sailors as well as Will. He had read every one of his books, some twice over. He tried very hard to find ways of breaking up the routine within his Division. He discussed this with Fraser quietly one evening, and got the go ahead to try anything that did not conflict with the routine of the ship. Luckily the seamen of the middle-gun deck were mostly seasoned hands, the older men on the ship. Each watch had gun drill each day, so Will gave prizes each week to the gun crew who managed the fastest reloading after firing. He took to taking his chronometer so he could accurately time the crews.

When possible he had the landmen haul up a length of the main hawser, and practice nipping and un-nipping the cable to and from the messenger. He encouraged the landmen to learn extra skills, which would help them achieve Able Seaman status. He gave small prizes for the best fancy rope-work, though the Purser did not think much of the use of the ship's spare cordage. Will was helped by the presence of the ex *Artful* members of his section, who spread the word that he was a fair officer. Seamen admire bravery, and Will's reputation did him no harm. One only had to take one look at him to think 'pugilist'. As a result it was easier for him to keep discipline, helped by the fact that two of the quartermasters were from his old ship.

In the wardroom some officers liked to play at cards, which went with betting. Will was not a card player or a gambler, and politely turned down requests to join others at the table. He preferred to read or to play chess with anybody who was free. He was an average player, and didn't take it too seriously. Fellowes thought he was a great card player, but was always losing to others. In the end he owed so much that Fraser banned him from playing, so to Will's horror Fellowes decided he might be a chess genius. He wasn't, but hated losing, so Will refused to play with him. It was a great relief to the wardroom when Admiral Jervis decided to rotate some of the officers and Fellowes was sent off to join another ship in the fleet. The wardroom was so glad to be shot of him; nobody demanded payment before he left.

One day whilst on watch Will was approached by O'Connell the Second Master.

"Might I ask what that object you are holding does?"

"Will turned to hand him the board he was holding. "It is my way of keeping a journal of the weather without having to leave the deck whilst I am on watch." He explained.

"Can't shake the Master out of you, eh?" Commented O'Connell, with a grin.

"I suppose not! I have always tried to build up an idea of what the weather is likely to do by keeping a journal note. When I became a Watch-keeping Officer as well as the Master I couldn't pop into my Chart Room as easily as I did as a Master. I pondered the problem and then thought of this. I suppose it is loosely based on a Traverse Board. You put in a peg at the time you come on watch. Then in the first row a peg for the wind direction starting from north clockwise. Then a peg in the next row for what I think the strength of the wind happens to be between a flat calm and a full gale. Today I would call it about halfway say 5.

Then there is the state of the Sea. I try to judge the height and length between waves. Again this is between a flat calm and a full gale. The Essences are a different matter. [Until the early 1800s the word cloud was not commonly used to describe clouds. They were referred to as Essences.]

There is no official name for any that I know of; so I have named them myself. I would call the cloud to our West, where they are coming from "Low semi-fluffy".

"And then what?"

"I transpose them to my journal. The next time we have the same conditions I will look to see what happened the last time we had similar conditions. Over time I have built a fair understanding of what will happen. Here in the Med. It is entirely different to the Atlantic. Have you ever asked yourself why?"

"Aye. I have discussed it many times with Mr Blair. We are of the opinion that it has something to do with the fact that there is land all around us. I mean take the winds that come down from the North as you close the French coast at this time of year. You don't get anything like that in the Channel, do you?"

And so the discussion continued. Two days later Mr Blair, the Master, button holed Will in the Wardroom.

"O'Connell has been telling me about your wee toy. I should like to take a gander if I might?"

Will retrieved it from his cabin and explained the methodology again.

"And these Essences, how do you describe those?"

Will pushed a sheet of paper across the wardroom table on which he had sketched the various types.

Blair looked at the paper long and hard.

"I think we might be able to assist you. If you can give us

a copy of you drawing, we will nail it up in the cubby and get the Mates to write the number classification in the rough log. That way you will have a full daylight hour report available to you."

Victory would sail up and down the French Coast in line with the other ships of the line, with the frigates acting as scouts and messenger relays. It was frustrating to be able to see the enemy shore, and sometimes the masts of the French fleet bottled up in harbour, but not able to do anything about them.

Occasionally they would retire to San Fiorenzo Bay, to replenish stores and water, or if the weather looked set to blow hard from the South. Will still kept his journal, and noted the weather changes and what preceded the violent weather. The Mediterranean had its own unique weather pattern. Will discussed this at length with both the Master and Second Master. One moment you could have a flat calm and the next the wind would come at you from a totally unexpected direction, sometimes ferociously.

News of the war elsewhere was few and far between. Occasionally a ship would join from England, and everybody would want to know the latest news. Within their own world of the Mediterranean Sea, nuggets would filter down to the wardroom. The Gazette, if it ever arrived, was weeks old.

There were though, marked differences, coming down the chain of command. Admiral Jervis might be a strict disciplinarian, but he was fair and respected around the fleet.

When they were anchored in the Bay of Fiorenzo, Will was ordered to assist the Purser in trying to obtain fresh vegetables and fruit. Apparently the Admiral considered onions to be very good for his men. This was the first time that Will had set foot on the island. He was struck by the poverty of the land, even near the coast. The inhabitants lived a subsistence existence, so there was little available for the ship. The Admiral seemed to take more interest in the health of his crews than the previous incumbents. He ordered that hammocks and bedding should be aired more frequently. Gun-ports were opened far more often to let fresh air into the ship.

On many ships there were women aboard. Wives of members of the crew, or supposed wives. Often they serviced more than their husband's needs. Admiral Jervis did everything in his power to try and off load the 'ladies'. Unfortunately before the Admiral had arrived, ships crews had managed to get ashore in Leghorn and other Italian ports, Venereal disease was rife throughout the fleet, debilitating many of the crew.

It also seemed that supply ships were slightly more frequent than previously. For Will, if Officer of the Watch, it meant even more concentration. Mr Blair was responsible for the handling of the process, but it was still the Officer-of-the-Watch's duty to keep his ship in its convoy position.

Will had now got to know his fellow officers in the Wardroom. Fraser, the First Lieutenant, was a strict disciplinarian, but had a human touch. He expected his fellow officers to perform their duties to the highest standards. He had harsh words for anybody dropping below those standards. In the wardroom off duty, he was friendly, and informative, without letting himself appear to be one of the crowd. He was a good deal older than the other officers; with the exception of Lieutenant Locke, the Purser and the Surgeon. Will had been surprised that he did not have his own command, until one night on watch, he had confided to Will that their Captain, Grey, had asked him to stay as his First Lieutenant, and promised him a command when this tour of duty was over. Apparently Grey was worried that, *Victory* being the flagship, had to out-perform all the other ships in the fleet, and trusted Fraser.

Locke was a completely different character. A tall thin character, he knew his ships, and how to get the best out of them, as well as his men. He was a fair man, who disliked excesses of corporal punishment, so found other ways of disciplining those who misbehaved, when they came within his orbit.

Spenser, the third officer, a short stocky, thick set man, who on first acquaintance would seem to have been more at home in the army or marines than the navy, turned out to be a fine mariner. He was not above asking for advice from the Master or First Lieutenant, if he was not quite sure about anything.

Fellowes on the other hand, had never asked for advice. He thought he knew it all. This was disastrous, because he clearly was lacking in nearly all areas. Will was to learn from Dundas, that Fellowes had influence at the Admiralty. According to Dundas, Fellowes had been promoted to Lieutenant despite failing his exams. It transpired later that Fellowes' mother had been the mistress to a member of the Admiralty Board. Fellowes was supercilious to the point of being rude. He was always being reprimanded by Fraser, but it didn't seem to dent his self-esteem. He would never appear on duty or elsewhere without checking his appearance. His absence was a blessing, especially as his replacement, a Lieutenant Andrews turned out to be a merry fellow who added greatly to the good humour of the wardroom. He was powerfully built, with a round ruddy face, which normally had a wide grin.

Dundas was a frail young man, with a stutter. He had been bullied by Fellowes, and had at first seemed to be under Fellowes' influence. As the weeks had gone past he tended to gravitate towards Will, and seemed to become surer of himself. This seemed to rankle with Fellowes, who could not help but to make disparaging remarks. Now with Fellowes gone, he began to come out of his shell.

The Honourable Richard Gaunt, Will's immediate junior, was a good looking young man with an un-deniable amiability. He was the younger son of a Marquis, but never took advantage of it, preferring to be referred to as Gaunt or Dicky. He was a keen learner, who soon discovered Will's navigational skills, and sought to learn from him.

The most junior Lieutenant, Cartwright, was older than either Will or Gaunt, but had remained a midshipman as he had constantly failed his exams. He was a thick set man, with a weather beaten complexion. Now finally he had passed his exams and been promoted. He was utterly reliable, double checking everything, and well respected by the crew.

CHAPTER 20

There was one character that Will could not fail to be aware of – a certain Captain Nelson. His exploits were much discussed in the wardroom. Will learnt that this Captain had captured the imposing fortress at Calvi, just round the coast from San Fiorenzo. Will first saw the Captain when he came aboard the first time after Sir John Jervis had arrived as Admiral in command of the Mediterranean fleet. After that Nelson was a constant visitor, when his ship was with the fleet. In April, Will was the Officer of the Watch when Captain Nelson came aboard. Nelson left as a Commodore, promoted by Admiral Jervis and put in command of a small fleet to support the Austrian army in northern Italy. The slightly framed Commodore had chatted to Will, whilst he waited for his gig to be ready to take him to his ship.

Will was to meet him again on the occasion of Commodore Nelson being given the command of the larger *HMS Captain*.

After a period of sailing backwards and forwards across the southern coast of France, blockading Toulon and trying to entice the French fleet out, *Victory* returned to Corsica to re-provision. There they were met by seven British ships under the command of Admiral Mann. Will observed the Admiral being rowed across to *Victory*. Later he was surprised to learn that Mann was being sent back to Gibraltar to provision properly. This caused much discussion in the wardroom.

Once when sailing off Toulon, Will was amused by the commands of his admiral. As *Victory* set sail to pass astern of *Britannia* the order went out that the young ladies were to muster on the poop of *Britannia*. Will commandeered a telescope to see what all the mirth was about. As *Victory* glided past, there were a row of attractive young ladies waving. Later in the week, Will was to be able to inspect the young ladies in close-up. The Admiral was throwing a dinner party, and the ladies were rowed over to the flagship. Will, as Officer-of-the-Day, had the pleasurable duty of supervising their being lifted aboard. That night there was considerable merriment to be heard coming from the Admiral's quarters, where most of the Captains from the other ships in the fleet had been invited.

Then one night when Will was Officer-of-the-Watch, doing the morning watch from 4am to 8 am, the Admiral appeared on deck. Admiral Jervis was known to retire early at about half-past eight and to rise at two o'clock in the morning to work on his papers.

Much to Will's surprise the Admiral strolled over to have a word with him.

"Calvert, isn't it?"

"Aye Sir!"

"Thought so. Been watching you young man. Had very favourable reports from Captain Grey, who also showed me your record. Most impressive. Just the sort of officer we need in this Navy of ours."

Will didn't know what to say.

"Come from Cornwall, don't you?"

"Yes Sir."

"I was a Member of Parliament for a Cornish Constituency for a short time. Fine seamen the Cornish!" And with that he turned to mount the steps to the poop-deck.

Just when matters couldn't seem to get any worse, the

wardroom learnt that Corsica was to be evacuated. A fleet of twenty-six Spanish ships had been reported heading north in the direction of Corsica. The British fleet consisted of only fifteen sail of the line. The wardroom was full of rumours that they were waiting for Rear Admiral Mann to return with his squadron, so they would be a match for the combined Spanish and French fleets. The news was that the French were sending troops to retake the island. The British were trying to hold the island of Elba with its harbour, which meant even less ships were available to Admiral Jervis. To make matters worse the Corsicans, who had welcomed the British now turned on them through fear of retribution from the French when they arrived. Commodore Nelson was sent with transports to evacuate Bastia the Island's capital.

On the 18th October the French landed troops on the northern most tip of the island, some 20 miles from Bastia and Fiorenzo Bay, and started to march on Bastia.

Victory and the other members of the fleet available were now anchored in Fiorenzo Bay. Nelson successfully evacuated the British residents from Bastia just as the French troops arrived. He escorted the transports to Elba, and then rejoined the fleet in the Bay. With the French now occupying the island, Fiorenzo Bay became untenable as an anchorage. On October 23rd the fleet abandoned their refuge. Apparently the Spanish fleet were reported to have joined forces with the French at Toulon. On the 29th October at Mortello point, the British fleet razed the Tower to rubble, Will thought as target practice.

On the 1st November, Will was aware that something out of the ordinary was going on, due to the number of Captains that were rowed across to visit the Admiral. Later the wardroom was full of it. The British fleet had been ordered to retire to Gibraltar, as with the north of Italy now in the hands of the French under a young General Napoleon, there were few places from where the fleet could be supplied.

On the 2nd of November the entire fleet together with transports set sail for Gibraltar.

On the 11th November Admiral Jervis learnt that Rear Admiral Mann had disobeyed his order to return to Corsica, and instead had patrolled off Cape St. Vincent for a short period and then sailed back to Britain. Was this because he resented Admiral Jervis sending him back to Gibraltar to make sure he was properly supplied?

Based on Gibraltar the depleted British fleet were handy to descend on any Spanish or French Fleet trying to leave the Med. for Cadiz. The frigates kept watch on the Strait in case a Spanish fleet tried to join up with their ships at Cadiz, or worse still, join the French at Brest. It was winter, so the main fleet mostly stayed anchored in the Bay at the foot of the Rock.

Will took the opportunity to school his gun crews in his methods. The forward middle gun deck was equipped with 24 pounders. He explained that these guns could do immense damage if strategically used. Even with all the smoke about after the first broadside, it was often possible to recognise some part of the opposing ship. From this one had to use an informed guess as to where the best target would have been if there was no smoke. So if you could see the fore shrouds, one could gauge the distance below of the first gun-deck, their normal target. If you looked carefully before the first shots were fired, you could remember the relative positions of the gun ports to the shrouds above. It was far better to fire into an open gun-port than just hit the other ships side. Their whole ambition should be to silence the opponent as quickly as possible. If one could fire through the open port you were almost certain to kill or injury a number of the enemy gunners, which would slow their rate of fire.

If they were coming alongside a smaller ship, then the foremost guns would be loaded with grape shot and aimed as far forward as possible towards the other ship's quarter deck, to try to take out the senior officers and helmsmen.

Normally the carronades on the forecastle would do this, but Will reasoned that with their superior range the cannons could inflict a decisive strike much earlier. At anchor with the gun ports open, Will would go forward to join his crew if a ship was about to pass them. They would discuss exactly where they would aim their cannon for maximum effect if the other ship had been the enemy. It was taken as a sort of game to pass the time, but in reality it also made the crews think far more about placement of shots.

Each gun had a crew of six or seven men, the bigger guns below had larger crews. There was a Senior Gun Captain who was the most experienced of the whole of the gun crews. Each Gun had its own Captain who was responsible for the aiming, the elevation, pricking the cartridge and firing the gun. There was a second Captain who was in charge of the other side if both sides were in action. The number two trimmed the gun, adjusting the horizontal angle by use of a hand spike. He also helped with the tackle. Numbers three and four were the loaders who sponged out the gun. One of these would insert the sponge, in reality a cloth or rope splayed to hold water, twist it – called worming – to remove any residue from the previous firing. Anything combustible was shaken off, extinguished and the other end was used to ram a cartridge and wad down the barrel. Then the chosen shot was added with another wad and rammed home. This man had to be nimble to jump over the recoil tackle, so as not to get pinned against the hull when the gun was hauled out to its firing position. Using the tackle and handspikes the gun was run out by the extra men. The gun captain pricked the cartridge through the vent, inserted a quill filled with combustible material, aimed the gun and then pulled the lanyard attached to the gunlock to fire the gun. The cartridges were brought up from the magazine in wooden cartridge boxes to protect them from sparks, by the powder monkeys, who were young boys, or sometimes marines.

Will's guns were one deck up from the magazines, but even so he managed to add an extra marine whenever possible to carry the heavy shot to augment the existing powder monkey. The marines had to be the fittest aboard! Each day the gun-crews practised without firing. Each day Will varied the scenario. Early in his time aboard *Victory*, soon after the ship had become the flagship, the Gunner had come forward to see why the forward middle gun-deck seemed to be rather slower than the other decks. Will explained that they were practising sighting the guns for extra effect. Mr Rivers had grunted and with his hands behind his back strolled back to the quarter-deck to inform the Captain what was going on. That evening Will had been summoned to Captain Grey's cabin. There he found Fraser with the Captain. Quizzed as to his actions that morning, Will explained his theories of maximum effect. Captain Grey listened to him in silence. When Will had finished he turned to Fraser and commented that they had before them a 'thinking' officer. Fraser asked about broadsides, and Will had replied that with a broadside, one had to do as commanded, but with the following rounds, where there was so much smoke, maximising the effectiveness of each gun would achieve a better result. He asserted that he was pleased that his guns were 24 pounders, not 32s, as the lighter gun was easier to aim. Captain Grey called for Mr Rivers, and a lively discussion took place. Will was surprised that Captain Grey would countenance such an exchange of views. But the result was that he was given permission to use his methods, unless specifically ordered not to do so. Little did Will know that Captain Grey would discuss Will's ideas with the Admiral himself.

CHAPTER 21

The fleet had a bad time at Gibraltar. There were frequent gales and bad weather. Boredom in the wardroom was as intense as ever. Fraser one day enquired if anybody had any unusual experiences to relate. Locke told a long and convoluted story about his time during the American War. So each meal the next officer had to tell a tale. When it came to Will's turn, he described the strange people who inhabited the South China ports, which led to many questions being asked and the realisation of the officers that Will had travelled far further than any of them. He was asked to describe in detail lands others had only vaguely heard about.

In the middle of what had been a gale ridden winter, yet another gale started to blow from the East. The British were anchored to the West of the Rock, protected from the Westerly's by the hills behind Algeciras. Just when the British were trying to prevent their ships from being blown ashore, a French fleet were blown through the Straits of Gibraltar. There was nothing that could be done about it. Aboard *Victory* it was all hands on deck. The strength of the gale made it impossible to put to sea, because they wouldn't have been able to work their way east enough against the gale to round the point to the south of Algeciras. The 74 gun *Courageux* managed to escape the Bay under the command of her First Lieutenant – her captain was ashore attending a court-marshal – but was driven onto rocks and was wrecked on the North African Coast. The 80 gun *Gibraltar* and the 74 gun *Culloden* were both driven ashore after their anchor cables parted. A few days later the 74 gun *Zealous* hit a reef off Cape Malabata in Tangier Bay. Indeed quite a few ships did the same thing, but with not so disastrous results. *Victory* was showing signs of fatigue. She was leaking badly and her timbers were liable to spring. She had been hard pressed during her time in the Mediterranean. There were no docks available for repairs to the British ships in the Mediterranean, and Gibraltar offered no dockyard and was low in provisions.

The wardroom later learnt that Lieutenant Fellowes, who had earlier been transferred to the *Courageux,* had lost his life along with 462 of the crew.

To add to the misery, the order came for Elba to be evacuated. Admiral Jervis sent Commodore Nelson to undertake this endeavour, but because he was so short of ships-of-the-line, he sent the Commodore in the frigate *Minerve,* together with the frigate *Blanche.*

It was a relief when *Victory* and the fleet sailed on the 15th December round the coast to Portugal and the mouth of the River Tagus. Portugal was their ally, so it served two purposes. The ships could be provisioned and re-supplied, whilst being within easy distance to prevent a Spanish/French fleet calling at Cadiz, or passing on north to Brest.

Their troubles however were not over. There was a lack of pilots to help them enter the mouth of the River Tagus. As a result the 74 gun *Bombay Castle* ran aground. Every effort was made to try and get her off, but they failed. *Zealous* was leaking so badly that she had to go into Lisbon harbour for repairs. *Gibraltar* still suffering from her ordeal off the Rock in the gale, had to be sent home to Britain.

Will was allowed to go ashore a couple of times, and admired the City, but not knowing anybody, nor speaking the language, he found it a fruitless exercise. He now spoke passable French, having discovered that *Victory's* Surgeon spoke it fluently. He had prevailed upon the bored medic to instruct him at every opportunity. French however was not the language to use in Lisbon, even if they had understood.

Admiral Jervis had issued a strong order that nothing should be done that might offend the Portuguese, so seamen were under strict control of officers at all times on the rare times they had to go ashore.

Ships at anchor are very boring places for a cramped crew. Petty fights broke out more than when they were at sea. At sea the men had a full routine, and were constantly employed. In harbour or at anchor, there were only routine chores to occupy the time. Christmas was now upon the anchored British fleet, and there was plenty to eat and plenty to drink, curtsy of the Portuguese allies ashore. Will thoroughly enjoyed the festive spirit in the wardroom, which without the late unlamented Fellowes was a much happier place. His replacement, Lieutenant Andrews, was an amiable soul, who fitted in well.

Another accident meant that they were even shorter on ships. On the 11th January 1797 when the British set out to escort a Portuguese convoy bound for Brazil, the 98 gun *St George* collided with a Portuguese frigate and lost her mast when she ran aground. She was refloated, but had to undergo major repairs. Then ten days later the 32 gun *Meleager* sprang her bowsprit and had to be sent into Lisbon for repairs.

With even less ships to face an expected large fleet of Spanish ships, the British ships managed to escort the Portuguese well out into the Atlantic and so avoid the threat from the Spanish. Leaving their Portuguese allies, the British ships turned back to head for Cape St. Vincent, to be able to intercept any Spanish ships trying to get into Cadiz.

On the 1st February the fleet was abuzz with lookouts sighting five ships-of-the-line appearing from the North. It turned out to be much needed reinforcements sent out from England to replace Mann's ships which had shamefully returned to England.

Will noted in his journal the size of the fleet that night.

Victory	100 Gun	Admiral Jervis	Culloden	74 Gun
Britannia	100 Gun	Vice Admiral Thompson	Egmont	74 Gun
Barfleur	98 Gun	Vice Admiral Waldegrave	Goliath	74 Gun
Blenheim	98 Gun		Diadem	74 Gun
Prince George	98 Gun	Rear Admiral Parker	Irresistible	74 Gun
Namur	98 Gun		Orion	74 Gun
Captain	74 Gun		Colossus	74 Gun
Goliath	74 Gun			

At last there was a proper fleet of fifteen ships of the line, six of them three deckers. The wardroom was sure that they were now going to show the Spanish a thing or two if they tried to break-out of the Mediterranean. There were various rumours that the Spanish fleet had been seen passing through the Straits of Gibraltar, but there had been a gale shortly after, and it was not known what had happened to them.

CHAPTER 22

Early on the morning of the thirteenth of February, the frigate *La Minerve* was sighted heading for the fleet. She came about and her ship's boat was seen to be making its way across to *Victory* with Commodore Nelson sitting in the stern. The Commodore bounded up the side and was rushed to the Admiral's quarters. Very soon he was out again and the 74 gun *Captain* was being signalled to draw closer. The Commodore was then rowed over to rejoin *Captain*.

Word was soon out that he had brought news that the Spanish fleet had passed through the straits. Nobody had been quite sure if the Spanish would head for the West Indies, or try to enter Cadiz. They now knew, because Nelson had sailed undetected through the Spanish fleet. The British fleet now headed south to intercept the Spaniards in case they tried for Cadiz. In the afternoon the British sloop

Bonne Citoyenne signalled that the Spanish were 20 miles to the South East, and moving in an Easterly direction. [Bonne Citoyenne was captured from the French, with the name retained]

Very early the next day in misty conditions, the distant sound of single cannons, signalling the Spanish ships positions to one another in the foggy conditions could be heard. The frigate *Niger* broke through the mist to signal that the Spanish fleet was nearby. Then the Spanish fleet began to appear through the mist. As each moment passed it seemed more ships came into view. Will had positioned himself on the gallery above the upper deck, so was able to see what was happening. He relayed what he could see, quietly to his crew below.

There was a long wait to see what was going to happen. Will along with the other officers changed into their best uniforms. An hour after *Niger* had first sighted the Spanish, *Culloden* a 74 gun ship-of-the-line signalled. Will could vaguely see that she was signalling, but had no idea what the signals meant. Then *Victory* hoisted a number 13 signal flag, which Will recognised as meaning "Prepare for battle".

Will was now watching the poop deck carefully. He saw Captain Calder and Grey nod their heads and say something to Fraser. Fraser raised his speaking trumpet and shouted. "Clear for Action".

Will scuttled down from his position to make sure his gun crews were ready.

All around him, the gun crews were removing shoes, if they wore them, and replacing them with their soft slippers or bare feet. Water barrels, known as scuttlebutts, were brought out and placed strategically in case of fire, and to supply the buckets for the rammer's swabs.

Looking aft Will could see the wardroom partitioning being taken down, together with his own furniture.

Will double-checked everything was ready and informed the Midshipman awaiting the response, that everything on the forward middle gun-deck was ready.

Then came the steady beat of the drums calling all hands to their quarters, called "beating to quarters".

Will ordered the sand to be scattered on the deck, over the already soaking planks.

Then the Gunlocks were distributed to the gun captains.

Will wandered down his command checking that the captains had enough quills, spare flints, powder and lanyards. With each crew he cracked a joke to try relieving some of the tension. Satisfied that everything was ready, he strolled aft and mounting to the quarter-deck informed Fraser. He could now see that the Spanish fleet appeared to be in two sections. To windward there appeared to be a larger group of about 16 to18 ships, where-as the leeward Spanish ships appeared to number less, about 7 to 9.

There was a commotion on the quarterdeck, and a group of signal flags broke out from *Victory's* yard. A passing Midshipman informed him that the signal had gone out to form line of battle as convenient.

About half an hour later, the British fleet, now in an orderly line, *Culloden*, the leading ship opened fire on the Spanish. As each of the six ships ahead of *Victory* came within range, they opened fire, almost at maximum range.

Through his telescope Will had checked on their first likely target. He had estimated the height of her gun decks and the distance they were likely to be at when they first opened fire. This he relayed to his guns below, so that they could set their chocks for elevation. Each of his 24 pounders was double shoted for the first broadside. [Two cannon balls were loaded] Will was watching Fraser carefully. There would be a look-out posted forward, who would signal as the bows of Victory drew level with a Spaniard. As Fraser put the speaking trumpet to his mouth Will dropped down, ran forward to the foremost gun, steadying the gun captain to wait until he had a target. The guns below him fired, then through the open port Will could clearly see the Spaniard.

"Fire!" He ordered. The lanyard was pulled and the first of the 24 pounders crashed back on it restraints. Will was not able to see if the shot had done any damage as the other ship was almost immediately obliterated from view by the smoke from the guns below. "Remember to judge where the open gun ports are!" Shouted Will.

As *Victory* passed down the Spanish line, or what was in reality a group of three abreast, the Spanish ships turned to larboard. After what seemed minutes there were no ships to see. *Victory's* guns stopped firing. Will went to a larboard gun port and looked out to see that there were nine Spanish ships to windward, and that they appeared to be turning to larboard as well. As *Victory* turned to follow *Culloden* and the other leading ships, a Spanish ship came within range on the larboard side. The order was given to 'back sails', then after a short wait the order to fire was relayed and *Victory's* guns fired a blistering broadside and the huge Spaniard fell away. The gun-deck was full of smoke and fumes. The order to cease fire was given. Running up to the gallery deck above, Will could see that *Victory* was going about and that they were now obviously chasing after the main Spanish column. To starboard Will could see a British 74 gun ship in a state of confusion, which he recognised as being the *Colossus,* whilst astern a large Spanish four deck first rate was hauling off badly damaged by *Victory's* guns. Will asked if anybody knew the name of the Spaniard and was told it was the 112 gun *Principe de Asturias* . The ship was flying an Admiral's pennant.

There was now a pause in the proceedings on the gun-decks. There were no enemy ships within range. Will popped up to the gallery once more and could see that *Captain*, Commodore Nelson's ship, seemed to be wearing away and heading out of the line. Will watched as *Captain* made for the van of the Spanish group. Will could not stay up there as he had work to do, but he just had time to see *Excellent* turn to support. Back with his crew he informed them of the situation as he saw it.

It was now midday, but the crew would not be getting any hot food, because the galley fire had been extinguished. Will made sure that his gun crews got some sustenance and liquids. Everybody was still at their battle stations. It would be some time before *Victory* could catch up to the enemy. Will made sure that the crews relaxed, after checking that everything was still in place. There was no wardroom for the officers to retire to even if they had not been on duty. Thomas Tucker, Will's servant, brought a glass of wine, waited for Will to drink it and then disappeared.

The senior Gun captain offered to have Will's sword sharpened in case they had to board an enemy ship. Grateful for the reminder, Will undid his belt and handed the sword over. A powder-monkey took it up to the forecastle above where a sharpening wheel had been erected.

Will leant against the base of the foremast, feeling the vitality of the ship as she relentlessly overhauled the enemy.

At about two o'clock Will was re-united with his sword as *Victory* came within range of the Spanish ships. After the first broadside, they were ordered to cease fire as the Spanish ship they had been firing on had lowered her colours. After another short period of waiting, the order to fire was passed down. Will had no idea who they were firing on, or what was happening outside. Either side of her great hull, smoke swirled hiding the enemy for the most part from the gunner's aim. On the gundeck it was all sweat and smoke. It was difficult to see exactly what was happening within a few feet of one's position, the smoke was so dense. It clawed at the throat, making one cough and the eyes smart. It was the ears that really suffered. In the confined space the cannons' discharges echoed round the wooden walls, making it impossible to speak, let alone shout. The ears rang and head ached. One prayed for a rest-bite just to be able to think!

Will was just turning to walk back aft to the main mast, when 'Wham' - something hit him incredibly hard on the left arm. He was thrown to the ground. Midshipman Lindsay rushed up to see if he was alright and had to help Will to his feet. Will's left arm hung uselessly at his side, the pain excruciating. He couldn't see any blood, but it hurt like hell. Gritting his teeth, he staggered to the mast and propped himself against it, whilst all around was bedlam. One of the 24 pounders had been thrown on its side and two of the crew injured. Will ordered Lindsay to get the gun righted, pointing with his right arm at the men to be used from other guns. The hastily assembled group, using the handspikes and brute force, heaved the gun back upright. The lashings were quickly replaced. A second gunner appeared holding a set of quills. Lindsay positioned himself halfway between the gun and Will so that he could pass on Will's orders. Within minutes the gun was joining the others in pouring a constant barrage of fire at the unseen enemy.

For about an hour, the guns barked, recoiled, were sponged out, reloaded, hauled back to the open port and fired. The gun crews were sweating away and worn out. At every opportunity they would dip their hands in the fire buckets and slosh water over their faces and bodies.

Will was going in and out of consciousness the pain was so great. He had himself lashed to the main mast, so that he didn't have to expend any energy in trying to stand. When the guns finally fell silent, Lindsay asked for permission to have Will taken down to the Orlop and the Surgeon. Will refused, saying that there were many more seriously in need of the saw-bone's administrations. Secretly he was convinced that he would lose an arm, and that would mean the end of his service.

It was Lieutenant Locke who discovered Will as he made a round to note the killed and wounded for the captain. He ordered an inert Will to be carried below.

Will woke up an hour later to find himself lying in his cot, still in tremendous pain, but with his arm splinted and tightly bound so he could not move it. Above him he heard the sounds of the cabin screens and furniture were being replaced. Young Lindsay popped in to see how Will was getting on, and informed him that they had won a great victory. The Spanish fleet that remained had scuttled off towards Cadiz, much mauled, and the captured Spanish ships were under tow from the frigates. He also excitedly told Will that the Admiral had narrowly missed being killed when he had gone on the poop-deck to get a better picture of what was going on around them.

The triumphant British fleet made its way back to the entrance to the Tagus. Will was forced to remain in his cot, where the Surgeon came to see him and enquire how he felt. Apparently Will's left arm was broken above the elbow, but the Surgeon had managed to get the bones back in line and had splinted the arm, hoping that the bones might join up and heal themselves. He told Will that he was one of only five casualties aboard *Victory*. He gave Will some more Laudanum to help with the pain and told Will he was going to his own cot.

Will fell into a fitful sleep; waking to find that it was a new day. He could see daylight through the open door to his cubicle. Tucker appeared and asked if he wanted any breakfast. Tucker added that they were nearing the anchorage. Will felt too tired to eat and his arm was still extremely painful, so he lay back and tried to go back to sleep after managing to sup some liquid.

Fellow Members of the wardroom dropped in to see how he was doing, and he learnt that only one of the crew had been killed. He had been next to the Admiral on the poop deck, and his brains and blood had covered the Admiral. When his officers rushed to assist him, he brushed them away wiping his face with his handkerchief and asked for some fruit to cleanse his mouth. A Midshipman had the glory of providing his Admiral with an orange. Richard Gaunt looked in to cheer Will up, with an over dramatised version of how brilliant he had been on the upper deck. It was conveyed with lots of rolling of the eyes, and smirks. It cheered Will up a lot, so he was livelier when he had an unexpected visit from Captain Grey.

"I hear you did rather well, Calvert." The Captain said as he entered. "But that you had a rather nasty experience with part of the ship's timbers!"

"Curtsy of the Spanish, Sir!" Replied Will.

"Ah, yes, you can certainly blame them. I suppose you heard that Commodore Nelson distinguished himself, despite disobeying the Admiral's orders. He weared round when he saw that the Spanish van might get away. He even managed to capture two Spanish ships at the same time! Used one to get to the other – never heard of such a thing. *Captain* is a virtual hulk though, lost all her masts and rigging. We sustained a bit of damage, but you should have seen the enemy! A glorious victory when you consider that the enemy had twice the number of ships and, I suppose, near twice the number of cannon." He grinned at Will and added.

"So make sure you don't put any strain on that arm of yours." And with that he left the cabin.

Later in the day, Will managed to get a message passed to Fraser, asking who would supervise the anchor party, now that he was laid low. To Will's surprise Fraser put in an appearance an hour later, asking how Will felt. Will was honest enough to point out that he was still drowsy from the Laudanum.

"Pity! Could have done with you in charge, still might give Gaunt a go, what do you think?"

"I don't think he has ever supervised coming to anchor, but if you could send him to me, I can go through the routine with him. The Senior Petty Officer is an old hand, so he really won't have much to do. However it would be better that he looked as if he knew what he was doing."

"Very true – I'll send him down to you – in the meantime, well done during the battle. You might not know it but your gunners did a magnificent job. The Admiral expressed his satisfaction!"

A few minutes later Gaunt appeared. "I understand that you are to explain anchoring to me!"

"I am sure you know all about it." Replied Will; hoping that his friend's nose had not been put out of joint.

Will suggested that Gaunt ask the Master how much cable he thought would be needed before they got to the entrance, whilst he still had plenty of time.

"All you need to do then is to tell the Senior Petty Officer how much cable will be needed, and he will do the rest. The anchor crew will realise that you know what you are doing, and everything should go smoothly then. The crew know what to do. Leave them to it."

"Thanks – good idea about the Master – never would have thought of that, thanks." Gaunt looked genuinely grateful.

From his cabin, Will could guess at what was happening outside. The anchor cable would be flaked out on the lower gun-deck. The bower anchor would be lifted off the cathead and readied for dropping. He strained to hear the noises that indicated what was going on around the ship. Finally he heard the noise of the crew going to anchor stations, then the noise of the cable being raised. Pipes indicated that the sails were being taken in, then there was a pause, after which the whole ship seemed to shiver as she dropped back onto her anchor cable.

Later, with his door open, Will was able to exchange news with his fellow wardroom colleagues.

CHAPTER 23

Two days later, Will felt strong enough to get up. He managed to get Tucker to help him dress, except that his coat had to be placed over his shoulders with only his right arm in a sleeve. The other arm was strapped to his chest under his shirt, which had to be torn up the centre of the back to get around him. Tucker made a fair effort at tying the stock.

He was greeted with a small cheer from the members of the crew that saw him emerge onto the quarterdeck.

Fraser came over to see how he faired. Will was able for the first time to appreciate the damage that had been inflicted on the ship. The carpenters were working hard to effect running repairs, but it was obvious that combined with previous wear and tear, *Victory* would need the attention of the dockyard. He walked with Fraser forward to the belfry to get a close up look at some of the damage. Above them rope-work was being spliced, and sails lowered for repair.

Sitting cross-legged before the belfry were a group of sailmakers busy with their needles. Across the water the same action was taking place aboard a number of the closest ships at anchor. Fraser pointed out the *San Josef* one of the captured Spanish ships.

"Pity, in the confusion of the action, the *Santissima Trinidad* managed to escape, despite the fact that she had surrendered once." Fraser said sadly. The *Santissima Trinidad* was the largest ship in the Spanish fleet, with an estimated 136 guns, besides being the flagship of the Spanish fleet.

At that moment a Midshipman arrived to say that Lieutenant Calvert was summoned to the Admiral's Cabin. Will couldn't believe that the messenger had got it right, but Fraser nodded his agreement and told Will to follow the Midshipman below.

Will had never been inside the Admiral's quarters. He arrived outside the Admiral's door to be met by a marine, rigidly at attention. Will gave his name and the Marine announced him. A servant opened the door, and Will found himself looking across a dining table laid for dinner to a group by the stern windows in what was obviously the Admiral's day cabin. He manoeuvred around the table and approached the group that consisted of the Admiral with Captains Calder and Grey. "May I present Lieutenant Calvert, Sir." Captain Grey said standing to one side so Will was facing the Admiral, whom he had seen lots of times at a distance, and even spoken to that memorable morning. Will had heard a lot about this man; how he was a stickler for discipline, but fair discipline. Apparently he considered that a good ship depended on its officers.

Admiral Jervis looked piercingly at Will and then smiled.

"I have had very good reports about you, young-man!" He said. "I understand you had yourself roped to the mast so you could continue to control the firing of your guns." Will just nodded.

"Well I also have very good reports on your seamanship skills. I understand that you were the young-man who took over command of *Artful* and managed to sink two French frigates off Brest, is that correct/"

"Aye Sir!" Responded Will.

"Very good – I shall make sure that you have a very good report to their Lords of the Admiralty. I am sending you back to England with dispatches. You will take them personally to the Admiralty. Captain Calder, here, will let you know which vessel you will be returning aboard."

"Thank you Sir!" Will was stunned. Out of the corner of his eye he saw Fraser moving as if to leave the group. Will stepped back, conscious of the fact that he still had his hat in his right hand as he had nowhere else to put it. He did a sort of half bow and joined Fraser to leave the presence.

Outside, Fraser grinned at him. "See, you can get on if you do your job well. It is not all about who you know with the Admiral."

"But you must have said something?" Asked Will.

"I only reported what was true – you are an exceptional officer. I am proud to have had you with me."

Will felt chocked up, he had no idea what to say. He pointed at his hidden arm and indicated that he needed to go below.

In the Wardroom he found the Surgeon, who happily gave him a few drops of the laudanum. "Must not get too used to the stuff." He commented.

Now they were back at the mouth of the Tagus – they had anchored in Lagos Bay to effect repairs, whilst they waited for news of the enemy. The Spanish had scuttled back to Cadiz, after a brief attempt to retrieve their lost vessels, but had thought better of it and given up.

For Will it was routine as usual, but a couple of days later he was given a berth on a sloop that was returning to England.

Had Will stayed he would have been with *Victory* for a month and a half where they either stayed in harbour or made brief expeditions to show their strength off Cadiz. Then in April there was a new arrival of ships. With them came the brand new *Ville de Paris*. She was a grand sight being the same size as *Victory* but so obviously fresh minted.

Admiral Jervis left *Victory* with his Fleet Captain, Captain Calder, to hoist his flag on the newcomer. *Victory* stayed with the fleet, but had a new captain as Captain Grey had transferred to the flagship. Now a 'private' ship, *Victory* continued to do blockade duty until at the end of October when she returned to England for a refit.

On the voyage back to England, Will didn't stand any watches, he was a passenger. As soon as the sloop docked in Portsmouth, Will left accompanied by Tucker who was in charge of the sea-chest.

Once in London, he hired a carter to take himself, Tucker, and his chest to The Swan with Two Necks Inn in Lad Lane. He had been advised that he was most likely to get a place on the Coach to Plymouth if he booked from there. He fully expected to be invalided out of the Navy.

Once he had settled his things in his room, he spent a very different evening listening to all the gossip around him, before retiring. The next morning, in his best uniform, he hired a chair, so as to not muddy his hessians or uniform, and had himself taken to Whitehall. He knew that he had to bribe the servants and had come prepared, but he also carried thc sealed dispatch from Admiral Jervis, given to him as he left *Victory* by Captain Calder.

After informing the servant that he had a 'signal' from Admiral Jervis, he was asked to hand it over to the servant. Calder had told him on no account to do any such thing, as it would disappear. Will therefore stated that he had been instructed to hand it personally to a Mr Napean. Will passed his bribe and he was shown into a waiting room full of naval officers, all who seemed to have been there for hours. He found out in conversation with a number who deigned to speak to him, that some had been there for days. It was only when it came to light that Will had been on the flagship at the great battle; that more senior officers strolled over to speak to him. They all wanted to know what had happened minute by minute. Will informed them what had happened, hour by hour.

An imposing liveried servant appeared and called out his name.

"I understand that you have dispatches for Mr Napean. I am directed to take them to him immediately so he can study them before seeing you."

"I was ordered to hand them over in person."

"Well that is exactly what you are doing. I am Mr Napean's secretary. He ordered me to take the dispatches to him personally, so we are in the same boat." With which he put out his hand, but he also gave Will an understanding smile, so Will did as he was bidden.

To everyone's surprise Will was called after only three hours of waiting. He was shown into the impressive office of Mr Evan Napean, secretary to the Admiralty Board.

"Lieutenant Calvert?"

"Aye Sir"

"I have here a second report from Lord Jervis. In it he recommends you to the Board.

I already have another letter from the same Noble Lord; as well as letters from Captains' Calder and Grey. I also have here in front of me a copy of your service record. The Board does not normally promote such Junior Lieutenants, unless unfortunately there is influence. In your case, the sole influence is based, not on who you know or are related to, but because of your outstanding abilities.

I see that you were temporarily in command of *Artful* when she sank those two French Frigates in the entrance to Brest."

Will refrained from saying anything, and Napean continued.

"So Lord Spencer seems to have taken an interest in you! You are to be promoted to Commander. You will command the schooner *Snipe*, but she is still in the hands of the yard at Appledore. I see that you are still not completely fit!"

"I am well on the way to recovery, thank you Sir. Bones are knitting well. The Surgeon said that I should have full use of my arm again in a couple of weeks. I can move it about, but I am advised not to lift anything with it at the moment."

Napean looked up at Will, gave him a cursory look from head to foot.

"I suggest that you take advantage of the delay to get some leave in – see your family. We have an address in Cornwall I believe." He sorted a few papers.

"Ah yes. Well congratulations. If you do as well in your new command as you have done in the past, you may well be fortunate. Admiral Nelson was much younger than you when he became a Captain, but then he had influence at the highest level. We shall send your commission to your lodgings – you should give the address to the clerk on your way out. Thank you for attending so promptly. Good day to you Sir."

CHAPTER 24

Will decided to stay in London for as long as it took to have his new uniforms made for him. He asked a couple of officers if they knew of any tailors in London who specialised in Naval Officers uniforms. He was surprised to learn that it would only take the chosen tailors two days to have a dress and an undress uniform ready for him. When he went to the tailors in his dress uniform of a Lieutenant, he was delighted to be offered money for the uniform he was wearing. Apparently the tailors did a roaring trade in second hand uniforms for the Midshipmen who had just been promoted. Two days later. Will walked out of the tailors wearing his new undress uniform, as he was preparing to travel. The new uniform was the same as that of a Naval Captain, but only had three buttons on the cuff of the sleeve and only one epaulette on the left shoulder. He wore blue breeches; and because he was travelling, black hessian boots. He learnt from the tailors that the Commander's dress, along with other officers' uniforms had been changed two years before.

To Will's confusion the Mail for Plymouth left the Swan with Two Necks at 7.30pm. Apparently it travelled through the night. How it navigated he could not surmise, since the coaches appeared to only have a couple of lanterns. Perhaps horses could see better in the dark than humans.

There were no seats available on the coach for two days. Will had already taken the opportunity to visit the theatre and circus. He therefore decided to stretch his legs and get to know London better.

When the evening to travel arrived, Will watched Tucker help the staff stow his sea chest on the roof of the coach.

"Check their knots Tucker!" He called.

The man on the roof turned and seeing that Will was grinning up at him shouted back.

"Just because you be Navy doesn't mean you can tie better knots than us men of the road!"

Will was laughing as he climbed into the stage. He found that the other passengers were already seated. There was a space near the door on the right for him, which would mean that he had his back to the horses. Sitting in the seat next to his, and taking up more than his fair share, was a portly clerical gentleman with a low crowned black hat with a wide brim. Firmly clasped to his stomach was a large leather bound bible. Opposite the cleric was a large woman with an ample bosom over which there sat a flushed round face, pierced by a pair of beady eyes.

As Will turned to sit he found he was to face a young lady. She struck him immediately as uncommonly attractive. From beneath a green trimmed bonnet black haired ringlets framed a pale face with the darkest eyes Will had ever seen. They seemed to be observing him with amused interest. She was wrapped up for the trip in a quilted coat of expensive green fabric that disguised any shape.

Will had to squeeze in, trying hard to spare his left arm, whilst having to gather up his sword between his knees. He expressed his apologies under his breath. His arm would be in danger of being knocked by the door frame as the coach moved.

"You are hurt Sir!" The young lady looked anxious.

"A mere trifle, thank you "Will said smiling back.

Outside could be heard the final checks on the horses harnesses, together with the clop of hooves being brought down in frustration. Finally the coach was on its way, but not very far, because they halted outside the main Mail Office in St. Martin le Grande, near St Pauls Cathedral, together with other assorted Mail Coaches. After a few minutes taken up with lifting the sacks of mail aboard, the coachman 'geed' his horses and they clattered out and on through the streets of London, which rapidly became lanes framed by hedges and fields.

It was the Cleric who spoke first as the coach had settled down after leaving the Post Office.

"I find on these tedious journeys it helps to know a little about your travelling companions. If nobody objects I shall introduce myself. I am the Very Reverend Joshua Arnold, Dean of Collet St Mary. I am travelling west to visit my old friend the Bishop of Exeter. We were at school together, don't you know. I always travel by Stage; I find I meet the most unusual people, with the most unusual stories. A bit like Chaucer's Canterbury Tales, don't you know?"

Just at that moment they passed a brightly lit establishment, so Will was able to see the Gentleman beside him was beaming good will around the small space.

"And you Madam, might I enquire as to your name and the reason for travelling tonight?"

"Certainly Dean! And may I say what a pleasure it is to be travelling with such an educated gentleman. I am Hestor Yelland; I am this young lady's governess. We are travelling back to the Kenton estate in Devon. Unfortunately the Kenton coach suffered a broken axle. I wanted to delay our departure, but Miss Kenton insisted on travelling by the Stage. You thought it would be an exciting experience, didn't you my dear? I on the other hand would far prefer the comfort of the Kenton coach. So well sprung you know."

Will could not see the expression of the young lady opposite as it was now too dark to make out anything other than the occasion outline of one's fellow travellers.

"Miss Kenton has been doing the season. She was presented. So delightful. Such an elegant dress."

The Dean cut straight across the garrulous governess to ask Miss Kenton her full name and where she lived normally.

"My name is Isabella Kenton. My father is a Banker in Exeter. We have an estate in south Devon and a House in London. We divide our time between the two. As Hetty has told you I have been doing the season. My parents had to leave for Devon before the end of the Season, so they asked Hetty, my old governess to act as chaperone."

"You make me sound really old, Isabella." Interrupted the Governess.

The Dean's booming laugh came from the darkness.

"I am sure Miss Kenton had no such intention! She was merely using the word as an adjective to place your position in historical context."

There was an audible intake of breath, which Will assumed came from the large bosomed woman sitting opposite the Dean. He could imagine her pulling up her crossed arms under her breasts as she did so, and it amused him to imagine the facial expressions of the two ladies opposite.

"And you, young Sir. A Naval Officer I presume from the uniform glimpsed as you mounted the coach.

"William Calvert, at your service."

"And your rank, Sir?"

"I am a Commander."

"If I may be so impertinent to point out, you appear to be very young for such a rank!" The Dean said in his clipped, singsong voice. Will did not need to say anything, because at that moment the coach was thrown about even more violently than usual.

"There Isabella, I told you how dreadful it would be by Stage. I hope now that you will listen to me rather better." The Governess was obviously getting her own back on Miss Kenton, but there was no reply. It was so dark now that it was barely possible to make out anything within the coach.

"It never ceases to amaze me how fast the coachmen are prepared to drive when it is so dark!" Commented the Dean.

"Reckless and suicidal!" Shouted the Governess; as they rocked precariously once again.

Will had to slither sideways so that his back faced the corner of the coach to try and limit the punishment being meted out to his left arm.

The lurching and banging seemed to silence the group and they sat in silence.

When the horses were changed in what seemed an incredibly short time, the little light coming from the lamps outside made it possible for Will to see that Miss Kenton was sitting watching him. She gave a shy smile when she realised he had caught her. The coach lurched forward, rocked back and was then rolling on again at break neck speed into the night.

The coach finally came to a welcome halt at Basingstoke to allow the passengers a toilet stop and a bite to eat with refreshment. Will got out first and handed down first Isabella and then the governess. He left the Dean to climb down on his own. The occupants of the coach were shown into a 'snug' room, which had a welcoming fire and candles lighting it. For the first time Will was able to really see his fellow passengers. The Governess took herself off to the toilet. Miss Kenton walked over to a chair near the fire and indicated to Will that he should take the chair beside her. After they had ordered mulled wine all round, Miss Kenton turned to Will.

"Does it hurt very much?" She asked: wide dark brown/black eyes behind long black lashes. Her black curls seemed to shine, reflecting the flicking light. Her pale skin was smooth and the lips had a hint of a smile at the corners. Will didn't think he had ever seen anything so enchanting in his life.

"Only when the coach jolts it." He said truthfully.

"How did it happen?"

"I rather think a Spaniard did not like the cut of my jib." Said Will with a smile for her benefit.

"You were in a battle?" She asked breathlessly.

"Battle!" Barked the Dean; overhearing the last part. "That wouldn't be the great battle off Cape St Vincent, would it?"

"The very same, Sir!"

"What ship were you on?"

"HMS *Victory*, Sir."

"The flagship?"

"Correct."

"Was it terrible?" Asked Miss Kenton, her eyes seemed to be watery.

"Very noisy and smelly!" Joked Will.

"I fear you are making light of it Sir!" Miss Kenton was leaning forward eager to learn more.

"Where were you?" She asked.

"On the middle gun deck."

"So what happened?" This was the Dean.

"You mean at the battle?"

"No to you!" Interrupted Miss Kenton.

"Oh I got struck by something when a cannon broke loose; it broke my arm."

"Were many killed?" It was the Dean again.

"Relatively few Sir, compared with the enemy."

"Did you meet the Admiral, Lord Jervis?" Asked Miss Kenton.

"Yes, several times."

"Rather strange, a Commander being on the lower gun deck of the flagship, I would have thought." Commented the Dean as the Governess re-entered the room, followed by their drinks and victuals.

"I was a Lieutenant then, Sir."

"Ah!" replied the Dean.

"What were you doing on the gun deck?" Asked Miss Kenton.

The Governess interrupted. "What's all this about gun decks?"

"Our young friend here was wounded at the battle of Cape St Vincent. We have a hero amongst us!" Expounded the Dean.

"Hardly that, Sir!"

"So tell us, what were you doing on the gun deck?" Repeated Miss Kenton.

"I was in command of the guns on that deck."

The lovely young lady took a sharp intake of breath, her eyes wide. "Could you see the enemy?"

He had not noticed them at first, but now she was leaning forward, he could see that her brown and black flecked eyes seemed to have a darker outside ring to the pupil, beneath the long curling lashes.

"It depended on whether we were engaged or not. At first I was able to watch the proceedings, until we were about to commit."

"Did you see Nelson disobeying his commands and leaving the fleet?" Asked the Dean; taking a huge mouthful of his food.

"Commodore Nelson reacted to the situation in his usual inimitable manner. He saw that the enemy van might get away, so pulled out of line to engage. It was a masterly stroke. Lord Jervis commended him after the battle. I was there, I saw and heard him."

"Oh! I had heard that it was strictly against orders." The Dean insisted.

"Lord Jervis expects his captains to act in the the best possible manner in order to bring their ships to battle as soon as possible to be effective."

The Governess, with her mouth full, demanded to be told the story of the battle from beginning to end. Will found three expectant faces turned in his direction. He found it hard not to concentrate on Miss Kenton, and had to force himself to regard each in turn equally as he told them his view of the battle.

Halfway through, he was interrupted by the call for the passengers to return to their coach in five minutes. Will found himself standing up at the same time as Miss Kenton to excuse themselves. He followed her out of the room.

"Pray continue when we are back in the coach." She said over her shoulder with a smile, before turning away to the ladies part of the Inn.

Back on the coach, once again settled in their seats, it was the Dean that demanded Will continued, as the coach moved off. When he had finished Miss Kenton clapped her hands together which set off the others.

"Bravo, dear boy, bravo." The Dean nudged Will, which caused him to hit his arm painfully against the side of the coach.

After Will's story, nobody seemed to have anything to say. This part of the journey seemed somehow smoother, or it might be they were getting used to the motion of the coach. Very soon there were very un-lady like snorts from the governess which became a steady snoring. A couple of minutes later the Dean joined the snoring game.

"Excuse my ignorance." Miss Kenton whispered, leaning forward. "But what is the difference between a Commander and a Captain?"

Will realised that she was at last free from the dominating governess beside her.

"A Commander is sort of half-way between a Lieutenant and a Captain. A Commander is the captain of his ship, but is also the Master, which means he is responsible for sailing her and the navigation."

"So you really are a Captain?" She asked, putting her head slightly to one side to ask the question, which Will found very appealing. When he could see that she was smiling it seemed to light up the whole of her face, but it was the eyes that he found most compelling.

"I suppose so, yes. This will be my first command. They used to call Commanders – Master and Commander, but a few years ago they dropped that and shortened it to Commander. I shall be taking command of HMS *Snipe,* a schooner, a type of vessel that I haven't sailed in before. It will be sharp learning experience, I fear."

"Did you start as a Midshipman?" She asked, still leaning forward. He leaned to meet her, so they would not disturb the two sleepers.

"No, I started out as a Master's Mate, because I had

already learnt navigation and sail control when I sailed with my father."

"Your father was a Navy man?"

"No, he was a Merchant Captain and owner with an interest in a fleet of merchant ships. I sailed all over the place; the Orient, America, the Mediterranean, and the Caribbean. He died, so I joined the Navy."

Isabella seemed amazed that he had travelled so widely.

"I haven't been anywhere! This is the first time I have travelled just with my governess. Normally I travel with my mother, but only locally, or occasionally to our house in London. This time it was my 'coming out'. I was presented, and attended a number of Balls."

"Sounds very exciting." Commented Will. To his surprise she made a disparaging noise.

"Not really, it is like a cattle market. You are there to be seen, rather like buying a horse. 'Is she fit to bear a child; does she have wide enough hips, and big enough bosoms to feed children? The young ladies are looking to catch the attention of those with money or titles. The men are after wives who will bring fortunes. At no time does love come into the equation!"

"I am sure you must have had a mass of admirers." Said Will; who had been surprised by the vehement reaction. Isabella sounded an un-lady-like snort, a trifle annoyed.

"Not you too!" She stated scornfully.

"I had hoped you would be straight talking!"

"I apologise if I have offended, but you are, if I may say so, very attractive."

She seemed to consider this for a few moments.

"Do you really think so?" She asked, and in a brief shaft of moonlight he saw that she was frowning delightfully.

"Most sincerely!"

"And you of course have known ladies from all over the world!"

"Hardly! I am a complete novice as far as women go. At sea you never see any ladies. You see the 'ladies of the night', when they come aboard to satisfy the seamen, but that is all."

Isabella smiled. "Really? Do they allow women onboard the ships?"

Will was embarrassed that he had spoken without thought.

"I apologise. I shouldn't have mentioned it."

"I am glad you did. It is so refreshing to talk to a real man. The types I meet are so - so controlled by convention."

To change the subject, Will asked.

"So were you successful in catching a gentleman's eye?"

Isabella spluttered. Then angrily, said.

"Oh yes, unfortunately! A complete noodle! He has no chin; he smells, and he has the most irritating laugh – a sort of bray, rather like a donkey. Trouble is he will inherit a title and has an adequate allowance. This, in the eyes of everybody, makes him a suitable match. If they were really thinking properly, they would consider the result – idiot offspring! It is the fact that I would be 'Lady', after the father dies, but then he has years left, so long as he doesn't drink himself into the grave. The likelihood of him leaving any money, when he dies is problematic, as he gambles recklessly. I have refused to have anything to do with his son."

She seemed angry even at the thought of it.

"What did your parents say?" Asked Will.

"Livid, absolutely livid! I threatened to run away – No not really, I am lucky, they would prefer that I married for love. I am an heiress, so something of a catch. That can be a distinct disadvantage, because you can never tell if the fellow fancies you or your money. I am grateful to my parents, they don't go about boasting about being well off."

It was at that point that the coach clattered through a cobbled yard to change horses. Both the Dean and the Governess woke at the same time with a start. It was still pitch black outside with only occasional glimpses of the reticent Moon.

After the brief interlude, the coach was on its rattling way. There was desultory conversation for a few minutes. Both the Dean and the Governess had partaken of large brandies. The Governess now paying rapt attention to the Dean as she had discovered he was a widower. Now the inside of the stage reeked of brandy. Soon the two imbibers were snoring away again. Will glancing at Isabella and realised that she was pretending to be asleep, her head was turned away from the Governess, but Will could see her eyes were wide open and she was watching him in the glass of the window.

Once she was satisfied that the Governess was deeply asleep, she turned to check on the Dean. The cleric was snoring loudly, his head cradled on a folded coat resting against side of the coach.

"Are you joining your new ship at Plymouth?" Isabella asked.

"No, I have to try to raise a crew in Plymouth – well Devonport – and then I have to go to Appledore to 'read myself in'.

"Read yourself in? Appledore? Sounds very strange!"

"*Snipe*, is being refitted at Appledore. When a captain takes command of a ship he has to read himself in. It is all set out by their Lordships at the Admiralty." Explained Will.

"Appledore is in North Devon, isn't it? Opposite Barnstable, if I remember my geography correctly."

"I am ashamed to say that I had not heard of the place. I had to look it up!" Grinned Will.

And so the conversation went on, interrupted every time there was a chance that either of the two other passengers were about to wake up.

Isabella explained that she didn't live in Exeter. Her parent's estate was south between Torquay and the small town of Totnes on the river Dart.

Will knew of Torquay, because he knew the south coast of England in detail. Torquay was the small harbour off which the Channel Fleet often anchored in Torbay. It was the Bristol Channel that he had never navigated.

When the coach arrived at Salisbury, the Dean left them, and they were joined by a tall thin man, who turned out to be a lawyer. The Governess was obviously taken by the newcomer, as she stayed awake to talk to him. For her it was unfortunate that he left the coach at its next major stop in Dorchester. His place was taken by a large red faced yeoman farmer, who had the same effect on the governess. She stayed awake to quiz him all the way to Exeter, so Will and Isabella were not able to continue their conversation.

At Exeter, Isabella was handed down from the coach by Will, who had to change coaches. In the process she slipped a small calling card into his hand. He realised that Isabella didn't want her governess to know, so he was only able to read it later.

As it was, they said their good-byes in a very formal manner. The Governess was fussing about onward transport to the estate.

Will's coach to Plymouth and Devonport was waiting to leave, so he had to check that Tucker and his sea-chest were transferred, before climbing aboard. The last he saw of Isabella was a forlorn figure gazing after him.

CHAPTER 25

Having left Thomas Tucker and his sea-chest at the coaching inn in Plymouth Dock, Will made his way to the steps, where years before he had met the Captain of his first Navy ship. He managed to hire a skiff to row him out to the Port Admiral's ship, anchored in the Hamoaze. Once aboard the flagship he had to wait for a couple of hours before he was shown to the Admiral's cabin.

"Ah! Calvert, come in and take a seat." The Admiral said, as Will entered.

"Been expecting you. The Sea Lord's orders arrived a day or so ago. I must say, they are most unusual, but the Fleet Captain and I will do everything in our power to carry them out. We have already started. His Lordship insists that your Schooner – err, the *Snipe* be crewed by experienced men. Luckily for us – and you – that is possible because a frigate is due to go into dry-dock shortly and her crew will be available. I think you will approve, as you know the ship concerned; *Artful*, your old ship!" And the Admiral smirked at his own joke, as much as Will's expression of incredulity.

Back on the quarter-deck of the Port Admiral's flagship, Will reflected upon his luck, as he waited for a boat to take him over to *Artful*. He realised he had been extremely lucky to have served on the ships he had, and under the captains he had. The posting to Admiral Jervis' flagship had been the greatest of all. Here it was recognised throughout the navy, you had the best chance of being promoted. His promotion to Commander meant that he had been elevated up the ladder way over many of his fellow Lieutenants. He also reflected on the fact that being a Commander could be the end of one's career in the navy. Too often, if you were in command of a sloop or similar ship, which was away from the area of influence, your chances of promotion disappeared. He would have to try his very best, to achieve the sort of recognition that would take him to the next level – Post Captain.

Will thought about his commission. In it he was ordered to:

Take said Snipe to sea to endeavour by all means possible to mitigate the threat of invasion, by destroying as many enemy transports as possible, together with any other enemy ships at sea or in port.

His commission stated quite clearly that *Snipe* was 'private' which meant that he was responsible directly to the Board of Admiralty and was not within the control of any fleet Admiral or other senior officer.

It felt strange being piped aboard his old ship, and to be greeted by many smiling and recognisable faces. James Craddock greeted him at the entry port, together with Hughes the Boatswain.

"I am to be the first Lieutenant in some barge called *Snipe!*" Craddock informed Will grinning from ear to ear.

"Really?" Asked Will. Delighted if it was true.

"Absolutely! Got my orders from the Admiral late yesterday. Just got to help get *Artful* into dock and then I am to bring round your crew to Appledore."

"No wonder the Admiral wouldn't tell me, who was to be my First. I hope you are not sore at my being promoted over you?"

"Heavens no! You deserved it, if anybody did!" And he slapped Will on the back in a friendly gesture.

"The Admiral told me to pick the best crew possible for you. Said that it was a very important mission – his words – and that you would need the best available. The Fleet Captain gave me a list of the complement. Of course you are free to change anything."

"So who have you picked out?" Asked Will.

Craddock led him over to the huge captain's desk where a paper lay. "Captain's left, got another commission, so I am temporarily in charge. Hasn't taken his personal belongings yet. Saw Wiggins ashore last night. When he found out what was going on, he asked to be considered for your Subaltern. He maintains he can clear it with the powers that be."

"Very good of him!" Commented Will.

"Hughes wanted to be your Boatswain, but he is getting a bit long-in-the-tooth for a small ship." Craddock added. "Tarrant, his mate is very keen. Good man too! I suggest Kemp and Gardner, as your Midshipmen."

And so the list of the crew grew. Apparently all were volunteers, which from Will's point of view, was fantastic news. His problem was that most of the crew were new to him, although the key players turned out to have been able to return to *Artful* by some means of other. Craddock promised Will he had chosen the best characters, both for their jobs and as part of a happy band.

Snipe was still in the hands of the dockyard at Appledore. It would be another two weeks or so, before *Artful* would be able to be docked. Craddock would then bring the crew round to Appledore by boat. Exactly which vessel they would be put aboard had not been determined, but was in the hands of the Admiral's staff. The reasoning behind the use of the sea rather than the shorter land route was that traditionally sailors were not trusted to complete their journeys over land. Many would runaway, to go back to their loved ones, given such an opportunity.

Will had asked for permission to visit his mother before travelling to Appledore and been told by the Fleet Captain, that now he was the Captain of his own ship, it was within his discretion, though once he had read himself in, he was expected to stay with his ship. [The process of 'Reading in' is where the new Captain reads his Commission to the assembled crew. Once he had done this, he is officially the Captain.]

Will arranged for Tucker together with his sea-chest to be taken out to *Artful* so they could be brought round by sea. He purchased a brace of saddle-bags into which he put his shaving things, a change of hose and shirt. His oilskin would be carried separately. The next morning Will took the first available ferry from Plymouth Dock [Now called Devonport] to Torpoint. There he hired a horse to carry him to his new Step-father's farm. The Farm was inland between Looe and Polperro, so nearer Torpoint than the old house at Fowey. Because of the terrain it took him five hours to reach the Farm. His mother was overcome to see her son, especially when she realised his rank. Will's mother's new husband – for that is how Will thought of him – was a silent but pleasant fellow, who left them mostly to themselves. Will stayed a couple of days, and then rode his hired horse back to Torpoint. He took with him his father's matched brace of pistols in their wooden box. To carry them he also took his late father's leather bag, which having long handles could be carried over one shoulder.

The coach for Barnstable left every other day, so Will found that he would have to wait a day. He was able to purchase a seat inside, which was a bonus as the weather threatened rain. He took the opportunity a whole free day provided, to visit the bank his father had used in Plymouth. He was very surprised to find that he was a wealthy man. A lot of his father's ships had been sold and the money had finally been paid. Asked what he wanted to do with his money, Will suggested the purchase of farming land and a house. His preference was somewhere in South Devon. The Manager promised to use his connections to see what was available. Will then gave him formal written authority to purchase anywhere that was particularly suitable, as he wasn't sure when he would be able to view anywhere for some time. He trusted the Manager as he had always acted honestly for his father. When he was leaving, Will asked if he knew a Banker by the name of Kenton in Exeter. The Manager knew him well, and implied that his bank was very sound. Luckily for Will, the Manager was more interested in seeing Will out, in time for the next client, than to ask him any searching questions.

The Coach from Plymouth to Barnstable, stopped at Plymouth Dock to pick up passengers, near Will's lodgings. Clutching his saddle bags, leather bag and oilskins he climbed up into the coach, to find that the other three places were taken. His travelling companions turned out to be a farmer returning to Okehampton, a Gentleman returning to Bideford, and a legal clerk on business in Barnstable. On the outside other passengers clung on for their lives, as the coach lurched across the poorly maintained highways to the north of Tavistock. The Turnpike franchise had yet to get to work on this less well worn route. Will had to book in to an Inn for the night when he reached Barnstable, as it was far too late to cross to Appledore.

In the morning he took the ferry across the river and made his way to where he could see a lean black hulled ship propped up on the dockside. She had two masts, slightly raked, but no top-masts. The rain was arriving in bursts from the sea the other side of the peninsular, so Will was wearing his oilskins and a southwester. As a result nobody knew of his rank. When he asked for the master shipwright, he was given a surly brush-off from the first man he asked.

Finally he found the master shipwright and introduced himself. He was a tall stooping man with bushy eyebrows over a hawk like nose. His face was deeply lined, but intelligent eyes regarded Will with amused interest.

"So you must be the young fellow who has come to take the *Snipe* off my hands at last." He spoke with a broad Devon accent, that even Will from the next county, found difficult. The master shipwright led him to a building near the slipways. Here able to shed his oilskin, he revealed his uniform. In the steaming office, the master shipwright showed Will the plans of *Snipe*.

"How long have you had her? I understand she was built in America." Said Will.

"Aye, Built just at the end of the American war, captured days before the end. She was brought over here in 1785. We partially rebuilt her for the Admiralty, then they placed her in 'ordinary' [What is now termed 'mothballing']. We took her up river and put her in a mud berth. We understand rot here, we takes precautions. We make sure the air can circulate below decks, and that there is nowhere where water can form into puddles and stay there rotting the wood; means less work when we do have to bring them out. The last time we brought her into the yard was when there was a panic over Nootka Sound. We was ordered to fit her out. That was in 1790. They put her back in 'ordinary' the next year. She had been prepared for the Pacific – we put in extra stoves. Now what with the war with France they have finally remembered her." The master shipwright commented, rolling out the plans.

"Never come across anything like her before! Built for speed, hence the slender lines. I remember when she was brought here, the prize captain – a Lieutenant – saying he had never sailed in anything as fast in his life. She's been here up on the slips a few times; checking you see. She was well built though, the fellows that designed and built her knew what they were doing. Not built as a fighting ship, she had gun ports cut very crudely in her gunwales. We have checked her all over, coppered her bottom and are ready to raise the top-masts as soon as the weather improves. We haven't as yet carried out any work below decks for officers and the like. Now you are here you can tell us what you want."

"Thank you. I understand that her ordinance will be supplied in Plymouth?"

"Yep! That's what we were told."

Will studied the plans with interest – this was to be his command!

The rain had eased for a time, so they were able to carry their foul weather gear across to the ship. Will could but admire the ships lines. She looked as if she wanted to leap off somewhere. A long ladder was lent against the side of *Snipe*. Without a pause the master shipwright started to climb the flimsy bending ladder. Will frightened the ladder might not take both their weights, waited until the fellow had disappeared over the top before scrambling up the ladder. He was greeted by a flat deck, which was in urgent need of holystoning, but looked well laid. He had arrived at almost amidships on the starboard side. There was a sense of speed just standing on her deck. They moved to the bows, so that Will could check everything as they made their way aft.

The bowsprit would project almost parallel to the water.

Her top-masts were in place ready to hoist. There was no sign of any anchors, which it turned out were stored ashore still. Will reckoned that there was enough room either side of the bowsprit for a cannon pointing directly forward. He made a mental note to discuss this. Between the two masts was a companionway, then a skylight, with chocks for a boat over it. Aft of the skylight was a capstan, and then the mainmast. Aft of the mainmast one came to the binnacle and the ship's wheel. Then there was another companionway. Again there was space aft for two cannons to be mounted facing directly astern. Will noted the fact, before descending to the deck below. He was surprised to find that there were windows to the stern which let in enough light to make yet another skylight redundant. The space was open and you could see right forward. The only piece of equipment that was already in place was a ship's cooker, just forward of the foremast.

Will stood, head bent as one could not stand up straight without banging one's head, and surveyed the space, watched quietly by the master shipwright.

"If you put in a normal captain's cabin, there would be no light for anybody else." Will commented.

"Aye that's why I didn't do anything hasty." Came back the reply.

"I suggest that we put my cabin there, with a built-in bunk and a desk there. That window will give me enough light to see to keep up with the paperwork, but it will leave all the other windows free to light a gunroom cum wardroom."

The master shipwright nodded his head.

"So we make the centre the wardroom – gunroom, with a table with benches either side running fore and aft. Then narrow cabins for the officers against the sides. I suggest a single cabin opposite mine for the First-Lieutenant. Forward of that another single for the Surgeon, well Assistant Surgeon. A single cabin next to mine, for the Marine Officer, Then double berth cabins for the rest."

The master shipwright was taking it all down.

"Might I suggest a complete bulkhead across here dividing the officers from the rest of the crew? We could put a hatch in here for passing the food. Trouble is there is very little space and if we have a door through, we lose the space for stowage of muskets and side arms." Commented the master shipwright; still making notes. Will nodded his agreement.

They wandered forward and the shipwright suggested placing the crews' tables under the skylight, leaving space down either side for the stores. This meant that the crew would not need to live all the time in candle light. Projecting out of the deck just aft of the foremast was a box-like construction behind the companionway

"New powder room, but no glass yet for the lamp. Need a lantern to see down here."

He continued. "She sails like nothing you will have ever sailed in before. Fast – I'll say she is fast, shows her heels to all and sundry. She needs careful handling, but lovingly treated, like any proud lady she responds beautifully when coaxed. Or so I am told!"

Will was surprised by the change in the shipwrights tone. He obviously really appreciated the ship.

"I expect she can sail pretty close to the wind?"

"I give them their due, those Yankee ship builders; they know a thing or two about speed. Yep! She sails so close, the wind doesn't know where to hide!"

"It strikes me she probably heels a lot?"

"That's why they designed the bulwarks so every drop of water is allowed to slip away."

"So not much use in a scrap!"

"I wouldn't know about that, not being a fighting man myself. Mark you when we pierced the sides for more guns, it did strike me that they would spend most of their time in the water!" Replied the Shipwright.

"Any chance of slipping in a couple of gun ports in the

forward gunwale?" Asked Will.

"What use would they be?"

"Well whatever the angle of heel, guns facing forward would always be pointing parallel to the sea, not at the bottom nor the sky!"

The shipwright stopped in his tracks, so Will not expecting the sudden stop bumped into him. The shipwright turned round and took a long hard look at Will before saying. "I never thought of that – of course you are right. I'll get my men onto it first thing. Have to strengthen the bulwarks to take the recoil."

"Not if we place the cannons on carronade slides!"

"Now you're talking! Will the Admiralty allow that?"

"As I understand it; the captain has the right to arm his vessel as he thinks appropriate. My argument would be that a schooner stands no chance trading broadsides, but given the speed and manoeuvrability, one has a chance if one can race in, give the enemy a couple where it hurts most and race out again."

The shipwright was chuckling now.

"Well your ship can certainly race, that's for sure!"

Set all over the lower deck were hatches to areas below for storage. There was no space in the bilges to stand up, so everything had to be lifted out from above. The officers' benches either side of the wardroom table would have to be able to be removed to access the flour store and the spirits store.

And so it went on, detailed discussion as to where everything could be placed. The ship had not been designed for a 60 strong crew that would be needed to handle her as a fighting ship.

Will contemplated his new charge and suddenly had a thought.

"Do you know of anybody in Barnstable or near-by who could make up sixty or so jumpers, and anybody who could make jerkins?" He asked.

The dock-master looked thoughtful.

"Not really my realm of expertise." He said. "But I shall ask around for you. You going to cloth your crew?"

"Yes, a smart crew tend to take a pride in their work!"

The master shipwright nodded his head sagely in agreement.

CHAPTER 26

Will had a lot of time on his hands. He didn't want to be looking over the shoulder of the dockyard workers all the time, so he based himself in the yard office making visits to the ship when needed.

The Shipwright had come up with a list of potential suppliers for Will's clothing list and Will sought them out to get estimates. He chose two groups of ladies who worked together, one to knit the jumpers in oiled wool to a set pattern, and another to sew together the white jerkins. He discovered in the back streets of Barnstable a hat maker who fell over himself to agree to make hats for each member of the sea crew. These would be black with a black rim, and for the sea-boat crew fancy ribbons in red.

Will discovered that *Snipe* would only be provided with a cutter and a jolly-boat. He decided to pay for an extra cutter himself, but since he was paying, he had all three painted shiny black with red gunwales. Two 'cats' or davits would be needed to support the jolly boat suspended at the stern. Furthermore the oars for all the boats would be painted with red blades.

Gradually the interior fittings began to go up. His cabin was larger than the others with a desk facing the window, drawers under the built-in bunk and a hanging cupboard. The other cabins were slightly smaller, had no windows and only hanging cupboards. There was no room for hanging cots so there had to be lee-boarded bunks with built-in drawers under them. On the same side as Will's cabin but next to the new bulkhead was a space for a steward's store, where a spirit stove could warm up any food needed. Under the stern windows, a window seat with storage beneath was constructed with comfortable cushions, so there was somewhere for the officers to relax. A change was made and a door inserted in the screen dividing the wardroom from the rest of the ship. The fiddles on the wardroom table had to be removable as it had to double as a chart table.

Over the companionways, canvas screens were erected to provide shelter as you ascended or descended. Will had a screen made for the quartermasters at the wheel, which would deflect most of the spray. It had provision also for the hammocks to be stowed in front of it to provide a shelter from musketry. It was shaped like an arrow, so that the water would be deflected to the scuppers.

The Shipwright put Will in touch with a local sculptor, who undertook to provide a figure-head within the time-scale. The final figure was painted white and had a long beak projecting under the bowsprit, with wings sweeping back either side of the bow. As this was not covered in the Admiralty requirements, Will had to pay for it himself. *Snipe* had now been slid into the water and was tied up to the wharf.

The top-masts were raised and all the shrouds secured. Will had a barrel mounted at the foremast crosstrees for a look-out. The sails arrived in dribs and drabs as they were completed. Each was hoisted and checked after its sheets, braces and lifts had been attached; when there was not too much wind.

Two weeks after he had arrived, Will received a letter from Craddock apologising for the fact that the crew had not yet left for Appledore. Apparently somebody had ordered a brig to carry them round, but there was no way that the crew could be accommodated. Craddock had gone to the Fleet Captain to notify him of the situation. The Fleet

Captain had blown his top, and immediately a merchant ship had been commandeered to bring the crew and all their gear around the coast.

Four days later a ship appeared at the mouth of the river, where it sat waiting for the tide to give it sufficient draft to reach *Snipe*. It took a good four hours for all the supplies and crew's gear to be transferred. Once that had been completed Will had the crew summoned on deck and read himself in.

Will was surprised by the spontaneous cheer that went up. It was usual for the Boatswain to offer up 'three cheers', but this had just happened without any prompting. Will thanked his men, and turned to Craddock.

"It is too late for the officers to transfer to *Snipe* this evening. I shall interview them each tomorrow morning. Inform them that they are to stay aboard the merchantman until then. Otherwise it is all yours Number One." He said and then dropped down the aft companionway.

Even though he had had precious little time to prepare, the cook was able to dish up a filling, if not too tasty a meal for all the crew. How he had managed it, Will had no idea, but he took the trouble of going through to the crew's quarters to express his thanks. The rum store was opened and all the crew given a tot, it was the sort of thing the Captain of *Artful* would have done, and Will had learnt the lesson.

Over their meal together, Craddock revealed the story of their delay. It transpired that no other than a certain Lieutenant Simmons had taken it upon himself to issue the order.

"Why should Lieutenant Simmons be given such a task?" The Fleet Captain had asked; explained Craddock. "He volunteered Sir." Came the reply. So the Fleet Captain had turned to his First Lieutenant and barked.

"We need a merchant vessel with enough space for the *Snipe's* crew and their chattels. See to it yourself this time and tell Lieutenant Simmons that I am up to his tricks!"

"So Simmons is still around causing mischief!" Will said shaking his head.

"Still as arrogant and stupid as ever. He won't last long – take my word for it!" Added Craddock; raising his glass.

The next morning the crew set to. They holystoned the decks, hoisted the yards up the top masts, and took aboard the anchors and their warps. At the same time a delivery of furniture was made for the wardroom.

Satisfied that the yards were securely in position, Will descended to his cabin, where he found Tucker in residence, tidying away his uniforms. The hanging cupboard was now in place as was the bunk, which at that moment had its draws open to various degrees. Facing the stern window a small kneehole desk was positioned with a small bookcase fixed to the side of the hull. This would be Will's first night aboard; he had slept the night before in the Barnstable Inn.

"Whilst your about it Thomas, see if you can find the shipwright. I have a favour to ask."

There was a knock at the door and Craddock entered.

"The gentlemen are settled now sir, if you want to see them."

"Right, ask Mr Kemp to attend." Will moved out of his cabin to sit at the wardroom table.

Kemp's tall figure filled the companionway stairs. He was a bony man with a balding head, and a complexion that told of years at sea. He marched forward and placed his papers on the table in front of Will, already turned to face the captain. Will recognised the foresight.

"At Ease Mr Kemp. Please take a seat."

Kemp looked extremely surprised, but the hint of a smile made his face less stern.

"So tell me about yourself." Commanded Will, but in a friendly tone of voice.

"Came up through the ranks Sir. I was a Gun captain, before I took the Midshipman's exam. Been a Middy for two years now." And he stopped there.

"How did you learn the navigational side for your exam?" Asked Will; intrigued.

"I asked the various Masters to teach me. I picked it up as I went along – the practical side that is."

"I take it you fought in the American War?"

"Aye Sir, Gun Captain on a second rate, then on a frigate. After the war I went merchant, that's where I learn the navigation. Worked my way up to first mate. When this war started, I thought it better to volunteer, so I went to my old frigate Captain and he took me on as a volunteer, so that I could take the exam."

"Mr Kemp I think you will be a great asset to this ship. I need somebody with experience as a watch keeper. I hope you can fathom out how I like to operate."

"Thank you Sir." Kemp stood up, but he appeared much more relaxed.

"Might I ask sir, which is the Master?"

Will smiled; despite himself. "I am. The title Commander is the new title for what used to be Master and Commander."

Kemp nodded and left the cabin.

The next down was David Gardner. He was obviously very self assured. Will estimated him to be about seventeen years old.

Gardner plopped his papers on the table, and Will noticed that the writing faced away. He noted the arrogance and the lack of planning. Will did not ask him to sit.

Will sat looking at the young man, not moving a muscle, letting time work to undermine the young man's self assurance. At last after a nervous clearing of the throat the young-man frowned.

Will deliberated let his eyes drop to the papers and back up meet Gardner's eyes.

"Sir?" Gardner queried.

"Mr Gardner, I require my officers to plan ahead. To think things through before they act. It is quite obvious to me that you haven't achieved that state of mind yet."

Gardner looked confused.

"When you present anything in writing to a senior officer, it is a matter of curtsy, and planning, to present the written word so that he can read it. You dropped your papers on the table – wrong! You didn't make sure that they were facing me – wrong! You are not standing to attention – wrong! You are slouching! I don't know what ships you served in before, but on this ship, I expect the highest possible standards. You are not in society here Sir! You are in the Navy, and a very small cog in the affairs of that Navy. I shall expect a much higher standard of behaviour, as befits a fighting man, not a lounge lizard! Do I make myself clear?"

Gardner had pulled himself to attention, and the hint of tears appeared at the corner of his eyes. This young man is spoilt, thought Will.

"Pick up your papers, get out of here, and wait until the other two gentlemen have finished, before presenting yourself again. And next time I expect a very different performance!"

Gardner picked up his papers and fled.

The next in was a Scotsman, a Master's Mate, by the name of Mackay. The man was of middle height with a beak of a nose between his intelligent eyes. He walked forward. Gently placed his papers on the desk, writing facing Will and stood at a relaxed attention. Will suspected the man was in his forties.

"Please be seated Mr Mackay." Said Will; indicating the bench opposite him.

"Thank you Sir." The broad brogue had a lilting lift.

"Am I right in suspecting that you were in the merchant navy before joining this crowd?" Asked Will; relaxing in his seat.

"Aye Sir, that is correct. I was high jacked when this war began!" But the words were belied by the smile.

"So the only question is - have you seen any action?"

"No Sir, unlike you Sir, my war has been very peaceful so far."

"You seem to have done some research."

"Just a wee word with a colleague, there. He was full of admiration for you Sir. I gather you were a navigator, before being promoted."

"That is correct."

"And the hero of the hour – two frigates in one go – that takes some doing in my opinion. No wonder their Lordships gave you a command. This is a lively lady, if I'm not mistaken!"

Will laughed. "We haven't tried her out yet. Probably tomorrow we shall check her handling capabilities. The shipwright here seems to think she is fast and manoeuvrable. The Sail-maker is checking the sails. Some are the original American sails, so I doubt if they will stand up to much. I have had some made here and I intend to have two suits of new sails provided when we gain Plymouth."

"But until that time we don't push her too hard, eh?"

"That's about the sum of it. I look forward to being better acquainted "

"Thank you very much Sir; an honour."

The Frenchman was the next to appear. His rolling gait as he came across the wardroom indicated a lifetime at sea, despite the rather dandified clothes.

"Monsieur le Captaine!" He said formally coming to attention in front of Will, but with his head bowed because of the beams. But unlike the others he was already smiling.

"Henri de Cornes – assistant surgeon, well that is what it says on my papers." He added.

His dress was fastidious, and he held himself proudly, but there was also a twinkle in the eye, that didn't escape Will.

"And pray, what is a Frenchman doing aboard one of His Majesties Ships?" Asked Will.

"I am a royalist, I flee the mob, I ship's surgeon in French navy. I volunteer to serve as such in your navy, but they do not consider a Frenchman capable of being a properly trained surgeon, I think!"

"Please be seated Sir!" Will found himself saying.

The man acknowledged the invitation with a slight inclination of the head, before arranging himself on the bench. He didn't present any papers.

"Do you have your commission with you?" Asked Will.

"Commission? Ah les papiers. Oui! Excuse me." He leapt up and shot out. There was a pause and then he was back. He carefully placed the papers on the table and then turned them to face Will, before enquiring with a movement of the head if he might sit again. Will indicated with a movement of the hand. He pulled the papers towards himself so he could read then.

"A moment please." Will said; and speedily absorbed the first page, which clearly stated the gentleman in question was assigned to the Schooner *Snipe* as an assistant surgeon.

"So tell me about yourself." Will said, sitting back to regard the Frenchman.

With a charming smile de Cornes replied. "I was trained in Paris as a doctor and surgeon. I wanted to see the world, so I joined His Majesties Navy – that is his late Majesty – n'est pas. When the revolution came I was abroad, but on return we were warned that the new authority did not appreciate us gentlemen – les Aristos – so I thought I had better disappear. I found a small boat, just big enough to venture across La Manche. But of course, I did not speak the language, and I had no money. I managed to find an English physician, who took me on, but he was a barbarian – a butcher! I stayed long enough to learn the language a little, and then it was necessary to find employment. So I volunteer to patch up your sailors. The clerks at the Admiralty don't read French, so had no idea of my qualifications. I went before a board who ask me questions, too simple questions, I think. They say I have to serve as Assistant Surgeon, before I allowed to be full surgeon. I say I serve five years as doctor and surgeon in French navy – no they say those are the rules

– Ba to silly rules! So here I am, at your disposal." The man smiled broadly, and Will couldn't but take to the man.

"What about your family?" Asked Will.

"I have no family now, I think. They have been all murdered by the mob. My family estates are in the hands of barbarians. I just wonder what happen to our loyal servants. Very sad!"

"We shall have to get you a proper uniform when we get to Plymouth, in the meantime, settle in. I have deliberately avoided having a grand cabin to myself – there would be no light and very little room for the other officers, so we all dine together – very revolutionary – n'est pas?"

The Frenchman responded with a broad smile of appreciation, then stood, bowed and said. "I look forward to that pleasure, Monsieur err – Captaine Calvert!"

There was a crash, followed by a stream of oaths said under somebody's breath, then finally a ginger haired young man of about Gardner's age descended the companionway, clutching a canvas bag under one arm. He stopped at the bottom of the steps, stood to attention and said.

"Fairley, Sir; Master's Mate."

"Come forward Mr Fairley, and show me your papers."

The young man shuffled forward, placed his bag on the end of the table and proceeded to search inside. He gave a sigh of satisfaction and pulled out some papers which he carefully arranged before placing them in front of Will the correct way round. He then stood rigidly to attention again, placing himself between the deck-head beams.

Will glanced through the papers. "Sit yourself down Mr Fairley."

The youth edged forward and carefully arranged himself sitting erect with arms by his side.

"Three different ships, I see." Commented Will; but the fellow sat silent, eyes straight ahead. "Your last ship, a frigate; tell me about her."

Fear seemed to fill Fairley's face. His face went bright

scarlet.

"Not a happy ship?" Asked Will.

"No Sir!" Came the strangled reply.

"Yet the Master gives you a good report. Was it the Captain that was the problem?"

Fairley stared at Will, surprise written all over his face.

"It is all right, I promise nothing goes beyond these wooden sides."

Nervously the youth nodded.

"And?"

"There was nearly a mutiny Sir!"

"Tell me what happened."

"It got so bad, half of the crew or more had been flogged – not for no good reason, the Captain just found fault with everybody – officers included. He was drunk all the time. Got so bad the officers locked him in his cabin. The First Lieutenant then got himself rowed over to the Flagship. Next thing we knows is that three Senior Captains came aboard, with a whole lot of them Marines. There was lots of shouting and swearing, and then the Captain was led out between huge Marines. He was kicking and cursing, like you never heard on the lower deck. The First Lieutenant never returned. We got a Lieutenant commanding – temporary like – until a new Captain arrived. Everything settled down then, but I got transferred back to England, and to this ship."

"Well we don't do drinking, and we don't do swearing – much, but we do have discipline. That is vital. By the way I was a Masters Mate once, so there is always hope."

For the first time Fairley's rigidity relaxed and he even gave a hint of a smile.

Next it was the return of a much chastened Midshipman Gardner. He advanced nervously, presented his papers – the correct way round – then stood rigidly at attention.

"Mr Gardner, on what ship did you serve?"

"Before *Artful*? The *London*, Sir; Third rate; ship-of-the-line."

Will tried to recall the ship or the name of the captain, but he failed. "Which station?"

"Mediterranean, Sir!"

"And the name of her captain?" Will had noticed that the young man had failed to mention the name of the captain which was normally given after the name of the ship.

The young man looked embarrassed. "Captain Gardner, Sir."

"Your father?"

"No Sir, my uncle."

Will pondered for a time, then said.

"I am afraid this may be very different for you. Here you are expected to stand out as an exemplary officer, standing watches and responsible for the behaviour of your watch. This is the greatest chance you will ever get to prove yourself by your own merit, not by the influence of others. It is probably the first time that you have been given such responsibility, not only for the ship but the entire crew. Think before you act. Ask questions; never be too proud to seek advice. I shall be keeping a sharp eye on you and be testing you to the limit. It is only under such a regime that I shall be able to assess your capabilities as an officer and so provide you with a means to advance in the service."

"Sir!"

"All the officers on this ship dine together, myself included. I suggest you listen carefully; there is a wealth of experience in this gunroom… and beyond. Just one last word of advice….pride is a seaman's downfall."

For the first time in this interview the Midshipman looked straight into Will's eyes.

"Might I be permitted to ask a question sir?"

"Carry on."

"Did you really sink two French frigates at the same time?"

Will relaxed and smiled.

"I see you have been asking questions, a good sign. Yes it is true that the frigate I was serving in did sink two frigates."

"Thank you Sir!"

The last to descend to the wardroom was the smiling face of Marine Subaltern Wiggins. He came clattering down to the ladderway, gave an exaggerated salute, winked and then came forward saying.

"Fine little yacht you have got yourself, Will!"

Will stood up and clasped the Subaltern's hands. "God it is good to see you again, you old rogue. Thanks for conning your way aboard."

"Knew if you were around; there might be a bit of excitement!"

CHAPTER 27

That evening Will sat at the end of the table in the gunroom/wardroom, his back to the windows, with the officers seated around the table. Craddock sat to his immediate right, with de Cornes opposite. Beyond Craddock were Kemp and then Fairley. On de Cornes' side sat Gardner, then McKay, with Wiggins in a chair at the other end of the table facing Will.

Will opened the proceedings after they had had a glass of wine.

"I shall be reading the Articles and Instructions to the crew at Divisions tomorrow morning. I don't think it necessary to write down my instructions in such a small command, but there a few points I need you to bear in mind. Some of the crew of *Snipe* are known to me as they served with me on *Artful*.

We won't employ starters, [Short pieces of rope or cane, used by quartermasters to chastise seamen] the crew know what is expected of them and will do it to the best of their ability. They are fine seamen to a man, they are also seasoned fighters. Mr Kemp I am sure knows all about discipline, and that a man's pride in his job and his ship is the single most powerful motive. I do not tolerate officers who abuse their position. Any Officer, who takes advantage of his rank, is not going to stay on my ship for very long! Mr Gardner, I expect you to seek the advice of the First Lieutenant, Mr Kemp or myself, on all matters until you are sufficiently experienced to act alone. On matters of navigation, we are blessed with two experienced navigators, so you will always have one of them at your side. Try and learn from them. We are singularly blessed to have aboard a highly trained and experienced doctor and surgeon. I don't expect that we shall see much action, but it is comforting to know we don't have a butcher aboard.

My old friend Spencer here; may appear to be an idle lay-about, but by God, I should want no other man at my back in a scrap. Now I should like to ask each of you in turn to give us a brief résumé of their most recent experiences. Mr Kemp."

Kemp looked slightly embarrassed, but swallowed hard.

"I volunteered when the war with France began. I was before that, first mate on a merchant vessel trading with America and the West Indies. I was serving on *Sparkler*, a frigate with the Mediterranean fleet, then *Artful* for a few weeks. Unfortunately no opportunity occurred for me to sit my Lieutenant's exam. The Port Captain at Plymouth advised me to join this ship, as it would give me the best chance, he said, to study naval warfare. Having spoken with Lieutenant Craddock here I think I now understand what he meant!" He smiled broadly at Will.

Gardner looked as if he was about to speak, so Will cut in. "Mr McKay."

"Aye Sir. I have been a Master of Merchantmen for more years than I care to say. I was poached by the Admiralty as they needed Masters with experience of the North Coast of France. Quite why I was sent to this ship I don't understand, because the Captain here is a very experienced Master with a good knowledge of the French Coasts, as I understand."

"Ah, but not the North Coast, Mr McKay. Surgeon?"

"Merci. I was a naval surgeon in the King of France's navy after I qualified as a doctor and surgeon in Paris. I am a royalist, so I couldn't stay in France. I had to flee to Britain, so I offered my services to your Navy."

"Spencer?"

"Not much to say, really. I am a Subaltern of Marines, who was with Will, sorry, our Captain in *Artful*, and I asked to join him when he took command of this ship."

"Thank you Spencer, Lieutenant Craddock - James."

"I too was on *Artful*. I was a Lieutenant, but I continued to study my navigation under Lieutenant Calvert, who taught me most of my skills."

"Mr Gardner." Will finally asked.

"I was on the *London*. I understand I was sent to this ship to gain more experience."

"Well said, Mr Gardner."

It took a further week, before Will felt that the crew were sufficiently knowledgeable with this new type of ship, to take her to sea. Will explained to the officers exactly how he planned to turn the *Snipe* around so she would be facing the sea. He told the officers to explain this to the crew before anything was undertaken.

As a result, the crew moved to their positions without having to be shouted at. First the Jolly boat was brought alongside. An extra long cable was taken from the bow to a post on the far side of the river, passed round it, and brought back to the ship. The Jolly boat then made its way to the stern where another cable was taken to a similar post slightly towards the seaward side. Again it was passed round and brought back.

The bow cable was taken through a block to the capstan. At slack tide, the springs were released and then the bow warp brought aboard. The capstan was manned, and gradually *Snipe* was brought round until she was sideways on to the river. The aft cable was then taken round the capstan and the first cable let go. Further work on the capstan hauled the ship round until she was facing the sea. Once the bows had been secured; the stern cable was hauled aboard and stowed away. The bow and stern lines were then rove round their respective posts, so they could be slipped and retrieved.

The wind was blowing gently from the South-West, which was ideal, when the tide was at its highest point. The Jolly boat was hauled up on its davits, so it swung across the stern of the ship. The Jib and Fore Staysail were hoisted, but not sheeted in. When Craddock reported everything was ready, the two sails were sheeted in, and as *Snipe* slowly gathered speed the bow and stern cables were let slip and retrieved. Will had never navigated this river before, and neither of the Master's Mates had either. They had charts, but they weren't that good. Will had however during the time he had waited for *Snipe* to be readied in the dockyard, had himself taken down river at low tide, so he could get a feel of the river. Will didn't want to go aground on his first voyage under his command, so he had also arranged for a Pilot to be aboard.

Once they were free, the Fore Course and the Main Course were hoisted and sheeted in.[Gaff and boomed sails attached to Fore Mast & Main Mast in Gaff rigged schooners.]

Snipe really began to rejoice in her freedom from the shore. They passed Skern Point with a couple of cables to spare, before turning North West, to head for a buoy called the Outer Pulley. Now it was the time where having a Pilot aboard could really pay-off. There is a constantly moving sand bar at the mouth of the Torridge Estuary. They passed the buoy marking the bar, but then had to come round into the wind and wait for the Pilot cutter to try and catch up.

"Excitable little lady you've got here Mister!" Commented the Pilot as he prepared to drop down to the cutter.

Back with the wind filling the sails, they tried *Snipe* out at every point of the compass. The expression on the faces of the crew said it all. There were broad grins, as the power and speed of the ship conveyed itself to them. As she cut through the waves, water and spume came up through the scuppers.

"How does she feel?" Will asked the quartermaster at the wheel.

"The man grinned, shifted his slug of baccey to the other side of his mouth and said. "Nicely balanced Sir!"

Will nodded, he felt elated. He was used to heeling ships as his father's smack had been a fore and aft rigged vessel. Craddock came to stand beside him.

"I think we might as well say goodbye to Appledore and make our way round to Plymouth." Commented Will.

"Aye Aye Sir!" Said Craddock, with the broadest of grins. Will looked round to see that both the Masters Mates were on deck, as well as both Midshipmen. de Cornes stood with Wiggins against the stern rail, gazing out towards the fast disappearing land.

"Mr Kemp, a course, if you please."

"Due West Sir, until we are well clear of Hartland Point, then we shall have to tack all the way to the Longships."

"It will be dark, long before we get there. I suggest we use the rest of what is left of the light to box our compass off Hartland, and then under reduced canvas, make a broad reach out towards the Atlantic during the night, before turning at first light for the passage round Lands End. I don't fancy trying it in the dark with a new ship and a new crew."

Kemp nodded his head. "Weather looks set fair at the moment. Wouldn't be a bit surprised if the wind didn't drop during the night and the wind veer."

CHAPTER 28

The trip to Plymouth turned out to be uneventful, except for the splitting of the Fore Course, which was an American made sail, so it was not much of a surprise as it was so old. The crew had replaced it with one from Appledore in an impressively short time, which gratified Will.

Snipe sailed majestically up to her mooring in the Hamoaze, with the crew in their new kit lining the side. This novelty had not gone un-noticed by the Port Admiral. However things began to become unstuck after that. They tied up to the gun-wharf, only to be informed that they couldn't have the guns Will wanted. The officious Superintendent stated flatly that schooners didn't have the type of guns Will demanded, and that he wasn't going to alter the normal arrangement for a Commander.

Will had himself rowed out to the flagship, and made sure that the Lieutenant who greeted him knew he needed to see the Port Captain immediately. The Port Captain was ashore, so Will demanded to see the Admiral. It took a bit of brow beating, but he was finally shown into the Admiral's day cabin. Here Will calmly laid out the facts. The Admiral sent for his Flag Lieutenant, sat down and wrote a signal to the Gun-wharf Superintendent.

The Flag Lieutenant accompanied Will back to the gun-wharf and handed the signal over. What the missive said, Will never knew, but there was an abrupt change in the man's attitude.

Will was not able to have Carronade carriages for his bow and stern chasers, because the guns would not fit. Four long barrel 12 pounders were brought out of storage, along with eight new 24 pounder carronades. It took three days for the guns to be hoisted aboard and the necessary fittings put in place. The Appledore Shipwright had neatly inserted extra strong ribs in the bow and stern of *Snipe* to take the force of any cannons fitted. He had also agreed to lay extra decking over the existing decks, fore and aft, to carry the weight and wear.

Snipe finally left Plymouth accompanied by a barge laden with extra shot and powder. *Snipe* wasn't large enough to carry the amount of powder and shot that Will required. The barge was crewed from *Snipe* as it would lie at anchor as a dumb barge in the Dart. He didn't want to have to retire to Plymouth or Portsmouth each time he ran short.

Next day *Snipe* and her consort entered the mouth of the river Dart. They sailed past the ancient port of Dartmouth, past the hamlet of Dittisham and came to anchor in the wide part of the river above the hamlet. Here they made sure that the barge was securely anchored fore and aft; and that her hatches were locked. Then they hoisted *Snipe's* anchor and sailed back down the river to anchor off Dartmouth Town. Will had himself rowed ashore, to meet the Mayor and elders of the Town.

Will wanted to make sure that the Town would look favourably on his ship being victualled by the port. He discovered that there was considerable interest being taken in the smart black schooner anchored in the river. The men of Dartmouth were knowledgeable about ships and shipping, but none had ever seen anything quite like the racy lines of *Snipe*.

Now they were ready to begin their 'work-up. Will had anguished over the very nature of his charge. Such a lively fore-and-after would have very little time to use carronades unless she was 'in irons' [When a ship is caught unable to turn to gain the wind] or running before the wind. At almost all points of sail she heeled markedly. Only the new cannons were available to be used when she had any speed on her.

They took *Snipe* back up to the ordinance barge and took on even more powder and shot. Whilst they were at anchor Will mustered his entire crew on deck. Luckily the rain was holding off as it often did at midday in this part of the world.

"Gentlemen, we are about to start on our new venture. For all of us this is going to be an entirely new method of fighting a ship. We are all used to firing broadsides and slogging it out with the enemy. *Snipe* is not suitable for that type of warfare. Therefore we must use different tactics. We must nip in and nip out. By that I mean we try to use the element of surprise, coupled with our undoubted speed and mobility to hit the enemy where it hurts. We have the honour of being singled out by their Lords of the Admiralty to take the battle to the invasion fleets assembling opposite our shores. In the past frontal attack has failed - singularly. Sir Sydney Smith had some success, but it did little to halt the build up.

So this is what we will be rehearsing for the next weeks. We will tow targets out into Lyme Bay, and we will practice charging in, firing our bow cannons. We will then go about turning fast and as we turn and the ship comes to a level keel we will use our carronades. Then when we are right round it is the turn of the stern cannon. There is no way we can trim our cannons, we can only adjust the elevation. Therefore it is up to us on the quarterdeck to aim the ship and the guns at the same time. What we need to practise is timing the swing. We must train ourselves to predict the angle off necessary to allow for the delay from the pulling of the lanyard to the time the cannon will be on target. We shall keep at it until we have perfected the moves. Then we will go frighten the French!"

There was a cheer from the crew.

"Any questions?" Asked Will; of a startled crew. They had never had a captain ask them their opinion on anything. There was a long pause; then one seaman raised an arm.

"Yes Guiles?"

"Won't the cannons misfire. They's always seem to be under water!

"Very good point! Yes, that is why the sailmakers are in the middle of making expendable gauntlets for the two of them. When we prepare for a scrap, we take off the normal covers and fit these temporarily ones. They will extend far enough back to have a flap over the flintlock. That can be pushed aside just as the lanyard is pulled. The ball will carry the gauntlet with it, but that doesn't matter, once we are in action. Any other questions?"

"Where are the targets?" Asked a fellow from the back.

"Is that Deadly?" Asked Will, to a chuckle from the crowd.

"They are being constructed at this moment in Dartmouth. We are employing a local shipwright. You are aware I am sure that we now have extra charge lockers conveniently positioned for all the guns. They are copper lined and as waterproof as possible. It should help stop any hold ups in reloading the guns." Will stopped and surveyed his entire crew before adding.

"The trimming of this ship is going to be of the utmost importance. Our survival depends upon it. We are not big or strong enough to stand and fight anything larger than us, so we won't try, we will sting them and scuttle off to fight another day. There is no glory in dying a failure. We must stop the French invading. It rests on our shoulders!" It was a gross exaggeration, but it buoyed up the crew, who cheered lustily.

The next morning at first light they hauled up the anchor and coasted down to Dartmouth where they took in tow two targets. Then under headsails they continued until they were past the 'Castles' that protected the entrance to the Dart. Sails hoisted, with Fore and Main Topsails set, they made for the middle of Lyme Bay. There they cast off the two targets.

Then the exercises began. They sailed away in a fairly choppy sea before making a headlong rush at the target. After the two bow guns had fired they would turn smartly to starboard, but first they had to get the run in correct. It was up to the gun captain to decide when he was within range. He would then hold up his arm to notify the team at the wheel. The quartermaster would adjust the bow angle until he thought that the first cannon would be in line with the target, and then as the first gun fired spin the wheel.

The first shot missed as did the second. Up in the crow's nest Midshipman Kemp had a slate to mark up the estimated fall of the shot relative to the target. Then as the booms came inboard on the turn, the carronades opened up. This time the third larboard side gun hit the target – just. *Snipe* continued to turn, the fore sheets being backed to speed her round. Once the stern came in line with the target each 12 pounder took its turn. Again they were off target, but not by very much. The targets were relatively small, so all-in-all it had been a good first try. Off they sped away from the target to turn and have another go. Again there was only one hit and this was from one of the two stern cannons.

Gradually as the day wore on, more and more strikes were made until the target disappeared. Then they had to hunt down the second target which had drifted away. Luckily someone had had the foresight to stick a short stumpy mast on the targets with a flag, so it didn't take too long to find it. Again it was frustrating. There were so many near misses. When they finally demolished the second target they returned to drop anchor off Dartmouth Quay.

It was obvious from their first attempts that the bow and stern cannons needed to be restricted on the recoil. They slipped down the deck to whichever side was lower. Will and Craddock went to inspect the problem. It was decided to put the cannons on rails. The carpenter made these up, but it was found that the cannons could jump out, putting the gun crew at risk. Will debated the problem with the senior gun captain and it was decided that there needed to be a restraint of some kind to hold them down. In the end they took the wheels off the carriages and had the Dartmouth Blacksmith make up metal rails to fit above the wooden ones. At the same time flat pieces of metal were fixed to the restraints to stop too much wear. Extra grease was required to make sure the cannons recoiled smoothly. The same treatment was applied to the two stern chasers. Now when the cannons were fired they stayed pointing at their target.

Ten days of solid practice and they were hitting the targets with monotonous regularity. It was time to go to war! The area they were commanded to patrol, was the same area that Sir Sydney Smith had patrolled some years before. There was a Channel Islands Squadron, but what Lord Spencer wanted was a concerted attack on all French vessels that might be used for an invasion or to support an invasion. His hope was that by using a schooner rather than brigs and sloops, the British would be able to move in fast and retire fast. The problem being that the French had Privateers based mainly on St. Malo, as well as matching sloops and brigs. The French also employed Gunboats, which were small vessels armed with a single cannon in the bows. They had proved quite successful in protecting the various types of vessel being built by the French to transport men, horses and artillery across the Channel.

Will had learnt that the French were attempting to construct a harbour on the tip of the Peninsula at Cherbourg. The latest reports told of quite a considerable number of troop transporters being assembled there behind a new breakwater. The problem was that the two bays that formed the harbour were closely guarded by forts at Querqueville to the West, Fort de Hornet in the middle and Fort Royal on the Isle of Pelée to the East. Will aimed to sort that lot out first.

As they raced up the centre of the Channel before a South-Westerly wind, Will set out his plans to his officers. They would sail past Cherbourg out of sight of land and then approach from the East. They would fly their own design of ensign based on those of the Baltic Nations. Because *Snipe* was such an unusual design, and not known to the French, he hoped to be able to lull the forts into thinking that they were a neutral vessel. He had the sail-maker and his associates hard at work modifying the ancient ripped Fore Course into a tarpaulin to cover the carronades and centre part of the deck. The old Jib and Staysail were to be draped over the fore and aft cannons. Timing was going to be crucial. Will aimed to pass the Fort on the Island of Pelée at midday, when he hoped the troops would be eating their lunch.

Snipe arrived off the Island of Pelée slightly later than intended, but passed between the Island and the breakwater without a shot being fired. *Snipe* continued heading straight for the town quay. On Will's order the wheel was put up and as *Snipe* came across the wind, the two bow cannons fired one after the other at Fort Artois, which dominated the bay.

The long barrelled 12 pounders had been loaded with bags of 2 pounder balls in sacks. The aim was to try and cause as much carnage and confusion as possible. Then the larboard carronades barked, throwing their heavy shot into the midst of the assembled landing craft. As *Snipe* continued to turn the stern-chasers added their weight to the proceedings. Then the starboard carronades opened up, one after the other carefully waiting until they had a certain aim on the enemy ships. There were a few brigs anchored close to the town, but *Snipe* ignored them. Because of her manoeuvrability *Snipe* still had enough way for the bow chasers to come into orbit. They had been reloaded in record time. Now they placed their chain shot in amongst the masts of the brigs. Still turning, although slowing, the larboard carronades once again were able to fire at the transports. Fort Artois managed to fire one of its cannons, but the shot went high over *Snipes'* masts. The sheets were hauled tight and like a race horse, *Snipe* picked up her heels and raced for the middle entrance between the two crumbling breakwaters. Port Artois tried again, but the shots fell just astern of the ship, her speed fooling the gunners in the fort. Now Will understood what the curious flat bottomed boats they had stopped off West Brittany were to be used for - transporting troops and equipment in an invasion.

Off the next port of any significance Barfleur to the east of the Cherbourg Peninsular, there is a rocky and treacherous entrance. There was no way that *Snipe* could get anywhere near, yet Will wanted to find out if the harbour was being used to hold transports. As night fell they coasted in towards the Port and anchored five cables off in two and a half fathoms. The two cutters were swayed out and manned by Wiggins' Marines with *Snipe's* seamen at the oars. Both cutters were under the command of the Midshipmen. Behind one cutter came the Jolly boat on the end of a painter. She was filled with small barrels of gunpowder. Old rags had been greased and bound round the oars to stop the creaks made against the crutches. Each oarsman was under pain of death to not make a splash. Luckily the water was fairly smooth, with only a short sea running.

The boats navigated by the generous lights that showed in many of the windows of the houses round the Port. Will waited anxiously; he had not gone with the cutters, because he wanted to show his trust in the Midshipmen. Will wasn't worried about Spencer Wiggins, the Officer commanding his marines. He had served with him on *Artful* and knew that under that joking exterior there was a very brave and serious officer.

At midnight, the first of the explosions rocked the Port. From *Snipe* you could see the flames beginning to leap up from the middle of the Port area. Then there were further explosions, followed by musket fire. Will had no idea whether it was his marines who were firing, or if there were any French troops in the Port. The conflagration continued, but the firing quietened down to a few desultory shots. Will ordered a lantern to be lit and suspended low over the water as a guide for the returning boats.

It wasn't until first light that the boats returned. The men scrambled up the sides and the boats were secured on lines to be towed until *Snipe* was clear of the land.

"Well that was quite a show!" Exclaimed Wiggins; when he had regained the quarterdeck.

"What happened?" Asked Will, with Craddock at his side.

"We were challenged on the way in, but the Surgeon shouted back in French, which seemed to work."

"de Cornes was with you?"

"Yes, I thought you had sent him in case we had any injuries."

"No! But go on."

"Well we landed to the north of the Port, and made our way over to the quay. Once there we signalled for the Jolly Boat to be rowed round. We unloaded the Jolly boat onto the quay and sent her off, before setting to work. We overcame a guard – he was half asleep – and then placed the barrels in the boats. Not the fishing boats - don't worry we followed your orders to the letter. Then we lit the fuses. By that time somebody had realised they were being attacked and raised the alarm. I had my marines lined up, double deep on the quay, so we were able to keep anybody inquisitive away from the fuse lighters. Then the powder began to go off and the harbour was lit up like daylight. A couple of your boys got hit when scrambling up the side of the quay, but nothing serious. We got them back to the boats and pushed off. Only thing was we had forgotten about the Jolly Boat, so had to go back to cover the two oarsmen. I think we managed to destroy most of the transports, or at least make them un-useable."

"What took you so long getting back?"

"Err, we lost our way rather. Gardner was in the lead boat, and I think he got his bearings wrong, so Kemp had to row around until we located him, and put him right. Easy to do in the dark – and by God it was dark after all the fires and explosions."

At that moment de Cornes strolled up.

"I didn't give you permission to go on the expedition." Said Will.

"My pardon. I thought that I might be needed. I didn't

realise I needed to be told."

"Well I hear you fooled the lookouts, so my compliments; but next time.... ask!"

"Oui mon Captaine."

That morning they sailed as close as possible to the rocky outcrop that is the Isle de Tatihou which is off the entrance to the bay of Saint Vaast-la-Hougue. There is a fort on the Isle, but they only realised that *Snipe* was British when it was too late to do anything about it. There was nothing of interest sheltering in the bay, so they continued on down the coast to the two small Islands of St. Marcouf, which were occupied by the British. Earlier in the year the French had attempted to take the islands with a large flotilla of gun-boats and landing boats. The small British company of 500 men managed to hold off a force of over 5000 French, with reports that something like 900 French soldiers had been killed or drowned and there had been casualties of over 400. The garrison had suffered one killed and four wounded. So *Snipe* made sure that an ensign was flying from the end of her fore-gaff, so that they would not be fired on. They luffed up and sent the Jolly boat in with Craddock to glean any information which might be useful, whilst taking the opportunity to retrieve the cutters.

When Craddock came back he had an extra passenger. Will had been warned of his imminent arrival and had come up to see him come alongside. The passenger sitting beside Craddock was muffled up in a boat cloak. Craddock came aboard and strode aft to Will.

"The Major in charge of the Islands asked me to bring this gentleman over. He is apparently an agent, and needs to get to England as quickly as possible." He said breathlessly.

"Does he have a name?" Asked Will mildly.

"He hasn't spoken to me at all, except to say thank you in French."

"Right, signal him to come aboard. Ask the Surgeon to

join me." He commanded of one of the Midshipmen standing close by.

The man climbed up the side and vaulted athletically to the deck. Will waited for him to come aft.

"Merci Monsieur!" The man said, bowing low.

"Do you speak English?" Asked Will.

"Oui – yes, mon capitaine."

"And you desire to get to England as quickly as possible?"

"Yes – it is necessary! I have important information for your government."

"Why couldn't you send a letter?" Asked Will.

"Ah, you obviously do not comprehend the problems this side of La Manche. If I wrote a letter, how do I know it will get to the right hands? No, not good! Also, if ship is taken, and letter is read – many die!"

"What if you are captured?"

"I kill myself, rather than tell!"

Will turned, and called to Craddock. "Retrieve the Jolly boat and get under way Number One."

Turning back to the man; Will could see his relief. His whole body seemed to have relaxed so much it looked as if he might collapse.

"You alright?" Asked Will.

"Very tired, Monsieur, very tired!"

"Mr Gardner, escort this gentleman below and find him a vacant bunk to rest upon."

Gardner looked at a total loss. "There aren't any spare bunks Sir."

"Mr Gardner, then you shall be a gentleman and offer this gentleman your bunk."

Gardner looked horrified, but nodded his head and managed a strangled "Aye Sir!"

Will turned to check on progress astern as the Jolly boat was hoisted into position. The Frenchman thanked Will as he passed.

"Mr Fairley, I think it is your watch, isn't it?"

"Aye Sir!" Came the reply; Fairley standing to attention by the wheel.

"Set us a course for Portsmouth, but make sure we start as far off the shore as possible."

Fairley went over to Mr Kemp and conferred with him before going below. Will knew that he would be studying the charts and laying a proper course, but he had had the initiative to consult with Mr Kemp to get them out of the area first.

Snipe had been resting head to wind between the two low lying islands. The sea all around was littered with rocks. There were strong currents running between the islands. Of all the officers, Kemp was the best person for the job of guiding *Snipe* out of the area.

Will had been keeping a close eye on his officers. Craddock he already knew he could rely on. He had learnt that Craddock had volunteered to join *Snipe* directly he heard Will would be commanding. He should have –by-rights gone as a First Lieutenant on a frigate. Kemp he admired for his obvious seamanship. He had also shown himself to be cool under fire, and enthusiastic about Will's ideas. Gardner still had a lot to learn, though to give him credit he had obeyed Will's orders about the firing of the carronades to the letter. McKay and Fairley were both very proficient navigators and sailing masters. They seemed to have fallen in love with their ship. They were always enthusiastic about her sailing qualities.

Once free of the islands, they ran before the wind almost due east until they could no longer make out the Cotentin Peninsular. Then in a freshening South-Westerly, they had a broad reach towards the Isle of Wight. In the evening their mysterious visitor joined them for supper. He gave a name, but the wink for Will's benefit, warned him it probably wasn't the man's real name.

Although the distance from where they turned North to head for Portsmouth was only 76 nautical miles as the crow flies, and *Snipe* was quite capable of averaging over ten knots, the total distance they had to sail because of the tides was nearer to a hundred and twenty to the Spithead.

It would have been necessary for *Snipe* to have returned to England anyway, as having so little storage; she was already low on powder and ammunition. Normally it would have been a return to Dartmouth, but the Agent would get to London far quicker from Portsmouth. Will managed to get some well earned sleep on the passage across the Channel.

As they turned to approach Spithead they could see the masts of the Channel Fleet at anchor. Will didn't really want the hassle of being signalled to report to the Admiral, so they took down their large ensign and hoisted an old and soiled one so as not to be signalled to, before they made the entrance to the harbour. Will reckoned that they probably wouldn't consider taking a second look at *Snipe* in the distance, because she was not your usual frigate or sloop.

Will had decided on South Jetty as his preferred landing place, rather than anchoring.

He set the two Midshipmen something of a dilemma, as they had to work out the flags signalling their intentions as they entered the narrow entrance to the harbour. He had no plan of staying in Portsmouth Harbour with its naval etiquette. It might take longer to replenish his stores, but he wanted to honour his pledge to the elders of Dartmouth that he would be using them as *Snipe's* home port.

He had no idea whether there was a Port Admiral's ship in 'ordinary' to salute, but he made everybody keep a sharp look out for any pennants. As it was, with their rapid progress they came smartly up to the jetty, dropping a bower anchor as they slowed to come alongside. The bower would help them get off the jetty if the wind was blowing them against it. Will had the French Agent standing ready to drop down onto the quay directly they came alongside. Immediately he was ashore, the capstan was manned and the sails sheeted. *Snipe* swung away from land, the bower was recovered and she did a neat pirouette, and was heading for the harbour mouth, before anyone ashore had reacted.

Snipe could sail so close to the wind, and tacked so easily, that Will took the Needles route out of the Solent. It meant passing the entire Channel Fleet, but by taking an inshore route close to the Isle of Wight in the fading light, they got through without being challenged. It was a few minutes after High Water and all agreed that the tide set in a Westerly direction. As they passed Cowes, they really began to feel the benefit of the tide. They were virtually spat out past the Needles at over fourteen knots relative to the land. Fortunately the tide stays running Westerly for five hours, and *Snipe* close-hauled seemed to relish the sail. They were halfway across Weymouth Bay before the tide turned against them, but even then it was insignificant compared to the previous five hours.

It was late in the evening that *Snipe* coasted up the river Dart, using the light reflective winds off the high banks to help her to her anchorage off Dartmouth town Quay. It had been an exhilarating sail.

CHAPTER 29

Will ordered a 'make-do-and-mend', whilst he went ashore to speak to the Mayor and then the various shop keepers. He was accompanied by Midshipman Gardner, as he wanted him to learn from his experiences. Will arranged with the merchants for fresh fruit and vegetables to be bought in from the near-by farms. Flour and other essentials were available from the bakers for a price. The butchers were more than happy to supply fresh meat.

Whilst Will was ashore, Mr Kemp took each cutter loaded with barrels ashore to be filled with fresh water. The Watches took it in turns to supply the men to man the boats. Craddock had not needed to specify that the men wore their smart jerseys; they appeared on deck wearing them, and carrying their hats. It was obvious that the crew felt an immense pride in the little ship.

Some miles away at his large country house, Banker Kenton was entertaining some local aristocrats and wealthy farmers. It was in the course of their conversation over the meal that one worthy from near Kingswear told of the smart black hulled beauty that had anchored in the Dart. The speaker had no idea what type of vessel she was; just that she was incredibly smart and attractive. He pondered the thought that she might be a British privateer, but scorn was poured on that idea, because England didn't have privateers, did she? It was Isabella's father who asked if she was staying long. The Kingswear Gentleman had no idea, but admitted that he had seen her boats carrying barrels ashore, so supposed that she might be around for a few days. Quizzed as to what flag she was flying, the informant had to admit that he thought it was an ensign and that it was Royal Navy. Much to Isabella's delight, her father stated that he wanted to have a look.

The next day the Kenton carriage carried the Banker, his wife and his daughter, the relatively short distance to the hamlet of Stoke Gabriel, where they had sent ahead to hire a boatman to sail them down the Dart. It was a pleasant day and Mrs Kenton had arranged for the servants to bring a picnic hamper and wine. The Dart was extremely beautiful at any time of year, full of birds, otters and other enchanting creatures. Sure enough a couple of cables downstream from Viper's Quay below the village of Dittisham, they sighted the strange black beauty calmly riding to anchor off the Town of Dartmouth.

The schooner seemed to be the centre of much activity. Boats were being rowed out to lie alongside, where the yards were used as derricks to lift the contents from the boats aboard the schooner. Other craft loaded with passengers were being rowed round by enterprising local boatman keen to make a penny or two.

The boatman took his craft as near as possible to the stern of the Schooner so they could read the name. Isabella gasped without thinking.

"What is the matter, my love?" Asked her mother.

"When we returned from London by the mail we travelled with a gentleman, a Naval Gentleman, who said he was taking command of a ship called the *Snipe.*"

"I wonder if it could be the same man?" Queried the Mother; aloud.

"What's that?" Asked Banker Kenton; overhearing his wife.

"Isabella travelled from London with a gentleman who was to take command of a ship by the same name as this one's."

Isabella had feared her father would be angry, but to her surprise he ordered the boatman to take his boat even nearer to the side of the black hull.

"Do you know the fellow's name?" Asked Isabella's father without bothering to look at her, he was too busy scanning the ship before him.

"Commander Calvert, I think he said his name was." Replied Isabella, not wanting her father to become too interested, although her heart seemed to be beating at an alarming rate, and she was sure everybody around her must be able to hear it.

A young man's face appeared looking down at them from *Snipe's* deck.

"Your captain – is his name Calvert, by any chance?" Shouted Banker Kenton.

The young man looked a bit surprised, but smiled down on them and replied. "Aye Sir. Did you wish to speak to him?"

Banker Kenton was slightly thrown it appeared, because he turned uncharacteristically to his wife for assistance. That Lady had no qualms. "Yes!" She shouted up.

The head disappeared, but a few other faces came to see who was shouting up to their ship. Each and every one of them seemed to be remarkably well dressed.

Then William Calvert came to look down. "You wanted to speak to me...." His voice trailed off as he recognised Isabella, sitting prettily in the middle of the boat.

"Why Miss Kenton; what an unexpected pleasure." Will said smiling broadly.

"My parents." Was all that Isabella could think to say.

"Really? Well why don't you come aboard? Boatman bring her round to the other side." Will stayed where he was but turned to order. "Mr Gardner, kindly have a boatswain's chair rigged to bring our visitors aboard, starboard side." And he disappeared.

Their boatman had difficulty getting his boat to turn and come about, to lie alongside, as there were so many other smaller craft milling about, but it gave the Kenton's time to admire the thrusting bowsprit and the white Snipe figurehead which seemed to support it.

Finally with much help from the boats that were unloading, who generously allowed the boat carrying the Kentons to manoeuvre inside them, they came to rest against the core fenders that hung from the shiny black hull. A board with a canvas arrangement above was lowered complete with a smartly dressed matelot to the waiting boat. This Tar showed Isabella's mother how to sit in the 'chair' and then on a whistle she was shot up in the air and neatly deposited on the holystoned deck of the schooner. Then the chair was dropped for Isabella.

On deck Will came forward to formally introduce himself, and Craddock his First Lieutenant. Isabella's mother smiled graciously at this strong faced young man with a broken nose and square jaw; that she thought was rather attractive in a strange way.

"Welcome aboard His Majesty's Schooner *Snipe* Ma'am. I trust you are having an enjoyable day so far." His eyes switched from looking at Mrs Kenton, to the new arrival, who was Isabella.

"Miss Kenton! An unexpected pleasure indeed. I trust

you are well?"

"Very, thank you Commander."

"I am flattered that you have remembered, after such a brief introduction, my name and even my rank. May I introduce my First Lieutenant, James Craddock?"

Craddock bent over first Mrs Kenton's and then Isabella's outstretched hand.

"Mr Kenton?" Will asked politely as the Banker shook himself free of the boatswain's chair. Will realised that the man was rather ashamed of having to be hoisted aboard.

"I apologise for the chair, but getting aboard a ship is an acquired science." And he put out his hand to shake the banker's.

Kenton was looking about him with undisguised admiration.

"She is a very pretty ship, Mr Calvert." Will ignored the mistake regarding his rank.

"And the crew are so smart! I have never seen anything so well turned out!"

"Thank you for the compliment, Sir. I feel it adds to the loyalty the crew feel towards their ship. I am sure that you would like some refreshment on a day such as this."

"Thank you Captain." Mrs Kenton replied on behalf of her family.

"Excuse me a moment." Said Will; and turned to stride aft to Gardner standing by the wheel.

"Mr Gardner, be so good as to check the wardroom and see that it is tidy, and that the officers' cabin doors are shut. Tell Tucker to prepare glasses for wine, well polished and that he should look his smartest. I shall be bringing our guests below shortly."

Gardner smiling; answered. "Aye Sir." And dropped down the stern companionway.

What Will missed whilst he was telling Gardner what to do, was the conversation that took place a few feet away. Mr Kenton remarked on the lack of cannons. Henri de Cornes standing close by remarked. "I doubt if my compatriots feel that way. Henri de Cornes, Surgeon, at your service."

"Isn't this rather a small ship to have a Surgeon?" Asked Kenton.

"I rather think that with our Captain they expect rather a lot of action!" Craddock said, just as Will came back to join them.

"I am sorry that everything on deck is rather a mess at the moment." Said Will. "We are re-victualling. Being small we can't carry very much to tide us over a long period."

"Your Surgeon sounds French, isn't that rather strange?"

"Ah! Henri here is a French Royalist. He was a surgeon in the Royalist French Navy. We are extremely lucky to have him aboard."

Henri made an extravagant bow, which amused the ladies. Will to kill time, explained about the ship's wheel and her binnacle, as they slowly made their way aft.

"Would you care to join us in our humble wardroom — that is the officers' quarters for that refreshment? I am afraid that we only have wine, no cordials, or if you really want to experience the navy life we have rum."

"A glass of wine would be just fine, thank you." Said Mrs Kenton; firmly.

Will led the way aft. "I suggest you descend backwards, the steps are rather steep."

Mrs Kenton turned and slowly made her way down closely followed by Isabella and then Mr Kenton.

"James, Henri; kindly join us below." Said Will: as he followed Kenton below.

Much to Will's relief the wardroom was not only tidy, but the table had been polished within an inch of its life. Spencer Wiggins sat reading a paper on the window seat at the stern. He was resplendent in his scarlet uniform. He stood up as the ladies descended and then waited to be introduced. Thomas Tucker appeared from Will's cabin wearing his short white jacket with white gloves on his hands. Time in a flagship had taught him a thing or two about etiquette. The ladies sat elegantly on the cushions of the stern seat. Kenton took Will's chair without being asked, so Will deposited himself on one of the benches with Craddock, Wiggins and de Cornes on the opposite bench. Thomas disappeared into his tiny cubbyhole and came back with glasses that he polished carefully. Then he brought a bottle of Will's best Claret, which he de-corked and poured a small amount into one glass and offered to Will to taste. Will nodded his acceptance, and Thomas carefully poured one glass at a time, handing each to the ladies first and then to the gentlemen, before disappearing back into his tiny pantry.

The ladies had been admiring the view from the stern windows. Now they turned to raise their glasses as Kenton called a toast to *Snipe*.

"Where is your cabin?" Asked Mrs Kenton.

"That one there." Replied Will; indicating the door from which Thomas had appeared.

Isabella rose swiftly to peep inside. "It is tiny!" She remarked as she regained her seat.

"I decided to do away with tradition. Normally the Captain's cabin takes up the whole of the stern of a ship. However, that would have meant no room for my officers to relax in, and no light. So I had it arranged this way. Since I spend most of my time on deck, it really doesn't trouble me."

Kenton had been watching Will carefully. "Do you eat with your crew then?" He asked.

"Not with the crew, I eat with the officers down here. We do eat the same food as the crew, but a little later. The crew have their food served first, then the Petty Officers, then the Officers. It has always been so, in the Navy."

"Don't you fall out of your beds?" Asked Isabella.

It was Craddock who answered. "We have boards to stop us doing so. In the bigger ships we have cots that hang from the beams, so they stay put as the ship moves about."

"The crew have canvas hammocks that work the same way as the cots." Added Will.

Then Craddock turned the conversation by asking if the Kentons lived close by. There then followed a discussion about the countryside around them, and the difficulties of travelling the narrow lanes of Devon.

The general conversation was later interrupted by Mr Kemp appearing on the companionway and quietly explaining that the Kenton's boatman was worried about getting back before the tide meant they could not get ashore at Stoke Gabriel. On deck Isabella managed to squeeze Will's hand for a second as she said goodbye. Her eyes though did the talking. Luckily Kenton and his wife were busy talking to the boatman.

CHAPTER 30

Next morning *Snipe* moved up the river to anchor just upstream from the barge and their ammunition. One of the cutters was used to transport the powder and shot back to *Snipe*. Will had insisted that the powder be made up into its bags aboard the barge, rather than being brought aboard to be filled later. They needed to save every inch of space they could.

The replenishment of the shot and powder took all day, so they stayed at anchor for the night up river from Dittisham. On the first favourable tide the next day, they sailed out of the Dart and back into the Channel. Will had a course set to take them up the Channel past Dover and into the North Sea. He was going to explore the Low Country harbours for any craft that might assist in any invasion. He felt that after their last escapade, the French might be too interested in schooners for a time. As usual there was gunnery drill as they sailed east.

Will's destination was marked on the chart as Cape Holland, and was the mouth of the river that led up to the city of Rotterdam. The United Provinces had been over-run by the French, and were now being forced to build flat-bottomed boats and gun-boats for an invasion of England. The entrance to the waterway was surrounded by very low lying land, so it was possible to see a long way inland from *Snipe's* crow's nest.

The look-out reported no sign of any shipping. Will didn't dare take *Snipe* up the waterway, as there would have been very little space to turn round. There might be shipping up the river at the city, but if there were he needed intelligence before committing his ship.

The sail-maker and his crew had been ordered to cut up old sails to make a long strip to cover the bulwarks of the schooner on either side, disguising her gun-ports. Will hoped that because of her unusual appearance *Snipe* would appear to be a merchant trading vessel, rather than a man-of-war. Now they were cruising the coast in a westerly direction, constantly marking their depth so that they could sail as close to the land as possible.

They came to the wide mouth of the River Maas which you could tell from the amount of silt that flowed out to the sea. The wind was from the south-west and quite steady. This estuary led to one of the Batvian Navy's principle ports. It would be a dangerous and audacious move. Will hoped that most of the ships of any size would be anchored or moored, so a quick in and out might be achieved before anybody could respond. The Port of Hellevoetsluis was approximately five miles up the river on the northern bank. As they rounded the corner there was the port, but to everybody's surprise there were very few ships of any merit to be seen. All Will could think of was that after the Battle of Camperdown the year before, the remains of the Batvian fleet must be elsewhere, probably at Texel to the north. *Snipe* coasted in closing on the naval vessels present. There were four brig/sloops, anchored in a line. Three were obviously in commission, but the fourth had no topmasts or yards set. Anchored in trots were three Batvian style gunboats and a trot of Peniches and smaller Caiques.

The weather was closing in. Low rain bearing clouds

threatened again from the west. The crew on deck had been kept to a minimum, to reflect the cargo carrier role they were impersonating. *Snipe* dropped her anchor just to the east of a low lying island in the middle of the estuary.

Will reflected that it might have been better if the hull was not quite so smart and glossily black. Luckily with the reduced visibility it would have to be a very sharp pair of eyes that noticed.

Will gathered his officers together in the wardroom and explained what he intended to do. He then asked for any comments. There were a few detailed points raised, but otherwise all agreed it was feasible given the weather conditions.

Heavy rain came with the night. Once it was dark enough to disguise what they were doing, the cutters were uncovered and swayed out. They upped anchor and moved slowly closer to where the brigs and landing craft were anchored. Judging they were within fairly easy reach of the enemy they dropped the anchor. *Snipe's* sixteen marines were divided into two groups. Wiggins was in charge of one group, the Sergeant and Corporal in the other. The marines did not carry their muskets; instead they had four pistols each carried in canvas holsters: two at the hip and two hanging at their chest. Across their back a cutlass was reached over the shoulder. On their feet instead of their boots they wore rope soled canvas slippers, the preferred wear aboard Snipe as boots made too much noise for those below deck when the marines were on sentry duty. Over all they had wrapped around them oilskins. Up forward two topmen dressed all in dark clothing, faces, hands and feet all blackened with coals from the fire; crouched ready to be the first to climb aboard the enemy vessel. They sported carpenters' mallets on cords, poniards, and cutlasses. The mallets were for swiftly rendering a lookout insensible. The twelve oarsmen all had cutlasses strapped to their backs under their oilskins.

In the first cutter Will was accompanied by Boatswain Tarrant and Midshipman Gardener.

In the second, Master's Mate McKay and Surgeon de Cornes accompanied Spencer Wiggins.

It was hard to see anything in the rain and pitch black. The two cutters rowed in the direction of the decommissioned brig/sloop. Once they had found her, they parted company. The first cutter, drifted with the tide down the larboard side of the brig/sloops, and the other on the starboard side towards the leading ship. Will's larboard side cutter's target was the mainmast shrouds. The other cutter's the starboard foremast shrouds.

In the dark, once they had found their target, they let the rope fenders along the cutter sides absorb any bumping, as the top men reached up and swung themselves into the ratlines. Will peering up, saw two vague shapes disappear. A few moments later there was a sharp click, click; the signal for the others to swarm aboard as the lookouts had been dealt with. Will dropped his oilskin onto the bottom boards of the cutter alongside the other discarded coverings and swung himself up, closely followed by Tarrant. Next came all but the coxswain and one oarsman, then lastly the marines.

The crew had spent the last hours before leaving *Snipe* in practicing working in pairs below decks. Members of the crew had slung hammocks and climbed into them. The pairs, working by shuttered lantern light had to climb silently down the ladderways and then one of the pair would pass a short piece of rope round the body in the hammock, passing the rope through a bight on one end of the rope and pulling it tight before securing it. This captured the prostrate character in the hammock incapable of much movement. At the same time the other member of the pair rammed oakam into the mouth of the victim and tied a piece of canvas round the head to hold it in place, so gagging the unfortunate.

Once borderers were all on deck, carrying their shuttered lanterns, they dropped down the ladderways to the sleeping crew of the brig/sloop. Will, Tarrant and Gardner dropped down the stern ladderway to head for the officers' quarters.

Here they found three gentlemen fast asleep in their nightshirts and caps. It was obvious from the empty earthenware bottles that the Dutch gin had been consumed in quite large quantities the evening before. Awoken with a sharp prod it the ribs, they found it difficult to comprehend that they were prisoners in their own ships in their own harbour.

Had there been any shots fired, it had been prepared for by the expedient of the topmen who would have laughed loudly and sung a ditty de Cornes had taught them in Walloon which was very rude. It was hoped that other vessels would think the crew were drunk.

Will accepted the surrender of the officers and their crew and placed them on their word of honour not to try and escape or to warn others. Anybody doing so would be deemed not fit to live! There was now a decision to be made. Should they try the same stunt on the brig/sloop behind them? Leaving eight Marines under the command of Midshipman Gardner, the sergeant and corporal, together with six seamen from *Snipe* they regained the cutters and cast off. The tide was now slack, so they had to paddle back to the next brig/sloop in line. Here they boarded in exactly the same way, but this time it didn't go according to plan. One of the marines lost his foothold as he tried to catch hold of the ratlines and fell back into the cutter, nearly capsizing it. His cry of anguish forced out of him by the pain could have been fatal. Luckily the Surgeon who was already on deck must have realised what had happened because he swore loudly in Walloon as if he had stubbed his toe or some similar fate had befallen him.

This time the Batvian officers were more on the ball. One was obviously the officer of the day, because he opened the wardroom door to find a poniard placed against his throat by the huge bulk of Boatswain Tarrant. Forward there were struggles, but the small crew were overcome by the element of surprise, and the brig/sloop was *Snipe's* for the taking.

Will felt that two brig/sloops in one night were quite enough. He would have a very depleted crew to sail *Snipe*, let alone capture and hold a third vessel. There were though the Peniches and Caiques which were unmanned.

Leaving the rest of the marines with Subaltern Wiggins and McKay, together with another six seamen on the second prize, the cutters were rowed over to the anchored landing craft. Selecting a Dutch style gunboat and French style Caique; these had their anchor warps cut and were towed back to lie astern of each of the brig/sloops. Will then sent the other cutter under command of his coxswain to cut out a third vessel, a three masted small Peniche. This would be *Snipe's* towed charge.

Now Will had to decide who to put in command of the prizes for the attempted trip to Ramsgate. He decided to let Craddock take command of the first with Gardner remaining to assist. The second prize would be under the command of Midshipman Kemp with McKay to assist. This would leave Will with Master's Mate Fairley and Surgeon de Cornes to keep watch on *Snipe*.

Back aboard *Snipe* the cutters were retrieved and stowed as before, upside down over the amidships skylights. Everybody was soaked to the skin, but aboard *Snipe* at least they could change into dry clothes. Those on the captured ships would have no such luxury.

At first light, there was no light! The rain had eased slightly, but the clouds were still low and blacked out the slightest trace of any hint of dawn. Two hours later there was just enough light to be able to see the outline of the shore. The anchor was raised and slowly *Snipe* made her way to towards the entrance to the estuary, riding the ebb tide. The schooner's responses were greatly dulled by their tow. As they passed through the entrance to the North Sea, the lookouts reported that the two Brig/sloops had been seen about a mile ahead of them.

As they fought their way further out to sea and the effect

of the land disappeared, the sea became much lumpier. The wind strengthened and spume began to be blown off the top of the short sharp waves. Instead of cutting through the waves as normal, *Snipe* now rolled badly and tried to climb each wave. Will began to regret trying to tow out the Peniche, which was not really worth much in Prize Money, but might be of interest to the Admiralty.

Had they been lucky or was it down to planning? He wasn't too sure which it had been that had resulted in so easy a cutting out operation. Certainly now the luck seemed to be deserting them. He was worried that *Snipe* could be broached or even turned over if the Peniche went off at an acute angle.

"Mr Tarrant! Cut the tow!" He ordered.

"Cut the tow, Aye Sir!" Replied Tarrant; hefting a razor sharp boarding axe. A couple of seamen pushed a heavy solid block of oak under the strop to which the tow line was attached.

It took two blows and the cut end raced out of the gun-port through which it had been thread.

It took, what felt like minutes, for *Snipe* to appear to realize that she was free. The motion eased and she began to cut through the waves in her usual casual style.

"Ship on the starboard quarter" Called out a Lookout.

All turned to look, but already the curtain of rain had obscured whatever was out there.

"What was it?" Asked Will joining the Lookout.

"Brig/Sloop, Sir!"

"Was she towing?"

"Not that I could see, Sir."

Surely they couldn't have overtaken the two Brig/sloops and their charges? Was one of them in trouble? These thoughts crossed Will's mind. After a long wait, the curtain lifted suddenly revealing a brig/sloop in the distance. She was on a parallel course. "Batvian flag. No tow!" Called the Lookout; peering through his scope. Will just had time to confirm the prognosis.

In this sea state there was little that they could do. It was surely far too rough for them to try and engage an enemy which was better armed and was a more stable gun platform? On the other hand *Snipe* was far more manoeuvrable than a brig/sloop.

Will checked that both booms were vanged on both sides. [A tackle attached to the boom to stop the boom from accidently crashing across in heavy seas.]

"Stand –by to gybe!" Will ordered.

"Man the fore and aft cannon. Shot and chain."

The gun crews ran to their stations.

"Bring her round gently Quartermaster" Ordered Will; standing beside the helm.

Up forward Will could see the gun crew disappear under the canvas that protected the foreward cannon. They would load the larboard gun with normal shot and the starboard would have chain shot for the enemy rigging. Grease would be applied liberally to the metal slides that were fixed either side of the gun carriage to the deck.

Snipe seemed to relish the change in her fortunes. She ploughed straight through a wave tossing the water negligently aside and over her decks to come round to her new course. Men manning the boom vangs eased them out, controlled round belaying pins. Sheets were trimmed and *Snipe* was now running before the wind and waves.

Up in the bows, the gun captains signalled they were ready. At the last moment they would pull off the canvas covers. Just before the gun was fired, the restraints would be whipped off. These stopped the cannon sliding backwards and forwards on the rails.

Everybody who was not actually engaged on vital work gazed ahead through the sheets of rain. Then suddenly the curtain lifted and there straight ahead of them was the brig/sloop fighting her way through the sharp choppy sea. Both bow gun captains had their quadrants held before them, regardless of any spume that crashed over them.

It was up to the Quartermaster at the wheel to try and make sure that the bows were on target on the upward roll, as this was when the captain's liked to fire the cannon. On *Snipe* this was comparatively easy as the quartermaster had a clear view forward under the storm foresails.

Crash, crash, crash, the bows forced their way through the waves; the little ship choosing to go through rather than over the waves. Suddenly the canvas over the foreward cannons was struck aside. The restraints whipped off, the lanyard on the tompion [Cap fitted to end of gun barrel] freed the mouth of the gun. First the starboard cannon fired. Then on the next upward lift the larboard barked.

Unfortunately the rain decided to move in on the act and obliterate their view.

"Put up your helm!" Ordered Will.

Snipe turned away from her target. He didn't want his ship to get within range of the brig's guns. It was unlikely that they sported long barrelled 12 pounders, but he wasn't about to take that risk. They were now close hauled and sailing away from their quarry.

Will had to picture in his mind what the Batvian Captain would do. Would he turn to follow *Snipe*; or continue on his course? It would be impossible for the Batvian to sail as close to the wind as *Snipe*, but they might not realise that fact. Will decided to go round in a circle so as to hopefully come up on the vulnerable stern of the enemy.

The sheets of rain had settled back, obliterating anything and everything. Gradually *Snipe* came round and gybed as she completed her turn. There was nothing! Everybody stood silently listening for the slightest clue as to the presence of the Batvian Brig. Up forward the gunners had managed to reload their cannons.

Will decided to do a figure of eight pattern to see if they could at least catch a sight of their elusive prey. They continued on a broad reach before gybing round to come back close hauled. Suddenly the curtain of rain lifted and there only a couple of cables in front of them was the brig/sloop's starboard broadside facing them. Even before Will had really taken in the situation both of *Snipe's* bow chasers spoke and it was clear to see that the aft three gun ports of the Batvian ship had been crushed, leaving a gaping hole in the gunwale by the quarterdeck.

The Batvian cannons fired and one ball hit the turning *Snipe* starboard amidships, up ending one carronade and damaging another beside it. Two of the crew were hurt. The fore course was punctured by a ball that bounced off the top of a wave and sailed high and through the canvas leaving a large hole. Another ball passed close over the heads of the stern chaser crew.

Snipe was closing the stern of the Brig and Will had the sheets let go so that the schooner came up on an even keel and the carronades could be employed for the first time.

The Batvian Captain must have realised the peril that faced his ship, as *Snipe* would pass less than a cable away and could not fail to score a number of devastating hits. Just as the bowsprit was coming level with the Batvian's quarter, the Batvian ensign was seen to be hauled down fast and a white sheet was hung over the side to re-enforce the signal.

Snipe came round to lie half a cable off the larboard quarter of the brig. Will grabbed a speaking trumpet and shouted across in French, for the brig to head to Ramsgate and to anchor in the Downs. A figure appeared on the brig's quarterdeck and waved acknowledgement.

CHAPTER 31

When *Snipe* finally dropped anchor off the town of Deal in what was known to the Navy as 'The Downs', there were four ships-of-the-line anchored off the town, together with two frigates and a quantity of smaller naval vessels. The two cut-out Brigs lay at anchor to the north of the British ships. Directly *Snipe* had dropped her anchor; Will set out in one of the cutters to visit his prizes. The nearest to hand was now under the command of Midshipman Kemp, though his uniform belied his age and experience. Will met the Batvian Captain, a Lieutenant, who didn't seem to be unduly fussed at being taken prisoner. It transpired that his family had been badly treated by the occupying French forces. Will assured him that he and his crew would be treated well by the British. Taking McKay with him as well as a couple of marines, Will was rowed to Craddock's charge. Here the Batvian Lieutenant was so angry that he had been locked in his own sleeping cabin, with a marine on guard. When the Lieutenant was brought before Will he was truculent and seemed to think that it was not right to capture ships in their own ports at night. In fact Will thought that the man was slightly un-hinged. He was returned to his quarters with the guard. Leaving Gardner in charge, Will returned to *Snipe* where he left Craddock and McKay. His next visit was to the now anchored Brig that they had captured in their battle at sea. The Batvian Lieutenant in command met Will as he climbed over the ship's gunwale. The Batvian presented his sword with his left hand as his right was swathed in bandages. Looking across the deck of the Brig Will could see why the Lieutenant had surrendered. The deck was a mess. Half of the starboard side cannons were scattered in grotesque positions where they had no right to be. The dark stain of blood was evident, although there were signs that the crew had tried to clean it off. Lined up across the quarterdeck the crew was in a sorry state. Half were bandaged and it seemed from the small number that there must be others below.

"I am sorry that we should have caused so much hurt. How many were killed and how many injured?" Will asked in French.

"Five were killed, including my First Lieutenant. Twelve have bad injury, five not so bad." Replied the Batvian Lieutenant; in English.

"You speak English?" Will asked in surprise, although it was an obvious question.

"I have spent a number of years in England, before we were at war."

"Ah! Don't you just hate war?"

"Agreed! Your little ship; she is extraordinary. Your gunnery incredible! How your people managed to damage us so badly in such a sea I shall never comprehend. Your first shots came out of nowhere. You took our fore-top gallant mast away and upended cannon. Then you disappear! We are looking everywhere for you. Then just as suddenly there you are! Bang, bang; total chaos!"

"Me thinks that a lot of luck came into it!" Replied Will. He handed the Lieutenant's sword back to him and added. "A worthy opponent."

As they were talking, one of *Snipe's* topmen had hoisted the British Ensign over the Batvian to show that the Brig was a British prize.

CHAPTER 32

Banker Kenton was extremely surprised when he received a reply to his letter to a fellow banker based in Plymouth, only four days after sending his own missive. The recipient had obviously jumped to false conclusions.

With regard to your enquiry about Commander Calvert, I have the honour to inform you that the Commander has more than sufficient funds to purchase your estate. I wish you luck you're your sale.

Kenton reread the short note, and sat back to consider its implications. Why should his fellow banker think that he, Kenton was selling? The Commander must be searching for an estate to purchase in the area. There could be no other conclusion. He was surprised that a young naval Commander should be able to afford an estate as large as his. How had the young-man come by such funds?

Kenton wrote back to the Banker informing him that he thought there must be some mistake. His Estate was not for sale. There was however an estate a few miles to the south of his on the shores of the river Dart which he understood might be for sale.

That night he told his wife what he had done.

"And such a pleasant young-man, and obviously well considered by his crew." She said; dreamily.

There was further news of the young Commander. It might be a week old, but Banker Kenton read the Gazette when it finally arrived in Devon. In it he was surprised to find a copy of a letter from Commander Calvert to Mr Evan Nepean Esq. At the Admiralty.

Copy of letter from Commander Calvert of His Majesty's ship Snipe to Evan Nepean Esq.

Dated at sea December 5 1797

Sir,

I am pleased to acquaint their Lordships of the successful cutting out of two Batvian Brig-sloops, together with a Batvian Gun Boat and Peniche. I can further report that subsequent to the cutting out, His Majesty's Schooner Snipe was involved in action in the North Sea with another Batvian Brig during a violent rain storm. The said Brig was successfully overcome and is now being brought back to the Downs in company with HMS Snipe. The cut-out vessels are already on their way to Deal.

I have the honour to be. &c. &c.

William Calvert

Commander.

Kenton read and reread the letter. It was short and to the point. How typical of the fellow; thought Kenton. He rushed out of his study to find his wife. She was in the Blue Sitting Room reading a novel.

"My Dear; I have something for you to look at!"

"Not more boring financial news, I hope!" Said Laura Kenton; putting down her book and taking the proffered paper.

"God Gracious!" She exclaimed. "I hope he is alright!"

"Well at least we know he is alive, my love. He wrote the letter!"

"Oh yes; that is some consolation I suppose: such a nice young man!"

"Not short of a penny either if he is capable of purchasing this estate!"

"Are you thinking what I am thinking; my Dear?" Asked Mrs Kenton. "And Isabella seemed very taken by him!"

"I shall post lookouts for the return of the schooner. If you write an open invitation, it can be sent out to the ship immediately it arrives back."

Kenton knew then that his wife was of the same mind as himself. The possible suitor that he had approved of for his daughter's hand could not possibly be as well endowed as the Commander. Clearly Calvert must have influence at the Admiralty to have risen so quickly, so he could possibly achieve much higher rank. If his daughter was to be married to an Admiral at some point, that would give great prestige to Kenton and his bank. In the meantime, he wrote to his banker acquaintance, to find out more about the Commander.

Leaving the Brig in the hands of his few marines and six seamen, Will returned to *Snipe*. He collected Thomas Tucker and the mail for the Admiralty and was rowed across in the Jolly boat to the largest of the ships-of-the-line. It flew no pennant, but he was fairly certain that the senior Captain of the Downs Squadron would be aboard.

Will was met at the entry port with the normal honours given to a captain of a ship visiting another. A Lieutenant greeted him and led him aft to the Admiral's cabin. An elderly Captain rose from behind the large desk and came forward to greet him.

"Am I right in what I have been told; your little schooner brought in five prizes?"

"That is correct Sir!"

"Might I ask by what right are you operating in our area?" It was said without a hint of malice.

"*Snipe* has an independent commission from the First Lord himself. We were instructed to investigate the Batvian coast. As a strange ship, it was thought we should be able to gather more intelligence than if any of your own ships were to attempt the same thing."

"And you have that Commission?"

Will pulled out the original papers from his pocket and handed them to the Captain, who returned to sit behind the large desk. He scanned the papers and then handed them back.

"Seems to be in order. My Admiral will be asking me when he returns. Now pray tell how you came about such a feat?"

So Will went through the whole story in detail; emphasising the rehearsals before the cutting out operation. When he had finished, the Captain sat gazing at him.

"You are not conventionally armed then?" He asked.

"No Sir! We have long barrelled twelve's. A brace fore and aft."

The Captain nodded his head. "Because?"

"Because we can fire those without having to come onto an even keel. The carronades are; with a fore and after, looking at the sky or the bottom of the hogging most of the time!"

"And who came up with that plan?"

"I was given permission to arm as I required."

"Well you bagged yourself a pretty prize. Pity you didn't come within our orbit. Could do with some prize money at my time of life!" The Captain gave a wry shrug.

"Might I take the liberty of asking if our mail can be brought over to be sent with yours?"

"Of course. Anything else?"

"Well Sir; we could do with some marines to guard the prizes, until prize crews can be assembled to take them wherever the Admiralty desires. I have hardy enough men to sail *Snipe* as it is, without being able to man any guns."

"Right! Leave that with me. Your men will be relieved by midday tomorrow."

"Thank you Sir."

"I should warn you. Provisioning here is a nightmare. You have to load your boats on the shingle. Nearest proper victualling yard is Dover, which is a pain."

"I haven't had the experience of dealing with prizes before. Might I ask exactly what the procedure is?" Queried Will.

"You have obviously notified the Admiralty that you have prizes?"

"Yes Sir!"

"Right they will send assessors to value them. They will also send somebody to take charge of the prisoners. That will happen far faster than the assessing. Once the prisoners have been removed, crews will be sent to take them wherever the Admiralty in their wisdom deems most suitable. In this case it will undoubtedly be Chatham."

"At what point can we leave them?"

"Well once we have put our people aboard to release yours, you could in theory depart. However I know my Admiral will want to speak to you when he gets back from London, so I would advise waiting until then. Do you have any damage?"

"Aye Sir. Our starboard side is damaged at gunwale level. We also have three or four carronades which will need replacing. I haven't yet had a full carpenters report. I shall send a copy over to you immediately I get one. From my cursory inspection; I think that at least four ribs will have to be spliced, which means a visit to the dockyard. I have said as much in my report to the Admiralty."

"Where are you based?"

"We operate out of the Dart. It means we can put to sea in nearly all conditions, when required. It also means we don't have to explain ourselves to every passing Captain who would try and get us to act as a messenger ship."

"Dart is it? Not sure I have ever been in there. So you should, I imagine be sent to Plymouth for repairs, as that is the nearest base."

"I should imagine so, yes."

"Well Commander, you have certainly drawn attention to yourself and your little ship. I look forward to reading of more of your escapades."

The Captain was as good as his word. All of *Snipe's* crew were back aboard in time for dinner the next day, which did not go down too well with the cook. Craddock had to go ashore at Deal and try and gather together more provisions; a task which he found irksome.

Three days later the prisoners were taken off on barges. Will was called ashore to meet with the Admiral commanding the Downs Squadron at Walmar Castle. The Senior Captain was there and made the introductions. The meeting was short and to the point. Will felt that the Admiral was making a point, but he was at least civil.

Another four days and orders arrived instructing *Snipe* to make passage for Plymouth, where the dockyard had been informed that repairs were needed. Will paid another formal call on the Admiral, before at dawn the next day they upped their anchor and in calm seas and a fluky wind started for Plymouth.

Off Selsey Bill, Henri de Cornes asked if he might join Will pacing the quarterdeck.

"So what are you going to do about her?" Asked Henri.

"Who?" Replied Will; thinking of ships.

"The lovely young lady you have lost your heart to!"

"Is it that obvious?"

"There are signs. You sigh a lot, which you never used to do. You also spend long periods gazing towards the land;

usually in the direction of where the young lady lives; unless I am mistaken."

"There is nothing I can do. Who would take on a mere Commander and in time of war/"

"Ah! But if you don't try, you will never know!"

"So what should I do?"

"Write to her."

"About what, pray?"

"Just say how enjoyable it was meeting her again and wasn't it a co-incidence that they should be sailing past *Snipe*. Then you can say that you have to be in Plymouth for a time for repairs to the ship, but that you hope to be able to return to the Dart after that, and hope that she and her parents would do you the honour of allowing you and your officers to dine them."

"And you think that will get a reply?"

"The lady is well brought up. She will be forced to reply; not that I think she needs an excuse."

Will realised what an innocent he was when it came to the affairs of the heart. Will wrote more than one letter, each time deciding it would not do and throwing it into a spittoon. In the end he changed tack, and wrote to Mr Kenton asking him if he would be so kind as to enquire regarding local properties for sale. He added that he had been informed that there was one on the North bank of the Dart not too far from Totnes that sounded interesting. It would be of immense help if he were to have some local knowledge as to the reasons for the sale before visiting any estates. He added that his ship would be in Plymouth for a month or so undergoing repairs, so he was taking some leave to try and see if he could complete a purchase if a suitable property was on the market. He had to leave the letter unfinished as they entered the Sound.

It was the usual round of visits that had to be made when they had dropped anchor up the Hamoaze beyond the other ships. The Port Admiral was the first, and then the Superintendent of the Dockyard. As Will had thought, there was a waiting list for ships to be repaired. He was surprised to find that Snipe was to be moved ahead of others, but it would still be at least a fortnight before the yard could start work. Added to that, Christmas would mean at least three more days. Will had completely forgotten about Christmas.

Back aboard Snipe he discussed leave with Craddock. Craddock pointed out that Will should be there when Snipe did go to the Dockyard. He added that since his mother lived in Berwick, there was no time for him to be able to get there in time for Christmas. Much better if Will was to take any leave first.

So Will completed his letter to Mr. Kenton by saying that he hoped to be in Totnes on the 21st December, but had not had time to book rooms at The Royal Seven Stars Hotel in the town. He said that he had written however to the Steward of the estate that belonged to a Baronet and was for sale; to warn him that he hoped to see round it on the 22nd or 23rd December.

He ended by being asked to be remembered to his wife and his daughter.

He then got Thomas to take the letter ashore and engage a fast rider to take it straight to the Kenton Estate. At the same time Thomas was to hire a coach for the trip to Totnes. That afternoon Will went ashore to visit his bankers in Plymouth. They confirmed that all of the interests in the Merchant Fleet had now been sold at a very good price, due to the need for ships; both for the Navy and for Trade. He was a wealthy man. Whilst ashore Will would have liked to have purchased some ordinary clothes to wear in place of his naval uniform, but there was no time.

CHAPTER 33

Very early the next morning Will with Thomas at his side set out for the trip to Totnes. He was glad that he decided to hire a coach rather than ride, because the morning greeted them with a damp outlook. Despite the rain and the appalling state of the roads, they arrived in Totnes in time for dinner. *[Dinner was normally taken at about 3pm.]*

Will was surprised to find a letter awaiting him. It was from the Kentons' inviting him to dine with them next day. If they did not hear otherwise, they would send a coach to pick him up from the hotel. There was no response from the Estate's Steward.

As is quite normal for that part of the world, the clouds parted and the sun came out as they emerged from the Hotel after eating. Together they climbed the steep High Street and Will found a tailor who was prepared to make him a suit which would be ready immediately after Christmas. It was the first time Will had visited Totnes and he found it charming.

The next morning the smart equipage, which could only be the Kenton's, arrived outside the Hotel. Thomas was to hire a horse and ride to the nearby village to try and find out as much about the estate as possible from the locals. Will trusted Thomas as a sharp observer of everything he saw. The coach's springing was superb, but the lanes between Totnes and the hills above the little seaside village of Paignton were very narrow, so the pace was slow.

Kenton House was set on high ground with views over Torbay. The approach to the house was very different from the lanes that took you to the house. The drive was gravelled for a short way before the Gates and Lodges. The length had obviously been chosen carefully because it just gave time for the gate-keeper to open the gates to let the coach roll through without slackening its pace. The house itself was hidden from view until the last moment when the drive turned into a turning circle in front of the imposing frontage. It was of classical design, with a portico which the coach rolled to a stop under. There appeared to be three main floors. This side of the house faced inland, so from here there was no view of the sea.

A footman came running out of the house, as a groom appeared from behind the house. Will stepped down to be greeted at the main door by an imposing figure.

"Commander Calvert. Welcome to Kenton Court. My name is Humphreys; I'm the Butler to Mr and Mrs Kenton. They are expecting you."

A footman appeared from behind Will and relieved him of his boat cloak and hat.

"I shall show you straight through to the Blue Room." The Butler continued.

The Hall was as impressive as anything Will had ever seen. A fine staircase rose against one wall seemingly unsupported. The whole was lit by a glass dome above. The floor was of white tiles with small black ones inset at the corners. Mirrors on both sides reflected the light, making the whole a bright and welcoming place.

Humphreys opened a door to the back of the hall and announced Will. He found himself in a much smaller room than he had expected. The walls were covered in pale blue silk, which was obviously the reason why it got its name. The view from the window looked over the Bay. A plain marble fireplace held a blazing log fire.

From a chair by the window, Mrs Kenton rose to greet Will with the broadest of smiles.

"Commander. How lovely to see you again."

Will advanced and bowed his head over her outstretched hand.

"Hello William." The well remembered voice came from behind and he turned to see Isabella sitting on a couch behind the door through which he had entered. Beside her a fire screen kept the heat from her face. A door burst open behind Mrs Kenton and in marched Mr Kenton.

"My dear fellow, so good to see you. Not too bad a journey I hope?" Came the cheerful greeting from Mr Kenton.

"Very smooth and what a fantastic position you have here." Countered Will.

"Come and sit by me." Isabella said, and Will was for the first time able to drink in her beauty as he crossed to take his seat on the couch beside her. Her hair was free, the dark locks resting on her shoulders framing her face. The dark eyes searching Will's. She wore a dark blue dress that almost matched the colour of his uniform. The dress was pulled in tightly below the bust, accentuating her figure.

"You are not injured then?" She asked; as Will sat.

"Injured? No; why so?"

"We read about your exploits in the Gazette." Mr Kenton explained.

"The Gazette? I am sorry you will have to explain." Will knew there was such a paper, but had hardly ever seen one, let alone read it.

"The Gazette had a copy of your letter to Mr Napean." Isabella stated quietly.

"Really? I didn't realise that it would be made public!"

"It said that you captured five ships. In your letter you said that Snipe was in need of repair. We were worried that you might have been hurt. Was there much damage?"

So Will was forced to give a detailed explanation as to what had happened.

Isabella's face was a picture of concern. Will realised that he had been telling her the story, so had to force himself to turn his attention to her parents as he completed the tale.

"Why the Gazette should bother to print my letter, I cannot fathom!" He ended.

"The public is eager for any good news in this long drawn out war." Commented Mr Kenton.

Then Mr Kenton turned the subject to the property Will was interested in.

"The house is in a very fine position. It is owned by a Baronet who is an inveterate gambler. He owes money everywhere. He has to sell the property, but keeps trying to put it off. He hasn't visited the place in years. The Estate Steward is a good fellow, who has tried to keep the place in reasonable order, but is not allowed to spend anything on it. There are five tenanted farms that bring in a reasonable income, which is probably the reason why the Baronet tries to keep hold of the place."

"You obviously have a very good spy network!" Commented Will; laughing.

"Well it is common knowledge here about."

"The Old boy was a great character. He used to come for about a month in the summer. He used to be very social. I never took to the son, even then. Loud and very arrogant! He hardly ever came here. His father was always tut, tutting over his gambling and the company he kept. The mother died young, and I gather the young man was never the same. Not that that is any excuse!" Added Laura Kenton.

Will noticed that Isabella hadn't joined in, so turned to her.

"Have you ever been to the house?" He asked.

"No. That was before my time. My brother didn't take to the son either."

It was the first time Will had heard reference to a brother.

"Your brother?" He asked surprised.

"Oh he died three years ago."

"I am so sorry to hear that." Will didn't really know what to say.

"Henry was three years older than Isabella. He caught some kind of ague. It was terrible. He didn't stand a chance." Mrs Kenton distress was palpable.

"Anyway; we must concentrate on Will's designs on the estate. Do you know what price the Baronet is asking? Because believe you me it will be highly inflated." Interjected

Mr Kenton.

"I understood from my Banker that he was asking between a thousand and two thousand guineas."

"My spies, as you would have them, suggest that the Baronet owes at least twice that amount in gambling debts."

"What happens to those debts?" Asked Will.

"Depends on to whom he owes the money. Normally 'Gentlemen' pay up. Here we have an aristocrat who can't or won't. Sooner or later his friends will melt away and he will find nobody will play with him. At that point it generally turns nasty. Evil Bankers like myself have been known to buy the debt at a discount and then force the debtor to sell everything. If that was to happen in this case, the man would lose a fine estate in Buckinghamshire and another in Norfolk."

Will felt he was entering an entirely alien world. "What should I do if I like the property?" Will asked.

"Wait my boy, wait. View the property and then pause, then go back and have a more thorough investigation. If you still like it, then you get your Banker to negotiate on your behalf, unless you have a 'man' in your employee, which I doubt in your case."

"When are you viewing it?" Asked Isabella.

"I am awaiting a reply from the Steward."

At that point Humphreys entered to announce Dinner.

Laura got up and crossed to a door behind Will that he had not noticed. The new room was about the same size as the Blue Room with a small square table set for four people. A fire in a similar simple marble surround made the room pleasantly warm.

Will sat opposite Isabella, who had her back to the window. This meant that Will was unable to see her expression clearly, as she was silhouetted against the light.

"Four of the farms are tenanted; the fifth is the home farm." Continued Kenton; as he sat himself down.

"Might I ask why you want an estate, when you spend most of your time at sea?" Asked Laura Kenton; with an encouraging smile.

"I am advised that property is the best investment. I shall need a base when the war ends, as I shall probably be put on half-pay, if I am lucky." He didn't dare to look at Isabella; because it was a lame excuse. He really wanted the property so he would have a home to offer her if he ever managed to woo her.

"How big a house are you looking for William?" Asked Isabella.

"I have no idea. I am not even sure how big the property near Totnes is. I just asked for information about any estates that might be on the market near the Dart. This property was apparently for sale, so I came to look."

"You don't want anything too small." Mr Kenton said; and then sipped on his soup.

"You need to have enough space for a family, in case you get married." Laura added.

"I have first to fine somebody who would take on a mere battered Navy Commander. You know what they say; to be a Commander can be to be forgotten."

"I doubt very much William if the Admiralty is going to forget you, if you manage to capture five enemy ships in one go!" Stated Mr Kenton; with a broad smile.

"Just make sure you marry for love!" Isabella said firmly.

"I don't know very much about the marrying business." Muttered Will.

"In Society it is de rigueur to marry for a title or for money – preferably for both!" Isabella sounded quite annoyed.

"I am afraid that my daughter has already been approached because I am a banker." Mr Kenton said; smiling at his daughter.

"It is like a cattle market! I mean imagine being married to that loathsome idiot who asked for my hand last season. I would far rather die a spinster than spend any time with him!"

"Is that why they say there are so many chinless wonders

amongst the Aristocracy?" Asked Will.

"Very probably!" Returned Isabella; smiling at Will.

Will was feeling uncomfortable with all this talk of marriage, when the lady he had lost his heart to was sitting opposite."

"I wonder if I could ask a tremendous favour." Will asked; as a footman removed his plate.

"What is that?" Asked Mr Kenton; but it was with a smile.

"I know nothing about houses or property. I have been at sea ever since I was twelve, and doubt that I have spent more than a few weeks in a house during all that time. Could you come with me to advise me; that is, when I know that I can look around."

"What a lovely idea!" Mrs Kenton said.

"That is probably a very sensible suggestion." Added Mr Kenton.

Will hoped that they would include Isabella, but wasn't sure how to suggest such a thing.

"You mean you need a woman's touch." Stated Isabella.

Will had to stop himself from sighing loudly his relief.

"Let us know when and we can pick you up at your hotel." Mr Kenton said.

"That really is very kind of you. Thank you!" All the Kentons smiled at him, and he realised that a cloud had obscured the sun so he could now see Isabella's face clearly. She was smiling that soft smile he loved so much.

Will asked how they passed the time in the country and all three started to explain, correcting and laughing amongst themselves over the parties and outings that they made; that filled their winter days. Gradually Will found himself relaxing and soaking up the warmth that seemed to pervade this extraordinary family. When they had finished Dinner, Laura suggested that Isabella should show Will her new horse.

"I'll get hold of some carrots and join you." Said Laura.

A footman was sent to tell Isabella's maid to bring an outside coat. Isabella led Will into the hall where they were soon joined by a maid with a coat over her arm. Isabella thanked the maid and put the coat on with Will's help. He could smell her hair, he was so close.

"This way!" She said and pushed her way through a swing door into the Servants quarters. As she passed she explained what was behind each door. Butler's Pantry, Kitchen, The private Sitting Rooms for the Butler, Housekeeper, Cook and the Servants Hall. Finally they opened a door and were outside on a path between orderly beds.

"Herbs for the Kitchen." Isabella said: waving a hand towards the beds. "It will be great fun looking round the house. Thank you for inviting us." Said Isabella smiling up a Will.

"I need all the help I can get!"

"What was your family home like then?" Asked Isabella.

"It was a town house overlooking Plymouth Harbour. I suppose by most people's standards it was quite a big house for the town. I only sold it recently. My Aunt lived there after we moved until she died."

"Where did you go then?"

"Fowey. Now that was a really fantastic position. The house looked out over the estuary and Harbour. It had a wonderfully light Sitting Room. My father had a study where he could sit and watch all that went on below in the harbour."

"Do you miss it?"

"What the house? Not really, I only lived there for about six months until my father died. "Then I joined the Navy."

They had arrived at a covered passage which led to the stable yard. To their left with an arch between them were coach houses, whilst the rest of the four sides were made up of stables.

Another arch pierced the stable block opposite the coach houses.

"Far side - carriage horses, near side - our mounts, middle block – guests' horses." Said Isabella; explaining the layout. They entered a stable door in the nearside and came face to face with a row of stalls full of curious heads. Isabella rubbed each horse's nose as she told Will their name and to whom they belonged.

The first in line was a huge bay with a fine head. "Oracle, my father's favourite mount. Not much of jumper, but a great stayer."

Isabella patted the horse's neck and then moved on to the next waiting, curious head. This was a more refined chestnut with intelligent eyes. Even Will could appreciate that. "Claudius, father's second horse; great jumper, not much of a stayer. No disrespect, old fellow!" She kissed the horse's nose.

The next was a white horse that Will remembered was called a grey. It was slightly smaller than the other two horses, but looked very well.

"Blondie, my mother's horse. Mother doesn't ride out so much now. Poor old love misses her outings don't you?" She said to the horse.

Next was a light bay with a knowing eye. He came from the back of the stable to blow down his nose at Isabella, who laughed.

"Jasper, lovely ride, calm and as safe as houses. Getting on a bit but still a lovely fellow, aren't you? Yes."

They moved on to a dappled grey which was smaller than the others and lighter boned.

"This is Starlight, my old mount. She will be put to foal later. I really out grew her ages ago, but she is such a lovely ride." Isabella rubbed the horse's neck and whispered in her ear something Will could not hear. They came to the end stable. A black beauty sauntered over to deign to inspect the newcomers.

"And this is my new horse, aren't you?"

"What's he called?" Asked Will.

Isabella blushed slightly and turned an impish smile to Will.

"Commander!"

"Really?"

"I only got him about a month ago."

Will stared at the beautiful black animal that was rubbing his nose against Isabella's shoulder.

"He is a wonderful ride. Powerful, yet you feel so safe on him!"

Will thought it wise not to ask why the horse was called Commander.

"He really is quite something, even I can see that!" Will commented; in admiration.

"Do you ride William?" Asked Isabella; turning to look straight into his eyes. The dark pupils seeming to be almost hypnotic.

"Like a sack of potatoes. There aren't many horses to ride on ships!"

"But you ride?"

"I sit on a horse and try to guide it. I wouldn't call it riding exactly."

"I could always teach you!"

"That would be wonderful! I just hope there will be an opportunity."

"We'll make sure there is then, won't we?" Isabella said; as a Laura's voice made them turn.

"Had to get them to dig some out. So what do you think of the newcomer?" She asked as she fed a carrot to each horse down the line.

"I am no judge, but to me he looks a very fine animal."

"You should see Isabella mounted on him. Turns all heads!"

The three of them said their goodbyes to the horses and left the yard by the rear arch. Here to the left could be seen paddocks with rail fences. Straight ahead a wall gave a hint of a walled garden. They turned to follow the wall to the right and came out onto a terrace with a fine view out to Torbay. There were only a few Merchant ships anchored in the bay.

Back in the house, Humphreys met them with the news

that a young man had arrived with a message for the Commander. The Steward had sent a message to say that the Commander could view the house the next day.

"Was he wearing naval uniform?" Asked Will.

"Yes Sir. I think it was naval. It was plain blue with brass buttons. However I don't think it was a midshipman's uniform."

"That will be my Clerk, Thomas Tucker. Where is he now?"

"I had him taken to the Kitchen. He looked as if he could do with some sustenance."

"Thank you Humphreys!" Will turned back to the ladies.

"Is that the young man who served us when we were aboard Snipe" Asked Laura.

"Yes, he doubles as my servant and clerk. He is very intelligent. I hope to make him up to Midshipman, when I have a ship with enough room."

Isabella smiled. "He worships you, you know!"

Will had never thought about it. "I doubt that!"

Isabella just nodded her head.

CHAPTER 34

The next day Will waited at the entrance to the Hotel. It was one of those December Devon days, where the sky was clear and the sun was trying its best to make out it was summer. He was surprised to see coming over the breast of the bridge a smart landau drawn by four horses with two postilions, and a groom sat at the back. Sitting facing forward were Laura Kenton and Isabella, whilst sitting with his back to the horses was Mr Kenton. The Landau drew up in front of Will.

"Good morning!" Cried Mr Kenton; a broad smile giving Will a warm welcome. The Groom was already down from his position at the rear to open the door and fold down the steps for Will.

"What have you got there?" Asked Isabella, pointing at the large leather case that Will had under one arm.

"My writing box. It is for Thomas who will be taking notes of the sizes of the rooms and position of doors and windows."

"So is he coming with us?" Asked Mr Kenton.

"No: he should be here any moment to lead the way on horseback."

At that moment there was a clatter of hooves and Thomas appeared mounted on a hack.

He rose in his saddle and saluted the Landau, before manoeuvring alongside the lead horse to speak to the lead Postilion.

Will climbed into the carriage and sat beside Mr Kenton opposite Isabella.

"A belated Good Morning; I think is due!" He said arranging the writing box to one side.

"Well the omens are good. What a lovely day for a trip out!" Exclaimed Laura.

"Is it far?" Asked Isabella.

"Thomas tells me it is about four to five miles only. However the lanes are extremely narrow so one can't travel fast."

The Landau turned to re-cross the bridge and was soon out of the town and onto the narrow lanes. They twisted and turned climbing steeply. Their view of the Dart disappeared so that they could only see a valley. After about one and a half miles they turned to their right down an even narrower lane towards the village of Stoke Gabriel. The lane dropped sharply to a stream and then rose quickly to a cross roads. They continued straight on by-passing Stoke Gabriel and dropping down again to cross a stream before rising again to their destination.

Although this was a turnpike road, the surface was very uneven. It seemed strange but there was no view of the Dart, even though they appeared to be at the highest point between two valleys. The Landau slowed and Will twisted his head to see for himself the reason. Up ahead Thomas' horse was sideways on to the lane and he was gesticulating at something or someone. Then the carriage moved ahead and it was clear to see that a cart had been backed into a field to allow the carriage to pass. They came to a bend in the road and there ahead of them they could see a copse of trees. Thomas had stopped and indicated that the Landau should turn to the right down a track that had seen better days. There was no lodge and there suddenly before them was an imposing house with what must have once been a gravelled turning circle in front of it.

The house was obviously of the early Georgian period with pleasingly proportioned windows either side of the front door which had a carved pediment supported by two pillars. On either side, were three equally spaced sash windows.

As the groom lowered the steps to allow the passengers down from the carriage, the double front doors opened and a tall thin man wearing a coarse jacket over breeches and gaiters came out to meet them.

"Good Morning! Commander Calvert?" He looked to both Mr Kenton and Will.

"I'm Commander Calvert." Said Will; climbing down before turning to hand down Laura and then Isabella. He turned and walked towards the Steward. "You must be Simpson the Steward."

Simpson did a small stiff bow. "I am afraid that the house is in somewhat of a state. No money has been spent on it for a long time and there are no servants to do anything. I have opened a few shutters so that you can see where you are going, but if you want to see more, then I am afraid we shall have to open more."

"Which means more to close afterwards!" Added Will.

A look of gratitude and surprise crossed the man's face. Then he led the way through the front doors. There was a small lobby immediately with an open arch to the main hall. Here a centrally placed stairs rose to a landing.

"I am afraid that the dome is covered in grim and verdigris." Commented Simpson; looking up. Indeed it was an eerie green light that pervaded the whole hall. One could just make out that there were mirrors on the walls. Simpson moved to the left and opened double doors onto a large room. This time the light came from a couple of windows whose shutters had been folded back. The carpets had been rolled up and every bit of furniture was covered in dust sheets. The walls were papered in a light green design, which offset the white marble fireplace. Dust sheets covered whatever was hanging on the walls on the fireplace side.

"This is the Ballroom." Remarked Simpson; with a sweeping gesture of his arm.

"I remember this room from when I was a girl." Said Laura. "The Ballroom! Behind those sheets I think you will find there are mirrors down the wall facing the windows. What has happened to all the curtains?" She added.

"Stored in huge trunks in one of the bedrooms. It was the last thing that the housekeeper had done, before she left."

They walked down the long room on the beautifully laid parquet flooring. At the far end a single door opened onto a flagstone floored lobby with a servants' staircase rising upwards and also downwards. To one side was a small pantry. To their right was a baize covered door with another in front of them. Simpson pushed open the one straight ahead and they walked into what appeared to be a small dining room to Will.

"The Breakfast Room!" Announced Simpson.

Isabella walked over to the un-shuttered window. "What a beautiful view. Look Will; that must be Galmpton Creek down there." Will joined her to look out over verdant green meadows to a glimpse of water.

There were two windows on either side of the room which was on the corner of the building. To the right a white marble fireplace sat unused. The table and chairs were covered in dust-sheets. Beyond the fireplace with a mirror over and pastoral scenes on the walls, a door opened onto a With-drawing room. French windows were set in the wall opposite another white marble fireplace. The shutters were open, so the sun shone across the bare floor. The carpet was rolled up to one side, whilst what were obviously settees sat either side of the fireplace covered in the now ubiquitous sheets. The French windows gave onto a wide terrace with magnificent views down to the Dart and across to Dittisham.

Isabella walked out onto the terrace, and was joined by her mother.

"Lovely views to the river." She commented. Will joined her to look out. The light seemed to play on her shiny hair.

Simpson led on to another door near the outside wall on the far side and opened it. It turned out to be a small parlour about the size of the Blue Room at the Kentons. This room had windows on two sides, both with views down to the river. It was a joyously bright room, with pale yellow wall paper. Here again the carpet had been rolled up and tired sprigs of lavender had dropped their seeds on the floor. The room had a corner fireplace with a marble mantel.

Simpson turned right and opened the doors to a Library. The leather bound books gave it a cosy feel. At the far side was a fireplace; whilst immediately in front of them was a large dust covered object which Will imagined was probably a desk. Kenton circled the room reading titles here and there. There was only one window with its shutters pulled open. The closed shutters had spring leaves with bells hanging from them.

"Not much of a deterrent, if there is nobody in the house!" Commented Mr Kenton.

"Sir Percy hasn't paid anybody for a long time. I'm only here until I can find another situation." Stated Simpson sourly.

Simpson then opened a door which led them back to the Hall, and then turned almost immediately back through open double doors to what was obviously the Dining Room. The chairs were all hidden under dust wraps, but the table could be seen in pride of place down the centre of the room, again covered. The carpet had been rolled up.

"Seats about twenty four." Simpson said.

They wandered down the room to the far end where a single door led to a flagstone lobby with another set of stairs, which were quite obviously intended solely for servants. Beyond them was another Butler's Pantry which this time was considerable bigger than the first. Laura and Isabella wandered around opening cupboards and peering inside. The Pantry had a door that opened onto the Hall.

"The Gunroom." Said Simpson, opening a door that they had failed to notice as they entered. "So the shooters and hunters don't drag all their dirt through the Hall." Commented Simpson.

They mounted the fine staircase which lacked a carpet. At the top they found it rolled up and pushed to one side, again showing evidence of the lavender that had been rolled up with it.

The landing ran round all four sides of the Hall.

"There are eight Bedrooms all with Dressing Rooms off." Stated Simpson; opening a door to one of the rooms. The bare bones of a four-poster looked slightly comical. Again everything else was smothered in dust sheets. In the nearest end to the windows in each wall there was a door leading to a dressing room and then another to the next bedroom. All the Bedrooms seemed to be much the same size. They went from room to room, finally coming out near another door which led to the servants' access to the floor. Here a stairs ran up and down. They went up to view the servants' bedrooms on the top floor. These were all small pokey rooms with just an iron bedstead and a chair each. The light for the narrow landing that ran right round coming from small windows high up near to the dome. Simpson indicated a ladder with a hatch above which led to the roof. They returned down the servants' staircase to the basement. Here were the cellars, with wine racks, mostly empty. There was one which had a locked grill.

"The Brandy store!" Commented Simpson; with a laugh. "Sir Percy sent a message to say I should ship the contents to London. Well he hasn't paid me for over six months so I thought why should I? I sent back a message saying that it wasn't possible, I didn't have the key. He wrote back saying I must. I wrote back saying he had it. That was how it was left."

"Your pension?" asked Mr Kenton.

"Nar, that would be stealing. No I just wanted to teach him a lesson."

They came to a steel bound door with three heavy padlocks on it as well as an enormous keyhole.

"Silver vault." Said Simpson.

"Anything inside/" Asked Will.

"Yes all the silver for the house."

"I won't ask you to open it. I should imagine that could get you into trouble." Returned Will.

"Thank you! Yes if Sir Percy was to ever find out I had opened it for anyone, then I would probably end up being transported.

"Is he the Magistrate?" Asked Mr Kenton.

"No, but he probably was on drinking terms with the present one!" Replied Simpson sourly.

They were walking down a stone flagged passage, passing the Kitchen, the Bakery, the Laundry and the Brew House. On the other side to these were the senior servants' sitting rooms. These didn't have shutters, but barred windows. Here the furniture remained uncovered as if someone had just got up and walked out. The servants' dining hall was the last room, before they went through a door to an open walkway that led to the stables. The stable yard was much the same as the Kenton one, having stables on three sides; with the fourth having coach houses either side of an arch. The arch was closed by two enormous stout wooden doors. There was no back exit.

"The Grooms' quarters are over the stables. Want to see inside the Coach Houses?" Simpson asked.

"Yes please." Replied Mr Kenton; for all of them. Simpson produced a key from the huge ring he held and opened the first. Inside were a coach and a phaeton. The Coach House on the other side revealed two dog carts and a shooting rig. There were no horses in the stables.

Simpson unlocked a small door in the huge doors to the Stable Yard and they found themselves back near the front of the house. The Kenton Landau was still in front of the House, but the postilions and groom were allowing the horses to graze the rough grass that had once probably been lawn. To their right was a walled garden, which was surprisingly well kept with neat rows of vegetables.

"I allowed the Gardeners to use this to grow themselves veg. It was the least I could do when Sir Percy failed to pay them."

"Do they still have cottages on the estate?" Asked Mr Kenton.

"Well they shouldn't, but I haven't the heart to turn them out. Where would they go? I was hoping that if the estate is sold the new owner would take them back on."

"What has happened to the rest of the staff?" Asked Isabella.

"Scattered here and there. Most have families from around here. Trouble is there isn't that amount of places for domestics. The Grooms drifted away. I know some are still about. I met a couple the other day in Totnes: living from hand to mouth."

The party retreated from the Walled Garden and walked back past the front of the house.

"I wouldn't mind looking around again, if you don't mind." Said Will.

Simpson shrugged. "Fine by me. I'll leave you to it. If you want to go down to the river, beware there is a Ha-ha. There are steps in about the middle to a gate: difficult to see with the grass so overgrown."

"Might take a look and then come back to the house." Said Will.

"I think we'll wait up here and wander around the house. You two go; we'll see you inside." Said Laura.

Will and Isabella headed towards the river, finding the steps and the rusty Iron Gate. Will had some trouble shifting the gate, but finally managed it to allow Isabella through. The field beyond had obviously been laid to pasture because the grass was quite short. They wandered down to a wood, with all types of tree. The path was steep, so Will took the opportunity of taking Isabella's arm to help her. Being winter most of the trees had lost their leaves, but it still provided a screen from the house above. They came to a jetty jutting out into the river. Will tested it and it held his weight. Isabella followed him. Here they were out of sight of anybody else, because of the river bank. Isabella's foot seemed catch on a plank because she fell forward. Will caught her and held her. They were virtually embracing each other. Isabella turned her head up and Will couldn't resist the temptation to kiss her on the lips. The response was passionate and they were locked in a tight embrace. Will had to try and step slightly back whilst still holding her, because he was sure she must be able to feel his arousal. Finally she stepped back slightly, a beautiful smile on her upturned face. She put up a hand to Will's face and gently stroked it.

"I suppose I shouldn't have done that!" Said Will; with a choke in his throat.

"I'm glad you did!" Replied Isabella. She took his hand and placed on her breast. He could feel the softness and the harder nipple through the fabric.

"Can you feel my heart?" She asked. All Will could do was to nod.

"What happens now?" Will asked finally; getting his own racing heart under control. "We haven't known each other that long. Do I ask your father or what?"

"Well." She paused and turned her head slight to one side. "You haven't asked me anything yet!"

"Well if I was to ask you to marry me, what would you say?"

"That isn't a proper proposal! Is it?"

"No! I've never done this before...."

"I should hope not!" Isabella giggled.

"Isabella Kenton would you do me the honour of agreeing to be my wife?"

"William Calvert, I am flattered by your proposal. I am very sorry to say that you might regret this, but my answer is a very definite Yes!" And she flung her arms around him and kissed him hard on the mouth.

"What happens now?" Will asked; when they finally drew apart for breathe.

"You ask to see my father in private. Then you ask him for his permission to seek my hand in marriage. But! But don't do anything until after Christmas."

"Why after Christmas?"

"You'll see. Trust me."

They wandered back up to the house, decorously a foot apart.

Once inside the house, it was with far more interest that they both scrutinised every room. They came upon Thomas busy writing away in one of the Bedrooms.

"How's it going?" Asked Will.

"Getting there Sir. Only two more rooms on this floor."

"Don't bother with the servants' quarters; otherwise you will be all night. I am dining the Kentons at the Hotel, so I will see you back there."

"Aye Sir!"

Isabella laughed. "Is that what you say aboard ship?"

"Aye. I mean yes Miss Kenton." Stuttered Thomas; a red glow climbing up his neck.

It was during Dinner at the Hotel, that the Kentons invited Will to spend Christmas with them.

"It will be such fun to have you. We have a supper party on Christmas Eve; then we have a dance on Boxing Day. All the locals are invited. Christmas Day we spend very quietly as we give the servants the day off, so they can spend it with their families." Laura Kenton informed Will.

Will was over come. He thanked them effusively, and explained that he couldn't remember the last time he had spent Christmas en-famille.

When the Kenton's Landau had finally disappeared over the bridge towards Paignton, Will hurried out of the Hotel. He realised he had no presents to give them. He asked at the first jewellers if they made enamel brooches. They didn't but sent him up the High Street to a small Jeweller who did.

Will asked if, for a premium, the little man could make up a special design of a brooch before lunch time on Christmas Eve. The man mumbled something, and then looking up for the first time at Will's anxious face asked what design he wanted. Will asked if he knew what a Snipe looked like. The man shook his head with a very perplexed look. Will asked for pen and paper and drew a similar design to the proud figure head of his ship.

"What colour do you want it? Asked the man.

"White!" Replied Will.

"You want just a plain bird?"

"No, no. I want it to be surrounded by gem stones. Diamonds if you can manage it."

"You can afford such a trinket?"

"If you can make it before Christmas Eve midday, Yes!"

"The little man thought for a bit. "You will have to let me have money for the stones, because I don't keep that many. I shall have to buy them from fellow Jewellers here about."

"But you could make it for Christmas Eve Midday without fail?"

"Yes!" Replied the man.

The fellow then drew a ring around Will's design so that the bird looked as if it was flying through the ring.

"I'll see if I can get enough diamonds to go round the ring and a small one as the bird's eye. Otherwise I shall intersperse the diamonds with other precious stones."

"That looks wonderful!" Said Will; gazing at the drawing.

They agreed how much the man would need for the Stones and Will went down the street to a corresponding Bank and presented them with a Bill of Credit on his Plymouth Bank. After much discussion in the back of the Bank, the money was finally paid over. Will hurried back to the Jeweller and handed over the amount agreed.

Leaving the Jewellers, he now wandered up the High Street seeking something to give Mrs Kenton. He found a very pretty silk shawl and then sought a present for Mr Kenton. He finally found a star globe mounted in a fine mahogany box with brass corner pieces, which was in good condition, but was quite old.

Now that he was to spend Christmas with the Kentons, Will arranged for Thomas to go back to Snipe so that any signals could be sent straight to the Kentons. Will gave Thomas a hand held compass with a pelorus on top, as used by the Army. It was small and would not offend others. He gave written instructions that a dozen bottles of the finest wine should be sent aboard for the Wardroom with six bottles of Brandy. Craddock would know to allow the crew a double measure of Rum. He had already left instructions that "Wives" should be allowed aboard whilst the ship was waiting to go to the dockyard. This would keep the crew happy.

CHAPTER 35

The following day Mr Kenton arrived as agreed, but not alone. Isabella dressed in a black riding habit with a jaunty black hat sat side saddle on Commander. Behind her a groom led Jasper, already saddled.

"I'm so nosey, I couldn't keep away! I hope you don't mind?" Isabella said; with a challenging smile.

"Couldn't keep her away. Told her farms were boring, but she said she found them fascinating. First I've know her take an interest in agriculture!" Commented Mr Kenton; jovially.

"I need all the help I can get!" Said Will; mounting Jasper.

"You might find you need to let out the stirrup leathers a couple of notches: make it more comfortable." Said Isabella.

Will did as he was told, and did indeed feel that would be a safer option.

Mr Kenton let Isabella lead off with Will at her side, as the street was too narrow for the three of them. They crossed the bridge and headed for Stoke Gabriel's Port Bridge. It was here that Simpson had said he would meet them. Sure enough, after a short wait he appeared from the other side.

"Good Morning. I hope I haven't kept you waiting." Simpson called as he rode his heavy horse towards them. Drawing up alongside and turning his horse. He swung an arm over the horse's head.

"All you now see ahead of you are two tenanted farms belonging to the Estate. The home farm is nearest to the house. I farm that, supposedly for Sir Percy, but really now to keep my family fed. The other two farms are to the north."

The first Farm had quite steep fields going down to the river, but once you made it to the lane the land flattened out. Most of the land was to pasture. A herd of cows contentedly chewed the cud on the field to the south of the farmstead. The farm itself was surrounded by a small wood. Simpson led the way into the farmyard, where an ancient bent fellow shuffled out of a cow shed.

"Morning Walter! All well with you?" Cried Simpson. The old boy knuckled his forehead.

"Aye, Mr Simpson. Any news on the rent?" The old fellow asked.

"Very quiet at the moment. Let's hope it stays that way. Just showing some visitors around the estate."

The old boy waved his hand and disappeared back into

the shed.

"Good farmer. His son helps him and should by rights inherit the tenancy. They supply Stoke and Totnes with a lot of their milk and dairy produce. His fields go on beyond the main lane to the village. I think it best if we go down to the lower lane and then make our way to the next farm that way; if that is all right by you?"

As they rode out of the farm, Mr Kenton commented. "Keeps his hedges in good shape. Sure sign that he tends the land well!"

Simpson nodded his assent. When they came to the bend before the steep hill, Simpson reigned in his horse.

"The farms' lands divide here. The boundary continues to the river." He then trotted on. Will found that using the deep seat; as advocated by Isabella, made it much easier to trot. They turned right and came to the second farm.

As they rode up, Simpson said. "Grows a lot of corn for the mill: keeps beef cattle on the lower pastures. Bit of a difficult character at the moment. Prickly you know, what with the threat of higher rents or being thrown off the land. If you don't mind staying here I shall just make my number and we can go on to the Home Farm. So saying Simpson disappeared through the gate to the yard.

He wasn't long. He came out with a sombre expression on his face. "Poor fellow doesn't know whether to seed or not! Now the Home Farm starts at the crossroads, with land going over to the lane. I used to grow everything necessary for the main house. Now I keep poultry, pigs, some cattle and a few milkers.

"This is where the estate lands end. Everything on the south side belongs to the estate."

"It is very beautiful!" Commented Isabella; who hadn't spoken since they had set off.

"Very muddy too!" Laughed Simpson; seeming to relax at bit.

They turned back and cut up the lane to the village of Galmpton. As they entered the village a clergyman appeared, coming out of one of the cottages.

"Morning Vicar!" Cried Simpson.

"Good Morning to you Mr Simpson. Still no news?"

"I am afraid not. All seems to have gone very quiet."

"I have just been visiting Mrs Dunwitch. Very worried that she is going to be thrown out of her home. This whole business is so unsettling!"

Simpson nodded his head and they moved on.

"I hope you have all the accounts up to date, so that if an offer is made on the estate the Commander would know exactly what the income would be?" Commented Mr Kenton.

"That be as it is now, or as Sir Percy would like it to be?"

"The former!" Said Will; emphatically. Simpson looked relieved. He put a hand inside his coat and pulled out a folded paper.

"I have written out the income of each farm as it was due last Quarter Day." Said Simpson; handing the paper to Will, who put it securely away inside his uniform jacket.

They left Simpson to ride back to Totnes. Once they had left the village they rode three abreast with Isabella in the centre,

"So what do you think?" Asked Isabella.

"So long as the rents are reasonable..., I think yes. Only thing is I haven't an idea what I do next!"

Mr Kenton laughed.

"I suggest then, if it is agreeable to you, that you leave it up to me."

"That would be wonderful....but are you sure?"

"Absolutely. These things take time, and you will probably be at sea, or taken up with the Admiralty. No, my Bank can handle this!"

At Midday on Christmas Eve Will returned to the little Jeweller. The man grinned hugely when he saw Will enter his little workshop.

"Ah! The fine young Captain returns. Well I think you will like this and so will your sweet heart – though say it myself."

He disappeared into the bowels of the workshop to re-appear with a small wooden box coved in green velvet.

"My wife made this for you. She said the brooch had to have a suitable case."

The little man proudly opened the small box and inside lying on a velvet bed sat the most exquisite rendering of a Snipe, wings delineated by fine gold wire. A tiny diamond sparkled as the eye, whilst around the ring diamonds framed the whole.

Will was speechless. It was beyond all that he had hoped for.

"It is incredible. You are a genius. Thank you... and your wife for making such a beautiful object in such a short time."

CHAPTER 36

Retrieving his belongings, now packed in two panniers on a hired horse, Will mounted Jasper and set off for Kenton House. He was particularly careful at observing as much as possible of the two Farms which belonged to the estate as he passed.

He was greeted by Humphreys and a footman when he arrived. Jasper was led off by a groom. Humphreys showed Will up to the bedroom he had been allocated. It had a fine view out to the Bay. A young footman appeared who stated his name was Edwards and he was to be the Commander's valet during his stay. Will changed out of his boots and Edwards brushed his second best uniform jacket.

Will then descended to the Hall and wondered where the family might be. He need not have worried. Isabella appeared from the Blue Room.

"We were told you had arrived, but I couldn't wait! I came to look for you. You alright? Everything alright?"

"Absolutely!" Replied Will; looking around to see if there was anybody about, before giving her a peck on the cheek.

Isabella squeezed his hand and led him into the Blue Room where her parents sat. Kenton shot to his feet and came to welcome Will as Isabella said; jokingly "Look what I found lurking in the Hall!"

Will shook Mr Kenton's hand and went forward to kiss the back of Laura's outstretched hand.

"Come and sit by me." Commanded Isabella; taking her usual seat on one of the two couches.

Will obeyed and got a dazzling smile as he was about to sit down.

"So what have you been up to since I last saw you?" Asked Isabella; but the friendly smile belied the question.

"Researching Totnes. I know it is only a small town, but it has a very fine array of shops to suit all tastes. I hadn't realised that one need not travel far to get whatever one needs."

"Yes it is charming, isn't it?" Laura replied.

"Doesn't seem to stop you demanding I purchase things in Exeter! I swear I spend half my time as an errand boy, when I should be attending to Bank matters." Commented Mr Kenton.

Laura Kenton just smiled benignly at her husband.

"So did you do any shopping?" Asked Isabella.

"Rather window shopping, although I did find a rather tempting Butcher."

"Butcher! The man is a philistine!" Cried Isabella. And she gave Will a friendly poke in the ribs.

The next day Isabella took Will out riding across the Kenton Estate and down the hill to the little village of Paignton and the beach. Here they were able to let the horses canter in the seawater, which Isabella informed Will was very good for them. The sun came out which was a bonus. On the way back they let their horses walk slowly up the hill, whilst Isabella explained in detail what would happen for the rest of the day. Having exhausted that topic, the conversation reverted to their own feelings and hopes for the future.

Isabella had plans for their new home, if they managed to purchase it, which she assured Will her father was very confident about achieving.

"He has influence in the most extraordinary places. You might think that just being a Banker in Exeter would be very limiting, but Exeter is the centre for most of the West Country, which means most of the West Country members of Parliament and Nobles have dealings with the Bank. Of course the Kenton Bank also deals daily with London Banks, so father knows most of the most influential Bankers in the City. That means he has met most of the most influential politicians of both parties."

"So how come I end up being engaged to you? You could have had your choice of the cream of Society!"

"Love Will, love!"

"Then I must remain in debt to Diana, the Goddess of Love.... I am right it is Diana isn't it?"

"Yes!"

Back at the house Will found Edwards and asked if it would be possible to have a bath. Edwards looked extremely surprised, but rushed off to organise things. About an hour later a line of maids and footmen entered Will's bedroom carrying jugs of hot water. Edwards had already dragged a copper bath into the room and laid towels around it. Once the bath was filled and the temperature checked, Will was left to scrub himself clean from head to toe. A hot bath was an indulgence he hardly ever had the opportunity to partake of; being used to washing in cold water from a bucket.

It was therefore a very clean and refreshed Will who descended the stairs to join the Kentons in the Hall to await the guests.

"It is just our immediate neighbours: we'll be twelve in all." Explained Isabella. "The Cottons and their daughter Cecilia. She is a year older than me, but has not Come Out. Her parents can't afford it. They don't have many assets, so

Cecelia has to use all she has got to try and land a man. I might add she has a pair of very outstanding assets, but she is not the brightest; if you see what I mean. She will try and eat you alive....you have been warned. Then there are the Torrs; Lord and Lady Torr and their son the Honourable Archibald Torr. He is something of a dandy. He will be after you as well."

Will registered his surprise.

"His parents are very worried that they will never have a grandson to inherit."

"Couldn't you put the young lady together with the Honourable Archibald?" Asked Will; with a wicked grin.

"I still don't think there would be progeny!" Giggled Isabella. "And a sweet couple Sir Edward Driffield and Lady Driffield. She makes everybody think she is completely deaf. Funny how she seems to know what exactly has been said, the next day. Father tried an experiment. He whispered in her right ear a 'secret'. Then later he told her another in the other ear. A week later she remembered the secret that she had heard in her right ear, but not her left. That is why she has been placed on your right."

And who prey is on my left?"

"A young lady who has yet to be officially spoken for; but who has already agreed to be married." She whispered.

"Ah!" Will rubbed one finger up the side of his nose. "I await that pleasure!"

Just then the Torrs were announced and Will was introduced.

"A sailor! My, we are in luck!" Cried the Hon. Archibald in a falsetto voice.

Will saw the young man's father wince behind him.

Luckily the Driffields were at the door, so Will was able to turn his attention in their direction and did not need to respond. They were closely followed by the Cottons. When Cecelia saw Will her eyes widened, and Isabella nudged Will. She was quite pretty but rather plumper than Isabella and she was well endowed. There was no avoiding them, and they were definitely out to be admired. The dress barely covered them before being tightly drawn below them to accentuate them. She had mouse coloured hair that was arranged in ringlets with a blue bow. Placing herself in front of Will she gave a little curtsy, and said.

"A real live Naval Officer, so exciting!"

"Let's go through to the Salon" Said Isabella; taking Cecelia by the arm and guiding her through the door. Will followed, but found that Driffield stepped in to talk with him.

"Commander Calvert. I understand you were reported in the Gazette recently. Read the letter myself. Fine piece of malarkey! I am myself a Colonel, you know. Late of the 29th. Tell me, do you buy your Commissions as in the Army, or what?"

"No Sir. We have to pass exams. Then it is a question of moving up the Navy List. Of course there are exceptions. Admiral Nelson is one in particular."

"Ha! But he had influence at the start!" Reposted the Colonel. "What about you, young man? You strike me as being very young for your rank!"

"I was lucky. I served on the flagship. Earl St Vincent marked me out."

"Good! That is what I like to hear. Now in the Army, any idiot with money could buy themselves a senior rank. Not much use when you face the enemy! I had to work my way up, as my father could only afford a Lieutenancy. Still it was a good life!"

At that moment, a footman inserted a tray of drinks between them, and the Colonel's wife dragged him away. Isabella appeared at his side.

"Just checking!" She laughed. "So what do you think of the young lady?"

"Too obvious!"

Isabella wrinkled her nose at Will.

The table in the Dining Room had been shortened: leaves had been taken out, but the centre was dominated by a huge silver centre piece with hot house blooms increasing its size. As a result neither side of the table could engage the other easily. The places had little cards with the names of the guests written on them so everybody would know where to sit. Cecelia was very disappointed to find that she was placed on the opposite side of the table from Will. On his right Will found he had Lady Driffield and on his left Isabella. Beyond Isabella Sir Edward sat near enough Mr Kenton to make the conversation flow.

The first thing Lady Driffield did was to turn to Will and tell him in a loud voice that she was totally deaf, so ignore her and concentrate on the lovely Isabella. This suited Will and he found that after the first platitudes Sir Edward spent his whole time facing away from Isabella. This meant they were able to converse for the whole meal virtually uninterrupted.

After the meal they all repaired to the Salon where Cecelia made a beeline for the piano and started to play. Will was no expert, but even he realised that she was not very accomplished.

She first played a couple of pieces for piano which allowed low conversation, but then she started to sing lullabies; she was definitely not in tune. The assembly sat listening politely, but you could sense the strain they were under. Will wondered if Isabella would play, but she remained firmly in her place beside him.

The next day was Christmas Day and all the staff was supposed to have the day off. Will arose early as usual and wondered out by the door to the stables to take a turn on the terrace. There was low cloud which mingled with the fog over the Bay. He breathed in the fresh air and stretched his limbs as he walked backwards and forwards. He knew there would be no riding today. He kicked himself for not having asked what the form was for the morning. He knew they would be walking to the church over the grounds at half past ten. He judged the time to be about seven, but without a clock he was not too sure. He wandered round to the stables and found that the horses had been attended to and were happily munching on fresh hay nets. Making his way back into the house by the route he had taken on the way out, he heard a noise coming from the kitchen. He stopped and had a looked in. A plump maid was humming to herself, whilst stoking the range. She turned and caught sight of him.

"Happy Christmas Commander!" She called out; a wide smile across her otherwise plain features. I'm Polly, can I get you anything. I have a nice fire going in the Breakfast Room."

"I thought all the staff had the day off." Stuttered Will.

"Oh they do! I don't have anywhere to go, so I would have nothing to do. Anyway the Kentons are so good to us, I think it nice to give something back; don't you?"

Will nodded; very surprised.

"What would you like for Breakfast then? The kedgeree won't be ready for another half hour or so, but I can fix you an egg and some nice bacon."

"That would be splendid." A bemuse Will replied.

"Hot Chocolate will be coming up very soon. You just sit yourself down and I'll be in, in a minute."

Will thanked Polly's back because she was already at work on the stove.

Will had finished his breakfast and was just considering his next move, when Mr Kenton entered.

"Morning William. I see Polly has been busy. Always gives up her Christmas to make sure we are catered for. Between you and me, I think she is probably a better natural cook than Cook herself. I expect you'll poach her when you get your place. I shall be sorry to see her go. Always cheerful, yet has nothing really to be cheerful about. Her parents died when she was very young. Laura took her in when she was just twelve."

He stopped as there was a noise from the other side of the door and Polly came sailing in carrying a tray with silver dishes set out on it.

"Morning and Happy Christmas Mr Kenton Sir." Polly said; as she set down the tray on the sideboard and made a small curtsy.

"Morning Polly and a very Happy Christmas to you. And once again thank you for looking after us."

"A pleasure Sir." And she was gone.

"She will now take trays up to Laura and Isabella and think nothing of it." Kenton said as he got up to help himself from the sideboard.

Church was an ordeal. Will sat in the Kenton pew well aware that everybody was gossiping about him. The Vicar seemed to think that he had a captive audience because he appeared to involve every part of the service ordained for Christmas Day. He did all the Collets, Epistles and prayers which seemed to go on forever. When he mounted the pulpit, Will noticed out of the corner of his eye that Mr Kenton pulled out a leather cylinder that looked as if it might contain a cup. What Kenton pulled out surprised Will: it was a miniature timer, similar to those they used on ship. The sand ran through from one glass globe to another. Kenton set this up on the shelf in front of him and settled back. The Vicar glanced down at Mr Kenton and cleared his throat. Each time the sand ran out, Kenton would lean forward and turn the timer over. The fourth time Kenton turned it; he sat back and seemed to go to sleep. His head fell forward onto his chest. Then after a few minutes he started to snore loudly. The snoring became louder, until there were titters from the congregation. The Vicar started to lose his thread, and finally gave up the unequal struggle and stopped, glaring down at the slumbering form just below him.

After that the service seemed to finish quite quickly. Will following his host noticed that the Vicar appeared very strained when he shook Kenton's hand on the way out, but

Mr Kenton appeared not to notice anything.

CHAPTER 37

It was a cold buffet for Dinner, laid out in the Breakfast Room. As they relaxed afterwards, Will whispered to Isabella asking when they exchanged presents.

"Why? Have you bought anything? We didn't think you would have, so decided to not embarrass you." Whispered back Isabella.

"Well I thought that's what one did at Christmas!"

"Yes, Yes, normally."

Isabella got up and went across to her mother who looked as startled as Isabella had.

"Oh that's wonderful. Mr Kenton, kindly fetch the presents." Laura cried.

Kenton looked up with surprise. "I didn't think we were doing presents this Christmas!"

"Well we are, so go and get them; there's a dear."

"Excuse me." Said Will and followed Kenton out of the room to fetch his own.

"You brought something?" Asked Kenton; as he crossed the Hall towards his study.

"Yes. They are in my room."

"We weren't expecting anything you know." Muttered Kenton as he departed.

Back in the Blue Room with the fire made up so it blazed cheerfully they exchanged presents. Then they opened one each in turn. Isabella was reduced to tears when she opened hers. She leapt up and gave Will a kiss and a hug, even though her parents were present. The Kentons had combined to give Will a present. It was a handsome pocket watch, which left him speechless.

Proudly wearing her brooch, Isabella did a twirl round the room and then stopped suddenly.

"Will, can you dance?"

"Never tried."

"Mother, be an angel and play for us. I must teach Will to dance before tomorrow."

They moved into the Salon where Laura took her place at the piano. Isabella placed cushions on the floor to represent the other dancers, then she stood in front of Will and explained the basic steps of the first dance he had ever done.

It was a bright frosty start to Boxing Day. Isabella and Will went for a ride, trailed by the usual groom. Isabella looked radiant in her black riding habit. They spent most of the morning covering the Kenton estate. Then Isabella stated that she was going to rest before the events started.

Dinner was to be later than normal, because the Kentons were throwing their Christmas Ball.

The Salon had the furniture removed with only the couches remaining with their backs to the walls. The carpets were rolled up and removed. The wooden floor polished. Mr Kenton's Library cum Study was transformed into a buffet. The double doors to the Blue Room from the Salon were removed to make a clear space between the two. The Breakfast Room became yet another buffet area. The Rugs in the Hall were removed so that it too could be free for the circulating guests. In one corner of the large Salon a dais was put up and swags of material tacked to the front ready for the musicians.

Isabella knocked on Will's bedroom door and asked if he was ready. Together they descended the main stairs to take their places in the receiving line. Humphreys in his best uniform with gold buttons; took the cards from the guests and called out their names. Each guest either shook hands or curtsied as they passed the receiving group.

Already the hired musicians were playing in the Salon. When all but the laggards had arrived Isabella took Will onto the floor and they danced, joining the line. Will found that the other dancers were only too willing to guide him; if he went off course; with a smile or a laugh.

At first he hated it, feeling that he was making an exhibition of himself; but after a while he began to enjoy it. It was certainly good exercise! In between dancing he found himself being guided by Isabella to meet various people. Many were her friends, but others were obviously introduced as they had influence locally. Isabella never let slip that Will was intending to buy locally, nor that they were about to become engaged.

By the end of the evening when most of the guests had left, Will managed to ask Isabella about when to try and seek her father's permission to approach her with a view to marriage. Isabella seemed to think it was a great joke and told him anytime from the next morning. She had not wanted an announcement to be made that night, because the whole proceedings would have been ruined for both of them. Will could understand the logic, but went to bed a very troubled man. How was he to ask Mr Kenton for his daughter's hand in marriage?

Overnight the weather changed. Heavy rain fell from a leaden sky. Edwards informed Will that Miss Isabella would not be riding out that morning. As Will was finishing a roll filled with butter and raspberry jam, Mr Kenton walked into the Breakfast Room.

"Morning William, not a bad turnout!"

"No Sir! A very amiable crowd, if I might be allowed to be judgemental?"

"Quite so. Thought you did yourself proud; considering you had only learnt to dance the day before!" Kenton said; as he sat with a plate laden with sausages, bacon and mashed potatoes.

"I wonder if I might ask another favour of you, Sir?" Said Will.

Kenton looked expectant.

"I understand that you are travelling to Exeter tomorrow. I wonder if I could beg a ride, as I have to go to London to call on the Admiralty."

Kenton looked very surprised. It wasn't what he had expected at all.

"Certainly! Enjoy your company."

Later Will plucked up courage and asked Humphreys to let him know when Mr Kenton was in his study. It was only an hour later that Humphreys quietly let Will know the master was to be found at his desk. Will went and knocked on the door.

"Come!" Came from inside.

"Hello Will! Didn't expect you; take a pew."

Will crossed to beside the desk, but did not sit down.

"Thank you Sir. There is matter I should like to broach. I know I have not known your family for very long, but you have been extremely kind to me. It is therefore with some trepidation, that I should like to ask you for your permission to, to....err..."

"Ask my daughter for her hand?" Kenton completed Will's faltering sentence. "Thought you were never going to ask! Of course, my dear fellow; the answer on behalf of Laura and myself is - yes!"

Will swallowed hard as his future father-in-law roared with laughter. Will thanked Kenton as his hand was shaken firmly by his future father-in-law.

It wasn't until sometime later that Isabella and her mother came down to the Blue Room, which had been restored to its former state. Will was by himself; Mr Kenton being in his study.

"Morning William. Recovered from last night's ordeal?" Asked Laura; with a beaming smile.

"Just about!"Replied Will; who had risen as the two ladies had entered. Isabella looked questioningly at him, but he decided to play her at her own game. Isabella walked over to the window to look out. "What a miserable day!" She cried.

"Oh! I don't know." Came Mr Kenton's voice from the doorway. I think it is rather an auspicious day. It is not every day that I give my permission for my daughter's hand in marriage."

"Good God!" Isabella stared for a moment at Will. "You asked him?"

Will nodded smiling broadly.

"Oh at last! Now I can give my future son-in-law the hug he deserves!" Cried Laura rushing over and not only kissing Will, but giving him a warm hug. Isabella had in the meantime gone to her father and enveloped him. Then she turned and ran to Will, throwing her arms about him at the same time telling him off for not letting on when she had first entered the room. Champagne was called for, and all the servants told that they too could have a glass.

Will could never remember feeling so happy.

London was muddy and filled with evil smells. Will had been forced to hire a coach to bring him to the City, because he would have had to wait for a week to get a seat on the Stage. Now he paced the waiting room of the Admiralty together with a number of Post Captains and others all seeking some preferment. He had given the Admiralty doorman a large tip, saying that it was a season of good will. Now he waited to see if it achieved anything. He noticed that he was ignored by most of the senior ranks.

Two hours later he was called. This caused something of an altercation, because a red faced senior Post Captain complained loudly that he had been there the day before. The clerk just shrugged his shoulders and stood aside to let Will through the door. As they made their way to Mr Napean's room, the man muttered. "He'll never get a posting with that amount of alcohol on his breath!"

"Ah! Commander Calvert!"Mr Napean said as Will walked in. "Don't bother to take a seat; we are off to see the First Lord himself. Have a good Christmas?"

Will, rather uncharacteristically replied that he had, in that he added he had become engaged.

"Good for you! Anybody we might know/" Asked Napean as they walked the corridors.

"I doubt so Sir. She is a Miss Kenton of Devon."

"Not Banker Kenton's daughter?" Napean had stopped and was searching Will's face.

"Yes Sir!"

"You lucky young man! Not only a very considerable beauty, but she must be one of the most eligible young ladies about. I must tell Lord Spencer."

"Tell me what?" A voice asked from behind them and they turned together in surprise to find that the Noble Lord had just come out of a doorway behind them.

"Commander Calvert is engaged to Banker Kenton's daughter."

"My congratulations, Calvert. Obviously you have taste as well as a flair for getting the backs up of our enemies."

They walked into the large room that was the First Lord's base in the Admiralty.

"Now, got a special assignment for you, since you seem to be able to take that yacht of yours into places where others fear to go!" But it was said with a smile, as his Lordship sat behind his desk.

"St Valery-sur-Somme, we are informed by our agents is a major source of their growing fleet of assault vessels. Your mission is to destroy as many as possible and the resources to build the damned things. I leave it up to you how you mange this, but if you do, I can tell you it will do you no harm at all! Napean here will brief you and give you the necessary paperwork."

"Thank you my Lord."

"And our heartiest congratulations!"

The interview was obviously over as Mr Napean was already making for the door.

Back in Napean's office a servant was sent for to take Will across to the neighbouring building which was the Aliens Office.

"Come back here when you have finished." Were

Napean's parting words.

Will was guided out of a back door and through another rear entrance to the Alien's Office. Here the servant led him up a number of back stairs to an anonymous door. Here the guide stopped and knocked twice, then another three times. The door was opened a crack and a voice asked who the visitor might be. On being given Will's name, the door was opened to allow him in. The servant remained outside.

"Grantly." The tall thin bespectacled gentleman said as he shook Will's hand. "Come through and take a pew."

The second room was larger than the first and furnished more as a gentleman's library than an office.

"Obviously you are trusted by those fellows next door, or else you would not be here. However what I am about to impart must remain a secret... a state secret. We have as you probably are aware a number of agents working for us across the Channel. It is as a result of their efforts that we know what the Frenchies are up to most of the time. St Valery-sur-Somme is as you are probably aware a very small fishing port on their north coast. Strangely it is where William the Conqueror set out from. Anyway we have it on the best authority that they are building a great many of those flat bottomed troop carriers. We informed the Admiralty, and they hummed and erred, then finally the First Lord took an interest and came up with you! I have read the Gazette, so can understand why he should choose you. What I didn't know was that your little ship was badly damaged. How soon will she be ready?"

"I am hoping that she will go into be repaired next week. It should take about a fortnight before she is ready to sail again. However I should point out that St Valery, as far as I know is a very shallow port. I do not have sufficient large scale charts to be able to say if it is possible to get Snipe in and out. Therefore it is not something that can be undertaken lightly."

Grantly leant back in his chair and observed Will carefully.

"I would have been disappointed if you had said otherwise!" He stated. "Our Agents warned us of the perils. Apparently there are shifting sand bars at the entrance. For that reason we have asked for an up-to-date French chart. Not easily come by, I should add. I have every expectation that one will become available, so I should be grateful if you could keep in touch. We shall also keep you posted as to any changes that occur. Just thought I should like to meet you, since Spencer has singled you out."

With that he stood, shook Will's hand and guided him out. The servant was waiting to take Will back to the Admiralty. Will was taken straight back to Mr Napean, who handed him his special papers. These on inspection restated the fact that Snipe was under the direct orders of the Admiralty Board and that no Officer should interfere with her purposes, or try and take her under their command.

"The Admiralty have already set up a system of fast riders to take messages between Kingswear and the Admiralty. We shall await your confirmation that your ship is back on station. I have already sent a signal to the Superintendant of the Dockyard giving your repairs priority." Napean finished.

Will spent the night in London, before taking his hired coach back to Exeter. Here he managed to get a seat on the Stage to Plymouth. Will returned to Snipe to find that she was much as he had left her. A couple of ratings were on the Captain's list for having got themselves senseless over Christmas, so Will gave them extra fatigues as it was Christmas. He also ordered the main brace be spliced, meaning that the crew had an extra issue of rum, to celebrate his engagement. The crew had according to Craddock already laid bets on his coming back engaged or married to the ship's mascot, as he put it.

The next morning very early he had himself rowed across the Tamar to the village of Torpoint where he hired a horse to ride to his step-father's farm. He found the going far easier, now that he had done so much riding, and had benefited from Isabella's instruction. His Mother was overjoyed to see him, and even more thrilled to find that he was engaged. She obviously had not heard of his exploits, so he chose to keep her in the dark, so as to not worry her. He stayed two nights before returning to his ship.

It was Craddock's turn to go on leave, even though he had to travel right up North to see his people. As always there was a mountain of paperwork to deal with, all neatly put in order of importance by the faithful Thomas.

Three days later the signal came for them to go to the dockyard. Once alongside the dockyard crew took over. Because it would be impossible for the crew to stay aboard as the ship would be laid on her side, they were shipped across to a ship-in-ordinary. Will took a room in a nearby hostelry. Once satisfied there was nothing he could do; Will returned to Kenton House and his Isabella for a further week. When he got back he was distressed to find that the wood used for the spliced ribs, was not as seasoned as either the carpenter or he would have liked. He was informed it was all that was available. It took another week before Snipe was finally out of the hands of the dockyard. Her damaged carronades had already been removed to a barge, so they now had to wait for the ordinance barge to return with their replacements. Craddock arrived back the same day as the Carronades finally arrived, together with fresh powder.

CHAPTER 38

It was good to be back at sea, even if the weather was pretty foul. Snipe seemed to relish it as well as she scythed through the waves. Will took her on a course for the mouth of the river Seine. After leaving Start Point on their starboard beam, they headed for the 'Nez Bayard, the north-west pint of the Cherbourg peninsular. Then keeping just over the horizon they headed for Le Havre. They made their land fall just as the Sun decided to come out in the early morning. Turning to run along the French coast following the 3 fathom line they made their way up to St Valery-sur-Somme. As they approached they deviated to the two fathom mark. This meant taking a series of running fixes, which Will was keen that Midshipman Gardner should carry out alongside the two Master's Mates, to give him practise.

Using the most powerful telescopes at their disposal they surveyed the coast and the little port set back up the narrow estuary. The local French fishing boats ignored them as they sailed past. It being low tide it was clear to see how narrow the channel was to the port. There were plenty of mud banks; but very little width to the waterway. When the tide turned they turned to run down the coast as close to the shore as they dared. It confirmed Will's worst suspicions. No gunboats came out to challenge them, but then they were not flying the ensign. The coast south of St Valery-sur-Somme reminded Will very much of the coast south of Dartmouth called Slapton Sands, which gave him an idea.

Back at their mooring in the Dart, Will pondered his problems. How on earth could they achieve their aims? He managed to find Henri de Cornes on one of his late night exercises' walking the quarter-deck.

"Henri, I know this is a lot to ask, but I have a problem I should like to discuss with you."

"If it is about marriage, I am not your man!"

Will laughed. "No it is business. We are supposed to attack St Valery as you know. I am worried that it is too narrow and too tidal. The only way I think one could be sure, would be to take a look close up from ashore."

"You mean land?"

"Yes, but I don't think I could carry it off. My French is not up to the mark. I can't send anybody else because I couldn't be certain of all the facts I need to have at my disposal. Do you think it is even a starter?"

Henri tried to make out Will's features in the half light. They continued to pace backwards and forwards. Finally Henri stopped.

"If we were to both go, then there is a very good chance we could get away with it."

"But that would put you at too greater risk!"

"Nonsense, no more than you. I speak English well enough to fool any Frenchman, so I would just pretend to be a British Naval Officer."

"We could be shot as spies!"

"We could be sliced in half by a French ball the next time. I see no more risk than we put ourselves to each time we engage the French."

"You really think we could get away with it?"

"Absolutely: with your detailed planning, it is more than a 0certainty!"

Will sent a signal to the First Lord. In it he reported that Snipe was once again under command; and that for their first shake-down cruise, they had taken a close look at the entrance to St Valery. He repeated his fears that the depth in the port might not be great enough for Snipe to be able to turn around and get out of the port after any incursion. He therefore proposed that he should undertake a close reconnaissance of the town and harbour himself. He anticipated that he and his Surgeon, a Royalist Frenchman serving in Snipe, should pretend to be agents from Paris come to inspect the progress of the building of the 'landing craft'. To this end he was writing to the Aliens Office to ask if it would be possible for their Agent to provide mounts inland, so it would appear that they had ridden from Abbeville. In the meantime he was going to undertake rehearsals for the landing on the beaches of Slapton as these were very similar to those a few miles down the coast from their target.

The first rehearsals were made during the day. Snipe anchored off the Sands in two fathoms. Her cutters were then sent in with a contingent of marines to secure the beach. Particular attention was paid to noise. For four days they left Dartmouth early in the morning and repeated the landings using different crews to man the boats and interchanging the marines.

Once the marines had leapt off the cutters as they ran up the sand, they dispersed to form two lines either side of the intended landing point but well insight of it. Next they practised in twilight, leaving candle lanterns and strikers buried in the sand for the returning men to be able to signal to the ship. One problem that arose during this exercise was the difficulty of finding the exact spot in the dark. The dropping of fake lobster pot markers helped at sea, but when Henri and Will tried to find the lanterns in the dark, it took them until morning.

It was agreed that a cross should be placed above the designated landing point, but a few yards to the north. The cross would appear to be a religious mark commemorating a drowning.

The lanterns had to be buried above the high water mark, as they would be landing and departing at Spring Tides. To aid the location of the lanterns it was decided to place the remains of a lobster pot two paces to the East.

Will had also written to Grantly at the Aliens Office to ask if it would be possible to have drawings of the apparel that might be worn by Commissioners from Paris. Henri de Cornes had pointed out that they would need tricolour cockades. It was after this that they left Henri for a couple of days in Dartmouth trying to obtain old clothes that might be worn by such Commissioners.

Only after they had spent six nights approaching Slapton Sands and landing members of the crew and retrieving them, did Will feel that they were sufficiently prepared for the undertaking. One of the greatest problems was the navigational aspect of the enterprise. There were no permanent lights along the coast of France to aid them. It was therefore vital that the first approach was made just before the lack of light made it impossible to be exact.

Now that they had completed the first part of the exercise, Will felt it was time to invite his fiancée and her parents to dine aboard Snipe. Because the wardroom was communal, he first asked his officers for their permission. As a result an invitation was sent out, reminding Isabella that Dinner aboard a ship was at about three in the afternoon.

The Dinner was a great success. Isabella was radiant, and her parents extremely gracious. Mr Kenton in particular showed a side that Will had only just begun to appreciate. He had a fund of wickedly amusing stories, which kept the whole wardroom in fits of laughter.

Three days later as they lay to their anchor off Dartmouth Town, a boat arrived alongside from the Kingswear side. The passenger was well dressed and asked for Commander Calvert by name. It transpired that the gentleman had been sent by the Aliens Office. He had with him not only up-to-date charts, but a selection of French made clothes and articles. This was an enormous bonus. The charts proved that Will's fears were correct. The clothes collected from Émigrés were sorted, and tried on by Will and Henri. Henri was to be the senior official, so his clothes were to be of a slightly higher standard than Will's. Both would wear multi-collared capes, very like coachmen's capes, which the officials tended to use. They would both wear leather riding breeches and boots. Henri had a hat with a cockade, nicely faded, to give support to the idea that he was an official from Paris. Will had a cap, a Phrygen cap, much worn by the revolutionaries. Henri was advised to cut his hair short, which was the latest fashion in Paris. Will was to free his hair at the back so it hung down around his head and to make sure it looked dirty and greasy. There were also Assignats, the latest form of revolutionary money and coinage, some dating back to before the revolution. However the biggest bonus was the fact that the gentleman also brought a crude map which indicated the farm where an agent would have a selection of horses available. It would be a five mile hike to cross the flat lands to where the ground started to rise, which was where the farm was located.

All that was needed now as a Spring Tide, a fairly calm sea, and not too much moon light.

It was another week before the tides would be right. The St Valery tidal anomaly had been carefully worked out. Three days before the absolute highest Spring tide, Snipe left Dartmouth to attempt her mission. Spencer Wiggin's Marines had been handed out dark blue coats instead of their bright red ones, and their white piped belts and pouches, had been swapped for plain canvas pouches.

As Snipe approached the French coast in the last of the light, they were faced with the sight of a large number of small fishing boats still out to sea. It was not until long after dark that the sounds from the fishing boats faded and they knew that the coast was clear. The problem was that they had no certain knowledge of exactly where they were. The attempt had to be aborted. Will had extra rope attached to the second bower anchor, and the next night they approached again. There were still a number of fishing boats sitting between them and the shore, but this time they were able to anchor and fix their position. Finally just when they had lowered the cutters and were about to start loading the marines, the clouds parted and they were lit up for all to see. It was obviously going to be a clear night now, so the cutters were retrieved and Snipe hauled up her anchor and went back out into the centre of the Channel.

It was not until two nights after the highest tide, that the clouds came back, and the sea settled enough to make a landing possible on such an exposed coast. The anchor was raised and slowly Snipe crept in towards the land. At the four fathom mark the anchor was lowered. The cutters already in the water were brought alongside and loaded. The marines were divided into two sections. The Larboard one commanded by Spencer and the Starboard by the Sergeant of marines. Will was in one cutter, Henri in the other. Thomas came with a spade to bury the shuttered lanterns and leave the remains of the lobster pots. Able seaman Allwood, who had become Calvert's coxswain, had the cross ready.

In a moderate sea, the cutters silently approached the shore. Directly the prow touched the sand the Marines climbed past the oarsmen and dropped as silently as possible onto the sand to disperse in either direction. A whistle, repeated from the other side, told them that the marines were in place and all was clear. Thomas raced up the beach and climbed the low sand dune alongside Allwood. They then separated pacing the distances needed for the marker and the cache. Once they had returned to the cutters Will and Henri watched as the cutters were turned and pushed out into the waves to return to Snipe.

Will and Henri had a rough idea of where they were, but they had no way of reading the rough map in the darkness. They had spent hours memorising the route. They had to walk about half a mile inland until they struck a cart track. They then had to follow this track for a further one and a half miles to a fork. Here they were to take the right fork and continue further two miles until they came to a wood. Then they were to turn to their left and follow the line of the wood on another track until they came to a remote farm. Here they were to wait in an outbuilding until dawn. Quite why they had to wait for dawn had never been explained. Luckily although it was a leaden sky, with only the faintest sign of moonlight; the rain failed to arrive. It was either luck or good judgement, but the walks Henri and Will had taken to the top of the hill above Dartmouth, now stood them in good stead. It was estimating the distances on land that they found difficult. They very nearly missed the fork in the road, but luckily by keeping to the right they had discovered it almost by accident. It didn't appear to be the most used route. When they finally found the farm and the outbuilding, it was to find that somebody had thoughtfully piled in fresh straw and hay. They lay down and wrapped their multi-collared cloaks about them and settled down for the dawn to arrive.

It was the whistling that altered them to the approach of somebody. The outline of a figure was visible in the opening. It stopped and then said in English. "Good Morning!"

Both Will and Henri got up and crept towards the figure from either side.

"Ha! You have arrived! I was expecting you days ago. What kept you?" The Man had a decidedly French accent, but obviously spoke fluent English.

"Too much moonlight and fishermen." Will said and added "Bon Jour!"

The man laughed. "Good to have you here. I won't ask what you are up to... less known... less to tell!"

When Henri spoke the man responded in French, adding "At least this gentleman will be taken for a Frenchman!"

He led them further on from the farm, which partly explained why they had to wait for the morning. It was a good mile and was through a dense wood. Here they discovered a broken down farm, but in one of the out buildings were six horses of various sizes and colours, munching contentedly on hay nets. It was light enough now for the man to estimate the height and weight of Will and Henri. He picked out a strong looking dappled grey for Henri and a light bay for Will. From another building he came back with saddles and bridles. He left the two to tack up, only to return with worn saddle bags and holsters.

Both Will and Henri carried rough leather satchels, but the saddle bags would be more convincing. They transferred their pistols and writing paraphernalia to the newly arrived French equipment.

It was now light enough to see where one was going; that is if you knew the route. The man explained that to appear to be coming from the Abbeville direction it was necessary to cut inland until they came to a track which ran roughly north-west to south-east. They then could turn east and follow this track to the canal. Once they came to the canal, they should turn left and use the towpath. It would be quite natural for someone to use this route from Abbeville.

It was obviously going to be one of those 'iffy' days. The Sun was being very coy about showing itself, but on the other hand the clouds were high and it could well be that the rain would hold off. Before they left the man told them what to do when they left St Valery. This was a great relief, because they doubted that they would have been able to find their way back.

They walked the first part through the wood, getting the feel of their mounts. Will blessed the fact that he had done so much riding recently. Poor old Henri wasn't so lucky. He hadn't ridden for a considerable time, but it was clear that he knew how to ride. He sat very well.

When they reached the canal it was obvious that there had been considerable traffic along it. The towpath had been cut up by a multitude of hooves. They trotted alongside of the canal until ahead of them they could see the lock gates and just before them a barge which was looked to be in the process of being unloaded. A stack of timber was neatly placed on the far side of the tow path. The un-loaders must have stopped work the day before and would probably return to complete their job. As they passed the lock gates there were more stacks of timber of different sizes. Then there were Caiques in different stages of construction. To one side there was what looked like a giant still. From the top a tube ran down to a long length of canvas.

"Vapeur!" Said Will; quietly, hoping that Henri would understand he meant a steamer. Henri nodded his head.

They stopped at a curious array of poles driven into the ground in an arc. It soon became obvious that these were the bending posts for the steamed timbers. There were different sizes of arc and in the one nearest the village there was still a rib held in place by timbers and wedges against the posts.

Will followed Henri to the quayside, where the tide was out. A Peniche was tied up. From the length of the vessel

Will tried to estimate the length against that of Snipe. The tide was right out, it being spring tides and Will's fears were confirmed. There was very little space to turn a ship the size of Snipe. They sat there on their horses taking in the layout of the small port.

From the houses a soldier emerged and walked over to the quayside, pulled open his breeches and peed into the mud. As he adjusted himself, Henri called him over in a peremptory manner.

"What regiment?" Demanded Henri in French.

"Artillery." Answered the elderly soldier.

"How many of you are in the village?"

The man looked puzzled. He thought for a moment and then said. "Sixteen including our officer. The others are on duty at the Fort."

"Ah!" Exclaimed Henri as if this explained everything. "Where is your officer?"

"Still in bed, I should think!" And the man spat as if to imply that all officers were rubbish.

"No you imbecile, where is he billeted?"

"Oh, the hostelry. It is just up the street...can't miss it."

Henri waved his hand dismissively and the soldier trotted away. Henri was playing his part well. He had that certain attitude that implied he should not be trifled with. Will had understood most of what had been said, if not the detail.

Henri pointed towards the sea, and Will turned his horse to follow Henri through the walled village and out the other side. They followed the track that led them around a muddy bay and then wended back on the inshore side of the promontory. At the end they could see that there had been a fort or earthworks erected. As they approached they realised that although the cannons faced the sea and entrance to the estuary, there was nothing covering the harbour. The entrance to the fort was just a gap in the earthworks on the southwest.

They trotted right into the centre of the fort. An ancient sergeant staggered up from where he had been seated by a fire and came to ask what they wanted. There were five cannons which Will estimated to be probably eighteen pounders. The soldiers were bivouacked in tents, whilst in the centre a huge trunk seemed to do the duty of a powder store. Each cannon had four balls piled beside them. The soldiers emerged from their tents rubbing their eyes and finishing dressing. Discipline was obvious non-existent.

"Yer?" Was all the sergeant got out before being berated by Henri for not being properly dressed and not standing to attention when addressing a representative of the Directory. [The Directory was the new form of Government in Paris after 1795 and the White Terror.]

The man quickly stood ramrod straight. Will slid from his horse and climbed the side of the redoubt. He wanted to see how the channel cut its way through the sand banks at the mouth of the estuary. Meanwhile Henri continued to distract the soldiers.

"Who is in charge?" Demand Henri, ignoring the man and taking a sweeping look around, as the soldiers began fall into line.

"I am." Replied the Sergeant.

"Where is your officer?"

"In the village."

"When do you change the guard?" Henri was now directly addressing the Sergeant.

"In about an hour."

"So how do you manage that?"

"The off duty guard comes here and we change over."

"Will your officer be here then?"

"I don't know. Sometimes he shows up, sometimes he stays with his whore."

Henri nodded.

Will clambered back down the slope and remounted.

"Carry on!" Ordered Henri as he wheeled his horse and trotted out of the fort. Will quickly followed him as they returned to the village.

By the time they arrived back in the village, people were

beginning to stir. Soldiers were beginning to collect outside what was obviously the hostelry from various billets. Henri and Will reined in before the place and handed their reins to a stable lad. They removed their holsters and saddle bags and made their way into the Hostelry.

"Attention!" Called Henri in the dark entrance hall. A barmaid appeared to enquire what they desired. Her dress and person was filthy.

"Food and wine!" Countered Henri. The barmaid indicated a doorway to the right with a nod of her head and disappeared into the bowels of the place.

Inside were dirty wooden tables, with the remains of much of the evening before's, tankards and food. Behind the one clean table in the corner a rotund army officer sat eating his breakfast. Beside him a trollop with her breasts barely covered lent against him and picked food from his platter.

With one sweep of his arm, Henri sent tankards and dishes crashing to the floor. The Officer tried to stand, apprehension written all over his debauched countenance. Henri then sat down and indicated that Will should follow his example. The Barmaid came rushing it to see what was happening. She took one look at Henri and then the floor. She didn't need an explanation, this stranger demanded service.

"Is the food edible?" Asked Henri, without even bothering to pass the day.

The officer gave a strangled assent. The barmaid came back in with a platter of coarse bread and two tankards filled with what smelt like vinegar.

"I said wine! Not this disgusting cattle feed! Take it away and bring me a bottle of your best, or the landlord!"

The barmaid scooped up the tankards and fled.

"Do you all live like pigs in the country?" Demanded Henri; coupling the officer with the locals.

Will doubted if the officer had ever seen any service in the field, as the man seemed terrified of Henri.

"Might I ask...err... if you... don't ...err..object.....who you might be?" The man finally managed to get out with a stutter.

Officials from the Ministry of War, Paris. Come to inspect this God forsaken place.

"You are not...err...mil....itary....then?"

"We eat Generals for breakfast! They taste better than the fodder in this place!" Retorted Henri; leaning back and giving the whore a disdainful inspection. The woman flaunted herself at him. Henri's expression of disgust spoke volumes more than any words.

The Barmaid returned with an unopened bottle and two moderately clean glasses. She then fumbled under her skirts for a cork screw revealing a plump and none too clean thigh.

"I see you have eggs for the Lieutenant, but not for us? How come?" Demanded Henri. The girl bit her lip and fled.

"I am a Majjjj...jor." Expostulated the officer.

Henri just looked at him, and turned his attention to the wine bottle and the forgotten corkscrew. He proceeded to extract the cork and pour a small sample into a glass. This he then held up to what light there was from the window and inspected it, before swirling it round in the glass. His nose came down and loudly sniffed at the contents. He then cautiously took a sip. He made a face; but nether-the-less poured some more into the glass before taking a mouthful. He totally ignored Will sitting at the end of the table.

"You may pour yourself a glass, Citizen!" He said as he leant back once more. Will poured himself a glass and took a sip. It wasn't wonderful, but it was drinkable.

"Err...excuse...err...me." Said the Major and slid out from behind his table and fled the room. The whore stayed to place her elbows on the table and leant her chin on them.

"Take me back to Paris, Citizen?" She said, in what Will supposed she thought was a seductive voice. Henri ignored her. There was a pause and then the Barmaid returned with two platters on which were fried eggs and bacon.

Neither Will nor Henri had much to drink, though they

did finish the food. Picking up their gear, Henri dropped an Assignat on the table and they went out with Henri demanding that their horses should be ready. The soldiers were lined up with the officer talking to a sergeant as Henri and Will mounted their horses. Will indicated with a slight movement of his head that they should head south back to where the Caiques were being constructed.

Henri had taken the hint and when they arrived back at the boat building area called for the superintendant. A little man came bustling out of a nearby stone built hut.

"You the superintendant here?" Demanded Henri.

"Oui Monsieur." Replied the little man.

"How many of these craft are you making?" Henri asked in French

"Ten, at the moment, Citizen."

"Where are your instructions?"

Without hesitation the man shot back into the hut and came out with a roll of plans under one arm and a sheaf of papers that he handed up to Henri.

Henri read them carefully. "You are instructed to build five Peniches. I see no such craft, except for the one tied up at the quay."

"No Monsieur..Citizen... We can't get the right timber for the keels for the Peniches."

"And the rest of the wood doesn't look very well seasoned either!"

"Indeed not Citizen."

Henri wheeled his horse round muttering profanities, or what Will thought sounded like them.

Back on the quay, Will was able to quietly thank Henri in French. He then carefully reconsidered the scene before him. The tide was coming in, but still had a long way to go. The river turned west where they sat on their horses, so that it had been impossible from the sea to gauge exactly what was going on. Now it was clear. On the opposite side tied to posts but resting on the mud at the moment were eleven completed Caiques. At the top end of the quay, before the area where they were building the landing craft, fishing boats were tied up side by side. Beneath their horses' heads, the single Peniche lay tilting slightly away from the quay, but from their higher position of the horses' backs one could see that there were no guns, and in places grass was beginning to grow at the corners of the decking.

Will lent towards Henri. "We shall have to move this thing, to be able to turn Snipe around." And he checked again to make sure nobody was within hearing.

Henri nodded. "Fini?" He asked.

Will nodded his assent, and they turned their mounts and rode back through the village towards the sea. On their way they passed the relief column of soldiers who were certainly not marching in step. Strolling would be a better definition.

Once they came to the sand dunes, they turned west, and followed the line of the shore until they came to a scrubby wood that hid them from the village and the fort. This was where the agent had told them to wait. They dismounted and tethered their horses to trees near a patch of scrub grass. They were prepared to wait for some time. From the seaward side of the wood they could see the cross which was their marker.

It must have been an hour or so after midday, judging from the position of the feeble Sun, that they heard movement. From the landward side the Agent appeared carrying a satchel, with a rug thrown over his shoulder. He dropped the articles on the ground, put a finger to his lips and then checked in each direction that all was clear. Then he came back and said quietly.

"I have brought you some food. Did all go well?"

Will resumed his position of authority by answering. "Better than I could have wished. There is still a problem with the width of the river, but I think at the top of a spring tide we can just about make it."

"Bon!"

The Agent opened his satchel and produced French

loaves, filled with butter and ham. To wash it all down he had brought a flask of Calvados Brandy.

After they had eaten, Henri asked. "What's with the rug?"

"Ah! That is to throw over the grey. It will be less conspicuous. That is if anybody is bothering to take a look from the church towers around here. On this side of the Somme there is less risk. The other side is teaming with soldiers. The nearer you get to Boulogne the more there are. On this side you have to be nearer to Dieppe, before it becomes more militarised.

"How often do they change the men at the fort?" Asked Will. The Agent laughed. I have never known them to do so. The fellows there are the Ancients. They are of no use anywhere else. Certainly not for landing on an alien shore!"

In the middle of the afternoon, the Agent left riding one horse and leading the other, now rugged up. He left heading in a south westerly direction. Will and Henri settled down to wait.

Before it got too dark they were relieved to see the outline of a schooner out to sea. The problem would be the fishing boats. Since it had been high tide at about half past one in the afternoon, it would be low tide again at about half past eight that evening. From what they had observed, it seemed likely that all but the smallest craft would have to be back in port by around seven that evening. Even the most knowledgeable fisherman would have trouble finding the entrance to the estuary if the moon did not come out. Will prayed that the heavy cloud cover would continue.

The two stood in the cover of the wood and watched as it got darker, then quite suddenly all the fishing boats seemed to make a bee-line for the port, a few going the opposite way as if to Le Tréport.

The retrieval went as planned and rehearsed. Will and Henri dug out the lanterns, lit them and held them one above the other, making sure the shutters allowed the light to been seen only on a narrow arc out to sea.

Once back aboard Snipe Will made sure he drew on the chart, the route that a vessel should take to enter the Port. By the time his command had dropped her anchor in the Dart, Will had completed reports for the First Lord and for the Aliens Office. In his report to the Admiralty he set out his plans for the destruction of the Caiques and the timber in St Valery. He planned to take Snipe up to Dittisham to start rehearsals for the attack, but before they moved he had himself rowed over to Kingswear and hired a horse to ride to Kenton House.

Isabella was out visiting, but he received a rapturous welcome from Laura Kenton. Will explained where he was taking his ship and invited the Kentons to dine aboard, if only they could get to the landing stage at the northwest of Galmpton Creek, from where they would be able to see Snipe and be seen. It transpired that unfortunately Mr Kenton was in London, so the ladies could hardly come alone. A disappointed Will retired to his ship.

The rehearsals that were undertaken on the meadow to the west of Dittisham Village were the carrying of barrels. To burn the Caiques and the timber, it would be necessary to douse them liberally in oil. Wood was collected from the woods around and piled as neatly as possible. Then with the little oil they had been able to obtain in Dartmouth, they experimented on the best methods.

It would take some time for the Admiralty to respond to Will's missives, so he had himself rowed over to the landing stage he had told Laura about, and walked the two and a half miles to the Kenton Estate. This time Isabella was there and they were able to spend most of their time together.

CHAPTER 39

By the time the Admiralty had responded and approved Will's plans the window of opportunity had passed. It would be another month before the tides were at their highest and there was a New Moon. In the mean time Snipe was ordered to proceed to Plymouth and take on another ten Marines as Will had requested. He needed the extra Marines to provide cover at the Port, whilst his own marines occupied the Fort. They were also to load the necessary small barrels of oil and igniters.

Once back in the Dart, Will continued to pay frequent visits to his fiancée. They decided on a date for the wedding the next year in the hope that they would have a home to move into. Unfortunately, the word was that the Baronet had won some money and now didn't want to sell the estate. Mr Kenton didn't see it that way. The Baronet owed money left right and centre. What neither Will nor Isabella knew was that Kenton, through third parties, was buying those debts. It was only time before the addiction would make it inevitable that the Baronet would find himself in a position where he had to sell, like it or not.

Spring was giving way to summer, which made the attack on St Valery more difficult. It had to be at the period of the New Moon, so there was as little light as possible to reveal a landing, whilst the tide had to be as high as possible to make it feasible to turn Snipe around in the harbour. To make sure that the crew did not become lax, Will took Snipe on frequent cruises along the French coast. They paid particular attention to the waters off St Valery.

Finally the time came, and with the extra marines making things cramped aboard the schooner, they set off to try and achieve their aims. They were off the port three days before spring high tide. The problem was that with the longer daylight, the fishermen were out even later. Finally Will had to call off the landing as there was too much light. The troops on the Fort would have been able to see a landing along the coast and raise the alarm. The next two nights were similar, but then the clouds began to form, which also brought more wind and a more boisterous sea.

They crept in, picking out the buoys they had left. In two fathoms they dropped the anchor, and the cutters, which they had been towing, were brought alongside. Spencer Wiggins and his marines were embarked and taken ashore. Once the cutters returned, Snipe hauled up her anchor and waited for daylight. It had been arranged that the Marines would signal the ship if they had been successful in capturing the fort. They would then have to wait for the soldiers from the village to march down to the fort to be ambushed by Spencer's marines. Snipe would not approach the entrance to the estuary until that had been achieved. From out at sea, they watched the marines form up from the wood and march along the track above the sand.

Wiggins led the red coated marines straight into the fort without hesitation. The soldiers in the fort were caught completely off guard. It took some time for them all to be tied up, but finally the British flag was displayed over the rim of the fort so that Snipe's crew could clearly see it.

Still they waited until at last they could see through their scopes the relief column of soldiers for the fort shambling along the track to the fort. They disappeared from view. Again there was a considerable wait; then the flag was once again displayed.

Snipe under reduced sail made for the entrance to the estuary. To avoid the sand banks she had to turn virtually opposite the place on the shore where they had landed the marines, then run parallel to the shore a mile out gradually reducing the distance until the end of the promontory was due south. Inshore of the promontory someone had driven withies into the mud on either side marking the channel. Following these they sailed slowly up the channel until it virtually met the land. Here the channel ran right alongside the western side of the estuary until it turned to reveal the quay. The cutters were being towed behind but as they rounded the bend one was manned on the larboard side. Once Snipe approached the same Peniche tied up to the quay, the cutter was cast off dragging a warp from Snipe. This was then fixed to one of the stout posts that had been driven into the mud on the eastern side of the channel, where the Caiques were tied up.

Once alongside the Peniche, the remaining marines used the French vessel as a launching pad to get to the quay. Here they dispersed to arrange themselves in a defensive arc around Snipe.

They used whatever they could find to hide behind; crates, barrels and stacks of nets. Snipe's own Corporal led two of the marines in a run for the lock to the canal to stop anybody leaving or approaching from that direction. Once the marines were ashore, the Peniche's warps were removed and she was dragged forward along the quay. Now Snipe was able to secure her stern to the quay and the capstan was manned. Gradually they hauled her bows round until she was facing out to sea. Then the cutter took another warp from the larboard bows to the quay. Now the designated members of the crew were able to swarm ashore carrying their barrels of oil and the igniters. Led by Kemp and Gardner they could be seen ducking under Caiques and wood piles. Boatswain Tarrant with a boarding axe made light work of all the bending posts.

Gradually a small crowd of bemused French started to appear from the village, only to duck back when they saw the marines with their muskets levelled at them. The Superintendent of the boat building was marched out of his hut by one of the crew and then unceremoniously pushed into the small crowd. He soon realised the reason, his stone hut exploded, sending tiles and masonry high into the air. Fires were now blazing all the way from the canal lock back towards Snipe. Then more reluctant villagers appeared, including children. The marines who had taken the fort were now systematically clearing every house in the village on their way to the quay.

Standing on the quarterdeck Will finally observed the French 'Major' being prodded forward on the bayonet of the marine sergeant. Wiggins soon appeared carrying an extra sword that Will supposed had belonged to the man. Now the marines from the fort were close at hand, Will gave the order for them to rejoin the ship. From further up the quay, he heard Tarrant's bark and soon the outpost marines and the crewmen who had been setting fire to Caiques and wood fell back and climbed aboard. Now it was the turn of the marines who had formed the defence ring to work their way back until they were able to camber aboard. Their retreat covered by the swivel guns and the carronades.

The sails were hoisted, the warps cut and Snipe quietly began to leave the port following her route in. On her way out the starboard carronades fired their heavy balls almost point blank into the moored Caiques. Splinters of wood were flying everywhere.

As they passed the fort they could see the Major galloping on horseback towards the fort. Spencer turned to Will with a grin. "He will find all his troops neatly tied up! He can't fire any of the guns, they have all been spiked!"

CHAPTER 40

Twenty five miles off Cherbourg, the lookout called down that there were two frigates closing each other almost dead ahead. He could not at that distance tell the nationality.

Snipe was under full sail, as Will wanted to get back to the Dart to report; and to see Isabella again, if he was really honest with himself. *Snipe* was at her best point of sailing, carrying unusually top-staysails above the gaffs of both the fore and mainsail; making well over ten knots. A quarter of an hour later the new lookout reported that there was smoke, and immediately they heard the rumble of cannon fire from across the water. The water gurgling in the scuppers, *Snipe* raced towards the pair of frigates. Even at this speed it would take them an hour to reach the frigates. Now from the quarterdeck they could see through their telescopes, that the nearer frigate was slightly bigger than the one further away. Both were on a parallel course exchanging fire at extreme range. Soon they were able to make out the French flag flying from the mizzen gaff of the bigger frigate. As they watched they could clearly see that the Frenchman was out sailing the British frigate.

Snipe's gun crews hadn't needed to be called to their stations, they were there. They knew what Will's tactics would be. They had been successful in the North Sea; there was no reason why they shouldn't work here. The sails were reduced as they came nearer the two ships. *Snipe's* ensign had been lowered: they weren't going to announce to which nation this strange schooner belonged, that seemed to want to get close to the action.

As was normal the Frenchman must have been firing high at the rigging, because the British frigates fore-topmast tumbled into the sea, dragging the ship round. Now the results of the enemy gun fire could be seen to be inflicting damage to the upper-works of the British frigate. The British ship was still firing and at a slightly quicker rate than the Frenchman.

Allwood at the wheel of *Snipe* knew exactly what to do. Will brought his vessel round in an arc, so that she was at last pointing straight at the stern of the Frenchman. He was risking his ship if the French had stern chasers. Through his scope he carefully checked but could see no sign of them. He left it up to his bow gunners as to when to fire. Allwood stood to the larboard side of the wheel so he had a clear vision ahead. Nobody aboard the French ship seemed to bother about this strange 'yacht' that was coming up fast astern. Then the larboard bow chaser opened up. The gallery windows at the stern of the Frenchman disappeared.

Allwood gave a slight twitch on the wheel and the starboard cannon added its load to the first. It had been as usual loaded with ball, and it must have mostly gone through the hole made by the larboard gun. Now *Snipe* turned into the wind, sheets flying as the starboard carronades came into range. Carefully each one added its damaging load onto the target. The last two carronades were angled to aim at rigging and were loaded with chain shot. Their destructive power became only too obvious. The Frenchman's mizzen sail collapsed, bringing down with it the mizzen topmast. Canvas covered the stern of the French frigate as *Snipe* turned away and brought her stern chasers into action. This time they were moving away and the distance was greater. The balls seemed to skip across the water for the last bit, but they still had the power to damage, as the French frigate began to turn towards the British frigate.

Now the British frigate had the advantage. She was firing at the unprotected bows of the French frigate. Will turned his schooner through 360 degrees, so she was able to sail slowly back towards the French vessel. Suddenly Snipe seemed to shiver. Cries went up that she had been hit. There was no telltale smoke from the starboard side of the Frenchman, which meant that they must have been struck by friendly fire.

"We are taking in water fast. The carpenter is doing all he can." A voice called up from below.

"Get the starboard hammocks below immediately!" Shouted Will above the mêlée. He could hear the pumps being manned. The Carpenter appeared through the stern hatchway.

"I think we might need a sail pulled round on the outside, Sir"

"Mr Tarrant." Will turned to see the Boatswain already dragging canvas across the deck assisted by a group of seamen.

"Number One, see if you can get as many of the larboard carronades free from the deck and over to the starboard side." Will commanded. The carronades' base was bolted to the deck, unlike normal Cannons.

Luckily they were on the larboard tack, so the area where the ball had hit was not permanently under water. If he took in sail though, the angle of heel would be less, and they would scoop up much more water.

A top-man ran forward with a rope and crawled out along the bowsprit to feed the rope back under the Martingale to the other side. Then a spare fore-topsail was attached at its head and hauled under the hull. Then it was made taut with tackle. The Carpenter came up with a thin batten, which one of the crew sitting in a boatswain's chair nailed through the sail to the hull. Later, as *Snipe* was clinker built, another member of the crew was lowered over the side to ram oakum and wax into the spaces between sail and planks.

Snipe was still taking in water and the pumps had to be manned constantly, but the immediate danger of sinking seemed to have receded. There was no way that *Snipe* could continue the action, so they set a course for the Isle of Wight and ultimately Portsmouth. Will chose Portsmouth because his ship would be running before the wind and not having to sail too close. As night fell they were able to just make the bay off Benbridge on the Isle before it got too dark, it being a New Moon. Here at anchor, the pumps were manned all night.

It wasn't until late the next day that they finally limped into Portsmouth Harbour and ignoring protocol sailed straight up to come alongside a fifth rate tied up alongside the dockyard quay. They were at the north end of the quay, and Will had to plea with the First Lieutenant of the fifth rate to allow him to tie up against his ship, as there was no other space. The fifth rate's Captain was ashore. Gardner was sent off in the Jolly boat to apologise to the Port Admiral and explain the head-long rush. Will himself crossed the fifth rate's deck and went off in search of the Dockyard Commissioner and the Master Shipwright. Neither seemed to think that a mere Schooner warranted much attention, until Will pulled out his commission and pointed out that it came direct from the Board of Admiralty and that he reported to the First Lord direct.

Having sent off his reports to the Board, Will went back to his ship and had the first sleep he had managed for four days. Refreshed he wrote a letter to Isabella with the masterly under-statement that *Snipe* had had an 'accident' and needed a bit of repair. It took two long weeks before anything happened. All the while the ship's pumps had to be operated twenty-four hours a day. This meant that there was very little sleep for most of the crew, until they became immured to the noise. Finally instructions came that *Snipe* was to be repaired as a matter of priority, which caused a bit of a stir in the dockyard. By this time *Snipe* had been warped around the corner of the quay and lay isolated in the creek. Will was summoned to London at the same time. He had to leave Craddock to supervise getting the ship into one of the docks which became free.

In London Will was kept waiting amongst the hopefuls, despite a large tip to the gate-keeper.

Finally at the end of the second day he was taken up to the Secretary to the Admiralty Evan Napean's office. Napean did not look up as Will was announced; he continued to finish reading from a file. Will stood waiting until the Secretary finally looked up.

"Ah! Calvert. come with me." So saying he got up and led the way to the First Lords Room.

On entering Will realised Lord Spencer was not alone. Sitting to one side was Lord St Vincent with another gentleman on the other side. To the rear Grantly from the Alien's Office sat in a chair by the wall. Will bowed to each gentleman and waited.

"Commander Calvert, thank you for coming. Sorry about the wait. You know Jervis and this is Rear Admiral Gambier, a member of the Board. Mr Grantly you have already met.

Pray be seated, this is not a formal review. I have here in front of me two different reports. The first is your extremely detailed report on your attack on St Valery. Gentlemen, I should advise you that the Commander previously landed with a Royalist French Officer and made a detailed reconnaissance of the Port. It was a meticulously planned attack, which is why, in my opinion, it was so successful. Unfortunately the Aliens Office has asked us not to make this known to the public. I understand it could put our agents at risk. However, Calvert, the Board is only too aware and cognisant of the favour you have done this nation. The King himself has been informed.

Now to the second report. This gives another minute by minute summation of the Schooner *Snipe's* attack on a French Privateer that was engaging a British Frigate. Unfortunately, Calvert, I have another report from the Captain of the frigate that fails to mention that your schooner was in anyway involved!" The noble Lord stopped and waited for a reaction from Will. Will chose to not say anything, though he was seething inside.

A slight smile played on Spencer's lips.

"The said Captain has influence at Court and in the House. Admiral Gambier was kind enough to interview the Captain."

Lord Spencer turned to Gambier, who looked extremely solemn. He cleared his throat.

"Not what I would call the gentleman's finest hour! Before interviewing him, I took the opportunity of speaking to the captured French First Lieutenant. He was very explicit! He stated that they were caught out by the intervention of an audacious schooner that seemed to be able to fire her guns with uncanny accuracy from the bows. He had never come across that before. He went on to say that the French Privateer, because you were correct in your analysis it was a privateer out of St Malo; thought they had caught up with and were about to take the British frigate, when suddenly this schooner destroys the ship's steering and causes considerable slaughter on the gun deck. The Privateer's Captain was killed by one of the schooners carronades." Gambier stopped to see what effect this news was having on Will. Will tried hard to not show any feeling.

"It was only when the privateer was incapacitated that the British frigate turned to attack instead of trying to run away...his words not mine! He also stated that he could not understand why the British frigate was aiming some of her guns high. He was of the opinion that the enemy frigate was trying to hit the schooner. I had all this taken down, word by word. The man had nothing to lose, he is a prisoner."

"I then faced the said Captain, and demanded to know why he was risking his reputation by not acknowledging the debt he owed to the schooner that came to his assistance. By the time I had finished with him, he was in no doubt as to his options. Either resign quietly; or face a Courts Martial. He chose the first option. He has resigned his commission on the grounds of ill health. He and his crew will receive the Prize Money that is due. You and your crew will of course get yours." Gambier looked to Lord Spencer.

"Commander Calvert, I know you are an honourable man, so I take it that we can assume that the matter will go no further. The Gentleman, still has influence, and a discreet silence on your part will I am sure benefit you in the long run."

Will nodded his assent. He had nothing to lose.

"We shall have a new commission for you directly your ship is ready for sea. I shall await your signal."

Will took it that the meeting was ended. He stood up, bowed to each of the gentlemen present and turned to leave the room. Napean fell in beside him.

"I think you will agree that the matter has been handled with consummate diplomacy." Napean said as they walked back along the corridor.

"It could have turned very nasty for you, if you had pressed a case. The man is unscrupulous in trying to get his own way. The French Lieutenant was convinced he was trying to sink your ship. Now if the Captain says anything, he will have only himself to blame."

On his way back to his lodgings Will realised that neither the name of the Captain or the ship had been mentioned. He knew the name of the French privateer, but on consideration he realised that the Board were in essence protecting him.

Isabella was extremely disappointed when she received Will's latest letter. She read between the lines that the wedding would have to be delayed. She took the letter with her when she went to find her father. She read him the parts that mattered, not the parts where Will expressed his love and desire for her.

Kenton sat back and regarded his daughter. "What he has not told you, is what is cognisant here. I have it on the best authority that your William is regarded very highly at the Admiralty. What he has not told you is that he went to the aid of another British ship that was being attacked and managed to bring about the surrender of the French ship. That was how he had a 'little accident'. Now for reasons I can't go into, that is a secret. His new assignment also comes from on high. In fact direct from the First Lord himself. Again it is very secret, which is why he can't tell you anymore. I have been assured that your William has been marked out for higher command."

"All I want is for him to come back to me safely! Why can't that retched Baronet hurry up and sell! At least then we could have a home."

"He will, he will. But we must all be patience. Just wait and see."

CHAPTER 41

Snipe was still not ready for sea, but she was looking more like her old self. She was warped out of the dock, her sides freshly painted. They had a new Midshipman aboard, Gardner, whose connections meant that he was to go forward for his Lieutenant's exam. The officer who replaced him was an experienced older gentleman, previously in the merchant trade, who would be taking his exams very soon. Kemp had asked to have his exam for Lieutenant put back as he wished to stay with *Snipe*. Word had been brought back across the Channel that the young Corsican General Bonaparte was in charge of the invasion plans. This might have explained the upgrading of the defences around Boulogne. Certainly there was now field artillery in place at the mouths of the few places where the French were able to keep their assault craft.

Elsewhere, mutinies the year before, at the Nore and Spithead had passed the Schooner by: the crew knew about them, but thanks to Will's largesse, the crew had good food, good and adequate clothing, as well as a pride in their ship. Just as *Snipe* was ready to go to sea, Will was summoned back to the Admiralty.

Will had expected to be kept waiting at the Admiralty, but was surprised to be shown straight up to His Lordship. He was met by a group of gentlemen sitting around a table. Lord Spencer explained that he was not going to introduce the gentlemen present, because half of them spent their time in France. Grantly at the far end of the table gave Will a smile of recognition. Will was invited to sit at the table, and there followed a long discussion about the possible invasion. Will sat and listened politely until he was asked to give his impression of the boats the French had constructed for the invasion.

"Well frankly gentlemen, I would not want to cross the Channel in any of them, especially the flat bottomed troop transports. They are likely to fill with water in any seaway. The larger vessels, such as their Prams and Chaloupes could carry the horses. If there is a wind it is going to be very difficult for them; if it is calm the soldiers will be exhausted from rowing before they get to the coast. The problem the French have is that they must protect any invasion fleet, and frankly I consider that we are more than capable of making sure they never get ashore this side in any number. They have gunboats of various sizes, but the gunners will not be used to their weapons at sea."

There was no applause, not that Will had expected any, but there was much nodding of sage heads.

"The problem as far as we are concerned is knowing when the French attempt to start an invasion." The First Lord stated.

"Excuse me Sir. I would have thought that was fairly obvious. They must bring round the various boats and ships from all along the coast. They could be seen on a good day from Dover." Will was more confident now, but still surprised that they should have brought him in, rather than all the Admirals and Captains available.

He was soon to find out. It transpired that besides patrolling the channel, the powers-that-be wanted *Snipe* to land and extract agents to and from the French coast, and to carry messages backwards and forwards. Their reasoning behind the proposition was that of *Snipe's* speed and manoeuvrability, which had been noted by their Lordships. They considered her an ideal vehicle for such nefarious goings on. The reason Will had been brought to London, was so he would recognise any of the gentlemen around the table. There need be no questions asked.

The meeting went on for a couple of hours, during which Will began to understand the extent that the English had penetrated the French Government machine. As a lowly Commander, Will kept quiet, even if he would have had something to say.

At the end of the meeting, he was asked to wait. No refreshment was brought, and Will thought that he had been forgotten. Finally a servant came to take him to Mr Nepean's office. Here he was invited to sit down, whilst Nepean read a file in front of him. Finally the Admiralty Secretary, put down the file and gazed at Will.

"Been a busy fellow in the short time you have been stationed on the French coast. It has not gone un-remarked. This new venture is a sign of how we value your performance. It is a tricky business, you will have to decide on a new small home port – we leave that up to you. I shall have to know where you have chosen, as we shall have to set up a relay system to get the agents to London as quickly as possible. So it has to be somewhere where there are roads and be within easy reach of London! I have been informed that your senior Midshipman Kemp has now served sufficient time to take his Lieutenant's exam. The problem is, do we give you a new Midshipman, or do we increase the number of Lieutenants you carry. I have discussed this with their Lordships and they are of the opinion, that your ship will need all the experienced watch-keeping officers it can accommodate. That being the case - I suggest that Kemp is temporarily released, for the exam, and returned to you; whether he passes the exam or not. At present Jenkins is not due for the exam so he can stay – as long as you are satisfied with him."

Julius Jenkins was Gardner's replacement.

Nepean consulted his notes. "I understand that *Snipe* carries two cutters – one of which you purchased yourself. The Admiralty will refund you the cost of the cutter, as you will need two for your operations. I know that this means you are less likely to achieve the same level of prize-money already due to you again in the foreseeable future, but we desperately need to be sure that our agents get in and out successfully. In the past we have chartered mostly Luggers to do this work, but they are not Naval vessels, nor are their crew. The opportunity for bribery is very great. So are offers of drinks and entertainment – you take my drift? Tongues can be easily loosened. We have already lost two agents, as a result of information; we believe was given to our enemies."

Nepean gave a wan smile. "We know we can trust you and your crew!" He added. Then he pulled out a sealed letter which he passed across to Will.

"That is a letter to the Port Admiral, Portsmouth, instructing him to supply a replacement Lieutenant from his own staff, during Kemp's absence. Now I wish you well. I hope that you settle for a home port very quickly. Immediately you have done so, send a message to me. Good luck Commander." And surprisingly he put out a hand to shake Will's.

It was late, so Will put up for the night at the 'Swan with two Necks', and in the morning took the Mail to Portsmouth. On arriving at Portsmouth, he immediately went to see the Port Admiral to deliver the letter. Although it was late, the Flag Lieutenant confirmed that the Admiral was still aboard and took the letter. Will paced backwards and forwards awaiting the outcome. Ten minutes later, the Flag Lieutenant reappeared. "Commander, I am instructed to report to you tomorrow morning. I trust you won't mind my being sent as the replacement for your Midshipman. I must say both I and the Admiral were mightily surprised by the contents of the letter. You see we are a bit short on active Lieutenants, who would be available at such short notice and for so short a time. I volunteered. I have to admit I have heard of your reputation, and that of your fine schooner."

Will was very surprised. The Lieutenant must have been higher up the list than he had been when he had been made a Commander. A Flag Lieutenant offering to serve, how-be-it for a short period, was most unusual. The fellow seemed very keen and was grinning hugely at his own cheek.

"I am honoured; I look forward to you joining us tomorrow. I take it that Kemp should report here in the morning?"

"Oh, yes!"

The Flag Lieutenant showed Will over the side.

The next morning saw the departure of Mr Kemp, to be examined for Lieutenant, and the arrival of the Hon Archibald Bracken, late Flag Lieutenant. That afternoon *Snipe* sailed to seek out the most suitable 'port', which would be convenient for the North Coast of France, and suitable as a base, with easy travel to London. Before they had left, Will, Craddock, McKay, Fairley and Bracken had indentified which places they thought might be suitable.

Dover was ruled out as being too public, as it often held ships of the Channel Squadron.

Rye was a possible, but the mouth silted up badly.

Newhaven, seemed to be the best as far as convenience was concerned, as it had breakwaters either side of the entrance. It was more of a merchant port, with flour mills, and even ice houses, in the quarries. It also had, according to Bracken, whose family came from near Lewes, an adequate road system.

Shoreham, was really too far to the West, as was Chichester Harbour.

The Channel was fairly beneficent, the wind blew from the south and the sea was relatively calm. They sailed past Southsea village and taking advantage of the tide, popped into Langstone Harbour to have a look around, before they were back in the Solent again. Next it was Chichester Harbour, which had the same problems as Langstone, in that there was nowhere suitable to transport supplies to the ship, or for that matter, agents.

Littlehampton could not be approached except at high tide, Shoreham was a possible, but only as a fall back. They followed the coast along the low lying sandy beaches, until they came to Shoreham. Here they put *Snipe* in through the narrow entrance. Once a significant port, it had suffered from the inroads of the sea. *Snipe* anchored there for the night, but directly the tide was favourable next morning, departed.

After the small town of Brighton, the cliffs began to rise. The wind had veered and had dropped to a light breeze. To their larboard, the cliffs dropped down to sea level quite quickly, and there were the breakwaters to Newhaven. The channel was quite narrow, but navigable. Here it would be easy to tie up alongside the wharf. The Harbour Master in his little boat was alarmed, when he realised that *Snipe* was an English Navy ship. He didn't have many of them come a calling! He thought that they had come to land a Press Gang to take the young men from the town. Will was called to negotiate. He had to promise on the Bible that they were not there to do that. It took a lot of persuasion by Will, with veiled threats of intervention from on high, before the old boy agreed to let *Snipe* use the quay. When it was explained that she would be using the Port as a base, the harbour master was again in a state of panic.

"What about the merchantmen who use this port?" He asked.

Will assured him that *Snipe* would only use the quay when necessary; otherwise she would turn around and anchor near the swing bridge, fore and aft.

"What about payment?" The old boy asked.

"We are at war, you know! We are here to protect you. If you would rather that the French came a calling, well...."

"No, no, of course! Silly me, what was I thinking? I could lay you some moorings, if you are going to be here that often. I have some spare chain, so they would be very secure."

"That would be very kind. Why don't you come and join us for a noggin of rum, when you are ready?"

That sealed the deal. Snipe stayed tied up to the quay. Bracken was sent to use his 'diplomatic' skills to find a rider to take a message to London.

CHAPTER 42

Wiggins set marine sentries on the quay, to ensure that none of the seamen tried to go 'absent without leave'. It was also necessary to prevent the 'ladies' from around, jumping aboard to offer their services to the frustrated crew. Will realised that it might be an idea, when they were in port, to allow a few hand-picked women to come aboard to service the crew members. He therefore consulted the ever patient de Cornes. The Surgeon agreed to inspect the women, so long as he wasn't expected to take advantage of their services. Will ordered the sailmaker to construct a canvas screen forward, so that it might prevent any fighting.

The Hon Lieutenant Bracken, far from being scandalized, greatly approved of the idea. However there was an added problem Will had realised. The Lieutenant was sharing a cabin with Midshipman Jenkins. Bracken had assumed the position of 2nd Lieutenant without a murmur, although he was obviously senior to Craddock. Will called for the carpenter and together they inspected the wardroom area. It was agreed that a simple screen could be erected athwart ships under the companionway. Temporarily the midshipman would sleep in a hammock, until there was time to construct a new single bunk in the old cabin, and move the twin bunk structure to the new cabin.

The Harbour Master, after a fill of naval rum, for which he received a heavy beating from his wife, had the moorings set the next day. There were two buoys so *Snipe* could moor fore and aft. *Snipe* was towed by her boats out to the moorings, much to the discontent of the crew, until they learnt that women would be allowed onboard, each time they returned to this port. The Surgeon took over part of a warehouse, where the ladies were able to apply for permission to 'come aboard'.

Will waited for a reply from London, which came five

days after they had first arrived. They were to await instructions. Will gave the nod, and the first ladies prepared aboard; with much cheering and ribald remarks from the crew. Craddock had arranged a system of drawing lots, so there would be an orderly progress to the forward screened section.

That night, the jolly boat, which had been tied to the quay for the very purpose, ferried a swarthy gentleman across the river to *Snipe*. He came with a sealed letter for Will.

In the privacy of his cabin, Will opened the letter, whilst the 'Gentleman' sat in the wardroom next door, drinking wine. The letter instructed Will to take the 'Mr X' across the Channel to a certain point. There would be a reception party who would show lights in a 'V' formation, using the surrounding cliffs. There was a small sandy bay, 1½ nautical miles north of the little hamlet of Audresselles. They were to pick up another agent when landing 'Mr X'.

The time for the rendezvous was between midnight and four in the morning.

Snipe left Newhaven at a reasonable time in the morning, at the start of the forenoon watch, as eight bells were sounded. The time was eight in the morning, giving enough light for a safe departure, after the 'ladies' had been put ashore. The wind had got up and was blowing fairly strongly from the southwest. They had four hours before the tide would turn in their favour. Will calculated that they would be off Cape Gris Nez at about midnight, when the tide would turn against them. Because this part of the coast close-in was new to them, they ostentatiously sailed north a few cables off the French coast flying their now well used 'private' ensign. All telescopes available were used to seek out any likely marks that would be available to them in the dark. Audresselles village had a church, which would have been a good mark by day, but at night was useless to them. However it was to be hoped that at least one or two lights might be seen, which would give a rough idea of the village's position. If there was too much cloud, the very faint moonlight that would be available, might just give the possibility of making out the edge of Cape Gris Nez. It was as a result of their rehearsals off Slapton Sands that they resorted to their old system of dropping a few lobster pots with buoys. Bracken could not believe that they had come up with such a simple but brilliant idea. The lobster pots, complete with bait were anchored off where they needed to drop the Agent. *Snipe* then sailed on past Cape Gris Nez, so as to not arouse suspicion. In the falling light, they then turned as if heading for the North Sea. Directly it was dark enough, they turned about and set a course for the buoys. This was going to stretch all their navigational skills to the limit. Will had all the officers work out their own estimated routes and times, and then compared them. What they did know was that the buoys were at 3¼ fathoms, a cable's length off the bay. Either side the depths were considerably greater, so that was an extra pointer. The cutters were swayed out a good mile off the coast. Men were sent aloft with old cloth normally used for burnishing the brass-work, to wrap round the blocks, and grease for the sheaves. As normal the yards were already lowered and bound to their respective masts. With the wind to the southwest and it having eased as the night drew in, they were able to coast towards land.

An allowance had to be made for the tide, but according to all their records, the tide was virtually slack at this time, so close to the shore. Either side in the forward shrouds, the leadsmen kept heaving their leads, but instead of calling out the depth, they signed it by laying fingers across another seaman's palm, who passed the word down the line in a whisper. It was like looking for a needle in the haystack trying to find their buoys. Eventually an eagle eyed lookout whistled, and the word was passed as to the angle on the bow. A kedge anchor was lowered gently into the water. The jolly boat was lowered and brought round to lie alongside.

Will had no intention of putting the Agent ashore unless

he was absolutely certain that there were no French troops waiting for him. Spencer Wiggins with eight of his marines dropped down into the larboard side cutter, where seamen already sat waiting. The marine sergeant with a further eight marines dropped down to the starboard cutter. The marines were wearing their dark blue coats instead of their red ones. Then they rowed for the shore, their rowlocks padded and greased. There would be no shouting. The marines had been practicing bird calls, so as to be able to signal to each other. The cutters took shuttered lanterns, with a green glass inserted on one side, so as to be able to signal to *Snipe*. It was half an hour into the new day, when the first lantern's green light could be seen. This was closely followed further down the coast by another. Will said goodbye to the Agent, who carefully lowered himself into the Jolly boat, with a rope round his middle in case he lost his footing in the dark. The Jolly boat was commanded by Will's coxswain, Allwood with his crew. Suddenly a 'V' of lights showed in the area between where the green lights were evident.

Sometime later the Jolly boat returned with a different Agent aboard. A rope was passed down and the coxswain tied this round the agent, who then had to scramble up the side of the schooner. Will quietly welcomed the newcomer aboard and had him taken below to the wardroom. The cutters returned and once the marines and crew had been retrieved they were streamed astern, the Jolly boat already having been raised on the stern davits. The kedge anchor was hauled up, and the sheets hauled in. *Snipe* gradually gathered way and set a course for England.

It was early morning when *Snipe* nosed her way into Newhaven Harbour. She went straight to her buoys. The Agent, who had been given Craddock's bunk to rest in during the night, was rowed ashore in the jolly boat, with Bracken to assist him. Bracken led the man to the local staging Inn, where he roused the coachman, who had been sent from London for this very purpose. Horses were led out and attached to the fast curricle. Bracken watched as in the early morning light the Agent was whisked away.

Snipe lay to her moorings, and harbour duty took precedence. The decks were holystoned, rigging checked, sails aired and repaired, whilst below the carpenter continued work on the transformation to the wardroom. A small cabinet was added for the Agents next to the new one with one bunk, but no storage.

Here they waited for a week before a curricle returned with a sealed order for Will.

Again it was the same rendezvous, but this time to collect two agents. The same time for the pick-up had been agreed, but this time there would be no 'V' form of lights. The same routine was undertaken, but this time they dropped lobster pots in a line either side of their original buoys. They had had some problems with the local Newhaven fishermen in buying the pots, because the fishermen thought they were going to take their catch. It was only when Craddock showed them a corked and sealed bottle with paper inside, and they were told the pots would be used for leaving messages close to the French shore, were they mollified. They carried out the same procedure with the cutters and jolly boat as before and successfully took off the two agents.

This became the norm. They would await instructions, race across the Channel, and deliver or pick up agents. Will had become worried about always using the same pick-up point. He sent a letter to London, suggesting that they be given a number of points where the pick-ups could take place, but that it was essential that they had time to carry out a detailed reconnaissance of the areas, before being told which place.

Nepean replied a few days later agreeing to the idea in principle, but saying that the present small bay would have to be used until the agents had come up with alternatives. So for the next three months, *Snipe* crossed an average of once a week on her clandestine activities. Will wrote every week to Isabella, but he had to be very restrained in details of his activities. She wrote back equally often, in the most amiable manner. She had suggested in one letter that she and her mother might try to stay with acquaintances that lived near Lewes. Will had written back that it was a great idea, but because of his duties, he was unable to leave his ship even for an hour or two, being on-call at all times.

The shuttle service continued, not without its problems. The weather was not always kind, and both landings and retrievals had to be aborted. There was the occasional skirmish with the enemy, usually gunboats. It was also very tiring as they were constantly under strain. Finally a letter from Nepean arrived containing a list of bays and beaches chosen by various agents. There was a comment at the end in his usual terse way, pointing out that some of the descriptions were to say the least – vague in detail. Will had a conference of his officers where they all spread out the charts and tried to identify each chosen location. Most of them were either side of Cape Gris Nez; obviously because this was where the agents were used to travelling. There were however some that were further south of the town of Boulogne. This part of the coast was dominated by white cliffs, with the occasional creek or file breaking them up. Each of the named places had a very rough description in French. Will didn't like too narrow defiles, as it would be impossible to put Spencer's marines in ahead to secure either side against surprise, if the location had already been discovered.

It was now the end of February, with frequent bad weather, which meant that they sometimes had to keep returning to the bay on consecutive nights until the agent turned up. However in the first week of April, a letter came from Nepean, saying that there was a week in which there were definitely not going to be any requirement for *Snipe* to transport agents, so instructed Will to research each of the suggested landing sites and code them with a letter.

Snipe was beginning to suffer, she had been almost constantly at sea in all kinds of weather, and she was beginning to look and feel her age. Cordage was fraying and constantly having to be replaced, the sails were ripping as the seams gave way. The ship's hull was beginning to leak badly, meaning that the pumps had to be manned almost constantly. Will had written to the Admiralty informing them of the deterioration, but there had been no reply. He had even added it to his reports to Mr Nepean.

Snipe set out on the hazardous expedition to review each of the places on the list. They started with a bay just to the north of Cap Gris Nez, which turned out to be a possible, but overlooked by the headland. It provided more shelter than their normal bay from winds from the southwest and west. The bottom though was more dangerous. Further north still the bottom had been unkind to a number of ships in the past, and would be impossible at night. So they turned their attention to places south of the port of Boulogne. This meant slipping past the port at night well out to sea, as the French had begun to anchor a row of gunboats of various shapes and sizes off the port. They would have to tack against the prevailing wind, so they put out to the centre of the Channel, and sailed west until they could turn and head for Cap de la Hève just north of Le Havre. Then a few cables off the cliff lined coast they made their way back north. Saint-Jouin-Bruneval was the first gap that they approved of, followed by a beach and gap just south of the village of Ètretat, which was hidden from view by a cliff projection with a strange keyhole in it. And so the list went on, with suitable locations being given their code letter. The small gap near the village of Vattelot-sur-Mer was given the letter 'G', which was out of sequence, in case any letters were to fall into the hands of the French.

They deliberately avoided anywhere too near a port where the French navy could secrete a brig or a few gunboats. When they came near to places like Fécamp or Dieppe, they sailed out away from the land until they were hull down. Then they would sail back in to continue their survey. The weather was holding up for April, with a bright sunshine, but a cold wind. As they worked their way north the wind began to veer round to the northwest, and the speed increase, making it perilous to be that close to the cliff ranged shore. They indentified about half a dozen places that really suited them, before hauling off and returning to Newhaven, before the wind and waves got up to a near gale.

CHAPTER 43

The locations on a chart and their letters had been sent to Mr Nepean, and gradually more agents began to use the different locations. Once more they were going backwards and forwards across the Channel, without respite. As summer came, the seas were mostly kinder to them and their approaches to the coves were easier. However the longer daylight hours, gave them a shorter time span in which to make their runs in and out. In the middle of August they had delivered an agent to one of the landing spots south of Dieppe, when they discovered at dawn that there were two French ships, a Prame and a Chaloupe appearing out of the gloom. It would have satisfied the crew to immediately rush in and take them on, but Will had more important factors to consider. He had no clues as to how important the Agent might be, but he had to protect him at all costs.

The two French vessels turned to confront *Snipe*. The schooner was not responding so quickly to the helm after all the time at sea. Two to one were far too greater odds. Will cleared for action, but told his crew that they would have to try and avoid the enemy if at all possible. The wind was fresh from the west, which was a point in favour of the French.

Running before the wind was their best gauge, where as *Snipe's* was sailing close hauled, which she could do, but it meant sailing towards the oncoming enemy. A broad reach was needed, which held for a couple of hours, but the French were slowly and remorselessly gaining on the schooner. *Snipe* turned to put the wind on her quarter, so she was heading more for home. Still the enemy pressed on. It would have to be a confrontation after all. Will surveyed their position; he made up his mind and ordered *Snipe* to come about. There was a cheer from the crew as they smelt action. Now they were plunging into the sea, and spray was being thrown up over the crew each time the bows shovelled up the water. The guns were still covered by their tarpaulins, but soon they would have to be removed.

The two Frenchmen were sailing in a close formation, with the windward one slightly ahead of the other. Now *Snipe* was racing towards a face down. The leading Chaloupe fired first, her bow mounted cannon throwing chain shot at the schooner, obviously trying to wreck her masts and rigging. *Snipe* was bows on, and the shot narrowly passed her side. *Snipe* was still heeling at an angle, which normally would have made firing impossible, but with her cannon rails, Will felt he had to risk it. The order was given and first one and then the other of her forward facing cannons barked. One was loaded with chain shot, the other with canister shot. It was some time since the crew had fired in anger, but their self control and discipline showed. The foretopmast of the Chaloupe slowly collapsed over the side, dragging the ship to starboard and into the path of her consort. Will brought *Snipe* up into the wind and the carronades fired before the French crew had realised what was happening. This time it was normal shot. As *Snipe* came across the wind, the stern chasers fired canister shot. The French though were now in a position to return the compliment as *Snipe* tried to race away. The shot was as usual for the French aimed high. The mainsail was ravaged; the maintopmast was struck, and looked in danger of falling, which would have put *Snipe* entirely at the mercy of the Prame which was now coming round the bows of her ally.

Boatswain Tarrant, had the top-men up in a flash, to grab hold of the severed stays and tie on new lines, which were swiftly secured. Craddock had the spare Main attached to the hoists that they kept attached to the peak and throat of the gaff and the tack and clew of the boom. This meant that they could hoist a new sail without having to lower the old one. It was this device that saved them, because with the new sail drawing they were able to begin to creep away, but not before the Prame had placed a few well aimed balls into the stern and larboard quarter of the schooner. The jolly boat was flotsam, the wardroom windows smashed, and who knew what damage had been done to the wardroom and cabins. Another shot demolished part of the larboard bulwarks. Will turned *Snipe* before the wind to allow her starboard side carronades do their duty. The highly trained gun captains didn't fire a broadside, each one waited until he had the perfect aim. The heavy shot tore away the enemy catheads, and her bower anchors either side dropped like a stone, dragging the ship to a slow pace. Gybing round, *Snipe's* reloaded bow-chasers put bar shot into the enemy rigging. Will allowed the larboard carronades have their say with canister shot. After a complete circle *Snipe* turned for home licking her wounds. It wasn't only the ship that had suffered. One seaman was dead, and five had been injured. By a stroke of luck, the cannon ball that had entered the wardroom had finished up a spent force against the base of the mainmast, but had not done very much damage. De Cornes had been in his cabin getting his instruments out, so had only had a splinter wound, which he patched himself.

The Agent had been lying in his bunk, trying to keep out of the way, and had witnessed a ball pass his head by inches to lodge against the hull, after it had glanced off the mast. The Carpenter reported that some of the hull planks had sprung, and that every time they heeled to larboard, water came in faster than the pumps could remove it. Will ordered

Craddock to have the powder stores battened down to try and prevent the powder getting wet, and so useless.

Bracken, with his eye to a scope reported that the two enemy ships seemed to have given up the chase. Then the reason became obvious, the lookout hailed the deck to report an English frigate. It must have responded to the sound of cannon fire, and was fast approaching over the horizon.

Will would have liked to have made for Portsmouth for much needed repairs, but the Agent had to be got to London fast, and the curricle would be waiting at Newhaven. *Snipe* limped into Newhaven as the sun was setting. Instead of trying to come to the buoys, Will laid her alongside the quay. The Curricle was summoned, the Agent sent on his way, but he also had a quickly scribbled report from Will boldly stating that he was taking *Snipe* round to Portsmouth the following day. Any messages should be forwarded there.

Early next morning *Snipe* edged out between the breakwaters, and turned to tack her way along the coast to Portsmouth. As she passed between the forts on either side of Portsmouth harbour mouth, a sailing skiff met her with the harbour master's aide. *Snipe* was sent to a buoy up the harbour to await further instructions. Bracken asked if he could be rowed across to the Flagship, which Will agreed to immediately. He had to get a complete report written up before he visited the Flag.

An hour later Bracken returned with a Lieutenant, who turned out to be a beaming Kemp. Bracken was to return to be the Admiral's Flag Lieutenant. Dinner that day was a boisterous farewell for the Hon. Archibald Bracken and a welcome return for the newly elevated Lieutenant Kemp. The Wardroom was a mess, but they had managed to save the table top and place it on a couple of sea-chests. One bench was supported at one end by an empty powder barrel. Will didn't drink more than a toast or two, as he had to report to the Admiral. He already knew that Bracken had paved the way. Just as he was about to descend into one of the cutters, a boat arrived alongside with instructions from the flagship, for *Snipe* to proceed immediately to the main basin.

The cutter was employed to turn the schooner round, rather than transport Will, and under reduced rig they made their way down to the entrance to the naval basin of the dockyard. Horses were tethered to either bow and slowly the schooner was dragged into the basin. Warps were used to haul her round to lie alongside the west side of the basin. Immediately the Admiralty Master Shipwright appeared on the quayside, complete with clerk to take notes. He was soon joined by others, who discussed what they could see, before filing aboard and introducing themselves. Soon *Snipe* was crawling with foremen and shipwrights, eagerly discussing what needed to be done.

Will watched as the dockyard force went about their inspection. Then a messenger arrived for the Master Shipwright, who read it, looked up at Will, grimaced and then came forward.

"Had a signal, via that new fangled telegraph, from London." He paused dramatically and then said. "Instructed to carry out only essential repairs; and to get you back to sea as soon as possible. Comes right from the top... I think, because it says 'Spencer' at the end."

Will groaned aloud. "She needs a bit more than that! We have to man the pumps at all points to the wind, except running. My Carpenter keeps nagging me with new problems virtually every day."

"I commiserate, but orders is orders!"

So it was a quick patch-up job. The shipwrights swarmed all over the schooner. New windows were fitted to the wardroom; the bulwarks repaired, and new stays attached to the mainmast. The riggers said she needed new shrouds, but there was not time to replace them. The leaking timbers were repaired by the expedient of attaching lines to the two masts at the trees, and hauling *Snipe* over onto her side against the quay. Only badly damaged timbers were replaced. Then shipwrights in punts placed canvas patches over the offending areas, and tarred them.

Will was horrified, but his complaint to the Port Admiral was rebuffed. Three days later *Snipe* was hauled back out of the basin, and made her way back to the buoy. Here Hoys arrived with victuals, and then ordinance barges laid alongside to replenish her powder and shot. The next day the patched and battered apology for the elegant schooner slipped out of Portsmouth Harbour at first light and returned to Newhaven.

There were letters awaiting them at Newhaven. Isabella had written three letters, all expressing her affection and describing life in Devon. There was yet another letter from Will's Bank explaining the difficulties they were having in trying to tie down the Baronet to a sale of the Estate. The man kept changing his mind, and making ridiculous demands. They suggested that Will give up and try to find another estate. The next letter was in a strange hand, and turned out to be from Mr Kenton. In it he wrote that he had learned of the obstructions raised by the said Baronet. He had taken it upon himself to make enquiries in London and elsewhere. The fact was that the Baronet owed money everywhere. His wife refused to have anything to do with him, and had instructed lawyers. It would only take a small debt, other than a gambling debt to put the nobleman in the debtor's prison. Kenton had taken the precaution of buying such a debt for a modest amount to help his future son-in-law. He had sent a strongly worded note to the Baronet, informing him that if he did not repay the debt, papers would be served. He had also managed to locate a close friend of the Baronet, one of only a few left, to nudge him to sell the estate quickly at a reduced amount. He understood the Baronet had kept raising the asking price. Kenton now awaited the outcome. There was no mention of the plight of his daughter, engaged to a man she never saw.

Then there was the usual dreaded sealed order from their Lordships at the Admiralty. Yet another pick-up.

CHAPTER 44

It was now early September, and the nights were drawing in. The rendezvous this time was letter 'K' the beach and cove near the hamlet of Criel-sur-Mer. As usual they laid their buoys during the day then made their approach at nightfall, slightly from the south of the location. There was a bigger village called Tréport up the coast, with fishing boats, which might also harbour a gunboat or two. The bottom was sandy, but on a direct approach there were shallower areas, some with rocks indicated on the chart, although with the schooner's comparatively shallow draft, they were not a hazard. With the tide there was little problem in putting *Snipe* a cable or so off the beach. Hatches cloaked, lights in the wardroom forbidden, until the shutters were safely in position and wadding pushed round the edges, they crept in. This was Kemp's first visit as a Lieutenant this close to this part of the shoreline of France. He had poured over the charts, but it was still going to be a nightmare to hit exactly the right part of the coast. Everything was by estimated calculation once the light had gone. There were no lights, other than a few which luckily sprang up around Tréport They were very dim, and you could not be a hundred percent certain that they were actually coming from Tréport, and were not French fishermen out catching fish at night by lantern light. It was all down to soundings once again.

As they closed the shore, the moon came out between the scudding clouds; the sea state was just within limits. They realised that they were facing blank cliffs. The question was, were they too far north or south? They turned to run parallel with the coast, but it proved to be the wrong way.

Unfortunately the moon had disappeared behind the clouds again. This time they had to put out further to sea to be able to tack. On each tack that took them towards the coast, it seemed they were faced with sheer cliffs. There was no way that Will was going to risk getting too close. He ordered the cutters to be lowered, and sent Masters Mate McKay inshore in one of the boats.

At last there came the hooded signal, they were looking for. They estimated it to be about 4 cables south of their destination. *Snipe* edged up the coast until she was off the lantern light; then dropped a kedge from the bows. Without the Jolly boat, the agent would have to be brought out in one of the cutters, which would then have to return to take off the marines. McKay returned to the ship and Spencer took his place with his marines, as per normal, and the two cutters rowed for the beach. There they waited. The hours slowly ticked by. At last Will got his group of seaman to do their impression of a frightened flock of seagulls through the speaking trumpets. The green lanterns flashed acknowledgement, and a few minutes later the cutters were back alongside. Just before the first hint of light, *Snipe* was hull down in the Channel. It had been an abortive exercise. They would now stand off the coast and return the same time that night. Again nobody turned up, so they had to stand-off and try again the next night. Again the same thing happened, there was no show. Reluctantly Will took *Snipe* back to Newhaven to send a report to Mr Nepean.

The trips across the Channel and the deployment of agents went on to the end of the year, with the weather getting worse and worse. Will was really worried about the condition of his ship, but his appeals went unheeded. There always seemed another agent to be transported. Whenever there was the time in Newhaven, the carpenter and his aides would try their best to replace patches of canvas and cover them with tar. Agents often commented on the battering the little ship took as it traversed the unfriendly seas. Many were violently sick, or bruised from being thrown around. It wasn't only the ship that was suffering; the crew were getting increasingly tired from the almost constant strain they were under. Often twice a week they were creeping in close to the enemy shore, half expecting artillery to blast them out of the water.

Will did get a Christmas present; at long last the Baronet had given in and signed the papers. The estate in Devon now officially belonged to him. Isabella sent him a charming painting of the house, which she had painted herself, and had framed. It now hung in Will's cabin, alongside the miniature he had commissioned of the lady in question.

For Christmas Day, Will managed to get the good shopkeepers of Newhaven to supply him with an adequate range of fresh meat and vegetables to give the crew a special meal. The officers carved the various joints for the crew, and many toasts were made. The day after Boxing Day, they were at sea again, fighting a freezing Northerly gale. Any landing on the coast of France was going to be virtually impossible. Instead of approaching the coast after dark, this time Will took *Snipe* in during the late afternoon, to witness breakers crashing against the small beach which had been chosen. He hoped that the Agent in question would perhaps be there already and see that they had at least tried. It was a long and tiring haul back to Newhaven. The crew had been ordered to stretch lines fore and aft on either side and laterally across the aft deck. In inclement weather Will had laid down strict rules that everyone on deck, officers included, had to be attached to a line by a short piece of rope with a bowline knot around the waist of the man, with another round the line. This had saved quite a few of the crew from being washed overboard in bad weather. The deflector in front of the binnacle and wheel had proved its worth. It stopped at least half of the water soaking the two helmsmen. Even with their canvas overcoats and hats, the crew were soaked to the skin within minutes of arriving on deck. In such weather Will instituted a very different routine. Nobody was allowed to stay on deck for more than half-an-hour. Since hot drinks and food were impossible, small tots of Rum, helped to restore the circulation.

Will wondered if Mr Nepean had ever been to sea, as his pleas were falling on deaf ears. He took the risky strategy of writing to Lord Spencer the First Sea Lord, explaining the risks they were being forced to take, and the likelihood of a disaster, if *Snipe* could not be repaired.

Still they were being ordered to sea, still the weather was appalling. Twice the cutters were swamped, and it was extremely lucky that nobody drowned.

In the middle of January, a signal arrived saying that *Snipe* would be relieved of her duties at the end of January for the time that it took to make good the necessary repairs.

It was the second week of January; *Snipe* was carrying an Agent for rendezvous 'W', which was a small sandy break in the cliffs just down the coast from the village of Yport. As usual the cutters had gone in with the marines to secure the area. The new Jolly boat, bought by Will from his own funds, was waiting to take the Agent ashore. Will was worried because there was a freshening on-shore wind. Everybody was waiting impatiently for the green lanterns, but there was no sign of a light.

Suddenly there was the sound of a shot being fired, followed almost immediately by a ripple of musket fire. There was nothing that *Snipe* could do to help. If she fired her guns, she was as likely to hit her own as any enemy. They couldn't send in reinforcements as both cutters were ashore. There was only the Jolly boat. The firing continued in spasms. The wind was blowing in the wrong direction to be able to hear any voices. The wind was building and Will had to make the painful decision to order the sails to be sheeted in and for them to sail out the kedge anchor. Just as they began to move round, another stronger gust forced *Snipe* on her beam ends. The sound like a small explosion from forward was unexplainable, but the schooner was not responding to the wheel. Will ordered the kedge rope to be cut, but that did not help. Men came piling up from below shouting that water was rushing in. *Snipe,* now broadside to the wind, was relentlessly blown towards the beach broad side on. Will ordered the crew to grab any musket and cutlass they could lay their hands on and to be ready to jump when the ship struck. It came sooner than expected, there was a grinding sound, and the whole ship shuddered. Then they were lifted to be thrust against the sand again. *Snipe* was well and truly aground. Waves were now building on the windward side, but on the shore side it was still possible to get the crew to swing out on ropes and drop on the beach. Will waited until the last of the crew were ashore and then followed them. The firing had quietened down, and now there was only the occasional shot. Will sent Craddock and Kemp to explore either side of the cove to try and locate the marines. The Boatswain was whispering in the dark the names of the crew members to check if everybody was present.

The Carpenter sidled up to Will, though how he knew it was his captain, Will didn't know.

"The timbers gave way up forward. Patch must have come off." He whispered.

"Thank you." Replied Will, but without any satisfaction.

It seemed like hours, but it was probably only about half-an-hour later that a limping Spencer Wiggins found Will.

"Ambush!" He muttered.

"You all right?" Asked Will

"It's nothing, just a scratch. Couple of my boys took a bit of lead, but I think they will live. The buggers have run off, but they are sure to be back with reinforcements."

"Boatswain, did our guest get off?" Called Will; quietly.

"Aye Sir!"

"I am here Monsieur. " The Agent said; a few feet from Will.

"I suggest you get going. Go up to the right to gain

height and then make your way inland. Make sure you keep below the skyline. Good luck!"

"Merci! I am sorry about your ship!"

Spencer Wiggins formed the marines up in a double defensive ring facing inland. A break in the clouds allowed the moon to reveal the plight of their stricken ship. She was being bumped up the shelving sand with each wave. Soon the tide would turn and leave her stranded. Whilst she was still on the move, Will did not want his crew endangered by letting them back aboard.

At first light it was possible to see that the water had retreated leaving *Snipe* high and dry. The carpenter went back on board and returned with his tools and balks of timber. They had lost one kedge anchor, so Will had the cutter stood by to take out the remaining one to be used if they were given enough time to try and refloat their ship. Will had a firkin barrel of rum brought ashore, so that the crew could at least have a drink to warm them up. The carpenter and his crew could be heard working away on the far side of the ship. Will walked round to view the damage, as soon as the water was low enough and there was enough light. There was an added problem though, that made the carpenter's work probably useless. The starboard side, the side she was lying on, was also damaged, and would have to be repaired before she could be floated. This would mean somehow lifting the ship. Normally Will would have had the kedge rowed out and dropped with a long line attached. Tackle then would have been connected to the masts to haul the ship up so timbers could be inserted to hold her. With the wind still making the waves break, the cutter would probably be tossed over and the kedge lost.

There was no sign of the wind abating as it grew lighter. Wiggins' lookouts reported movement inland, but were unable to tell if they were troops or not.

Soon after nine o'clock, it became obvious! Mounted

men could be seen riding in formation. The cavalry were on their way. Will ordered each member of the crew to retrieve any small item that was particularly precious to them. There was no point in making a stand; they were eventually going to be overrun, whatever they did. Will went round talking to each member of the crew, thanking them for the loyalty and preparing them for the ordeal to come.

Wiggins ordered his marines to stand in a line and then to place their muskets on the ground in front of them. A white tablecloth from the wardroom was attached to an oar and raised, so that it could be clearly seen. Will looked round and realised that there was no sign of de Cornes. He had done the smart thing and melted away. Will ordered all the crew to not mention the Surgeon, just as a rider appeared in the gully. The horseman approached slowly, his horse sensing the fear was shaking his head, eyes wide. Will had expected an officer, but this fellow was obviously a sergeant. He drew up about a hundred yards from *Snipe's* crew.

"Anglais?" He shouted, eyes darting from side to side, as if afraid of being shot down at any moment.

"Oui!" Replied Will walking forward, arms outstretched each side, so the man could see he was not armed.

The man looked past Will to *Snipe* lying on her side behind. His jaw dropped and he looked really puzzled.

"Restez la!" He said and turned his horse to canter back down the defile that led away from the beach. After a moment or two he disappeared amongst the trees.

"I should sit down. I think we could be here for quite some time." Said Will to the crew in a matter of fact manner.

"Mr Tarrant, I suggest that the crew return to the ship and make sure they have proper footwear and that they bring warm clothes and their foul weather gear."

The Boatswain organised the crew into small groups to each collect their things. Will went over to his officers who were sitting close up under the cliff.

"I suggest you collect your things now whilst you can. James would you mind supervising my boat-cloak, razor, oh and the miniature of my fiancée, please. I better stay here in case anybody shows up."

CHAPTER 45

About half-an-hour later, the Carpenter came over to Will. "I been back to have another look-see at the hull. There is no way I could repair it, even if I had all the time in the world. She be sprung either side."

"Thank you Mr Warren, I came to that conclusion myself. Trouble is - it looks as if the replacement timbers were not properly seasoned. I shall put in a report, if I ever get the chance. You did everything you could to keep the poor lady going. The irony of it is; we would have been going into dock on our return. I had finally been given permission."

"Dear Lord!" The Carpenter exclaimed. "We wasn't supposed to, were we?"

Craddock came up with Will's boat-cloak over his arm, and a canvas bag-like object.

"Mr Tarrant organised the sailmaker to tear canvas squares, so that the men will be able to carry their things over their shoulders. This is yours. I am afraid that the miniature has gone."

"Gone, it can't have!"

"Well I searched everywhere, I took the liberty of checking your sea-chest – the catch was open – but no sign of it. Your sextant, celestial-globe, pistols, and clock have all gone as well."

Will shook his head. Nobody but the crew had gone aboard, and he was certain that none of them would have gone aft to the wardroom, or for that matter have stolen his possessions.

"Henri has taken his instruments, I looked in his cabin."

"And no sign of Thomas?"

"None, I am afraid. I asked around. One of the crew admitted he had seen three men disappearing along the beach to the south."

"Well, all I can think of is that Thomas must have taken the things with him, but why the miniature?"

"He must have had a reason." Commented Craddock.

"I suppose so: Thomas is no fool. I had hoped to sponsor him as a Midshipman. I still don't get the reason for the miniature."

"Perhaps....no, but on the other hand...perhaps he took it so he could find her."

"Find her?"

"Yes, if he went with the Surgeon....... Henri probably had a plan.... otherwise Thomas would never have left you. That must be it; Henri probably knows how to get back to England. The Agent would know anyway. Henri couldn't afford to be caught; he would have been shot or guillotined. Thomas has taken your instruments so they won't fall into the hands of the French. I bet Henri will send him down to Devon to seek out your lady. With the miniature, he would be able to find her quickly, identify himself, and let her know what has happened, and that you are still alive."

Will stared at Craddock for a few seconds taking in the information.

"I think you are right! That has to be the explanation."

Will patted Craddock on the back and strode over to the Boatswain.

"Everybody accounted for, Mr Tarrant?"

"Aye, Sir!" Tarrant knuckled his forehead." Save for the Surgeon and your servant Tucker."

"Ah yes, I know about them, don't worry. Perhaps you might ask the cook if it would be possible to rustle up some cold food for the crew." Added Will; surveying his men.

Tarrant looked around for the cook and then walked over to where the cook sat with other members of the crew.

It was not until mid afternoon that the French

reappeared. This time it was a badly dressed officer, on a broken down nag. He was alone and approached with the utmost caution. He reined in his horse and using his finger to point at each member of the crew he counted them. He did not say a word. He wheeled about and trotted away. There was another long wait for the crew, with the clouds building again, and rain started to come down. Finally the officer came back. He rode up to Will who was standing alone.

"Vous et vos hommes, attendez moi." He commanded in a guttural squawk. He once again turned his horse and waited for the crew to start to line up. "File à la" He added.

Will was puzzled; his French was not that good. He raised both hands, turning the palms in the air, to indicate that he did not understand.

"En file, un et un. Le sentier ...étroit!" And he indicated with his hands that the path was narrow.

"Merci!" Will said grinning up at the man, who visibly relaxed. "Mr Tarrant – single file, Spencer, your marines take up the rear."

Will stepped forward and the officer squeezed his nag into a walk. They began a slow procession through the narrow defile with thick woods on either side. Will glancing about saw that the woods hid French infantry watching them suspiciously. That must have been what had taken the time. They had to summon the soldiers and then put them in place. The path continued through the woods, though the banks on either side seemed to be flattening out.

Will turned to Craddock who was immediately behind him. "Must be a smugglers path."

"Very likely. No wonder our fellow had chosen this place."

"But his security wasn't that good, was it? They were waiting for him!"

"Good thing you had sent in Spencer first."

"Perhaps; but I can't help thinking that if we had just dropped the fellow we wouldn't have been in this predicament."

"But we might have drowned in the middle of the Channel!"

"Quite so!"

Will was not good at estimating mileage ashore. He had no idea how far they had gone, when the trees gave way to a wider lane, and a small hamlet could be seen up ahead. They were led up to a small church with a very English looking tower. There were soldiers in the fields either side and along the short track to the church. The church did not look as if it had been used for some time. There were weeds growing out of the stonework and an air of desolation about it. The Officer indicated they should enter the church. One by one they filed in. It was a poor apology for a church inside. There were no pews; no alter; it was bare. There were damp patches on the floor where the roof leaked.

Once all of *Snipe's* crew were inside the church, the doors were hurriedly shut, with a bang, and the lock turned. If there had ever been any glass in the windows, it was long gone. The rain came in, and there was a damp smell about the place. The sailors and marines wandered round looking in corners and investigating everywhere. The door to the vestry was unlocked, but there was no furniture in there. A door to outside from the vestry was locked. The only vestige that remained of anything religious was the pulpit.

One of the crew reported that the door to the tower was unlocked, and that there was a fine view from the top of the tower. One of the powder monkeys offered to pick the lock to the outside door of the vestry, if anybody had any wire. When told, Will thanked the lad, but asked him what he would do if he managed to open it.

"Escape!" Replied the lad.

"Where to?" Asked Will. The lad pondered the problem, then grinned and shrugged his shoulders eloquently.

There were no candles, so no light and it was getting dark. The crew began to find places to settle. Will, asked where he proposed to lie down, told everybody to find their own place. He would wait and see what happened.

Nobody came. The Boatswain had the lighter boys hoisted onto the shoulders of the tallest sailors and marines, to see if they could report anything from through the windows, but it was too dark to see anything.

Much later, when Will had found an empty spot where he could sit with his shoulders against a wall, the Boatswain found him.

"Fellows asking what they should do about the heads, Sir?"

"Good point Mr Tarrant! Don't really want to soil our own area do we?"

He thought for a moment and then had a sudden inspiration.

"Mr Tarrant, I suggest that anybody needing to pee or release their bowels should climb up to the top of the tower. Just make sure they hold on tight!"

The Boatswain laughed. "Crap on our enemies! How very Biblical!"

The next morning, the main door was unlocked, and the officer appeared with a couple of soldiers with muskets and bayonets. Behind him came a group of peasants carrying wicker baskets filled with coarse bread. They dumped these inside the doors and fled.

"L'eau?" Asked Will.

The Officer looked distracted. He frowned, turned and stalked out. The door was shut and locked.

The bread was almost inedible. The crew must appreciate their cook after this, thought Will. Because they were constantly able to get fresh supplies, the food had been, by any standards, good aboard *Snipe*. The reason, unbeknown to the crew, was that Will augmented the Naval allowance, from his own pocket.

It was not until midday, that anything further happened. This time, the doors were opened, the soldiers stood by the doors, muskets at the ready, and a hand cart was wheeled in with a barrel on it. Nothing was said. The doors were shut and locked. The barrel contained water; water as bad as one got used to on patrol after any time at sea. The crew lined up with their tin mugs to refresh themselves. As nothing was happening, and it would soon be getting dark again, Will climbed the short set of steps to the pulpit.

"My friends, I have no idea what will happen to us. That being the case, I should just like to say what an honour it has been to lead the finest crew any man could ever ask for...." A cheer went up.

"Three cheers for the Captain!" Shouted somebody from the back. The cheering was deafening. Behind the crew the doors were thrown open and soldiers rushed in, bayonets fixed. They skidded to a halt in confusion when they saw that the faces turned towards them were all smiling. Perplexed they did not know what to do. They muttered together and then withdrew. The door was locked and the crew of *Snipe* were once again left alone. There was no further contact; what was left of the January light left them. They had to feel their way about and settle down as best they could, hungry.

The next morning the doors were opened and the wicker baskets brought in, and the old ones retrieved. Will strode over to the door and stood there so that it could not be shut.

"Votre officier!" He demanded. A surly soldier came up to try and push Will out of the way, but the burly form of the Boatswain appeared and just lifted the man off his feet and deposited him on the ground outside. Tarrant then stood shoulder to shoulder with Will, so the soldiers could not shut the door. Neither of them ventured outside, they just stood there.

"Votre officier" Repeated Will. A sergeant stepped forward, drawing his sword. There was a universal growl of disapproval from those inside the church who could see what was happening. Will and Tarrant stood their ground, and the sergeant hesitated.

"Un officier, s'il vous plait." Said Will, with a smile. The sergeant shook his head, replaced his sword in its scabbard, and turned to march away.

Five minutes later the original scruffy officer came from behind one of the cottages. As he got near, Will said.

"Bonne jour, Monsieur. Mes hommes, Ils n'ont pas eu toute la nourriture."

The Officer looked baffled, and turned to the sergeant, speaking rapidly to him. The man looked ashamed and was obviously trying to make excuses. The officer took his gloves in one hand and struck the sergeant hard across the face, berating him. He then issued a string of orders. Soldiers scuttled off in all directions.

"Pardon Monsieur. Nous n'avons pas en plus de nourriture. Les soldats, ils sont manager votre nourriture! C'est la monde aujourd'hui!" The Officer said with an apologetic expression and raised his hands in an expressive gesture.

Will bowed to the man, indicated to Tarrant that he should stand aside, and shut the doors. An hour later, the doors were thrown open and this time a group of peasant women, dressed almost in rags, brought in steaming cauldrons with a kind of stew. At least it was hot, although what meat had been included was impossible to chew. The vegetables were not much better, but at least it lined the stomach.

CHAPTER 46

That night Will got the lad who had volunteered to pick the vestry lock to do just that. Then he and Craddock slipped out. The door was shut behind them. By what little light there was, they crept around the churchyard and found their way to the track they had arrived on. It was even more difficult to find one's way here because the overhanging branches cut out a lot of what remained of the light. It took them sometime, but finally they made it to the cove. Vaguely you could make out the shape of *Snipe* still resting on her side, with the masts pointing inland. Gingerly they worked their way to the cliff's edge and waited. If there were any sentries, they were either asleep or extraordinarily quiet. Very slowly putting each foot down gently in a rolling motion to avoid dislodging any stones, they crept towards the ship. Once on the sand it was easier going. They finally found themselves up against the hull. Will managed to find one of the lines that had been used by the crew to get ashore, and shinned up it, then swung to the sloping deck. Craddock followed immediately. There was still no sign of any guards. There was no point in going aft to the cabins; they wouldn't be able to carry anything useful back to the church. They concentrated on their objective. They groped their way to the forward companionway and then slid down to the deck below. Here a quick check revealed that nobody was asleep or on guard. Craddock located a lantern, which they were able to light with the sulphur matches that were stored nearby. Now it was possible to see what they were doing. Craddock went straight to one of the ammunition boxes which formed one of the cross-benches used by the crew. Lifting the lid, he was able to locate the fuse-cord stored there. He handed it to Will who shook his head to indicate he had no idea what length was needed. Craddock gave a wan smile and using his fingers like a pair of scissors indicated the length he thought would be correct. A knife from the galley was used to cut the cord. Will then carried the cord down to the powder store hatch. Pushing the cord in until he was sure that it touched the paper wrapped powder charges; he unwound the rest across the deck to the bottom of the companionway.

Will in a whisper told Craddock to get off the ship. He waited; then lifting the lantern slide, he made sure that the fuse was well alight. Blowing out the lantern, he clambered up the slopping companionway and grabbed a line, swung himself out and dropped on to the sand. Craddock had already disappeared. Will ran, keeping low to the cliff edge and then felt his way back to the cove entrance. Here he bumped into Craddock who was waiting for him.

They were halfway back to the church, when there was an explosion, followed almost immediately by a massive one. Will ran up the track and then whistled to Craddock to leave and join him amongst the trees. Sure enough a group of panting soldiers rushed past their hiding place heading for the cove. Keeping to the side of the track, ready to leap into the undergrowth, they cautiously made their way back to the village. There were lights everywhere, with the silhouettes of soldiers being formed up. By skirting the edge of the village and approaching from the opposite direction, using grave stones to cover their approach, they were able to regain the church. Here they felt their way round to the side door to the vestry, expecting there to be a guard outside. There was nobody there! A discreetly knocked signal was responded to immediately and the door opened. Craddock, followed by Will slid in and the door was shut and relocked behind them. They heard the sound of the latch bolt being activated.

"All right here?" Whispered Will.

"Nobody has checked here yet!" Replied the invisible seaman.

"Go find us something to clean our boots, will you?" Asked Will. "Better take your boots off and your oilskin, James. Put the oilskin under one of the windows where the rain comes in."

"Right!" Came Craddock's voice out of the dark. Will felt his way to a corner of the vestry and removed his boots and own oilskin. He knew exactly where there was a wet-patch; he had once been sitting there when it had started to rain.

"Here Sir" Came the seaman's voice.

"Over here." Replied Will. "Thank you."

Will carefully wiped his boots, making sure that there was no vestige of sand to be felt. He rubbed hard so that in the end the sole felt dry to the touch, as well as the sides. He then settled down where he always tried to find some sleep.

They were blessed by the stupidity of the Sous-Lieutenant and his soldiers. It took them well over an hour and a half to think of checking on the crew of *Snipe* back at the church.

The first they knew that they were in for a visit was the flare of torches approaching the building which could be seen through the open windows. Then the main doors were thrown open and a group of soldiers burst in, holding the torches high. The Sous-Lieutenant then marched in to be met by rows of seaman shouting for the lights to be put out. Unperturbed, the officer ordered that the sailors be counted. The sergeant went round pointing a finger at each member of *Snipe's* crew whilst counting out loud. Will chose that moment to come out of the vestry to enquire what all the noise was about. The sergeant lost the thread of his counting and, much to the jeering amusement of the sailors and marines had to start again.

"What was the noise?" Asked Will. The Officer glared at him. Then obviously a thought struck him, because he ordered one of the soldiers to check on the vestry door. The man returned to say that it was firmly locked and there was no key. The Sous-Lieutenant shook his head. The count was correct. The officer marched out, followed by his torch carrying team and the doors were locked after them.

For the next two days the routine remained the same. Bread was brought in the morning and then late in the afternoon a cauldron of what appeared to be the same, mostly vegetable stew, would be brought. With stone walls and floors; no glass in the windows; it was bitterly cold so difficult to get any sleep. There was no position you could get yourself into that was comfortable.

Will, talking to his crew, was well aware of the problem. He had exactly the same conditions as the rest of them. He decided to try and do something about the predicament. The third morning when the bread was brought, he demanded the French soldiers ask their officer to come and see him.

Much later the doors were opened and the officer walked in, to look round and then stand waiting for Will to go to him. Will decided to remain where he was. It was an impasse, which was finally broken when the officer attempted to leave the church to be blocked by members of *Snipe's* Crew. The two French soldiers threatened the crew members with their bayonets, but the sailors were not impressed, and the soldiers were obviously afraid of the numbers. Finally the French officer moved a few steps towards Will.

"Vous êtes un sous-lieutenant, Oui?" Asked Will; as he would have done a junior rating.

"Oui."

"Je suis un Capitaine! J'ai peut-être un prisonnier, mais Je suis toujours l' officier supérieur."

The sous-lieutenant looked amazed that the Englishman should assume the dominant role, but you could almost see his brain working.

"What do you want?" The Sous-Lieutenant asked curtly in guttural French

"Mattresses." Replied Will in French.

The Sous-lieutenant looked round the nave of the church.

"But you are prisoners!"

"But we are not animals!"

"Where would I find this number of mattresses, it is impossible."

"There are plenty of hay ricks out there, they would be better than nothing."

The Frenchman snorted, shrugged his shoulders and turned to leave.

"My men could bring it in.......under guard."

The Officer did not say a word, he marched out.

"What do you think?" Asked Craddock.

"Just have to wait and see. I think he is completely out of his depth, poor fellow. Conscripted, where from, God knows!"

They had set up a pattern, the officers exercised in the Chancel, whilst the seamen and marines used the Nave. They would take it turns to walk up and down the allotted area. The crew had taken it upon themselves to decide that the Vestry was also Will's 'cabin'. So the Chancel was now known as the Wardroom.

Nothing more happened that day, and they settled down to another uncomfortable night on the cold unforgiving floor. The next morning the apology for bread arrived as usual. Then halfway through the morning, the doors were thrown open and in strutted a very different type of officer. This fellow was smartly dressed with a tall fur hat with gold tassels and a splendid red plume. His coat was of superior blue cloth with white facings, epaulettes, white breeches tucked into highly polished riding boots, complete with spurs. His sword clanked at his side as he walked. He had an air of supreme confidence.

"Captain, prepare your men to march!" He ordered in French.

"Where to?" Asked Will.

The officer looked surprised to be asked a question, let alone in his own language.

"Verdun!"

"Where is Verdun?"

"To the East."

"How far?"

"You leave in five minutes!" Stated the French officer; ignoring the last question. He then turned and marched out; the doors banging shut behind him. The men collected what little they had with them, and stood around quietly discussing their future.

The doors banged open, and there was the Sous-Lieutenant.

"Officers first." He shouted in French.

"I would rather wait until all my men are accounted for!" Stated Will.

"The orders are Officers first!" The man replied.

"Who said?" Asked Will; quite mildly.

The Sous-Lieutenant looked quickly over his shoulder. "Le Captaine!"

"Ah! Well go tell the Captain, that in His Majesty's Navy, the officers always look after their men first!"

The Sous-Lieutenant shrugged his shoulders and walked out. Through the doorway could be seen a group of soldiers on horse-back. They did not look like cavalry; they looked rather drab; the cavalry were generally flashier. Will could see the Sous-Lieutenant walk over to the splendidly dressed officer who sat on a fine bay horse. There was a short conversation, and then the Sous-Lieutenant came back.

"The Captain says if that is what you want, let the men out first."

"Thank you!" Said Will in French, with a smile. "Right Mr Tarrant, over to you."

The Boatswain grinned at Will then turned and ordered the men to line up in a column of two and march out, heads held high. On his order the men formed up and then on the order "March" proceeded to march out two by two.

Wiggins had quietly ordered his sergeant to follow suit, so once the seamen had left the marines marched out, followed by the non-commissioned officers, and finally the commissioned officers.

Tarrant had brought his men to a halt, with the marines lined up in front. The officers strolled out and took up positions either side of Will, facing the Captain on his edgy horse, which seemed to dance on the spot.

"Captain Calvert, you and your men are to march to the fortress of Verdun. Sergeant Petite will make sure that there are no attempts at escaping. Anybody escaping will be shot. Do you understand?" The Captain said in French. Will turned and repeated the Captain's words in English.

Then he turned to the Captain. "You are not accompanying us?" He asked in French.

"Good God no!" Replied an affronted Captain, in

French. "Sergeant Petite speaks English; that is why he was chosen." He added.

One of the horsemen reined his horse round to face Will. "I am Sergeant Petite. You will obey my orders at all times."

"No!" Replied Will. "You will respect the fact that I am senior to you in rank. You will 'ask' me to convey to my men what you desire us to do. There will be no attempt to escape, so there will be no excuse for any use of firearms. If any are used, Sergeant, you personally will be held to account, when the Allies have defeated you!"

The Sergeant's mouth moved, but nothing came out. He turned to the Captain, but he was already trotting away.

"But you are prisoners!" He finally managed to say.

"We may be prisoners, but we still need to be treated with respect. We treat our prisoners with respect, we expect you to do the same. You may no longer have a King, but I hope you remain a civilised Nation!"

The Sergeant looked down at Will digesting what he had said. "Will you get your men to follow the leading rider?" The Sergeant finally said.

"Mr Tarrant, when one of the horsemen begins to move off, have our men follow him in good order."

"Aye Sir!" Said Tarrant; knuckling his forehead.

So the procession was led off. Tarrant took up the front position; then came the seamen, the young men and boys then the marines, followed by the officers. The soldiers on horseback rode alongside. There were about twenty horses, none of them in very good shape. Behind them all, a couple of ox-draw carts followed. Every hour the party came to a halt, and they rested for a quarter-of-an-hour; then they were off again. They followed the tracks that led east. Every now and again they would come to a village. Here the prisoners were halted. The local peasants were told to bring water, but no food appeared. In the middle of the afternoon, the Sergeant ordered a halt. The Ox-carts were driven into a field.

"Your men will put up tents." Stated the Sergeant; still on

his horse.

Will decided to leave out the 'please' demand. He just told Tarrant that he had heard the man.

Wiggin's marine Sergeant stepped smartly up to be alongside Tarrant and repeated the order.

"Sergeant; how many men to a tent?" Will asked the French sergeant.

The man looked confused. For the first time he smiled. "I have no idea. Depends on the size of the tent I expect. You will have a tent to yourself, the officers will have a bigger one, and the rest must sort themselves out. My men will erect their own tents. We can't have them falling down in the middle of the night!"

Will suddenly realised that the man's accent was very pure; it had no guttural quality to it. He waited until the Sergeant had demounted, then he walked over to him and said in a low voice.

"You were an officer once, weren't you?"

Sergeant Petite looked about him anxiously. "How did you know?"

"Your accent, the way you ride your horse. Very different from your men."

"I can see that I shall have to watch you very carefully!" Said Petite, but it was said with a smile.

"Do my men get any food?" Asked Will; conversationally.

"Yes, we all do, once the tents are up. The second cart has all the food and cooking materials in it. Which reminds me, thank you." He tied his horse to a small sapling, and strode off shouting for somebody, whose name Will had never heard before. It was obviously the cook, because a figure emerged from the second cart and started to assemble a trestle table.

It was not until it was nearly dark that everybody had anything to eat. When it came, it was a lot better than the food they had been given in the church.

The routine remained the same each day. There was bread for breakfast, then it was marching with stops as before, and a meal in the evening. Every third day, when they came to a larger village the canteen cart would stop, whilst they moved on. Later it would join them, often just as it was getting dark, for the evening meal to be cooked. It was obvious that the supplies were being foraged from the villages. The ninth day, there was trouble where the cook tried to commandeer food. The villagers frightened him off. That night there was no food. The next day, the guards were divided and half stayed with the cook to make sure he managed to get something for them to eat. This meant that there were only about ten guards to look after the ninety-six English prisoners. Will suggested to Petite that they wait for the others, which was accepted with thanks. By now Sergeant Petite trusted the crew of *Snipe* not to escape. Later riding alongside Will, who was marching on foot, he commented that he was surprised that they had not provided horses for the English officers.

"Ah, but it is a Republican Army now; they don't know how to behave properly!"

Petite laughed out loud. "I believe there is an expression in English 'to hit the nail on the head'?"

"Where did you learn such good English?" Asked Will; intrigued.

"My father was a diplomat – we lived in London for a time. He lost his head, and we lost everything. I was an officer in the cavalry, but I was accused of being an 'Aristo' so I was demoted to private. I have had to work my way up, but I am no longer in the cavalry, now I am with the infantry."

They were the last in the column, except for the two carts, which lagged someway behind.

Into the second week, Will realised that the escort had diminished. He walked over to have a word with Petite. The Sergeant saw him coming and got up to meet him.

"You appear to be a bit short in numbers." Commented

Will.

Petite raised his eyebrows and nodded. "They leave at night. It is an opportunity not to be missed. A horse to get them back to their wives. I can do nothing about it, the sentries, plead innocence. I know they are lying, but it is not going to get them back, so what is the point. If I was to try and punish them – the sentries – they would do the same the next night, and I would have nobody."

"So how far are we from the sea?" Asked Will; innocently.

Petite gave him a long look, before replying. "About thirty lieue."

"What is that, a Lieue?"

Petite laughed. "About two and three quarters of a mile."

Will did a rapid calculation. "About eighty miles?"

"Something like that!"

"Shame!"

"Why were you thinking of trying to escape?"

"Well, it had a certain appeal. But only if all your guards left us, and it was just you. We could then get you back to England."

Petite gave a rueful smile. "Impossibility, I am afraid to say. General Bonaparte has thousands of troops all along the coast. Even with your reputation – oh yes I was told about you – you would never make it with so many men."

"Shame!" Said Will; storing the information away.

It took over three weeks to march the whole way to the citadel of Verdun, which was where the English naval prisoners were imprisoned. By the time they got there, there were only ten guards, counting Sergeant Petite. It was strange, but as the number of guards diminished, the atmosphere between the prisoners and their escort became friendlier. Sailors and marines who collapsed on the march were allowed to ride on one of the carts for a day or two, until they were fit enough to resume their march.

At the gates to the Citadel; the English said goodbye to

their escort and were taken inside the walls. The Citadel was shaped like a star and had been raised as a defensive position with high walls holding back the raised ground on which the buildings sat. The officers were taken one way, the sailors and marines another. Will found himself in a barrack hut with five other officers, only one of which was a Post Captain, but he was a shadow of his former self. Will found that he was having to act as the senior officer in fact; if not in theory. Here he was to remain, incarcerated, with little to eat, and even less to occupy his mind. He had no idea when he would be released. Unlike the French officer prisoners, English officers who were the prisoners of the French were not allowed to give their parole, so they had to abide in conditions not much better than their men. There was no privacy in the barrack huts. The officers had rough wooden bunks with coarse banks to cover them.

Nobody had any idea how long the war would go on, so depression was very acute. Will had nothing to bribe the guards with, to receive any benefits. He did manage to get hold of a few books on agriculture, which his fellow imprisoned officers found hilarious. He devoured them, reading them again and again, and making notes in the margins. He did not join in with the gambling, or the card games.

The Post-Captain was obviously mentally ill. He would walk up and down the hut giving orders to a non-existent crew and then say he was 'going below' to lie down on his bunk and weep. He was not violent, but his antics did get on the nerves of his fellow inmates. Eventually, the French doctor decided he was mad and took him away. Will never discovered what happened to him.

Will did get to meet Craddock and his other officers during the time they were allowed to exercise. From him he discovered that over half of the members of the crew of *Snipe* had been removed to other prisons.

Will wrote letters to Isabella, suggesting in them that she was free to break their engagement if she wanted, as there was no end in sight, though he would always go on loving her, hoping that at least one letter might get through somehow. With nothing to bribe the guards, there was no way of making sure that any missive would reach Calais, let alone cross the Channel.

With Craddock they surveyed their prison to see if there might be some means of escape. What had been designed to keep people out, served equally well to keep them incarcerated. The trouble was that the war could go on for years!

APPENDIXES

Plymouth Harbour

West Coast France

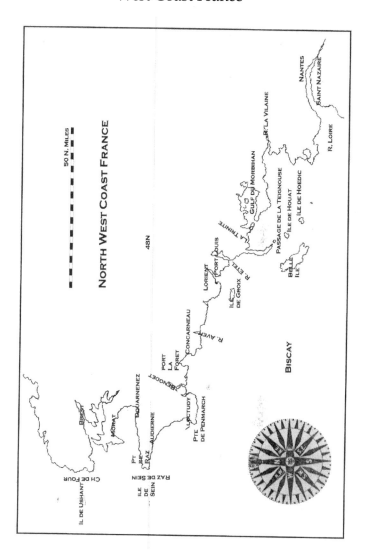

Brest Harbour

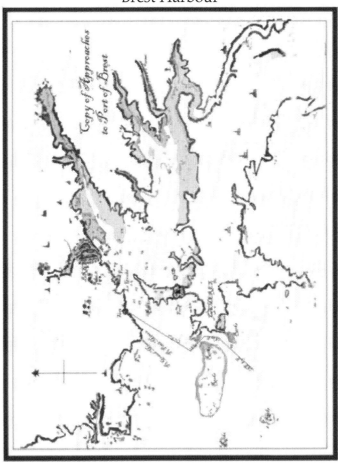

Cherbourg Harbour

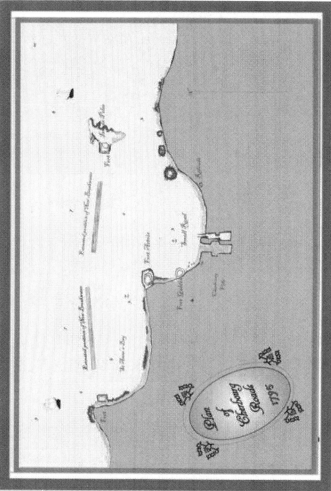

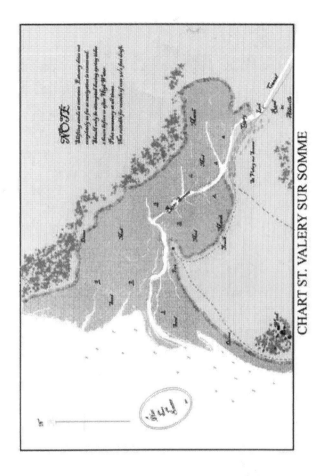

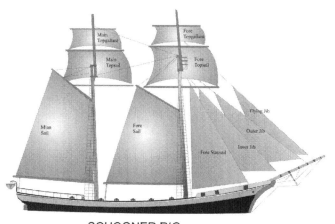

SCHOONER RIG

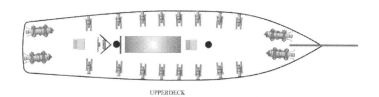

UPPERDECK

MESSDECK

PLAN OF H.M.S SNIPE

30174781R00197

Made in the USA
Middletown, DE
23 December 2018